PRAISE FOR MARTIN WALKER'S

The Resistance Man

"A passionate valentine to the splendors of the slow life." —*Washington Independent Review of Books*

"While most readers think the British have a line on cozies, Walker makes a great case for the French version. . . . [An] appetizing mystery." —*Booklist*

"Evokes all the history, culture, romance and fine food and drink you might expect of French village life." —*BookPage*

"Endearing. . . . Fans and newcomers alike will savor Walker's ability to smoothly fold suspense into his Périgordian soufflé." —*Publishers Weekly*

"[A] celebration of *la belle France*. But this time, Bruno, who's required to act as enforcer, sleuth, diplomat, comforter, impersonator, hostage negotiator and rescuer, reveals unexpected resources." —*Kirkus Reviews*

"An exemplary entry in the police procedural." —Bookgasm

MARTIN WALKER

The Resistance Man

Martin Walker is a senior fellow of the Global
Business Policy Council, a private think tank for
CEOs of major corporations, based in Washington, D.C. He is also editor in chief emeritus and
international affairs columnist at United Press International. His five previous novels in the Bruno
series are *Bruno, Chief of Police*; *The Dark Vineyard*; *Black Diamond*; *The Crowded Grave*; and
The Devil's Cave, all international bestsellers. He
lives in Washington, D.C., and the Dordogne.

www.brunochiefofpolice.com

The Resistance Man

A MYSTERY OF THE FRENCH COUNTRYSIDE

Martin Walker

Vintage Books

A Division of Random House LLC

New York

The Library of Congress has cataloged the Knopf edition as follows:
Walker, Martin.
The Resistance Man : a Bruno, chief of police novel /
Martin Walker. — First United States edition.
pages   cm
1. Police—France—Fiction.   2. Mystery fiction.   I. Title.
PR6073.A413R47 2014
823'.914—dc23   2013022876

Vintage Books Trade Paperback ISBN: 978-0-345-80480-8
eBook ISBN: 978-0-385-34955-0

Book design by Betty Lew
Map copyright © 2012 by Jamie Whyte

www.vintagebooks.com

Printed in the United States of America
10 9 8 7 6 5 4 3 2 1

*In memory of Christopher Hitchens and
Peter Scott, two Balliol College friendships
that lasted for over forty years*

The Resistance Man

Prologue

It was shortly after dawn on a day in late spring that carried all the promise of summer to come. The fresh green leaves were so bright they startled the eye, dew was already disappearing from the grass under the first rays of the sun, and the woods around the cottage were clamorous with birdsong. Benoît Courrèges, *chef de police* in the small French town of St. Denis and known to everyone as Bruno, could identify the different notes of warblers and hoopoes, woodlarks and woodpeckers, just a fraction of the birdlife of the beautiful valley of the River Vézère where he made his home.

Bruno wore his old army tracksuit in which he had just taken his morning run through the woods. His eyes were fixed on Napoléon and Joséphine, his two geese. These monarchs of his chicken run paced forward with slow dignity to study the quivering puppy held firmly in Bruno's grip. Behind the geese, twitching his head from side to side, came Blanco the cockerel, named after a French rugby hero. Blanco was followed by his hens and the two pheasants Bruno had added to his flock because he liked their smaller eggs and the careful way the hen pheasant would hide them in the undergrowth.

Raising a basset hound to be a hunting dog is slow work,

but Bruno was becoming convinced that Balzac was the most intelligent dog he had ever known. Already housebroken, Balzac would even abandon an alluring new scent to obey his master's summons. Now he was being taught that the birds in Bruno's chicken run were to be treated with courtesy as members of the extended family and to be protected against all comers. Balzac was eager to bounce forward to play and send the chickens squawking and jumping into the air. So Bruno held him down with one hand and stroked him with the other, speaking in a low and reassuring voice as the two geese advanced to see what new creature Bruno had brought onto their territory this time.

Bruno had already familiarized Balzac with the deep and sensual scent of truffles and shown him the white oaks in the woods where they were usually to be found. He took the dog on his dawn and dusk checks of the security of the chicken coop and thought the time was approaching when Balzac would be able to run alongside when he exercised the horses. Bruno suspected he'd miss the now-familiar feel of the large binoculars case strapped to his chest, where the puppy was currently stowed when his master went riding.

Napoléon and Joséphine, who had grown familiar with Bruno's previous basset hound, Gigi, came closer. Blanco flapped his wings and squawked out his morning *cocorico,* as if to assert that however large the two geese, he was really in charge here. The puppy, accustomed to sleeping in the stable beside Bruno's horse, Hector, was not in the least awed by the size of the geese. He cocked his head to one side to gaze up at them and made an amiable squeak of greeting. The geese cruised on past Bruno and his dog, leaving Blanco to stand on tiptoe and fluff out his feathers to enlarge his size and grandeur. Balzac looked suitably impressed.

Watching his birds and stroking his hound, Bruno could

not imagine a life without animals and birdsong and his garden. He delighted in eating apples plucked from his trees, tomatoes still warm from the sun and salads that had still been growing moments before he dressed them with oil and vinegar. At the back of his mind lurked the question of whether there would one day be a wife and children to share this idyll and enjoy the stately progress of the seasons.

He turned his head to glance at his cottage, restored from ruin by his own hands and the help of his friends and neighbors in St. Denis. Repaired now from the fire damage inflicted by a vengeful criminal, the house had grown. Bruno had used the insurance money and much of his savings to install windows in the roof, lay floorboards and create two new bedrooms in the loft. The plan had long been in his mind, but the decision to carry it out felt like making a bet on his own future, that in time there would be a family to fill the space.

On the desk in his study lay the estimate for installing solar panels on the roof, along with the paperwork explaining tax rebates he would receive and the terms of the bank loan he had been promised. Bruno had done the math and knew it would take him almost ten years to earn back his investment, but he supposed it was a gesture to the environment that he ought to make. Now, gazing at the honey-colored stone of his house topped with the traditional red tiles of the Périgord, he worried what the panels might do to the look of the place.

His reverie was interrupted by the vibration of the phone in his pocket. As he extracted it, Balzac squirmed free and began creeping toward the grazing chickens. Bruno reached out to haul him back, missed, dropped his phone, and a furious squawking erupted as the puppy bounded forward and the hens half flew and half scurried back to the protection of their hut.

"Sorry, Father," Bruno said as he recovered the phone,

having seen that his caller was the local priest, Father Sentout. He picked up Balzac with one hand and headed back to the house.

"Sorry to disturb you so early, Bruno, but there's been a death. Old Murcoing passed away, and there's something here that I think you ought to see. I'm at his place now, waiting for his daughter to get here."

"I'll take a shower and come straight there," Bruno said. "How did you learn of his death?"

"I called in to see him yesterday evening and he was fading then, so I sat with him through the night. He died just as the dawn broke."

Bruno thanked the priest, filled Balzac's food and water bowls and headed for the shower, wondering how many towns were fortunate enough to have a priest who took his parochial duties so seriously that he'd sit up all night with a dying man. Murcoing had been one of the group of four or five old cronies who would gather at the cheaper of the town's cafés. It had a TV for the horse races and off-track betting on the pari-mutuel. The old men would nurse a *petit blanc* all morning and tell one another that France and St. Denis were going to the dogs. Without knowing the details, Bruno recalled that Murcoing was one of the town's few remaining Resistance veterans, which could mean a special funeral. If so, he'd be busy. The decision about the solar panels would have to wait.

1

As if determined to make it his last sight on earth, the dead man clutched what at first appeared to be a small painting on canvas or parchment. Bruno moved closer and saw that it was no painting but rather a large and beautiful banknote, nearly twice the size of the undistinguished but familiar euro notes in his wallet.

Impeccably engraved in pastel hues stood Mercury with his winged heels before a port teeming with sailing vessels and steamships. Facing him was a bare-chested Vulcan with his forge against a backdrop of a modern factory with tall chimneys belching smoke. It was a Banque de France note for one thousand francs of a kind that Bruno had never seen before. On the quilted coverlet that was tucked up tightly to the corpse's grizzled chin lay another banknote, of the same style and value. Picking it up, Bruno was startled by its texture, still thick and crinkly as if made more of linen than paper. It was the reverse side of the same kind of note the dead man held. Against a cornucopia of fruits and flowers, a proud cockerel and sheaves of wheat, two medallions contained the profiles of a Greek god and goddess. They stared impassively at each other against the engraved signatures of some long-dead bank officials, and above them was printed the date of issue: DECEMBER 1940.

His eyebrows rose. For any Frenchman 1940 was a solemn year. It marked the third German invasion in seventy years and the second French defeat. But it was the first time Paris had fallen to German arms. In 1870, the capital had withstood months of siege before French troops, under the watchful eye of the kaiser's armies, stormed the capital to defeat and slaughter the revolutionaries of the Paris Commune. The Germans who invaded in 1914 were eventually defeated. But in 1940, France had surrendered and signed a humiliating armistice. German soldiers had marched through the Arc de Triomphe and down the Champs-Élysées and launched an occupation that would last for more than four years. France under Marshal Pétain's Vichy regime had retained some shred of sovereignty over a truncated half of the country, while the Germans took over Paris, the north and the whole Atlantic coastline. So it was a Vichy banknote Bruno held in his hands, and he wondered how long after the war's end it had remained legal tender.

There were more notes, for varying amounts, inside a black wooden box that lay open at the dead man's side. Alongside them were some old photographs. The one on top showed a group of young men and boys carrying shotguns, revolvers and elderly submachine guns. They were grouped around a black Citroën Traction Avant, one of the most handsome cars France ever made. A French *tricolore* flag was draped across the hood.

Bruno picked up the photo and turned it over to see the scrawled words *Groupe Valmy, 3 juillet, 1944*. Most of the individuals were dressed like farmers, some wore berets, and two had the old steel helmets from the 1914–1918 war. An older man sported a French officer's uniform with leather straps across his chest and ammunition pouches. He held up a grenade in each hand. Each of the men had an armband with the letters FFI. Bruno knew it stood for Forces Françaises de l'Intérieur, the name de Gaulle had chosen for the Resistance fighters. Another photo showed the same car and an ancient truck parked beside a train. The doors of a freight car were open, and men in a human chain were passing sacks from the train to the truck. On the back of the photo were the words *Neuvic, 26 juillet, 1944.*

"I've never been allowed to see inside his box before," said the woman Father Sentout had introduced as Joséphine, one of the dead man's three daughters. She eyed the photos but made no move to touch them or the banknotes. Her hands, work worn and gnarled, remained clenched in her lap. She looked to be in her sixties. The priest was packing away the breviary and holy oils he had used to give the last rites. Spots of oil gleamed on the dead man's forehead, where the priest had made the last sign of the cross, and on his eyelids.

"Eighty-six," the priest said. "A good age, a long life and he served France. Your father is with our Father in heaven now." He put his hand gently on the woman's arm. She shook it off.

"We could have done with that money when I was growing up," she said, staring dry eyed at the banknotes. "They were hard times."

"It was the banknotes that made me call you," said Father Sentout, turning to Bruno. "I don't know what the law says about them, being out of date."

"They're part of his estate, so they'll go to his heirs," said Bruno. "But those photos mean I'll probably have to plan for a special funeral." He turned to Joséphine. "Do you know if he had the Resistance medal?"

She gestured with her head to a small picture frame on the wall above the bed, below a crucifix. Bruno leaned across the bed to look closer. The curtains were open, and the sun was shining, but only a modest light came from the tiny courtyard. He saw the stone wall of a neighbor's house barely six feet away. A single lightbulb hanging from the ceiling in a dingy parchment lampshade did little to help, but he could make out the small brass circle with its engraved Cross of Lorraine hanging from a black-and-crimson ribbon. Beneath it in the frame was a faded FFI armband and a photograph of a young Murcoing wearing it and holding a rifle.

"I'll have to check the official list but it looks like he qualifies for a Resistance funeral with a guard of honor and a flag for the coffin," Bruno said. "If that's what you want, I'll make the arrangements. The state pays for it all. You can either have him buried at the big Resistance cemetery at Chasseneuil or here in St. Denis."

"I was wondering if he'd left enough to pay for cremation," she said, looking around the small bedroom with its faded floral wallpaper and a cheap wardrobe that had seen better days. "He was waiting for a place in the retirement home, so the *mairie* stuck him in here."

The old man had lived alone in the small apartment formed from the ground floor of a narrow three-story house in one of the backstreets of St. Denis. Bruno remembered when the *mairie* had bought the building and converted it for social housing. Four families were stuffed into the upstairs apartments, and another from the waiting list would be moved into this place as soon as the old man was removed. The recession had been hard on St. Denis.

"Paul should be here by now," she said, looking at her watch. "His grandson, my sister's boy. I called him as soon as

I called the priest. He's the only one my dad ever had much time for, the only other man in the family." She looked sourly at the corpse in the bed. "Three daughters weren't enough for him."

"I'll need your phone number to let you know about the funeral," Bruno said, taking out his notebook. "Do you know where he kept his papers, if there's a will?"

She shrugged and gave her number. "Nothing much to leave." She looked at her watch again. "I have to go. I'll take whatever food he's left." Through the open door they heard her rummaging in the small fridge and the food cupboard before she stomped down the narrow passage beside the garage that led to the street.

"Not much sign of grief there," said Bruno, taking out his phone to call the medical center. A doctor would have to certify death before Murçoing could be taken to the funeral parlor.

"He didn't have many visits from his family, except for Paul," the priest said. "All the sisters live in Bergerac. Joséphine told me she works as a night nurse, so she probably sees more than enough of the old and sick."

"How sick was he? I haven't seen him in the café for a while."

"He knew he was dying, and he didn't seem to mind," Father Sentout replied. "He had pneumonia but refused to go to the hospital. That was the sickness we used to call the old man's friend. It's a peaceful passing, they just slip away."

"I remember seeing him coming out of church. Was he a regular?"

"His wife dragged him along. After she died he didn't come so often at first, but this place is close to the church so he'd come along for Mass, for the company as much as anything."

"Did he ever talk about the money?" Bruno gestured at the open box on the bed and the banknote still held tightly in Murcoing's dead hands.

The priest paused, as if weighing his words in a way that made Bruno wonder whether there was some secret of the confessional that was being kept back.

"Not directly, but he'd rail against the fat cats and the rich and complained of being cheated. It was just ramblings. I was never clear whether he thought his daughters had cheated him out of the money from the farm or if it was something else."

"Is there something you can't tell me?"

Father Sentout shrugged. "Nothing directly linked to the money. I presume it's from the Neuvic train. You know about that, right? The great train robbery by the Resistance?"

Bruno shook his head. He'd heard of it but not the details. These days, the priest explained, the story was more legend than anything else. A vast sum of money, said to be hundreds of millions, had been stolen from a train taking reserves from the Banque de France to the German naval garrison in Bordeaux. Despite various official inquiries, large amounts had never been accounted for, and local tradition had it that several Resistance leaders had bought grand homes, started businesses and financed political careers after the war with the loot.

"If that was his share, he didn't get much," Father Sentout concluded, nodding at the banknotes on the bed. After the war there had been so many devaluations. Then in 1960 came de Gaulle's currency reform; a new franc was launched, each worth a hundred of the old ones. "That thousand-franc banknote is probably worth less than a euro, if it's worth anything at all."

Bruno bent down to pry the note from the cold fingers. As he put it inside the box with the photographs, he heard footsteps in the corridor, and Fabiola bustled into the small room, her medical bag in tow. She was wearing a long white coat of freshly pressed cotton, and her dark hair was piled loosely atop her head. An intriguing scent came with her, a curious blend of antiseptic and perfume, overwhelming the stale air of the room. She kissed Bruno on both cheeks and shook hands with Father Sentout, pulling out her stethoscope to examine the body.

"He obviously didn't take his medicine. Sometimes I wonder why we bother," she said, sorting through the small array of plastic jars from the pharmacy that stood by the bed. "He's dead, and there's nothing suspicious. I'll leave the certificate at the front desk of the clinic so you can pick it up. Meanwhile we'd better get him to the funeral home."

She stopped at the door and faced Bruno. "Is this going to stop you from getting to the airport? I'll be free by five so I can do it."

"It should be okay. If there's a problem, I'll call you," he replied. Pamela, the Englishwoman Bruno had been seeing since the previous autumn, was to land at the local airport of Bergerac just before six that evening, and he was to meet her and drive her back to St. Denis. Pamela, who kept horses along with the *gîtes* she rented out to tourists, had been pleased to find in Fabiola a year-round tenant for one of the *gîtes,* and the two women had become friends.

Bruno began making calls as soon as Fabiola and the priest left. He started with the veterans' department at the Ministry of Defense to confirm a Resistance ceremony and then called the funeral parlor. Next he rang Florence, the science teacher at the local *collège* who was now running the town choir, to ask if she could arrange for the "Chant des Partisans," the anthem of the Resistance, to be sung at the funeral. He rang the Centre Jean Moulin in Bordeaux, the Resistance museum and archive, for its help in preparing a summary of Murcoing's war record. The last call was to the social security office, to stop the dead man's pension payments. As he waited to be put through to the right department, he looked around the apartment.

In the sitting room an old TV squatted on a chest of drawers. In the top drawer, he found a large envelope marked *Banque* and others that contained various utility bills and a copy of the bill of sale for Murcoing's farm in the hills above Limeuil. It had been sold three years earlier, when prices were already tumbling, for eighty-five thousand euros. The buyer had a name that sounded Dutch, and the *notaire* was local. Bruno remembered the place, a ramshackle farmhouse with a roof that needed fixing and an old tobacco barn where goats were kept. The farm had been too small to be viable, even if the land had been good. Murcoing's last bank statement said he had six thousand euros in a Livret, a tax-free account set up by the state to encourage saving, and just over eight hundred in his checking account. He'd been getting a pension of four hundred euros a month. There was no phone and no address book. A dusty shotgun hung on the wall, and a fishing rod, its handle worn with years of use, stood in the corner. The house key hung on a hook beside the door. Bruno thought old Murcoing did not have much to show for a life of hard work and patriotism.

He wrote out a receipt for the gun, the box and its contents and left it in the top drawer. Beside the TV set he saw a well-used wallet. Inside were a *carte d'identité* and the *carte vitale* that gave access to the health service, but no credit cards and no cash. Joséphine would have seen to that. There were three small photos, one a portrait of a handsome young man and two more with the same young man with an arm around the shoulders of the elderly Murcoing at what looked like a family gathering. That must be Paul, the favorite grandson, who was supposed to arrive. Bruno left a note for him on the table, along with his business card and mobile number, asking Paul to get in touch about the funeral and saying he'd taken the gun, the box and banknotes to his office in the *mairie* for safekeeping.

As the hearse was arriving, Bruno's mobile phone rang, and a sultry voice said, "I have something for you." The mayor's secretary was incapable of saying even bonjour without some hint of coquetry. "It's a message from some foreigner's cleaning woman on the road out to Rouffignac. She thinks there's been a burglary."

2

Bruno sighed as he set out for the site of the burglary. It was the third that month, all at isolated houses owned by foreigners who usually only came to France in the summer. The first two families, one Dutch and one English, had been down for the Easter holidays and found their homes almost surgically robbed. Rugs, paintings, silver and antique furniture had all disappeared. The usual burglars' loot of TV sets and stereos had been ignored, and the thieves had evidently been professionals. No fingerprints were found and few signs of a break-in. Casual inspection might not have revealed that a burglary had taken place. Each of the houses had an alarm system, but one that used the telephone to alert a central switchboard, since the houses were too deep in the country for an alarm to be heard. The telephone wires had been cut.

To Bruno's irritation, the gendarmes had made a cursory inspection, shrugged their shoulders and left him to write a report for the insurance claim. He understood their thinking. Individual burglaries were almost never solved. The gendarmes preferred to wait until they had a clear lead to one of the region's fences and offer him a deal: a light sentence in return for testifying against the burglars. Then they could report dozens or even hundreds of burglaries to have been solved. This made their success rate look good on annual reports, which was what Paris wanted, and it led to bonuses and promotions. But it usually meant that few of the stolen items were returned to their owners. Bruno thought there should be a better way, and he'd suggested to the local insurance brokers that they ask their clients to provide photos of their more valuable items to improve the chances of tracking them down. Few of the householders bothered to do so.

But Bruno knew this house and was sure such photos would be on file. It was a small *gentilhommière*, the real estate agents' term for a building that was smaller than a manor house but bigger than the usual farmhouses of the region. Dating from the eighteenth century, it had an ornate entrance with stone pillars supporting a porch, two sets of French windows on each side of the entrance and five mansard windows on the upper story. Stone urns for flowers, still empty at this time of year, flanked the French windows, and each of the mansards had been topped with a stone pineapple, the sign of the handiwork of Carlos, one of the best of the local builders. The house had been impeccably restored, using old tiles on the new roof, and the old stucco had been chipped away from the façade to reveal the honey-colored stone beneath. The driveway was lined with fruit trees, and rosebushes flanked the vegetable garden. At the rear, Bruno recalled, was a swimming pool and a stone terrace with a fine view across the ridges that sloped down to the River Vézère.

Bruno had been invited here twice for enjoyable garden parties and another time for dinner. He had met the British owner, Jack Crimson, at the tennis club where the retired civil servant played gentle games of mixed doubles. He spoke decent French. He always signed up to take part in the annual tennis tournament, contributed to the prizes and made a generous donation each year to the children's tennis team. An affable man with thick gray hair, he was always well dressed. A little plump, but with the build of a man who'd been an athlete in his youth, he served excellent wines and had introduced Bruno to a deceptively potent English drink they called Pimm's. Crimson arrived each summer in a stately old Jaguar. When Bruno had seen that the house was filled with rare books, paintings and antiques, he had persuaded Crimson to take photos of them all for registration at the insurance office.

"*Ça va*, Bruno? I heard your van coming up the drive," said Gaëlle, the cleaning woman, greeting him from the front door. "They got in through the back and took all the good furniture, the rugs and paintings. They left the books. And they cut the phone line so I had to call the *mairie* on my mobile."

"Were all the shutters closed when you arrived?" he asked.

Gaëlle, a kindly and competent widow in her fifties, nodded. "I opened them myself to air the rooms. I always do. It's what Monsieur Crimson wants."

She led him around the side of the house to the rear door, where the wooden shutter on a French window had been forced open. One of the small windowpanes had been broken by a professional; some glue had been smeared on the glass, a folded newspaper attached and then punched to make little noise and a clear break. The same technique had been used at the earlier burglaries. Inside, darker patches on the walls showed where paintings had hung.

"This was the dining room," Gaëlle said. "You can't tell, now that the furniture's gone. He had some lovely old paintings of food, game birds and old-fashioned pots full of vegetables. They don't seem to have taken anything from upstairs."

"I hope you haven't been using that," he said, pointing at the feather duster she was holding. "They might have left fingerprints."

"I know, I watch those crime shows on TV. I just like to carry it."

"Have you called Monsieur Crimson?"

"I phoned his number in England right after I called the *mairie*. I heard some recorded English and then a beep, so I left a message. He'll call me back when he gets it."

Bruno took a note of Crimson's number and established that Gaëlle, who came twice a week to clean, had last been at the house four days earlier. He went from room to room with his notebook, relying on Gaëlle's memory for the missing items. The desk and filing cabinets seemed untouched in the room Crimson used as a study and library, but Gaëlle said an antique rug had been taken. At the side of the stairs was another door, a broken clasp and padlock lying on the floor.

"That's his wine cellar," she said, using the handle of her duster to turn on the light switch as she led him down the stairs. Bruno noted with approval the cellar's gravel floor and the care that had gone into the labeling of the stacks. It made it easier to see what had been stolen: vintage Pomerols and Sauternes and a case of 2005 Grand Millésime of Château de Tiregand, the prince of the Pécharmant wines.

"They knew what they were stealing," Bruno said, thinking that these were no common burglars. Cases of Cru Bourgeois reds and white Burgundies and even of champagne had been left in their racks.

As he returned to the staircase, Bruno noticed a small door beneath the stairs. He tried the handle, and it was open, leading to a dark cellar room that smelled of fuel oil. In the ceiling to one side he saw a chink of daylight.

"This used to house the oil tank," she said. "It hasn't been used for years. He's got gas now for the central heating."

Back upstairs, she led him to the side of the terrace, where she pointed to two metal plates held together by a sturdy padlock and said that was where the oil tank was refilled. Then she showed him some tire marks on a patch of lawn.

"I think they brought their truck around here to the back so they could load up easily," she said. "It rained all night the day before yesterday, so maybe that was when they came."

"You should be doing my job," he said. "It must be those TV shows you watch." Bruno followed the line of the telephone wire to the place where it had been cut. He called the security number at France Télécom to see if anyone could establish a time when the line had gone down. It had been shortly before 1:00 p.m. two days earlier.

"It's a shame," Gaëlle said, following in his footsteps. "Monsieur Crimson is such a nice man, always polite and generous, and he keeps the place very neat. You wouldn't know there wasn't a woman in the house." She looked a little wistful. "She died the year after they bought this place, his wife. He keeps a portrait of her in the bedroom. Luckily it's still there."

Bruno nodded but said nothing. The burglars must have known that Crimson would be away and that his house was very much worth robbing. They had come equipped with a truck large enough to take a dining room table, chairs and cases of wine as well as the paintings and a valuable old clock that Gaëlle said stood on the mantelpiece in the living room. That suggested inside knowledge, and that in turn meant, however unlikely it seemed, that Gaëlle had to be a suspect.

"Where did you have lunch the day before yesterday,

Gaëlle?" he asked, as casually as he could. Gaëlle eyed him steadily and replied, "With my cousin Roberte from the *mairie,* helping her bake stuff for her kid's birthday party. Don't worry, I know you have to ask."

He tried Crimson's number in England, but like Gaëlle he heard only the automated voice and the beep that invited him to leave a message. He did so, briefly and slowly, giving his office and cell-phone numbers and adding that he'd come back with a new padlock and clasp for the forced shutters and would try to secure the house. When Gaëlle pedaled away down the drive, Bruno debated with himself whether he should go the extra step. Remembering the fine dinner he'd enjoyed at Crimson's table, he decided that he should, and he rang Isabelle's number at the interior ministry in Paris. Again, he was invited to leave a message, and he gave Crimson's name and London number, asking if Isabelle could inform her Scotland Yard contacts to see if they could track him down.

How would the thieves get rid of such a mixture of stuff? Bruno wondered. Furniture, rugs and paintings could be sold at any *brocante* or at the antiques fairs that were held in town after town throughout the French summer. There must be thousands of them, everything sold for cash and no records of the sellers. Unless Crimson's possessions ended up with a very well-established dealer, the chances of tracking them down, even with the photos, were slim. The wine might be traceable, unless the thieves had very discerning palates and wanted it for themselves.

That triggered an idea, and as he reentered St. Denis, Bruno checked the time and turned off into the driveway to the *collège,* parking in front of the row of modest apartments where the teachers lived. Subsidized and almost-free housing was one of the ways the French state sought to lure well-qualified teachers to live and work in the countryside. For his friend Florence, a divorced mother of two toddlers with a science diploma who had found it tough to make ends meet, the teaching job had been a godsend.

Her arrival had been even better for St. Denis. Not only the mainstay of the town choir, Florence had also taken over the administration of the school sports teams. The dispirited and somewhat dowdy young newcomer Bruno had originally met had blossomed into a cheerful, self-confident woman with a widening circle of friends. She had earned the respect of her pupils and turned science into the most popular subject. She had persuaded the local recycling center to let her have all the discarded laptops and desktops so that she could repair them and launch a computer club at the school. *Sud Ouest* had run a story about the way all the club computers, when not in use, had been offered to the SETI Institute, to help process the reams of data from its radio telescopes that were scanning outer space for signs of extraterrestrial intelligence.

Florence was giving her children lunch when Bruno arrived. They waved their spoons and chanted "Bonjour, Bruno" when she showed him into the small kitchen.

"Have you eaten?" she asked. "I made Pamela's fish pie, and there's more than enough."

Bruno kissed the children and accepted gratefully.

"I know you like this part," said Florence, scraping off some of the crisp cheese gratin that covered the pie and transferring it to Bruno's plate. She poured two glasses of Bergerac Sec from the bottle in the refrigerator and handed one to Bruno. "I'm happy you gave me an excuse to have a glass of wine at lunchtime, but what brings you here?"

"Your computer club," he replied. "There's been a burglary, and a lot of good wine was stolen, and I was thinking that the thieves might try to sell it on priceminister.com or one of those other websites like eBay. Could your club come up with a program that would monitor those sites for these wines?" He handed over a copy of the list he had made of the gaps in Crimson's cellar.

Florence sipped her wine and scanned the list. "It should be possible. You have the vineyard, the year, even some of the shippers. Your burglary victim must keep good records."

"He's an Englishman, a retired civil servant. He has his cellar all cataloged like a filing system, along with what he paid for the wine. They took over ten thousand euros' worth. I can also get photos of the furniture, rugs and paintings that were stolen."

Her eyes widened. "Leave it with me. It's the kind of project that should get the kids thinking."

"He's the kind of man who'd pay a reward, so you can offer them an incentive."

"The thrill of the chase is all the incentive they need. You ought to see the way they've taken to hacking."

Bruno stopped chewing. "You're teaching them to hack? Is that a good idea?"

"They'd do it anyway. I'm just teaching them about computer security, how to build firewalls and search for malware. I don't let them practice on anything serious, but they've gotten behind a few of those pay firewalls some newspapers and magazines put up. The next project is to see if they can build their own version of an iPad, so they've been all over the Web looking for technical tips. The English teacher says it's done wonders for their English, so now Pamela is helping us to set up an exchange system with a school in Scotland. We've already got a Skype link with its computer club."

School had never been like this in his day, Bruno thought. This new generation was about to be unleashed on a rural commune where there were still farmers who drew their water from an ancestral well and in winter slept above their livestock for warmth.

"How are things between you and Pamela?" she asked, clearing away the children's plates and serving their dessert of stewed apple and yogurt. "I get the impression she's still depressed by her mother's death."

"She's due to fly back from Scotland later today after some complicated business with lawyers about the will and inheritance taxes," he replied, deliberately not answering her question. "Her finances are none of my business, but it seems like she'll be able to stay in St. Denis."

Bruno was not at all sure about the status of his relationship with Pamela. It was an affair where he sometimes felt he served at her pleasure, spending the night only at her invitation and not allowed to take anything for granted. Pamela guarded her privacy, but she could charm him with her warmth and generosity. And she could surprise him, bringing a flavor of the exotic and the unfamiliar. She was a woman unlike most of those he knew in St. Denis, and it was no surprise that she had forged friendships with Fabiola and with Florence, similarly strong and independent women with their own careers.

He kissed Florence and the children when he left, the taste of the after-lunch coffee lingering pleasantly in his mouth, and was just climbing into his van when his mobile phone launched into the opening notes of the "Marseillaise." He checked the screen and saw a Paris number that he recognized.

"I got your message," said Isabelle. "This burglary of yours is delicate stuff. Crimson is not just your usual British pensioner. His last job was running the Joint Security Committee in the Cabinet Office in Downing Street. Spies and their security people reported to him."

"You mean like M in the James Bond films?" He felt himself grinning at the absurdity of such a role being played by the genial old tennis player.

"Just like that. And he's an old friend or at least a long-standing colleague of the brigadier, so I've been ordered to St. Denis to take over the inquiry. This burglary may be more complicated than it looks."

3

Bruno could tell from the way the mayor took off his glasses and rubbed the bridge of his nose that he was not happy. His wife was in the hospital for some tests that sounded ominous. The project for the new sewers was well behind schedule, and the financial crisis meant that funds and grants from Paris were being cut. And now the commune was being hit by this wave of burglaries. The fact that one of the victims turned out to be an eminent Englishman with official connections in Paris was bad enough, but that neither the mayor nor Bruno had known that a retired British spymaster had been living on their territory for years was even worse.

Burglaries were supposed to be the responsibility of the gendarmes, but Bruno knew it would have been a mistake to make such a pitiful excuse. This was his turf and therefore his responsibility. However, Bruno knew how easily the mayor could be distracted by anything to do with local history.

On the shelf by the mayor's ancient desk lay a thick file of handwritten pages, the mayor's ambitious project of writing the definitive history of St. Denis from Neanderthal man through the Iron and Bronze Ages, the coming of the Celts, the arrival of the Romans, up to the present day. At various times Bruno had heard him wax lyrical about the Merovingian kings and the ancient Duchy of Toulouse, the Hundred Years' War against the English and the Albigensian heresy. There had been a whole year when the mayor spoke of little but the passage of the conquering Arabs from Spain and how they reeled back after Charles Martel defeated them at the Battle of Tours in 732. The mayor loved the coincidence that his three great French heroes shared the same name: Charles Martel, King Charles VII, who finally evicted the English in 1453, and, of course, Charles de Gaulle.

Bruno solemnly laid one of Murcoing's old banknotes on the mayor's desk, smoothed it out and said, "Loïc Murcoing died this morning and had this in a box on his bed. Father Sentout thinks it came from the Neuvic train."

"The Neuvic train, really?" The mayor replaced his spectacles and peered at the note. "July 26, 1944. It was the same day the Americans were making their breakout from the Normandy beachhead." His voice tailed off and he fell silent, his eyes fixed on some other place, some other time.

"They say it was a lot of money," said Bruno.

"Money? Over two billion francs, which means something over three hundred million euros. Did you know it all began as a plot between two of our prefects? One was a *résistant* and the other was condemned as a *collabo,* although perhaps that's too crude a word."

"I don't understand." Bruno was reeling at the idea of three hundred million euros in cash and wondering how much it had weighed, how it had been taken from the train.

"I suppose it was a credit to the wisdom of our prefects," the mayor began. There had been the Vichy prefect, a career civil servant named Callard, and Maxim Roue, the Gaullist one who would replace him after the Liberation. The two men knew each other and remained in discreet contact. With the

Allies already established ashore in Normandy and the Russian armies thundering through Poland toward Germany, Callard knew the Vichy regime was doomed. With an eye to his own future, he tipped off his successor that the Banque de France reserves were to be moved by train from Périgueux, where they had been stored to be safe from the bombing. The money was to be taken to Bordeaux for consignment to the Kriegsmarine. There was speculation that the German navy wanted to ship it out by submarine, perhaps to finance a new Reich in Argentina. Whatever the motives, the Resistance ambushed the train and took the money. A man calling himself Lieutenant Krikri left a signed receipt with the train guards for the full amount plus another fifteen hundred francs for the canvas sacks that held the money, each one sealed with lead and stamped with the seal of the Banque de France. Altogether, the haul had weighed six tons.

The mayor explained that various official inquiries after the war had concluded that the money was spent on pay and supplies for the Resistance fighters and money for their dependents. Even after the Germans lost Paris and retreated back into Germany, some of their garrisons held out in La Rochelle and elsewhere. The Allies couldn't spare any troops for them, so the Resistance took over the task, transforming itself into official units of the French army in the process. But the men still had to be fed and paid and their families supported. That was the official explanation.

"And the unofficial explanation?" asked Bruno.

"All rumor. Some of the local Resistance chiefs enjoyed very wealthy lifestyles after the war, Malraux, for one, although he was too close to de Gaulle to be touched. There was another, a man called Urbanovich, who suddenly became extremely rich with a big place in Paris and another in Cannes and ran one of the most expensive art galleries in Europe. Not bad for a Communist who was probably a Soviet agent. But nothing was ever proved."

"There must have been a lot of cash left over."

"That's why the rumors persist. But you should remember that there were no public funds for political parties until the mid-1950s, and parties need premises, staff, printing facilities and newspapers, particularly a new party like the Gaullists. I think you'll find that most political scandals can be traced to money, that or sex. If you're interested in all this, there's a woman historian at the Sorbonne who has a house the other side of Les Eyzies. Her name is Jacqueline Morgan. She's half American, half French; her father was a diplomat in Paris after the war and married a woman from the Périgord. I ran into her in the Bibliothèque Nationale when I was doing some research in Paris. She's gathered a lot of new material from the British and American archives on the Resistance and its postwar political roles. She's working on a book that should make quite a stir."

"Sounds interesting." Bruno would make a point of visiting her. "Murcoing had just over five thousand of those old francs in his chest. Not a lot to show for such a haul."

"The men who took part were promised ten thousand each, but a romantic young lieutenant called Gandouin said that for his men of the Groupe Valmy duty was its own reward. His men would take no fee. But at least one of the sacks of cash disappeared that night when they were moving the money."

"Whatever happened to him?"

"No idea. Perhaps I should have asked Murcoing, but it's too late now. I remember my father telling me about Gandouin. A lot of those young heroes died that winter, once they were re-formed into the French army and sent up to liberate

Alsace and then to invade Germany." The mayor looked up, forcing a briskness into his voice. "I suppose these banknotes now belong to Murcoing's heirs."

"Yes, I signed a receipt." Bruno leaned over and took the banknote from the mayor's hand.

"I'd like to have one framed and hung here in the *mairie* with a suitable plaque of explanation."

"You might ask Murcoing's daughter Joséphine if you could buy it from her. She struck me as the kind of woman who'd do a lot for a little money. You should have seen her perk up when I said the state pays for Resistance funerals. I've got her phone number here."

The mayor reached for his phone.

Bruno took the back road to Les Eyzies, a drive that always reminded him of cases and incidents past. As always, he admired the stupendous limestone cliffs that rose on each side of the river. Off to his left up the hill was the Grotte du Sorcier, the cave with one of the very few prehistoric engravings of a human face and a place dear in his memory as the spot where he had first kissed Isabelle. Farther up the valley was the site of the archaeological dig where the body of a young man wearing a Swatch had been found alongside a thirty-thousand-year-old grave.

He drove through the narrow main street of Les Eyzies, tucked between the cliff and the river, and mentally doffed his cap to the giant statue of Cro-Magnon man that loomed above the town. He took the sharply curving road that led along the Vézère Valley to the Lascaux Cave, and then at Tursac followed the mayor's directions to the small house of Jacqueline Morgan. A white BMW convertible with Paris license plates, its roof down, was parked beside a well-tended vegetable garden. Bruno noted with approval her choice of cherry tomatoes, eggplants, zucchini, haricots verts and some sweet corn.

Wearing jeans and a Columbia sweatshirt, clogs on her feet and a headband holding back a mass of iron-gray curls, Jacqueline Morgan took a cigarette from her mouth to extend a hand and greet him. She looked vaguely familiar; perhaps he'd seen her shopping in the market or standing in line at the post office. Behind her on each wall of the passage were loaded bookshelves. Bruno explained that the mayor had suggested she might be able to help him learn more about the Neuvic train and showed her Murcoing's banknote.

Her eyes widened. "I've never actually seen one of the notes before," she said. "Come in, come in, you're very welcome. The mayor has told me a lot about you."

Off to the left he saw a small sitting room with old furniture that looked comfortable, although hemmed in by more bookshelves that lined all the walls. She led him to the room on the right, again filled with bookshelves but with a large round table in the middle that contained a laptop, index-card boxes and several books. They were held open at certain pages by pens, a pepper mill and a handsome silver coffeepot. From the kitchen came the unmistakable scent of lamb being slowly roasted with rosemary and garlic.

"I clear all this away for dinner," she said, piling together some of the books on the table and clearing more from a chair to make some space for Bruno to sit. On the top of the pile sat a copy of Guy Penaud's *Histoire de la Résistance en Périgord.* "You caught me working on footnotes, a scholar's drudgery. I was just about to make some coffee. How do you take yours?"

"Black, one sugar, please. Are you writing a new book?"

"Yes, on Franco-American relations during the Cold War, a fertile field. I've written on bits of it before, on nuclear cooperation and American policy toward the French wars in Vietnam and Algeria, but now I'm trying to put it all together."

"The mayor seems to think it will have quite an impact, that you found lots of new material," Bruno said.

"We'll see." She went into the adjoining kitchen. Bruno heard a clatter of cups and the whir of a coffee grinder. She poked her head around the door and continued talking. "He's a good man, the mayor. It's such a shame about his wife. I'm making him dinner tonight after he gets back from visiting her in the hospital. Left to himself, he'd just have a sandwich, one of those men who are useless on his own."

"We're hoping she'll be able to come home soon."

"She's not coming home," came the voice from the kitchen. "You don't come back from galloping lymphatic cancer."

Bruno was stunned. The mayor had kept his wife's condition a secret from everyone, at least everyone but Jacqueline.

"You mean you didn't know?" she said, poking her head out again. "*Putain,* me and my big mouth. I'm really sorry, I thought his friends knew."

He was sure nobody else at the *mairie* knew either. Obviously the mayor's relationship with Jacqueline was closer than he'd thought.

"Let's forget it, okay?" she said, coming into the room. "And don't tell him I told you." She turned back into the kitchen, and he heard a metal tray being placed on a counter.

He'd never been close to the mayor's wife, who had rarely appeared at the *mairie,* but the news came as a shock. Cécile had never joined her husband in campaigning and seemed content to be a traditional wife, tending her home and her garden, politely greeting people in the market. She had stayed behind when the mayor had gone to Paris to work in politics and joined him there only once, for his investiture into the Senate.

Jacqueline reentered the room with a tray. "You were asking about the Neuvic train. Parts of my work led me into aspects of Resistance finance, which is why I got interested in the Neuvic affair, the slush fund to end all slush funds."

"Is this the manuscript?" he asked as he cleared some more space for the tray with its fine porcelain cups and saucers and a *cafetière.* He gestured to the typescript in front of him, Post-it notes in different colors scattered through the pages.

"No, mine is still in the computer, with copies sent elsewhere around the Net in case my hard drive dies. That happened to me once, and it was hell. What you have there are my father's memoirs, typed up from his handwritten journals."

"He was a diplomat, is that right?"

"Yes, he was in Paris after the war and then worked on the Marshall Plan, rebuilding Europe's economies. I first read about the Neuvic train fortune in those journals, where he called it the slush fund."

"The mayor thinks it was worth about three hundred million euros," he said.

She shrugged as she rested both hands on the plunger of the *cafetière* and began to press down. "The money aboard the Neuvic train was certainly a vast amount, worth about five percent of total government spending in 1946. Put it this way, the national education budget that year was 470 million francs, and the Neuvic train held about five times that."

The proportion staggered him. There were at least three official inquiries into the fate of the Neuvic money, Jacqueline explained, adding that they had all pretty much whitewashed the whole affair, claiming the money went to finance the Resistance fighters and their families and some was used to bribe prison guards. That was true up to a point, she conceded, but only for a fraction of the money, maybe half or a little more. Millions had been stolen.

"How much do you know about French politics after the war?" she asked.

"De Gaulle came to power after the Liberation of Paris in 1944 but resigned in 1946," he replied. "I'm not sure why."

"De Gaulle wanted a strong presidency rather than the unstable parliaments of the prewar days. The Communists, Socialists and Christian Democrats, who'd been in a coalition, naturally wanted a return to the party system, and they accused de Gaulle of wanting to be a dictator. Then the other two parties wanted to get rid of the Communists as the Cold War got under way, and the Gaullists started building their own party, the RPF. Politics are expensive, so that's where a lot of the money went, but maybe it was more virtual than real."

"Virtual? I don't understand."

She looked at him. "Suppose you're an American diplomat in Paris in 1946 and 1947, and the Communists are the biggest political party. Remember the Cold War is just getting started. What would American policy be?"

"Stop the Communists, I suppose. And try to strengthen the other parties, the anti-Communists."

"Right, and if you're an American diplomat, with all the money in the world, you'd use it to help the anti-Communists, right?"

"Yes."

"No, wrong," Jacqueline said firmly. "At least wrong if you do it in public where there's immediately a scandal about Americans buying up the French political system. But if some loyal Frenchmen with fine Resistance records start handing out wads of money with a nod and a wink and a discreet murmur about *le train de Neuvic,* nobody asks any questions, even if the money really came from the Americans."

"But wouldn't they have to change it from dollars?"

"Yes, but remember how the Marshall Plan worked. The

Americans gave dollars to the Europeans to buy food and goods and machine tools to restart their factories. They were repaid in local currency, which the Americans could do nothing with. There were no real exchange markets in those days. So the various American embassies suddenly found themselves sitting on this vast slush fund of French francs, Italian lire, Dutch guilders and so on. The money went to stop communism through funding election campaigns, subsidizing newspapers and student organizations and backing Socialist trade unions to undermine the Communist ones."

"Two slush funds, the Neuvic money and the Marshall Plan, and who knows which was which?"

"That's what I'm trying to find out," said Jacqueline. "That's why my father's memoirs are the key to all this. He was in it all the way through, from late 1945 to 1951 when the Marshall Plan became the Mutual Security Act."

"And how much was the Marshall Plan?"

"Altogether? About thirteen billion dollars. But another thirteen billion had already been sent in aid to Europe between the end of the war and the Marshall Plan starting in 1947. So the U.S. pumped in a total of twenty-six billion, at a time when the American GDP was just over two hundred billion a year. Thirteen percent of the GDP is pretty generous if you ask me, but not too expensive to stop Western Europe from going Communist. And it was certainly a whole lot cheaper than a war."

"I had no idea," said Bruno.

"Not many people do. If you want to know what really happened in history, it's like those two *Washington Post* reporters said in the Watergate scandal: 'Follow the money.'"

"The mayor is right about your book having a big impact," Bruno said. "I think you'll be rewriting the recent history of France."

"Oh, goody," she said, an impish grin lighting up her face, making her look years younger and much more attractive. "And wait till you see what I've dug up on secret nuclear cooperation. Your French independent nuclear weapons aren't nearly as independent as you think." She said it as casually as if she were talking about the vegetables in her garden. She went to one of her bookshelves and handed him a slim paperback. He looked at the title: *Le partage des milliards de la Résistance,* the distribution of the Resistance billions.

"That will get you off to a good start; most of the background is in there. Let me have it back when you're done. More coffee, or can I offer you something stronger? You look like you could do with a drink."

Even as he was thinking that a stiff scotch would be welcome, Bruno's mobile rang. It was Albert, head of the *pompiers,* the local fire brigade, which also acted as the emergency medical service.

"Got an emergency call from somewhere up in the hills by St. Chamassy about somebody badly hurt with head injuries," Albert said. His voice was faint, the signal weak. "We've just got here and the gendarmes should be on their way if they can find it." He gave Bruno directions. "And bring a doctor for a death certificate. The guy's dead. I think we might have a murder."

4

There was still no sign of the gendarmes when Bruno parked his van on the rough grass beside Albert's red emergency vehicle. A battered silver Renault Clio stood beside it. In front of the cottage on a small patch of gravel was a blue Ford Transit van, its side and rear doors open to reveal an empty interior. It bore English plates and a small GB plaque on the rear bumper. Beside the van lay a lumpish shape, two men standing over it—one was Albert, and the other was a stranger, carrying a plastic bag.

The house behind them was like many others in the district, with a red tile roof in the shape of a witch's hat and walls of light brown stone that in the sun turned to the color of honey. Wooden shutters hung on the windows, painted the usual pale gray that had become ubiquitous after the French navy sold off its vast stocks of paint very cheaply. To one side was a small barn and to the other a pocket-sized swimming pool, flanked by two cheap metal chairs that needed a new coat of white paint. A few empty flower pots were strewn about. The front door was open to show a floor of terra-cotta tiles. There were no personal touches, no patch of herbs or vegetables, no children's toys. It was a *gîte*, a farmhouse cheaply restored and transformed into a holiday rental.

"*Salut,* Bruno," said Albert. "This is Monsieur Valentoux from Paris, who called us. The silver Clio belongs to him. He was going to be staying here with the dead man."

"Monsieur," said Bruno as he shook hands with Valentoux, noting the pale, drawn face. He caught the smell of vomit, saw a patch of it by the rear wheel of the blue van. There were more spatters on the front of Valentoux's jeans and on his shoes, leather sneakers that looked expensive. His hair was short with blond streaks, and he wore a dark blue scarf around his neck, tucked into a cream shirt that Bruno guessed was silk.

"I put a cradle over the head," said Albert, looking down at the body. It was covered by a fireman's red blanket. Bruno knelt down and lifted a corner of the blanket and saw a spindly metal framework, rather like the ones he put over his winter seedlings.

"It's from my garden," Albert explained. "I was picking it up from my sister, and it seemed like a good idea to cover him up. He's been dead for some hours. It's not a pleasant sight."

"*Mon Dieu,*" said Valentoux. He raised his head to look at Bruno. "I couldn't even tell you if it's him."

"Perhaps the fire chief could help you to your car, monsieur," said Bruno, waiting until they left before uncovering the battered shape that had once been a human head. Blood had pooled beneath and behind the man's head. Bits of shattered bone and teeth stood out from the pool. The face was unrecognizable as human, the features savagely, perhaps deliberately, obliterated.

Bruno closed his eyes and tried to concentrate, forcing himself out from shock and back into professionalism by trying to think what weapon might have done this. Perhaps an iron bar, he told himself. He opened his eyes and looked at the rest of the body. One hand was blood-smeared and swollen, as if the victim might have tried to protect himself. The other hand looked to have been professionally manicured, the nails buffed and polished. An open and empty black leather wallet with brass reinforcements on the corners lay between the dead man's thighs.

The dead man was wearing khaki slacks and boat shoes without socks, a plain black T-shirt and a denim jacket. Only the jacket collar bore signs of blood, which suggested he had been knocked to the ground and then his head battered as he lay there. His attacker must have stood over him, probably straddling the body to apply backhand and forehand blows to the head. That was the only way Bruno could interpret the way the blood had spattered. They had experts on that, these days, at the Police Nationale.

He replaced the blanket over its cradle, rose and on his cell phone speed-dialed J-J, chief of detectives for the *département.* As usual, he got a recording, left a message and then sent J-J a brief text message.

On the floor by the passenger seat of the blue Ford was an empty bag of potato chips, some sandwich wrappings and a British newspaper, the *Daily Telegraph,* from the day before. Bruno took a pair of evidence gloves from his pouch. He noticed that under the seat was a magazine called *Antiques Weekly,* and some maps and other papers were in the door pocket. He examined one set of papers that seemed to be a rental agreement for the van for three weeks from a branch of Avis in a town called Croydon. The renter was identified as Francis Fullerton. Tucked into the Avis folder was a ticket stub from the 7:00 a.m. Eurostar train the previous day. Bruno checked that the registration number on the ticket matched that of the blue Ford. The other sheaf of papers was from

Delightful Dordogne, the local vacation rental agency run by Dougal, a retired Scottish businessman. The *gîte* was rented to a Francis Fullerton for two weeks, starting on a Saturday, as usual with such agreements. So why had Fullerton arrived early?

The rest of the van was empty. Bruno went back to the body and found some euros and British coins in a trouser pocket and a British passport in the denim jacket. He walked back to the Clio, where Albert and Valentoux were leaning against its side, smoking. Valentoux was still carrying his plastic bag.

"What's in there?" Bruno asked, gesturing at the bag. In the distance, he could hear a siren. The gendarmes seemed at last to have found the place.

Valentoux lifted the bag and looked at it in confusion, as if he'd never seen it before. He handed it to Bruno. "I was going to welcome him with lunch."

Inside was a baguette, a *saucisson,* cheese, fruit, tomatoes and a bottle of champagne, no longer cold. Nestling at the bottom was a small wrapped package. Bruno asked him to open it.

"I'd rather not, it's a gift," said Valentoux, and then caught himself. He took the package, tore open the silver bow and the gold wrapping paper. Inside was a gift box, which he opened to reveal a Laguiole folding knife with a wooden handle and corkscrew and a leather pouch. "Francis had always wanted one."

"What time did you get here?"

"About one-thirty, maybe a bit later. I left Paris before seven this morning to avoid the rush." He tossed his cigarette to the ground, crushed it with a violent twist of his foot, then took a pack of Marlboro Golds from his jacket pocket to light another. Then he offered the pack. Bruno shook his head, but Albert took one.

"Did you come by the autoroute? You should have a receipt."

Valentoux went around to the side door of his Clio and took a piece of paper from the well between the front seats. It was an autoroute *péage* receipt for that day from the exit at Limoges, stamped at 11:28 a.m. that morning. That would be consistent with his arrival at about 1:30 p.m. Bruno nodded and put it in his notebook.

"His call to the emergency service was made at one forty-three p.m., and he was transferred to us. He sounded panicked, said he thought his friend was dead," said Albert. "I got here about twenty minutes later and called you."

"What brings you down here?" Bruno asked Valentoux.

"I'm going to be working here for the summer at the drama festival in Sarlat. We were going to start with a couple of weeks together, just the two of us." His French was educated.

"How long had you been friends?" The approaching siren was louder now, distracting Valentoux.

"We were more than friends. I met Francis in London in January."

"How did you meet?"

"I was guest director at a small theater in Islington. He came to the opening-night party with one of the actors."

Bruno showed him the photo in the passport, and Valentoux confirmed that it was Francis Fullerton. He took a quick glance at the blanket-shrouded body and shuddered.

"What do you know about him?"

"We spent a lot of time together in London, and then he came to visit me in Paris last month. He's in France quite often."

"Why's that?"

"He's an antiques dealer. He buys British antiques, mainly furniture, and brings them here to sell at French *brocante* fairs. Then he buys French furniture here to take back to England. He seemed to do well out of it, never short of money and always generous." Valentoux's voice caught as he said this.

Bruno was about to ask why the blue van was empty and where Fullerton's clothes might be when his phone rang. It was J-J, returning his call. Bruno turned away to give J-J a briefing and directions, and then a familiar Twingo came in sight at the end of the lane, followed by the flashing blue light of a gendarme van.

"Wait here," Bruno said, and advanced to greet Fabiola for the second time that day.

"They were lost, so I showed them the way," she said, gesturing at the van, its siren finally silent. She took her medical bag from the back of her Twingo and walked across to the body.

Two young women in uniform climbed from the front of the police van, and a young male recruit unfolded his long limbs from a seat at the back. Ever since Capitaine Duroc had been suspended, the St. Denis gendarmerie had been run by a series of temporary commanders, all of them women.

The new one, Yveline Gerlache, had just arrived that week from Lorraine. So far, Bruno had met her only for a brief courtesy call and coffee at the *mairie*. They were to have been guests at a dinner party thrown by the mayor, but then his wife had been taken ill. Bruno reminded himself to organize a replacement dinner as they shook hands. In her late twenties and armed with a law degree, she had graduated the previous year from the officers' training academy in Melun. She was solidly built but with delicate features and unusually long eyelashes and her grip was as firm as a man's. Beside her was

Françoise, a gendarme whom Bruno knew well. Ordinarily he'd have kissed her on both cheeks, but Françoise held back, offering him her hand.

The lanky young male recruit was weighing himself down with a forensics bag, a camera and other equipment that he took from the rear of the van. He tried to add a roll of crime-scene tape to his burden, and some of the materials slipped from beneath his arm. He glanced nervously at Yveline, who looked at Bruno and rolled her eyes.

"You might not need all that," said Bruno. "The Police Nationale are sending a full forensics team. Their head of detectives is on his way. It seems that the dead man is a foreigner, an Englishman."

"So it's too sensitive for us clodhoppers from the gendarmes," Yveline said with a grin, but her eyes were not smiling.

"And much too serious for a country bumpkin like me," Bruno replied, and told her what he had learned. She heard him out and then asked: "What's their relationship? Lovers?"

Bruno shrugged. "I haven't asked, but I imagine so. The Englishman's an antiques dealer. His French friend Valentoux is a theater director. They were planning a vacation here together."

"A lovers' quarrel?"

"It's possible. But there's no blood on him. If he left Paris when he says he did, the timing of the phone call he made reporting the murder suggests he wouldn't have had time to kill the victim and then clean up. The autoroute receipt fits his story."

Yveline glanced across at Valentoux. He had at last put down his plastic bag and had a large white handkerchief pressed to his face.

"He's dead, sure enough," said Fabiola, shaking her head

as she returned from the body. "As brutal a killing as I've ever seen. Jaw, teeth, cheekbones and skull all shattered by something cylindrical and almost certainly metal. An iron bar, maybe one of those things you need to change a tire. Time of death was probably between six and ten yesterday evening."

Bruno still had his gloves on, so he opened the small hatch at the side of the Ford where the spare tire and tools were kept. Nothing seemed to be missing. Yveline had donned her own gloves and was looking in the back of Valentoux's Clio.

"Still, our theatrical friend could have killed him last night, washed and changed and driven away and then given himself an alibi on the autoroute this morning," said Yveline.

Bruno nodded thoughtfully and was about to follow her determined stride back to the body when Fabiola caught his arm.

"You're going to be stuck here with the body until they take it to the forensics lab in Bergerac. That means you won't be able to pick up Pamela at the airport. I can do it. Five o'clock, isn't that when her plane lands? But we'll expect you for dinner."

5

Bruno knew he would not quickly forget the expression on Yves Valentoux's face when J-J said he would be detained overnight at the gendarmerie for questioning. He had cast a look of hopeless appeal at Bruno before Yveline pushed the Parisian into her van. Already devastated by the death of his lover, Valentoux was now being treated as the prime suspect on what Bruno thought was thin evidence. J-J had brushed aside Bruno's discreet suggestion that he was being too hasty. Bruno acknowledged to himself that Valentoux's alibi deserved further probing and that his theatrical experience meant he could probably play the role of innocent with enough conviction to fool Bruno. But there had been something pathetic in the way he carried his plastic bag with the lunch ingredients, something genuine in his look of shock. And much as Bruno liked and respected J-J as a policeman, he was an old-fashioned type who made little secret of his dislike of homosexuals.

Bruno, by contrast, felt guilty about them. This stemmed from an incident that he recalled uncomfortably as one of his most notable failures as a policeman. It was a memory that kept returning, a frustrating and ugly event that he remembered as the swimming-pool affair. It had been in his first year as a municipal policeman, when he was still limping slightly from the bullet he had taken in his hip in Bosnia. He'd been part of the French contingent in the UN peacekeeping force, and the wound had led to his honorable discharge.

He had been summoned by a phone call late on an August afternoon when the heat had begun to subside, the time when people begin to rise from their after-lunch naps and the bakeries reopen for the evening trade. A voice he did not recognize, slurred with drink, had informed him there was a mess to be cleared up at a remote farmhouse at the far end of the commune. The phone had then been slammed down with a burst of laughter.

Bruno had checked the map of the commune on the wall of his office and phoned Géraldine, who ran the bar at the local tennis club and lived in that area. A disused farmhouse had been restored and turned into a *gîte* over the winter and a pool installed, she told him. It was mainly rented by British visitors, some of whom she'd persuaded to take out temporary membership at the club. Géraldine gave him directions, which he traced on the map with his finger and then set off.

It took twenty minutes to get there, a pleasant drive along country lanes, fields of sunflowers giving way to grazing cows in the meadows and then to sheep as the road climbed and the grass thinned out. As he rounded the last bend on the dirt track that wound up the hill, the scene appeared to be peaceful. The stone farmhouse had a new roof of red tiles, and the gravel forecourt was so new and white it almost hurt the eyes.

The front door was closed, and he strolled around to the rear, calling out *"Y'a quelqu'un?"* Then his eye was caught by the trail of blood that ran over the terrace of flagstones and led to a swimming pool at the rear of the house. Shards of glass glittered in the sun from an overturned portable bar, and at the pool steps he saw brownish swirls of blood hanging in the water. To the right of the pool was a white Range Rover with British plates, its windshield cracked and the headlights smashed.

A voice challenged him in English. He turned to see a middle-aged man in very tight swimming trunks standing at the sliding glass doors that led into the house. He had blood on his chest, a swollen lip and two black eyes, and he was holding a pair of fire tongs. Bruno saluted, addressed him as "Monsieur" and said he'd received a phone call reporting trouble. Bruno remembered thinking he'd seen faces like that after a particularly tough rugby match. He asked if monsieur needed to be driven to the medical clinic.

"An argument. Private. Much drink," the man said in broken French. Bruno looked past him into the house where another middle-aged man was helping a naked youth to limp his way down the stairs from the upper floor. Despite the bloodied nose and battered features, Bruno thought he recognized the young man. At the sight of Bruno in uniform, the youth turned as if to climb back up the stairs. Bruno gently took the fire tongs from the first man's hands and stepped inside the house. The two men on the stairs had also been beaten, with red marks on their bodies as if they had been hit with sticks. The older man, blood trickling from his mouth and nose, winced as he stood upright. The buttocks and thighs of the young man flared an angry red.

A pair of jeans and a T-shirt lay on a chair by the glass doors, a wallet peeking from one of the pockets. Bruno took it out, opened it and saw that the young man, Édouard Marty, had a French ID card and was eighteen years old. Bruno recognized the name. Just a few weeks earlier, Édouard had been at the tennis club with schoolmates, celebrating their graduation from the lycée in Sarlat. Édouard was going on to university, planning to study architecture at Bordeaux.

"What happened here, Édouard?" Bruno asked. The middle-aged man helping Édouard put a hand on the boy's shoulder as if to stop him from turning to answer.

"We were enjoying a quiet day by the pool when we were attacked by a bunch of thugs with pickax handles," the man said in good but accented French. His friend in swim trunks tried to interrupt, but the man on the stairs was too angry to be silenced. "They wore stocking masks over their heads. They beat us up, smashed the cars and drove off with two of our friends. Two more of us had to go to the clinic. One has a broken arm."

Beside him, Édouard sank to his knees on the stairs and lowered his head, his shoulders heaving with sobs.

After a brief but angry exchange between the two Englishmen in their own tongue, they refused to give their names to Bruno. It didn't matter; Bruno found registration papers in the Range Rover along with a copy of the rental agreement for the *gîte*. But it was clear that one had told the other to say nothing. Nobody had answered when Bruno asked if they had all been at the pool when the attack had come or whether some of them had been indoors. They wouldn't even confirm how many attackers there had been or if any of them had spoken. Édouard would not look at Bruno and remained silent throughout, shaking his head at Bruno's offer to take him to the clinic or to call his parents to take him home.

And there it had ended. Uncertain of the legal rights of foreigners, Bruno had felt powerless and frustrated. He had been alone; the gendarmes had been too busy with a traffic accident to be able to send any support. When Bruno reached the medical center, one Englishman had been treated for a fractured arm and a young Frenchman for a broken nose. The French youth had not shown his *carte vitale,* which would have qualified him for free treatment. Another Englishman in an Audi with smashed headlights had paid the medical fees and driven them away.

When Bruno went back to the *gîte,* the place was empty and completely tidied up. An envelope containing two thousand francs had been left on the kitchen counter, the words "for damages" scrawled on the outside. Édouard called his parents that evening to say he was joining friends for a vacation in England. His parents were too embarrassed to answer Bruno's questions in anything more than grudging monosyllables. Bruno had no statements, no formal complaints and no real basis for an inquiry, as the magistrate told him when declining to take up the case. What he should have done, Bruno now knew, was to seize the visitors' passports and their car keys, confiscate Édouard's ID card and say they could have them back only when they had made formal statements at his office.

Bruno knew that an injustice had been done. He had checked on the age of consent for homosexuals and established that Édouard and his English friends had committed no crime under French law. Édouard being gay had neither shocked nor offended him; he had been too long in the army to confuse anyone's character with what they chose to do in bed. He could have let the matter drop, but Bruno felt outrage that such deliberate violence could be inflicted on his territory with impunity.

He talked to several of Édouard's friends and tried to track down the other young Frenchman who had been treated at the clinic. It turned out he had given a false name and address in Bergerac. After a few days, all he had were the names of the four Englishmen who had rented the *gîte* and those of two of Édouard's school friends who had decided to take a sudden camping trip in Spain. One was the son of a local stonemason and the other the son of a dairy farmer, both of them tough-looking men in their late forties whom Bruno knew from the rugby club. They claimed to have been fishing and drinking together on the afternoon when the attack had taken place.

"From what we hear, a bunch of foreigners were trying to turn some local kids into fags," the stonemason had said when Bruno tracked him down at the house he was restoring. He would not meet Bruno's eyes. "Seems to me it's the foreigners you ought to be locking up." The other builders at the site had backed him up, muttering that there would have been more than a few bloody noses if they had known what was going on.

There was little more Bruno could do, but he called on Joe, his predecessor as the town's policeman, for advice.

"What's the problem?" Joe asked. "A couple of English queens get taught a lesson. They won't be messing around with any more of our youngsters. It's not the first time something like this has happened, and it won't be the last. I know there's a lot of talk about community policing these days. Well, this is community justice, and you interfere with that at your peril."

Bruno was shocked by what he heard. He was equally stunned when the mayor congratulated him briefly as they filed out at the end of a staff meeting at the *mairie*. "Glad you managed to tidy up that mess without any fuss," the mayor had said, with a reassuring squeeze of Bruno's arm. "That's the kind of policing we want around here."

As he turned into the driveway that led to Pamela's house, Bruno's mood lifted when he saw her with Fabiola and his own riderless horse leaving the stable. He sounded his horn in a double beep, parked and went up to take Pamela in his arms as she swung down from her mare. She kissed him squarely on the lips.

"If you must stand me up at the airport and then turn up late for the horses, I suppose a murder is just about acceptable as an excuse," she said as she hugged him.

"It's good to see you," he replied.

She put her hand to his cheek, kissed him again and turned. "We're heading for the ridge. See if you can catch us, or there's no dinner for you."

She slid from his arms and put her foot back into the stirrup to mount her horse. She tapped Bess's sides with her heels and trotted away while Hector ambled across to nuzzle at Bruno's chest, expecting his customary apple. Bruno stroked his horse's neck and gave him his treat. In the stable he greeted his puppy Balzac and installed him in the binoculars case that he strapped around his chest. He donned his riding boots and helmet, exchanged his uniform jacket for a plain one, mounted Hector and set out after the two women.

The day had been too busy for reflection about the reunion with Pamela. Theirs was an affectionate friendship, based on a common love of food and horses and convivial evenings that often enough ended in bed. But she had made it clear that she had no wish to deepen their relationship, or to make it permanent. Bruno wasn't at all sure what he wanted. He was comfortable in her company and content in their time together, but there was the constant thought that he wanted something more. It was not as simple as saying that he wanted children and she did not, that he wanted to experience a full family life. Bruno knew that he also wanted passion in his life, and for all the delight he took in Pamela and the sensuality she could display and share in private, passion and emotional fervor were not what he knew with her.

That brought his thoughts back to Isabelle, mercurial and tantalizing, fierce in her ambition and her determination to carve a brilliant career. Sometimes moody, sometimes capable of a deep and embracing calm, she stirred him in ways that were so profound he felt himself exulting in the great gift of knowing her. But they each knew, however often fate and sexual need drew them back together, that there was no future for them; that she was as committed to the career potential and power of Paris as he was locked in the deep peace of the Périgord.

Isabelle had called him as he was driving to Pamela's to say that her train had just reached Bordeaux and she had rented a car to drive to her hotel in Périgueux. Might he join her for dinner? Or perhaps your Mad Englishwoman has returned, she had added, with a touch of something in her voice that was part frost and part mockery.

"She's not English and she's not mad," he had replied, as he always did. The initial nickname the inhabitants of St. Denis had given to Pamela, who was Scottish, was no longer used, except by Isabelle. It was one of the few things about her that he found tiresome; such a casual dismissal of another woman was beneath her.

"I'll see you at Crimson's house tomorrow, or we could meet for coffee in St. Denis and I'll take you out there," he had said.

"We've got the GPS address. See you there early tomorrow." And she had hung up, leaving him to speculate what she had meant by "We" as he allowed Hector to pick up the pace and canter after the two women. Hector quickly narrowed the gap, treating Bruno to the delightful sight of his two friends bouncing in their saddles. Pamela looked especially magnificent, with her trim waist and that red-bronze hair flaring out behind her like a fox's tail.

Hearing the approach of his horse's hooves, Fabiola glanced back, waved and pushed her mare to a canter. Then all three of them launched into a gallop along the lower slope of the ridge. Bruno heard Pamela whooping with joy as she rounded the edge of the woods and sent rabbits scurrying and a flock of crows exploding noisily from the trees. Balzac gave one of his eager little barks, just deep enough to hold the promise of the full-throated bay of a mature hound. For the first time that day, Bruno felt at ease with the world.

His mood continued through the soothing chore of rubbing down and feeding the horses and the ceremony of opening the gifts Pamela had brought. For him, there was a bottle of Lagavulin, the magnificent scotch whisky that he had first tasted at Pamela's table. Fabiola received a cashmere sweater. Pamela had brought a leg of Scottish lamb, a whole smoked salmon and some Lanark Blue cheese made of ewe's milk that could only be found in Scotland. The lamb had been roasting in the oven since soon after Pamela's return, and the rich, luscious smell pervaded the kitchen.

Fabiola set the table and then went into the garden to pick the early strawberries and the first of the haricots verts. Bruno opened the wine he had brought, two treasures selected from his cellar to go with the food he was sure Pamela would be bringing. For the smoked salmon, he'd brought a Bergerac white from Château la Vieille Bergerie. For the lamb, he had sacrificed one of his last remaining bottles of the Grand Millésime 2005 from Château de Tiregand. The wines of Bergerac, he believed, were one of France's better-kept secrets. While half of him looked forward to the day when they took their place alongside the great vintages of Bordeaux, he also feared that he'd be less and less able to afford them.

The wines ready and the glasses polished, Bruno went out to the garden to dig up some potatoes. Back in the kitchen he washed and peeled them as Fabiola beside him prepared the beans, and Pamela began slicing the salmon at the big round kitchen table. Glancing up from the sink, Bruno could see Pamela's swimming pool and a corner of her grass tennis court, whose lumps and dips persistently frustrated his attempts to roll them smooth. The vivid green of late spring covered the slope that rose to the woods and the ridge that looked down on St. Denis.

"Shall I harvest some mint?" he asked. Pamela had introduced him and Fabiola to the British custom of eating mint sauce with lamb.

"Not today," she replied. "We're trying something different, something a little magical."

She laid the slices of salmon onto the plates, black pepper and quartered fresh lemons beside them, and began to slice the big round loaf of Meyrals bread she had bought on the way back from Bergerac airport. Then she took from her bag a small dark jar and chanted in theatrical tones: " 'Rowan tree and red thread, keep all witches deep in dread.' My mother used to say that every time we had rowan jelly. The rowan tree is meant to be good magic, you find it often in churchyards. We used to bring a bough of rowan indoors on Good Friday to keep away witches and the dark forces. And my father liked to squeeze a little rowan juice into his gin and tonic. Made into jelly, it goes well with lamb, so I brought some for you to try."

The potatoes and the haricots were bubbling in their saucepans as Pamela put a meat thermometer into the lamb and pronounced it done. She left it on the stove top to rest, took off her apron and ushered them to the table.

"Welcome home," said Bruno, pouring out the white wine.

"And welcome to you both," she said, clinking the glasses and giving the good news that her mother's estate was now settled and her financial future looked reasonably secure. Her worst fears had not been realized; her mother had not left everything to the Battersea Dogs Home or some charity that rescued old donkeys. She would be able to stay in St. Denis with her friends and her horses and never have to see her ex-husband again.

"So this is a very good day," she declared, and turned to Bruno. "And now I want to hear all about this murder."

"You mean that under English law someone can bequeath their property to anyone they like? In France it has to go to the family heirs."

"Yes, I know, it's part of your Code Napoléon. But come on, let's hear about the murder."

The bare facts were easily told. But it was hard to describe the growing skepticism of Yveline and J-J. Valentoux had gazed at them helplessly when they asked him to prove he had not killed Fullerton the previous day. The man was clearly in shock, still stunned by the sight of his friend so brutally killed and now aghast at the further stress of hostile questioning. He had insisted that he'd been at home in his Paris apartment overlooking the Buttes Chaumont the previous evening, reading the manuscript of a new play. He had no visitors, had seen nobody and so could not prove that he had not driven down to St. Denis, murdered the Englishman, driven back to Paris and then returned in the morning to establish an alibi. He was taken to the gendarmerie for questioning and detained overnight under *garde à vue*.

"If it's not him, we have nothing; no clue, no motive, no idea of a suspect," J-J had told Bruno. He had replied that short of fingerprints or DNA evidence, they could not even be sure the dead man was Francis Fullerton. J-J had nonetheless asked Bruno to call the British consulate in Bordeaux while he sent a query to the British police through the usual informal channels.

"Two gay lovers, they have a quarrel, crime of passion," J-J had said. "That's the working hypothesis, although I suppose whatever trendy young magistrate gets the case will say I'm prejudiced."

"Not if Yveline says it first," said Bruno. "Anyway, you are prejudiced. We both know that."

"That goes for most cops my age," J-J grumbled.

The only new piece of evidence came from the dead man's trouser pocket; two receipts that Bruno had missed in his initial search. Fullerton had twice on the previous day filled his van with diesel fuel, once in Calais and then at a station in the shopping center outside Périgueux. J-J had sent a detective to check the tapes from the latter's security camera. Since the receipt gave the time of purchase, it was a simple matter to wind back the tapes, and the man shown filling his van was wearing the same clothes as Fullerton and looked sufficiently like him for a preliminary identification. After filling his van, he had gone to the air pump to check his tires and had opened the rear doors, revealing that the van had been full of furniture.

"So that's the second mystery, apart from the murder," Bruno said over the smoked salmon. "What happened to the furniture? Did he deliver it somewhere before he picked up the keys to the *gîte,* or was it stolen by his attacker? And why did he arrive a day early? Valentoux seemed certain that they had arranged to meet today, and Fullerton had said he'd get an early train through the tunnel and planned to arrive here early afternoon today."

"And he has no alibi that could show he'd been in Paris yesterday evening?" Pamela asked.

Bruno shook his head. "He was racking his brains trying to remember, but he'd been at home since the late afternoon. We asked if he'd had food delivered, gone out for a drink, had a phone call—anything."

"What about his mobile phone?" Fabiola asked. "Can't you find out from that where he was?"

"Yes, but if he was trying to fabricate an alibi he could have left the phone at his apartment in Paris and still come down here to commit the murder. At least he gave us Fullerton's cellphone number, and we're trying to trace its movements, but there was no sign of it in his van or in the suitcase we found in the house."

"Are you sure they were a gay couple?" Pamela asked.

"Valentoux confirmed that when he was being interrogated."

Bruno did not mention the tension that had arisen with J-J and Yveline when Bruno had argued there was too little evidence to hold Valentoux for questioning. There had been another row when Bruno learned that Yveline had delayed sending a fax to the *procureur,* the public prosecutor, until after his office had closed. Under French law, once a crime had been committed, the *procureur* assigned a *juge d'instruction,* an investigating magistrate, to supervise the case. Delaying the formal alert to the *proc* was a fairly common police tactic, giving them more time to question a suspect. Bruno's response had been to go to his car to call Annette Meraillon, a young magistrate he trusted. When he mentioned Valentoux's name, she perked up to say she'd seen a couple of his plays in Paris and had been impressed. She promised to follow up.

It would infuriate J-J and Yveline, but that was their problem. Then, as he'd driven to Pamela's house, he'd heard a report of the murder on Radio Périgord. Albert must have tipped them off, but it meant that any inquiry from Annette could have been triggered by the media. That would leave him in the clear with his colleagues. Bruno put it from his mind and began to pour his treasured Pécharmant red.

When the lamb had been served, the rowan jelly tasted and praised along with Bruno's red wine, Pamela asked him, "So what do you think?"

"I don't think he did it. He seemed genuinely stunned by Fullerton's death. Maybe I'm overcompensating because of the way J-J and the gendarmes seemed to leap to conclusions. But I'm also wondering whether there's a link to this spate of burglaries I mentioned."

The coincidence had struck Bruno when Valentoux had described Fullerton's astute method of doing business, buying French antiques for sale in England and then doing the reverse in a neat back-and-forth across the Channel, taking advantage of the snob appeal of foreign antiques in each country. It was the kind of operation that would fit with burglaries, taking stolen goods abroad for sale where they would be less likely to be traced. Whoever had burgled Crimson's house had known which items were worth taking. Fullerton couldn't have done it, given the timing of his travels, but there was serious money to be made and perhaps a wider organization involved, and that could provide a motive for murder.

Over fresh salad from the garden and Pamela's Lanark Blue cheese, they finished the wine, and Pamela looked thoughtfully at the painting of an extremely plump pig that hung on her kitchen wall.

"I wonder if I should think about getting some special insurance. That's quite a valuable painting, and I've got some decent furniture." Pamela had been stunned to hear that Crimson's house had been emptied; they were frequent tennis partners and she knew him well. "I've never worried about burglaries around here before."

"You don't even lock your door half the time," said Fabiola. "I keep telling you about it."

"Nor does Bruno," Pamela replied. "And he's a policeman."

"I lock my shotgun and the shells away, but I've got nothing else worth stealing," Bruno said. "And Balzac's there most of the time."

"Balzac is still too much of a puppy to deter any thief. And there's your wine—you'd be furious if that got stolen."

After the fresh strawberries and the coffee, Fabiola helped them wash the dishes, then said a discreet good night.

"Would you like to stay the night?" Pamela asked, taking his hand. "I'd hate for you to be stopped and Breathalyzed by this new gendarme woman."

"It wouldn't be her. There's a new rule that gendarmes can't go on traffic patrol in their own commune, to stop them from recognizing a friend and letting him off with a warning. And yes, I'd love to stay the night, but if you're tired I can use your guest room."

"I could tell that's where you slept while I was away. Why didn't you use our bed?"

"Because it's your bed," he said. He'd been exercising her horses as well as his own while she had been in Scotland, so he had usually had dinner with Fabiola and then stayed over at Pamela's rather than drive home after a glass or two too many. It was on the tip of his tongue to say: I don't think of your bed as ours. But he'd caught himself, and said, "Your bed isn't the same without you in it."

"Silly Bruno," she said, kissing him. "In my bedroom the bath is en suite, much more convenient. Why don't we go up with a candle and take a nice hot bath together?"

6

"Murder in Périgord" said the headline in *Sud Ouest* the next morning. "Englishman brutally slain in *gîte*. Parisian man held for questioning."

"So you've got the guy already?" asked Fauquet with an inquisitive gleam as he served Bruno his coffee and croissant. Owner of the café tucked into the alley behind the *mairie,* Fauquet had become one of the main sources of the town's gossip. Along with his excellent croissants and powerful coffee, it was part of his stock-in-trade. "Albert was in earlier. Said it was a really vicious killing, the guy's head smashed to bits."

All along the crowded counter of the café, conversation stilled as customers waited to hear what new light Bruno might shed on the case. He knew them all well, local shopkeepers and office workers, people who worked at the *mairie.* Whatever he said would flash around town within minutes and probably be featured on the next news bulletin of Radio Périgord. And it would certainly be swiftly conveyed to Philippe Delaron, who spent much more time on his part-time role as *Sud Ouest* correspondent than he did running the family camera shop.

"Nobody's been arrested," Bruno said, and took a bite of croissant. He could hear himself chewing, such was the silence along the bar as the other patrons awaited information. "We were just talking to the guy who found the body and called the emergency service."

"That's the Parisian?" Fauquet persisted. "*Gai comme un phoque,* Albert reckoned. He was in here just now."

How had the French dreamed up the phrase "gay as a seal" to describe a homosexual? Bruno wondered. What did seals have to do with it?

Bruno finished his coffee, put a two-euro coin on the counter with some change, said *"Bonne journée"* to the crowded café and climbed into his van for the drive to Crimson's house. He was aware of a dryness in his mouth as he anticipated the reunion with Isabelle.

She was not alone. There was a large white, unmarked van parked at the rear of the house, and two men in blue overalls were taking in some electronic equipment. Isabelle was prowling the terrace. She still had a slight limp and was puffing at a cigarette as she argued with somebody over a mobile phone. As usual, she was wearing black slacks, a turtleneck, flat shoes and a long black raincoat. A turquoise silk scarf worn as a belt provided a splash of color. Her skin was bronzed from her vacation.

Part of him wanted to rush to her, take her in his arms and relive those moments when he'd felt closer to her than to any other human being. But another part of him felt—he groped for the right word—not dispassionate so much as detached, observing himself as he watched her, seeing her vulnerability as she changed her step to avoid an empty floral urn. Her profile came into view, the slim neck, the hair so short she looked boyish. Then she spun on her heel, chin out and head tilted high, imperious and hard. In that moment, he had a sense of how she would look in another twenty years, her ambition fulfilled and her heart cold, a woman at ease with power. He felt a moment of sadness that she might succeed in building a brilliant career and become one of the handful of people who ran the French state, returning each evening to a magnificent but empty apartment.

Her eyes widened in recognition as she spotted him. Did they soften? Bruno wasn't sure. She waved the cigarette at him in cursory greeting, turned and resumed her verbal duel. Bruno sighed, shrugged and began to examine the van, its rear doors open and revealing racks of electronic equipment. Behind it was a new-looking Peugeot with a rental sticker, doubtless Isabelle's.

"What's this?" he asked one of the men. He was carrying what looked like a very fat laptop.

"Ask her" came the surly reply, with a glance toward Isabelle.

"They're with me," she called to Bruno. "He's got a secure phone line in there and we're checking to see if it's been compromised." She returned to her call.

France Télécom had told him the line had gone down at 1:00 p.m. three days earlier. But would there not have been some kind of automatic alert on a special secure line? Why would Isabelle lie to him, unless she had been ordered to take this opportunity to make a different kind of search, or perhaps to install some microphones? Yet if they were going to plant bugs in the house of a retired British spy chief, they could have done it at any time. And presumably Crimson was experienced enough to take his own precautions.

"Sorry, Bruno, some idiot in the liaison office at France Télécom in Paris was trying to explain why they didn't notice the line had been cut." Putting her phone away she kissed him on both cheeks and hugged him with fierce energy in that way she had. The embrace lasted a second too long for social nicety, and her hand lifted to stroke his cheek. Over her shoulder, he saw the man with the big laptop watching with interest.

"It's good to see you again," she said, reaching into her raincoat pocket for her cigarettes. She had given up smoking when they'd been together during that magical summer before she had taken the job in the minister's office in Paris.

"And it's great to see you. How was Greece? And your leg?" Isabelle had taken a bullet during an operation against a ship-load of illegal immigrants the previous year. She now had a titanium implant in her thigh. The latest stint in the hospital had been for plastic surgery to repair the fist-sized hole in her flesh, and the cruise around the Greek islands was her convalescence.

"The docs say the operation was a success," she said. "There's still a scar, but it's fading and the cruise ship was fine. I lay on my deck chair and read trashy novels. It's left me with a strange suntan and a couple of extra pounds."

"You needed to put some weight on. The pounds don't show."

"How would you know?" she asked, and then gave him a flash of that private smile of hers, the one that came from her eyes. "Enough chitchat," she said briskly. "What do you make of all this?"

He explained about the previous burglaries, the perpetrator using the same method each time. He added that he'd confirmed the cleaning woman's alibi for the time the phone wire had been cut.

"Who's been handling the burglaries, the gendarmes?"

"Yes." He told her they had left it to him to file the insurance reports and he'd be e-mailing photographs of some of the stolen items to the national watch list.

"Big embarrassment in Paris," she said. "The minister called his counterpart in London to apologize, and the brigadier did the same with his contacts. They virtually promised the Brits we'd clear it up, get all the stuff back and send the thieves to Devil's Island. That's where you come in. The brigadier wants your local knowledge and has asked for you to be assigned to us to track down the burglars. I gave the prefect his letter last night, and I've got another one to give to the mayor."

As a municipal policeman, Bruno was officially employed by the mayor and council of St. Denis, part of the complexity of French judicial bureaucracy that had the gendarmes employed by the minister of defense and the Police Nationale by the Ministry of the Interior. But the ministry could always dragoon him into service when it thought his local knowledge might be useful. Bruno shrugged in reluctant acceptance of the inevitable. "You know we've also got a murder on our hands?"

"I heard it on the car radio. Who's the guy being questioned?"

"A Parisian theater director named Yves Valentoux. He found the body, and J-J thinks he did it as a *crime passionnel.* I'm not so sure."

"Leave that to J-J. The burglars are your priority. Apparently Crimson has been in Washington, but the Brits got in touch with him, and he's heading back."

Surprised and a little hurt at the way Isabelle assumed she could give him orders, Bruno carefully kept his face immobile. This was no time to start squabbling over turf. He changed the subject. "I brought some tools to seal the broken shutters, lock the place up again and secure it."

"We'll take care of that. I'll have someone here until Crimson returns." Somehow she had taken his arm and steered him out of earshot across the terrace toward the pool, still covered from the winter. Dead leaves lay thick on the plastic sheeting. Beyond it was a *potager* and young tomato plants had already been staked. He saw the filigree green of carrot tops, young zucchini and lettuce. Crimson must have a gardener to take care of the grounds. When had the gardener last been here? He would ask Gaëlle.

"I trust you had a pleasant evening," Isabelle said. "At the last minute I was squeezed into the prefect's dinner party. His wife took one look and put me way down the table, between the mayor of Ribérac and the headmaster of the *lycée*. Once they learned I was a *flic*, they talked golf, which made me miss you a little."

Her eyes sparkled with mischief, as they always did when she teased him. *Mon Dieu*, it was good to see her again.

"A career woman like you, perhaps you should take up golf."

"It takes too long. And we have a perfectly good gym at the ministry. My leg is almost healed, and I have this plan to jog to place Beauvau every morning, hit the gym and shower. I have my own locker, so I can keep clothes there."

That was Isabelle, always planning, always with some project. "You always wear the same clothes anyway. Everything black."

"When you first saw me, I was wearing jeans and that brown leather jacket." She grinned back at him.

"I liked you best when you used one of my shirts as a dressing gown," he said, and she slapped his wrist in mock reproof.

"Those days are over," she said abruptly and paused, giving Bruno time to wonder if this time she really meant it. He had heard it before, and he had said the same, but each time they met, something pulled them back together. Then she made her face serious, one of her sudden switches of mood that often left him floundering. "How's your Englishwoman?"

"She always wears the same things too. Riding breeches mostly and Wellington boots." A memory came to him of Pamela in a long green evening dress, her hair piled high.

"You smell a little horsey. I like it, very masculine." Her tone changed as if she were changing gear. "Do you have any leads on these burglars? The brigadier really wants this cleared up."

"Crimson's been retired for two or three years now. Is he still so important?"

"Guys like that never really retire. He's a consultant now with the Hakluyt Group, filled with his old colleagues from British intelligence and charging big corporations fat fees for political advice and well-placed contacts. At least, that's what they say they do, but in that world of ex-spies, who knows? If they're anything like our guys, they may be off the payroll but they're still in the loop. Do you know him?"

"He's active at the tennis club, and he comes to the rugby games when he's here in winter. He's friendly to everybody, and I've been invited to his house a couple of times."

"Who were the other guests?"

"At the garden party there were a couple of local mayors, a bank manager, Hugo from the wine cave and a lot of expats, mostly retired British diplomats and a couple of writers. At dinner it was the same mix but a smaller group. Oh, and the local deputy to the Assemblée Nationale."

"Any Americans?" she asked, a little too casually.

"Not that I recall. There aren't many around here. Why do you ask?"

She shrugged. "Just wondering how retired he really is. Apparently he was having some pretty high-level meetings while he was in Washington."

They were in a garden now, and he saw that the lawn had been mowed, but not recently. "If I'm going to focus on the burglary, I need to check on the gardener and see who might have known Crimson would be away."

He explained why he thought it was one gang and that the thieves knew their antiques. Bruno could search criminal records, but Isabelle would have access to much broader archives that would include suspected dealers who were too careful to have ever been caught. It would be useful to have that list, particularly if there were any local connections.

"How long are you here?" he asked.

"At least until Crimson gets home and settled in. Maybe we could find time for dinner. And I want to see our puppy." Balzac had been her gift to him after his previous dog was shot by a Basque terrorist.

"Come to dinner. You can see the puppy and tell me what your plans are if the government changes with the next election."

He said it lightly, but Bruno did not have to spell out his meaning. The interior ministry was always controversial, but there had been more and more scandals in recent months, over the wiretapping of journalists, over some alleged cover-up of campaign donations from a rich industrialist's widow and above all over a new department of the ministry, the Direction Centrale du Renseignement Intérieur. Combining the old police intelligence operation with counterespionage and antiterrorism, it had become a very powerful arm of the state. Critics, including the opposition parties, called it sinister and suggested that its boss was little more than the president's private spy. If he lost the forthcoming election, the new government was expected to launch a wholesale purge and change of personnel.

"I'm not involved in any of that political stuff." She turned to face him, looking vexed. "I thought you knew me better."

He held up his hands in mock surrender, smiled and said: "I'm on your side, you know that."

"It doesn't sound like it, Bruno." Her eyes narrowed. "Is this part of J-J's plan to get me back to Périgueux?"

"No, you'd hate it," he replied. "I can't see you spending a couple of years waiting to take over J-J's job when he retires," he went on, wondering how to take the heat out of the conversation. He tried to make a joke of it. "You'd be forced into a lot more tedious dinners with the prefect and you'd probably have to take up golf."

"So why did you bring this up? This is my career you're talking about." She turned away. "God, I hate being manipulated."

"Why did I bring it up? Because I care for you and because I'm worried about your becoming a political football, that's why."

Her back was toward him, shoulders rigid. Bruno knew Isabelle well enough to be sure that apologies would not work; she was not the sort of woman to be easily mollified. She insisted on straight talking, and he was in a mood to provide it.

"I don't know what your connection is to this new organization, but there's something in your ministry that's starting to stink. It doesn't matter whether you're part of it or not. The mud sticks."

She turned again to face him, still challenging but less fierce. "How come you're suddenly an expert on the election, let alone the internal politics at the ministry?"

Bruno had never been clear which particular section of the sprawling ministry employed the brigadier's team. It seemed to occupy some vague middle ground between Defense and Interior and the DGSE, the foreign intelligence service.

"I don't have to be an expert. You're attached to the minister's private office," he said. "If the government changes, you'll be assigned elsewhere. The new minister will want his own people."

"That's just an administrative convenience. I'm a serving police officer with the rank of *capitaine.* Nothing will change that."

"They can always assign you to traffic management in some cold, gray *département* up on the Belgian border."

She stopped herself from making a quick rejoinder, as if debating internally whether to say more. "Funny you should say that. I might get reassigned soon, even a little farther north than the Belgian border. I've applied for another job."

Bruno raised an eyebrow. "Anything you can tell me about?"

"Eurojust, the judicial coordination office of the European Commission based in The Hague. If it comes off, I'll be getting a promotion to commandant." She paused and looked back the length of the garden toward the house. "It's a four-year assignment." She let a silence build again as if expecting Bruno to comment. "The brigadier suggested I apply."

"Good for him," Bruno said, and meant it. He had wondered whether the brigadier, a ruthless operative and consummate political survivor, was the kind of boss who would take care of his staff.

"I don't expect he'll go down with the ship." She had taken his arm as if the brief row had never happened and somehow they were walking amicably together again. "Apart from your murder, what else is happening down here? And how's our puppy?"

"Balzac is fine, but I really need more time to train him.

And there is something else—have you ever heard of the Neuvic train robbery?"

"A Resistance thing in the war? I heard somebody gossiping about it when I was stationed in Périgueux."

"A couple of the old banknotes turned up on the deathbed of an old *résistant*. I have to organize his funeral. If there's anything in your files at the ministry, I'd be interested."

7

Bruno wanted to check the list of burglary victims against the owners who used Dougal's rental agency to find tenants for the months when their houses would otherwise stand vacant. A retired businessman from Glasgow, Dougal had started Delightful Dordogne out of boredom after his first year of inactivity and had now become one of the leading employers in St. Denis. The business employed his two daughters and their husbands, one French and one Dutch. His first grandchild was already spending his summer vacation helping Dougal keep track of the bookings.

"I've been expecting you since I heard about Fullerton's murder on the radio," Dougal began. "I suppose that's what you're investigating."

Bruno nodded. "Did you ever meet him, or was the rental arranged by phone and Internet?"

"I certainly met him. He called me Monday and asked if he could take the place a couple of days early. It was empty that week, and he seemed like a nice-enough fellow, so I agreed."

"Very trusting."

Dougal shrugged. "It's the way I do business. He'd already

paid for the original booking with a bank transfer. I've made you a copy so you'll have his bank details."

"Did you see him at all?"

"Yes, he came to the office here the day before yesterday just after five to pick up the keys and paid for the extra days in cash. You can see where I marked it."

Dougal led Bruno to the giant wall chart. It dominated the large, airy room in the old public laundry that he had rescued from ruin and converted into offices. The houses he rented were listed from top to bottom on the chart, and from left to right were columns for each of the weeks of the season. Crimson's name was not among them, although Bruno noted that the other burglary victims were listed along with the *gîte* where Fullerton's body had been found. Bruno ran his finger along the right line and saw Fullerton's name with a tick in the small box beside it to show the rent had been paid and another to show the cleaning had been done and sheets and towels installed and the swimming pool prepared. There was a small hand-drawn arrow pointing to the current week and a scribbled note that said: "Three days paid."

"I used to keep this on the computer as a spreadsheet," said Dougal. "But then I put it up on the wall so that the cleaners and other maintenance people could see when they were assigned to each property."

"So anybody who worked here could see at a glance when a house would be available for rent, which meant the owners were away?"

"That's so. You must be thinking that was how the burglars chose their victims, but most of my people have been with me for some time. I know them pretty well and trust the ones working for me now. Still, I can print out a list of all the employees if you want."

Bruno said he needed that and then a thought struck him.

"What if an owner doesn't want to rent out his house but still needs a cleaner or gardener or pool maintenance? Do you offer that as a separate service?"

"We do, mainly for the pool maintenance. There aren't many takers for the cleaners and gardeners. Most people have their own connections because it's cheaper. They pay cash, whereas we have to pay the social charges for our employees. It damn near doubles the overall wage bill."

"Is Monsieur Crimson one of your clients? His house is not on the list."

Dougal led Bruno around his desk to another wall with another chart that listed the separate pool and garden and cleaning services and pointed to Crimson's name.

"He comes to us for pool and garden work. He used to have cleaning as well but then Gaëlle realized she could do better on her own than working for me. We always make our people work Saturday mornings because that's the changeover day for most rentals. She said she wanted the weekends off."

One of his daughters, Kirsten, brought in two cups of coffee from the espresso machine in the kitchen as Dougal called up the Crimson file on his computer. Bruno greeted her, asked after the children and then copied down the names and contact details of the gardener and the pool-maintenance man.

"Any of your staff that you have doubts about?" Bruno asked when Kirsten had gone.

"Not anymore. One or two turned out to be unsatisfactory in the early days, but we weeded them out. We do take on some part-timers at peak periods but usually people we've used in the past. I'll add their names to the list."

"Could anybody else come in here off the street and look at the charts?"

"It's possible. We get a number of casual visitors, salesmen mainly or people trying to rent out their houses, and we use this as a waiting room if I'm busy elsewhere. But if they don't know our system, I'm not sure whether someone off the street would be able to read the charts in the way you mean."

Bruno gathered his printouts, thanked Dougal for his time and walked to the post office to look at the delivery rosters. Jean-Louis, the deputy manager, checked who had done the routes that would have covered Crimson's house and the *gîte* where Fullerton had been murdered.

"Pierre and Pascal," he said, looking out of his office window to the yard where the yellow postal vans were parked. "They're both on break now, so you can see them on the porch. We aren't allowed to smoke in the building anymore, so that's where they take their breaks."

Pierre had made no deliveries to Crimson's house on the relevant days and recalled seeing nothing of interest. But Pascal had delivered a letter and a couple of circulars to Fullerton's *gîte* two days earlier.

"I was on the late shift," he said, his Gitane bobbing from his lips as he spoke. "Must have been late afternoon, sometime around five o'clock. It's a long driveway, and as I was driving back I had to stop and reverse because of the *chauffagiste.* He was in a big white van, and he had trouble getting by me. That's how I saw the sign."

"What did it say?"

"Chauffage-France or France-Chauffage. I'm thinking of putting in central heating, so I remembered the address. It was in Belvès, in a *zone industrielle,* and I thought I might ask them for an estimate, see if they're any cheaper than the ones around here."

"Did you get a look at who was in the van? One person or two?"

"Just the driver, a youngish guy, I think, but I didn't really notice. I was trying to be sure I didn't take my own van so far over I'd end up in the ditch. The funny thing was, when I looked up the firm in the phone book I couldn't find any listing for a heating firm in Belvès."

"Could have been a new one, not in the phone book yet."

"That's what I thought," said Pascal, glancing at his watch. "So I looked it up on the master list we keep in the office that has all the new subscribers, and there was nothing on there either."

Pascal looked across to the yard where his friend Pierre was already loading boxes of letters into the back of his van. "My break is over," he said, rising. "Got to go. It's not the place where they had that murder, is it? They said on the radio it was up by St. Chamassy."

"There might be a connection. We'll check it out and may have to come back and take a statement from you. Did you see anybody at the house, or was there a car parked when you dropped off the mail?"

"Not that I remember. There might have been a vehicle, but I can't be sure." He shook his head.

"Do you remember anything about the driver of the van, what he was wearing?"

"The usual blue overalls." Pascal shut his eyes as he tried to remember. "One sleeve was rolled up, and he had a tattoo on his arm, very striking with thick stripes. It was like an abstract design, not the usual mermaid or anchor. When we slowed down to squeeze the two vans past one another, I got a good look at it. His arm was resting on the rim of the door, and we were so close we were almost touching."

"What about the van?"

"It was one of those extra-tall Renaults they use for moving furniture, big enough for people to stand up inside."

"You said white. What color was the sign?"

"It was in blue letters, pretty big. I could read it easily. It had the Belvès postal code. There was a phone number too, but I didn't write it down."

Back in his office at the *mairie,* Bruno called his counterpart in Belvès to ask what he knew of the industrial zone where the heating firm was supposed to be based. Bruno learned that it contained two construction companies, two warehouses, a commercial laundry and a firm that specialized in handmade staircases, but no heating company.

"What's in the warehouses?" he asked. One stored goods for a local chain of do-it-yourself stores and the other was run by a moving company that parked its big trucks in the zone's secure parking lot.

Bruno opened his phone directory and looked through the yellow pages for sign makers. The fourth one he tried, in Bergerac, had the previous month made two truck signs for a company called Chauffage-France, with an address in Belvès. The customer, a young man, had paid cash and said his name was Lebrun. The address he gave was the alleged workshop in the industrial zone.

"Had you seen him before?"

"No, but I wouldn't mind seeing him again," said the woman on the other end of the phone. "He was a good-looking guy."

"So you'd know him if you saw him again?" Bruno asked.

"Sure. And if I need to jog my memory we've got him on tape. We've got security cameras now, for the insurance. You could come and see for yourself. What's he done, this guy?"

Bruno evaded the question, but within the hour he was at the sign shop, part of a modern printing company that also did photocopies, business cards, posters and advertisements for billboards. The entire operation seemed to run on computers, and the manager had prepared for him a plastic folder with several frames already printed from the security camera tapes. He also e-mailed copies to Bruno's office computer so Bruno could forward them to J-J and the gendarmes.

They showed a young man in his twenties wearing dark blue overalls and a dark baseball cap that shadowed part of his face. The nose was clear enough, although the mouth and jaw were obscured by a mustache and small beard. There was one clear shot of his features, when a banknote slipped from his hand to the floor. The girl at the desk must have said something because he looked up smiling, almost flirtatious. Bruno was sure he'd seen that face before.

"Who was the woman I talked to on the phone?" he asked the manager. He was steered to a girl with spiked hair and a nose ring. He showed her the photo to check that it was the mysterious Monsieur Lebrun that she remembered.

"Do you remember what you said that made him smile?" he asked.

She laughed. "I asked him if he always threw money at girls' feet and he gave me this sexy smile and said it helped him see their legs better. I was sure he was going to say something else, maybe ask me out. But then he bit his lip, paid his bill and left quickly. It was a bit odd, that's why I remembered him."

Armed with the printouts of the photos, Bruno pondered his next move as he returned to his van. He could go through the rogues' gallery, the books of photos of people who had been arrested, although he assumed J-J's team would be doing that. If the guy had used the ZI address and postcode, he was probably familiar with it. He started the van and headed for the old hilltop bastide of Belvès.

He always enjoyed visiting the bastides, those fortified towns built in the Middle Ages along the shifting frontier between the French parts of the region and the lands held by the English. Built on grid patterns around a central market square, with a church at one corner that could act as a fortress, they still dotted the region. Together with the caves along the valley with their prehistoric art, their Roman ruins and Renaissance châteaux, the bastides were a constant and satisfying reminder to Bruno that he and everyone else who lived around St. Denis were part of an endless stream of history. He also relished the irony that while the bastides had been built to defend and reinforce the power structures of the Middle Ages, they had in fact helped to erode the feudal system. As incentives to get the peasants to move to these towns, where kings and barons hoped to make money from taxing the markets, they were offered freedom from serfdom. Along with the power of the English longbow and the crossbow to decimate the charges of the feudal knights in armor, the bastides had undermined the social and political order that the knights were dying to defend. That was often the way with political solutions, Bruno reflected: they produced dismayingly unexpected results.

Perched on its hilltop and still clustered around its central square, Belvès boasted a fine market and an antiques fair where Isabelle had bought Bruno a dining chair he loved. He smiled to himself at the memory of her purchase as he circled the old town and headed for the *zone industrielle* below. He paused only to make a courtesy call to the local municipal policeman, who said that Bruno was most welcome on his turf, and would he have time for a *p'tit apéro* after his visit? Bruno accepted the invitation with pleasure.

The zone was part of the urban sprawl that in Bruno's view defaced more and more of the countryside he loved. There was always a giant supermarket, a do-it-yourself discount store, huge furniture and sports shops and a discount gas station.

Behind this commercial center stood vast warehouses and small factories, each a single story high and built with vinyl siding and cheap metal roofs. The industrial zone had a sliding metal gate, which opened automatically once the security guard saw the police van. There were cameras on the roof of the guard's kiosk, dotted around the buildings and on tall lighting poles that could illuminate the parking lot where the giant moving trucks were parked.

The security guard did not recognize the young man in the photo. Bruno then called at building after building. Mostly he got apologetic shrugs, but at the office attached to the movers a woman in her forties with heavily made-up eyes, showing a generous amount of cleavage, lingered on the photo twice.

"You're not our local *flic*," she said. "What's up with this guy?"

"Routine," he said casually. "He could have been a witness to something, and he was driving a van with an address at this ZI."

"Not anymore, he isn't," she said. Bruno suspected that her desire to show she had information he wanted had trumped her instinctive caution when talking to a policeman. "We had to let him go. When was he driving this van? Was it one of ours?"

"No, it was another warehouse, but we're checking everywhere to see if we can identify the guy. Do you know his name?"

"Paul, handsome little Paul," she said. "We'll have something in the personnel files. He was with us just under six months, driving the small vans. He wasn't licensed for heavy goods."

"I only saw big trucks in the yard."

"Some customers don't have much furniture. And then we've got a sideline business, storing antiques and stuff for the *brocante* dealers who come down here every year for the summer trade. That's why we use the small vans."

"A nice guy, was he?"

"A bit too nice, if you get my meaning. I was interested in him at first, but I got the impression that women weren't his preference."

Bruno deliberately let his eyes linger on the cleavage. "His loss," he said.

Smirking, the woman rose from behind the counter, turned and swayed into a rear office, her hips swiveling in the tight skirt of royal blue that matched her eye makeup. She came back bearing a slim file and a teasing expression.

She tapped him on the chest with the file and then let him take it. Inside the file Bruno found a job application form and copies of an ID card and driving license. Paul Murcoing, he read, age twenty-eight. There were three different addresses listed for him in the six months he'd worked at the movers, one in Belvès and two in Bergerac. The elusive connection now came to Bruno. He'd last seen Paul in a photograph in the house of his dead grandfather, the *résistant*. If Paul and Yvonne had kept the family name that meant their mother had been unmarried. Idly, Bruno wondered if they had shared the same father.

The woman leaned forward on the counter, her hands together so her arms could squeeze the magnificent bosom into even greater prominence.

"I suppose now you'd like me to make you a photocopy."

"What I'd like you to do could get us both arrested," said Bruno, by now thoroughly enjoying himself. "But a photocopy would be very kind." He paused. "My name's Benoît."

"I'm Nichole." As she went into the rear office, she turned and waved her blue-tipped fingers and said: "Be right back."

Bruno called J-J's mobile to tell him that he had a suspect.

He gave Murcoing's name and last-known address, read out his aunt's telephone number from his notebook and added: "According to one woman he worked with, there could be a gay connection."

"Hang on while I look him up in the records," said J-J.

"Are you still questioning Valentoux?"

J-J grunted assent, and then Nichole returned with the photocopies.

"*Très bien,* Monsieur le Commissaire," Bruno said into the phone. "Right away."

He clutched the photocopies, leaned forward to plant a kiss on Nichole's cheek and said: "Got to go, that was the boss. One last thing: did Paul have any friends here in the zone?"

"He might have had one, but like I said, he wasn't interested in girls."

As he opened the door to leave, she called: "Hey, Benoît." He stopped and turned. "That was fun," she said, and blew him a kiss.

8

At the first address Paul had listed on his personnel form, Bruno found an elderly North African woman in a headscarf with an imperfect command of French. A young man in a tracksuit with a shaved head and a large single earring turned from the blaring TV set and said: "We've only been here three weeks." He had never heard of Paul Murcoing and never seen the man in the photo.

At the final address in Bergerac, a curtain twitched when he rang the bell. After a minute, a young woman in a dressing gown opened the door on a chain, yawning, and asked him the time.

"Eleven-twenty."

"*Merde,* I only got off work at six. What is it?" She clutched at the neck of her gown where it was falling away to reveal a large rose tattooed on the curve of her breast.

Bruno explained and showed the photo. She gave a nod of recognition. "That's Paul, sure enough. He doesn't live here, but he sometimes used to come to visit his sister." He tried not to look at the tattoo.

"Is she in?"

The woman shook her head. "Yvonne moved out a month

or so ago, maybe more. She said someone had offered her a room near where she worked, but she may have hooked up with some guy she met. She does that sometimes. I haven't seen Paul for ages."

"How well do you know him?"

"I was at school with Yvonne so I've known him for years, even before he came out. What's he done this time?"

"He's been in trouble before?"

She looked at him levelly and began to close the door. "None of my business."

"This is pretty urgent. He could be a witness in an important case. Do you know where Yvonne works, where I could find her?"

She sighed. "Promise I can go back to sleep if I tell you?" When he nodded, she said: "She does part-time cleaning in foreigners' houses up around Les Eyzies, some company run by an old Scottish guy who wears a kilt."

"You mean in St. Denis?"

She nodded. "Can I go back to sleep now?"

"Thanks," said Bruno. "Sweet dreams."

Back in his van he looked through the list of employees Dougal had given him. There she was, Yvonne Murcoing, on the list of the part-time staff. The name should have jumped out at him. The address Dougal had listed for her was the one he'd just visited. He called Dougal and asked if Yvonne was still working for him.

"She's out sick, but I think she's been staying in one of the staff houses we use." He gave Bruno a phone number and an address. Bruno called the number, but there was no reply. He tried calling J-J, got only voice mail and so tried one of his deputies, a young inspector in Bergerac who would have been assigned to any previous search for Murcoing. There was no news. At the most recent address Murcoing had given the warehouse, no one had seen him for weeks. Bruno then called Joséphine, Murcoing's aunt, and left a message, asking her to call him, that he had news about the funeral.

He took the back route from Bergerac through Ste. Alvère to avoid the traffic on the main road along the river. He parked opposite the gendarmerie and noticed Valentoux's silver car in the lot, so obviously he was still being held. Bruno walked across to look at it. He could see fingerprint dust on the door handles and mirrors. That meant forensics should have finished with it. He put on a pair of gloves and opened the door, wondering if they had checked for discarded receipts that could buttress Yveline's theory that Valentoux could have driven down a day early to commit the murder. He found nothing.

He was about to close the car door when a thought struck him. He opened the glove compartment and pulled out the car's manual. There was a section at the back where careful drivers could record their gas purchases and the number of kilometers driven and work out their consumption. But Valentoux had never made an entry. Tucked inside the manual was the little compartment where most people kept their *carte grise* and other documents that the police asked to see when a car was pulled over. There was a receipt from a *contrôle technique* garage, an inspection station where older cars were required to be tested every two years. Bruno saw that the car had been inspected nine days before. The form listed the number of kilometers on the odometer when the test was performed. He compared that with the present number. Valentoux had driven seven hundred and twenty kilometers in the past nine days. Paris to St. Denis was nearly six hundred. If he had made a second journey to kill Fullerton, he could not have done it in his own car.

Bruno entered the gendarmerie. From behind the desk,

Sergeant Jules shook his hand and said Yveline was in the interview room with the suspect. Bruno was directed to the room where J-J was working. Bruno handed him the *contrôle technique* and explained what he had found out. "But I suppose he could have hired a car and done it that way," he said.

"Only if he knew someplace that let him have a car for cash," said J-J wearily. "We've been through his credit cards and bank account. There's no sign of any odd transactions." He took off his glasses and eyed Bruno. "Is it you I have to thank for that phone call we got last night from the *procureur*'s office?"

"What phone call?" Bruno asked innocently.

"From your friend Annette Meraillon, asking if it was true we were questioning a murder suspect."

"My friend?" said Bruno. "She's a vegetarian feminist who thinks I'm a dreadful old meat-eating dinosaur like you. Anyway, she's too junior to be assigned a case like this."

"One of these days you'll go too far," J-J grumbled. He tried to glower at Bruno, but his heart didn't seem to be in it.

"How's Valentoux bearing up under the interrogation?" Bruno asked.

"He seems fine. He obviously has great faith in French justice. He keeps saying he didn't do it, has a little cry when he thinks of his dead friend and then dries his eyes and credibly answers everything we throw at him. He's been very cooperative, hasn't even asked for a lawyer. I was going to release him this morning when the *juge d'instruction* arrived, but Yveline was keen to have another crack at him, and I don't want to start an argument with the gendarmes. The *juge* is talking to him now."

J-J turned to a young woman sitting at an adjoining desk and handed her the inspection station receipt Bruno had taken from Valentoux's car and asked her to explain its significance to the magistrate in the interview room. Then J-J looked at his watch. "I wonder what your friend with the bistro is doing for his plat du jour?"

"Ivan usually makes *côtelettes de porc au céleri* today."

"So what are we waiting for?" said J-J. He lumbered to his feet and headed for the door at a pace that belied his bulk. A bowl of *potage de légumes* later, mopped up with part of a fresh baguette and washed down with a glass of Ivan's house red, J-J sat back and looked at Bruno.

"So you can put Murcoing at the murder scene at the relevant time, in a van with a forged sign, and you say he's probably gay, so that could be a connection with Fullerton. I ran his name through the records when you called. He's got two convictions for car theft, another for hunting without a license, and he was questioned last year on suspicion of selling stolen antiques but released for lack of evidence. He could be a suspect, but it's all circumstantial."

"And his sister is in a position to know which houses would be empty and open for burglary."

"That's the problem. Why would he want to rip off a *gîte*? There's no furniture worth taking."

"Maybe he knew Fullerton and knew he had a truckload of antiques with him."

"It's a bit thin," J-J said, surprising Ivan, who was about to serve the pork chops. "Not you, and not this fine-looking dish," J-J said hurriedly and then leaned forward to breathe in the aroma of the celery sauce. A wide smile appeared on his face as he waited for Ivan to return with the vegetables.

"I warn you, he's raised his prices," said Bruno. "Probably your fault for overpraising him. It's ten euros fifty now for the set lunch."

J-J swallowed his first mouthful, nodded in approval and sipped at his wine. "Soup, this fine pork chop with vegetables done to perfection, then a green salad followed by cheese and topped off with—what's the dessert today?"

"*Tarte Tatin.*"

J-J looked up to the heavens. "Thank you, God." He looked back at Bruno. "Plus a quarter liter of this very drinkable red, all for ten euros fifty? I don't know how he does it."

"It will be an extra euro twenty for the coffee, and then you'll probably want a glass of Monbazillac with the *tarte* and then maybe a digestif and suddenly your bill is twenty euros," Bruno said. "That's how Ivan makes his money."

"It's worth every penny and we'll economize. No digestif for you today. By the way, who's his latest girlfriend?"

Ivan's menu varied with his love life, which in turn was usually defined by those girls he met on vacation whom he could persuade to return with him to St. Denis. There had been a Belgian girl who seduced him into producing endless *moules.* The Spanish lover had introduced St. Denis to gazpacho and paella, which were greatly appreciated, although the sounds of crashing pans and murderous curses that came from the kitchen when she was angry with Ivan were also relished by the regulars. The new German girl had been a pleasant surprise; her Wiener schnitzel, hammered so thin it overlapped the plate, served with a succulent potato salad had become a local favorite that Bruno tried never to miss. Hugo from the wineshop had even started to stock an Austrian wine, Grüner Veltliner, in its honor.

"It's still the German," Bruno said, "but the signs aren't good. Ivan's been seen sitting alone at the bar and drinking after the place has closed." As a result, he explained, there was now keen anticipation in the town of Ivan's next vacation plans. One faction was urging him to explore Southeast Asia and bring back a Thai cook, while another was suggesting that the French Caribbean islands of Martinique and Guadeloupe might bring an exotic tropical spice to the plat du jour.

"And who's your latest recruit, the woman in the office?" Bruno asked.

"That's Josette. She's just completed her detective's course and transferred from Nontron. Married to a *motard*." J-J used the slang for a motorcycle cop. "Any day now I'm expecting her to announce she's going on maternity leave. She's the one who looked up Murcoing's record. We're putting an all-points bulletin out on him."

"So if you're no longer taking Valentoux seriously as a suspect, why are you still holding him?"

"I told you, Yveline wanted another go at him, and then Bernard had to question him. He's the *juge d'instruction* they assigned, Bernard Ardouin. He's pretty good, a Socialist, of course, but sensible. He used to play rugby for Sarlat. I told him I thought we'd wrung Valentoux dry, and he seemed to agree. I don't think there's much point keeping Valentoux any longer. He'll be out this afternoon."

"With a big sign around his neck saying 'gay murder suspect.' Can't you put out a statement saying he's been cleared?"

J-J shrugged and attacked his *tarte Tatin* as if he hadn't eaten for days. It disappeared in four large spoonfuls. "Sure you won't join me in a little Armagnac with the coffee?" he asked. "By the way, you didn't tell me Isabelle's back in town."

"I saw her this morning." Bruno explained Isabelle's interest in Crimson's background.

"I hate it when intelligence gets involved," J-J said. "Always screws things up. A little bird in the prefecture told me the brigadier has got you assigned to his team again."

"Afraid so. I'm supposed to find the burglars and get Crimson's stuff back."

J-J snorted. "I'm surprised at Isabelle. She knows how tough burglaries are to solve. She damn well should; I trained her."

"There may be one possible way into this," Bruno said. "You say it's thin, but what if there really is a connection with the murder? Fullerton's an antiques dealer, and Murcoing has an arrest for stolen antiques, even if nothing was proved, and that's what the burglars have been taking."

"And we have to find out what happened to that load of antiques Fullerton had in the back of his van."

"So it's all the more important that we track down Murcoing," Bruno went on. "Perhaps you could put through a request to the British police to see if anything's known about Fullerton. We know he was an antiques dealer, but maybe he was a crooked one."

J-J nodded, picked up his phone, called Josette and asked her to take care of it.

"Let me make sure I have your theory right," said J-J. "Murcoing could have had some dealings with Fullerton in the past, maybe doing the burglaries, and then Fullerton ships the goods back to England. He goes to meet Fullerton at the *gîte* to pick up Fullerton's latest shipment, which might even be stuff stolen in England. They transfer the stuff into Murcoing's van, and then they have a falling-out, maybe over money, and Murcoing kills him."

"And then there's the gay angle. We know from Valentoux that Fullerton was gay, and one of Murcoing's sister's friends confirmed the brother is gay. Maybe they fell out because Fullerton had found a new lover in Valentoux."

"That corpse was a *crime passionnel* if ever I saw one," J-J agreed. He sipped his coffee and called for the check. "So even though Isabelle and the brigadier want you focused on the burglary, you want to be part of the murder inquiry, because that's how you think you'll solve it all."

J-J opened his wallet, put a twenty-euro note and a ten onto Ivan's saucer, waving away the change, and tucked the receipt away with the rest of his cash. "Suits me," he said. "I'll make sure you're kept informed of everything we get: forensics, records, anything from the British police and the men I've got making the rounds of the local antiques dealers."

"And I want to be there when you question Murcoing."

"We have to find him first. Inspector Jofflin from Bergerac is in charge of that. Now let's get outside. I'm dying for a cigarette."

"I'll come back to the gendarmerie with you. I want to speak with Valentoux once you let him out."

"In that case, give me an hour to square things with Yveline and Bernard."

Bruno headed back to his office to deal with his e-mails, phone messages and the usual pile of mail. There was a message from the British consulate in Bordeaux saying that Fullerton's brother would arrive by plane in Bordeaux the following day to take care of the funeral arrangements. He'd rent a car and contact Bruno on arrival in St. Denis. The consulate had booked him into Les Glycines in Les Eyzies for three nights. There was an e-mail from the adjutant of the Fourth Régiment de Transmissions in Agen confirming that a squad of troops would mount a guard of honor for Loïc Murcoing's funeral, asking Bruno to verify the date and time. Bruno called Father Sentout to confirm the funeral arrangements and was about to call Florence when the mayor put his head around the door, came in, closed the door behind him and leaned against it.

"I had a phone call from Jacqueline Morgan. I gather you know about Cécile's condition," he said. He looked exhausted.

"Yes, I was really sorry to learn it." As he did whenever the mayor entered his office, Bruno stood up. His instinct was to go over and embrace the old man who had been the nearest he'd ever had to a father. "I will keep the information to myself."

"It's her wish." The mayor put a hand to his brow, then smoothed his fingertips over his temple as if trying to soothe a headache. "She does not want her final days filled with a stream of weeping visitors. Nor does Cécile want people to see her as she is now."

"I understand." He felt helpless, wanting to do something to show his sympathy and concern but with no idea what might be best. Bruno wondered how long this trial would last, not just for the mayor but for the sweet and loyal woman who was dying in the same self-effacing way that she had lived. How little we can really do for one another at the time when it's most needed, he thought.

"It must be difficult for you, returning from the hospital to an empty house. Would it help if you moved into my spare room?"

"Thank you, Bruno, but no. Jacqueline has taken on the task of seeing that I'm properly fed, and I think it's right to sleep in the room that Cécile and I shared for nearly four decades. It will be forty years next February, but she won't live to see it."

9

Like Valentoux himself, the theater director's silk shirt looked the worse for wear when Bruno met him at the gendarmerie and took him across the street to the Bar des Amateurs. He seemed bemused when Bruno asked what he'd like to drink. Valentoux shook himself out of his daze and ordered a beer, then pulled out a cigarette pack that was empty. They sat at a table outside, the sunshine dappled by the leaves of the plane trees that lined the street.

"What will you do now?" Bruno asked.

"Buy cigarettes, take a shower and see if the drama festival still wants a director who's suspected of murder. Then I'd better head back to the *gîte* where Francis died. I won't be able to sleep a wink, but it's the only place I have to stay."

"You can't go there. It's been sealed off as a crime scene."

"*Merde.* I'm in no shape to drive back to Paris. Can I take my car, or have they sealed that too?"

"You're free. You can pick up your car whenever you want. I was going to suggest you follow me back to my place, take a shower there and change, and you can have the spare room until you decide what to do." Bruno turned and called to the barman to bring him a pack of Marlboros and some matches.

"I didn't know you smoked," said Valentoux. "That's a very kind offer—why are you doing this?"

"I don't smoke. They're for you," Bruno said. "You've spent all night and half the day in a jail cell and interrogation rooms. You're out of cigarettes. I don't think you killed Fullerton, and neither does the chief of detectives. If any evidence to the contrary turns up, we'll know where to find you. Will there really be a problem with your job at the drama festival?"

Valentoux shrugged, pulled out his mobile phone and said, "I have three messages from them asking me to call right away. This job's supposed to last me all summer, and I turned down other opportunities to do it."

"Phone them. If there's a problem, I'll speak to them."

Valentoux called, exchanged a few sentences and then said, "There's a policeman here who wants to talk to you." Bruno took the phone, and Valentoux whispered, "Festival director."

"Chief of Police Courrèges on the line, Monsieur le Directeur. I understand you have some concerns about Monsieur Valentoux."

"The news reports have been troubling, but I understand Yves has now been released," the director said.

"He was never arrested, simply helping us to understand what happened. He was the one who found the body of his friend. He is completely free, and I know of no suspicions attached to him, whatever the media might be saying."

"I've been asked to cancel his contract."

"Excuse me, I thought you were the festival director," said Bruno, putting some frost into his voice. "Are you not in charge? Should I speak to somebody else?"

"I'm the director, but there's the board chairman, the mayor, the sponsors . . ."

"And there's a contract. If you cancel it, you'll have a lawsuit on your hands, and I'd have to testify that I had formally informed you that Monsieur Valentoux has been released with the thanks of the police for his assistance and without any shadow on his name. We don't want any unpleasant accusations of discrimination."

Bruno spoke over the protests that came from the director. "I suggest you give me your e-mail address, and I'll send you a message within the hour confirming what I have said, and I'll put a hard copy in the mail tonight. That should suffice for your sponsors and your board."

The director seemed to be mollified. "Okay," said Bruno. "I'll send those off to you and confirm to Monsieur Valentoux that his contract stands and he is free to come and see you tomorrow, if you wish. Thank you for your time and *bonne journée.*" He handed the phone back, took a long pull of his cold beer and watched Valentoux light a cigarette with shaking hands.

"Why are you doing this?"

"You've had a rough time. No need to make it worse," Bruno said. "Stay here, have another beer. I'll send off the e-mail and letter and pick you up back here in thirty minutes. Okay?"

As he walked back up the main street toward his office in the *mairie,* Bruno tried calling the house where Yvonne, Murcoing's sister, was staying and where she was supposed to be on sick leave. Again there was no reply. He called Annette to thank her for her intervention and explained that Valentoux had been released and that he'd be at the drama festival as planned.

"They've assigned Bernard Ardouin to the case, so you're in good hands," Annette said. "I told him that Valentoux had enough of a reputation in cultural circles to get the Paris newspapers interested. I also told him to make sure to talk to you about the case."

"You'll destroy your reputation," he said, smiling as he

spoke. He liked Annette, a keenly competitive rally driver who had once scared the life out of him by putting him in the passenger seat for a hair-raising drive around a forest track.

"What reputation? Anyway, if Valentoux is out and in the clear, I'd love to meet him."

"In that case, come and have dinner at my place tonight. He'll be there. Are you still a vegetarian?"

"In principle, but as you know it's almost impossible to live in Sarlat and not eat a little duck."

"Duck it shall be," he said. "We'll see you about seven-thirty. I have to exercise my horse first."

He hung up and climbed the old stone steps of the *mairie* to his office, where he sent off his e-mail and letter to the drama festival director and called Dougal at Delightful Dordogne to ask who else lived in the staff house with Murcoing's sister. He was given three names and cell-phone numbers. Two of the girls had been in his tennis classes when they were schoolgirls. He called the one he'd liked most, Monique.

"I'm trying to find Yvonne Murcoing," he said, after the usual pleasantries. "She's supposed to be at the house, but there's no reply."

"We haven't seen her for a couple of days," Monique replied. "She left a note on the kitchen table saying there'd been a death in the family and she'd been called away. I've got her cell number if that helps."

It was the same number that Bruno had been trying without success. "Have you met her brother?" he asked.

"Paul? Yes. He drops by from time to time, usually just to pick her up. They seem to be pretty close. She has a photo of him by her bed. We had a couple of takeout pizzas here together, watched a DVD he brought. I went to bed after a bit. The film was too arty for me, something Swedish in black and white, with lots of moody silences."

"Did you see him recently?"

"Not for a few days, but I've been out a lot. Should I ask the other girls?"

"Yes, please. Do you know if Yvonne has a car?"

"She drives one of those little Toyotas, I don't know what they're called. It's gray-silver, and it's not here now. I know she gets it serviced at Lespinasse's garage. He should have the registration number."

On the way back to the bar to pick up Valentoux, Bruno stopped at the butcher's and bought a kilo of *aiguillettes* of duck. These were long, thin strips of the finest meat that was left after the *magret,* the breast, had been removed. They were too often ignored or left on the carcass to thicken a stock, but Bruno loved them and planned to make them for dinner that evening. He had potatoes and the first of the strawberries under glass frames in his garden, lettuces, a lot of radishes and some early zucchini. Stéphane had dropped off some cheeses with the ham he'd been curing in salt since the ritual slaughter of a pig at the start of the year. That was all Bruno needed.

There was no sign of Valentoux at the table outside the bar, but Bruno looked inside and saw him standing at the counter, a large glass of what looked like whisky in his hand as he thumbed through the bar's copy of *Sud Ouest.*

"I see what the festival director meant," he said, closing the paper with its front-page headline on the murder of Fullerton. "It's only just hitting me that I'll never see him again."

"Let's get going," said Bruno, and led the way to the gendarmerie's parking lot so that Valentoux could follow him home. Once back at his house, Bruno showed his guest around and grinned as Valentoux enthused over the view and the vegetable garden.

"What a wonderful place to live," Valentoux said as he

turned back toward the house. "It's like something from a film set, hearing a cockerel crowing beside a picturesque house in the country."

"More comfortable than jail," Bruno said lightly, but inwardly pleased by the Parisian's reaction to his home. He gave Valentoux a towel, showed him the shower and guest room and suggested he get some sleep after his night in jail.

In the kitchen, Bruno filled a bowl with hot water. He poured a half glass of red wine into a flat-bottom dish, added salt and pepper and a crushed garlic clove and rolled the duck *aiguillettes* in the wine. Then he took a large jar of old-fashioned mustard, thick with seeds, and put three heaped tablespoons into the emptied warm bowl. He added an equivalent amount of chestnut honey from a jar he'd been given by Hervé, a bee-keeper who sold his wares in the St. Denis market. He mixed the mustard and honey together, added the wine and the duck and turned the *aiguillettes* until each one was well coated. He covered the dish with plastic film and put it in the fridge.

Out in the garden with his basket, he dug up a couple of his potato plants, picked radishes, strawberries and zucchini, as well as some spring onions. He took the strawberries and the onions into his chicken coop and plucked them there, leaving the green stalks for the chickens to fuss over. Back in his kitchen, he washed the vegetables, leaving them in the sink as he checked that he had sufficient flour and yeast to make beignets. He peeled and sliced the zucchini, added salt and laid it in a colander to drain. Then he added two eggs and a cup of milk to his flour and yeast, whipped the mixture into a cream and put it in the fridge to rest. He was just washing up when a clean-shaven Valentoux entered the kitchen wearing a silk dressing gown and carrying the bottle of champagne that had been in his plastic bag at the crime scene.

"I needed that shower," he said. "Bruno, I'd like to give you the champagne."

"Put it in the fridge, and we can drink it tonight. I have some friends coming for dinner, including a fan of yours who saw some of your plays in Paris. The other guests and I will arrive smelling of horses, since we have to exercise them. The guests are due at seven-thirty, and we'll eat about eight or so. I'm heading out, but I'll be back after I take care of the horses."

"I love riding. I had to learn for a film I was in, a costume drama about Catherine de Médicis. I'd really like to take it up again, but not today. I'll get some sleep, if that's okay. You're being very kind."

"I hope you like dogs. Better prepare yourself to meet a very affectionate and even more inquisitive young basset hound puppy. He's called Balzac, and I'm supposed to be training him. I'll bring him back from the stable where he likes to spend his days."

"Balzac's a great name for a dog."

Bruno dried his hands, picked up his cap and headed for his van. His first stop was Lespinasse's garage, where the owner scooted out from beneath an old Citroën he was restoring to look up the registration number of Yvonne's car.

"Is there a problem?" Lespinasse asked. A plump, jolly man who could still play a decent game of rugby, he wiped his hands clean with grease from a large open jar and then with a paper towel before turning to his files.

"No, it's her brother I'm looking for, and I thought she might be able to help me track him down. You know their grandfather died?"

"Old Murcoing? Yes, I knew him from when he had me up at the farm trying to fix his old tractor. It was a Porsche, so he said it should run forever. I bet you didn't know Porsche used to make tractors. Here's her registration number, a Toyota Yaris."

Bruno wrote it down, told Lespinasse that there would be a military funeral for the old man and made his way to the gendarmerie just down the street to ask Sergeant Jules to put Yvonne's car on the watch list.

"The magistrate was looking for you," said Jules. "I gave him your number but he had to get back to Sarlat. Nothing urgent, he said. He'll be back tomorrow."

"How's the new boss?" Bruno asked.

"Anybody would be an improvement on Capitaine Duroc, but she's only just arrived. Too soon to tell, but she's very polite. She's still got the officers' school polish on her."

"You'll rub that off soon, Jules," Bruno said. "Anything else?"

"Philippe Delaron was asking about that Englishman whose house was burgled. He said he'd looked him up on Google, and he thought there might be a story in it. Apparently the Englishman's a milord or something important. Delaron was holding back. You know what he's like when he's after a story."

Bruno made a mental note to do his own Google search and headed for the house where Monique lived, to see if Yvonne Murcoing might by chance have returned. The place was empty. It had been a long shot, but not a big detour from the route to Pamela's house. His spirits lifted and his mood mellowed as he drove up the familiar lane to the house where his puppy and his horse and Pamela all awaited. He was looking forward to an oasis of affection and calm after a long and frustrating day.

What greeted him was controlled chaos. A plumber's van and a large truck were parked in the courtyard, and there was the unmistakable whiff of a problem with the septic tank. Pamela, in overalls and rubber boots, was cleaning out her kitchen.

"Don't come near me, I stink," she called, blowing him a kiss. "Antonio says he's almost done."

Bruno nodded at Marcel, standing by the truck that was known locally as the honey wagon. Marcel had a steady business installing and emptying septic tanks all over the region. Somehow he managed to shed the aroma of his trade in the evenings when he'd spend his time at Ivan's bistro and the Bar des Amateurs, coated in the pungent smell of the cheap cigars he smoked constantly.

A new gust of fumes drove Bruno to the stable to be greeted by Balzac trying to scramble up on his legs while Hector gave a welcoming whinny. Bess and Victoria, Pamela's two mares, gazed at him incuriously and then went back to staring at the wooden planks of their stalls. He changed into his riding clothes, despite Balzac's best attentions, gave Hector his customary apple and saddled all the horses. He hadn't seen Fabiola's car, but he assumed she'd join them.

Pamela came into the stable dressed for riding and her still damp hair pinned back. She could change faster than any woman Bruno had ever known. She reached for her riding hat and kissed him. "We had a plumbing disaster this afternoon, but Antonio fixed the blocked loo and persuaded Marcel to come and pump everything out."

"And somebody was just enthusing to me about the delights of life in the country. You'll meet him at dinner, that drama festival guy I was telling you about last night."

"It's okay for him to wax lyrical. He lives in Paris where they have sewers, and on days like this I wish I did too. Fabiola called to say she's on her way. She was held up by a broken bone she had to set at one of the campgrounds. We spent half the morning moving her stuff across."

"Across to where?"

"Didn't I tell you? She's moving into the spare room in my house for the summer so I can rent out her *gîte*. Lucky you, you'll be sharing the bathroom with two women. With the rental I'll be able to install a second bathroom upstairs, at the end of the landing."

"Do I get to scrub Fabiola's back too?" He grinned and hugged her from behind.

"Don't even think about it."

10

Bruno returned home to find that Valentoux had explored his way around the kitchen and dining room. He had set the table and gathered wildflowers from the field behind the black-currant bushes. They filled the vase he had placed on the outdoor table, where Bruno's champagne flutes were gleaming. Balzac had raced ahead and was already making friends with their guest. A few moments later he spotted Pamela and Fabiola coming up the drive bearing bottles of wine. Balzac tore himself from Valentoux to greet them and then darted back to Valentoux again.

"You look a lot better than you did yesterday," Fabiola told Valentoux. "At one point I thought of declaring you in shock, but you seemed to be pretty lucid in answering Bruno's questions. My sympathies on the loss of your friend."

"I want to hear what you have planned for the theater festival," said Pamela. "But maybe we'd better wait until Annette joins us."

Bruno was pouring the champagne when Annette arrived in her small blue Peugeot with the wide tires for rally driving, sending Balzac into another frenzy of welcome.

Bruno excused himself and went to the kitchen. First, he

heated a pan of sunflower oil for beignets. The he readied a bowl of spicy salsa, removed from the fridge a pot of Stéphane's *aillou* (fresh cheese flavored with herbs and garlic), spooned it into a bowl and took both bowls out to the garden with some small plates and a pile of paper napkins. Back inside, he dipped the sliced zucchini into the light batter he had made earlier and then eased them into the hot fat. Once they were brown and crisp, he took the beignets out with a slotted spoon, sprinkled salt onto them and slipped in a fresh batch to fry. He took the first plateful out to his guests and left Pamela to show Valentoux how to hold the hot beignet in a paper napkin and then decide whether to smear it with salsa or *aillou*.

The sound of laughter greeted him as he emerged with the second batch, Valentoux deploying a range of voices to play various roles in the story he was telling. He broke off to applaud Bruno's return.

"I never had zucchini like this, and adding this *aillou* makes a perfect couple," he said. "It's like oysters and champagne or caviar and vodka, heavenly twins."

"Wait until Bruno introduces you to his foie gras and Monbazillac," said Pamela.

Nothing like food to get a conversation going, thought Bruno, smiling as he went for the final batch of beignets. But he wondered at Yves's surprisingly cheerful mood so soon after his lover's murder. Was it the thespian style, Bruno wondered, the tradition that the show must go on? He'd never come across someone quite like Valentoux before, a man so deliberately theatrical that Bruno suspected he'd never be able to tell whether Yves was being genuine or just acting.

When Bruno returned to his guests, Valentoux had opened a bottle of Clos d'Yvigne, the dry white Bergerac that Fabiola loved. She must have brought it. Knowing Bruno's fondness for Pomerol, Annette had brought a bottle of Château Nenin, which he had decanted at once so they could enjoy it that evening. Pamela had brought a Monbazillac from Clos l'Envège, which would go perfectly with the strawberries, and he'd put it in the fridge to stay cool. He put the marinated duck into the oven, sliced some ham from the haunch that hung from the main beam in the kitchen and put a plate of ham and his fresh radishes at each setting on his dining room table. He added some unsalted butter to each plate and sliced a big round loaf of bread from the Moulin bakery.

"À table," he called from the kitchen window, "and bring your wineglasses with you."

He steered Annette to the head of the table, he and Valentoux to her left and right and then Fabiola and Pamela, and explained to everyone how the ham on the plates came from a pig that had been treated since the previous summer to a regular diet of acorns and chestnuts.

"And I saw Bruno pick the radishes from his garden today," added Valentoux.

Valentoux copied the way Bruno smeared a little butter onto each of the plump, red radishes, dipped each one in salt and then alternated a bite of bread, a radish, a piece of ham and then a sip of the white wine.

Pamela helped Bruno clear away the plates. She stuck a fork into the potatoes and declared them ready as he removed the duck from the oven using bright red gloves emblazoned with a white Swiss cross. Fabiola had given them to him for Christmas.

"Aiguillettes de canard au miel à la befre moutarde à l'ancienne," Bruno announced as he and Pamela brought the dishes to the table.

"I thought that was honey I could smell," said Annette as

Bruno darted back into the kitchen to bring the carafe of Pomerol. "I never heard of that with duck."

"It should go well with this wonderful wine you brought," said Bruno, pouring it out.

"Tell us about the festival," said Pamela, looking at Valentoux. "What can we expect?"

Valentoux described the mix of old classics and experimental new theater, French and foreign drama that he had planned. The plates were cleared away, the cheese and salad placed on the table, and then Bruno opened the Monbazillac.

"Do you know where you'll be staying while you're in Sarlat?" Annette asked.

"Not yet. I was going to look for an apartment in the next few days. I'm not looking for anything grand. It just needs to be fairly central."

"I rent an old house with some friends on the rue des Consuls, just around the corner from the festival office," Annette said. "We each have a floor to ourselves, two rooms and a small bathroom, and we all share the kitchen, living room and garden. One of the tenants leaves this weekend for summer school in Italy, so his floor is free until the end of August."

"It sounds perfect. Can I come and see it tomorrow? And then take you to dinner?" The two of them agreed to meet at her house in Sarlat at six.

Bruno brought coffee, and as the dinner drew to a close, Valentoux proposed that he might cook and be their host at a similar event. Pamela was the first to agree, placing her foot firmly on Bruno's beneath the table; as usual, she'd slipped off her shoes as she dined. When they all rose from the table, she made it clear that she intended to stay the night, so Fabiola and Annette said their good-byes. Valentoux declared his intention to do the washing up.

In the kitchen, Bruno said, "I meant to ask you, did Fullerton ever mention the name of Paul Murcoing, a young man from this area who seems to have been involved in antiques?"

Valentoux froze. "I never heard that name. Is he somebody who might be a suspect?"

"Could be. Did you meet any of Fullerton's friends?"

"Only when we were in England, and none of them was French." Valentoux was scrubbing at a pan that was already clean. "This Paul Murcoing, is he gay?"

"Yes, and he's disappeared. We're keen to talk to him. Can you help?"

"I do know some people down here in the gay community."

"Frankly, I'd be grateful for any information about him. He's a bit of a mystery to me, and that bothers me because I know everybody in a small commune like ours."

"And you don't know any gays?" All the dishes washed, Valentoux had turned and was leaning against the sink, looking at Bruno with a slightly amused expression.

"Don't be silly. There are three thousand people in this commune. We get all sorts. But it tends to be very discreet, and Paul Murcoing doesn't fit into any part of the closeted gay world that I know around here. He's an urban type, an outsider to the countryside that I'm familiar with. I feel a bit lost in trying to track him."

"I'll do what I can. Where was this Paul based?"

"Bergerac mainly, but he worked for a while in Belvès, which is very like St. Denis. He seems to have worked mainly as a driver. Hang on, let me get a photo."

"I'll be outside. I need a cigarette."

Standing on the terrace, moths beating valiantly against the outside light, Bruno handed Valentoux a copy of the photo from the security camera.

"Good-looking—with a smile like that he could be very popular in Paris. Can I keep this?"

"Yes, I have copies. Pamela and I are going to leave very early in the morning to ride the horses, but I'll probably be in the café by the *mairie* by eight unless something comes up. I can recommend their croissants. Good night. And sleep well."

When Bruno came in from the bathroom, Pamela was sitting on the bed draped in a large bath towel. She had applied some fresh perfume, and his bedroom was lit by only a single candle.

"That was a lovely evening," she said as he started to unwind the towel. "I'm looking forward to its lasting awhile longer."

11

Bruno was enjoying his croissant at Fauquet's café when his phone rang just before eight.

"Have you seen the paper yet?" Isabelle asked, her tone of voice surprising him. She sounded sharp, almost shrill.

"I'm just looking at it." He gestured to Fauquet to hand him the café's copy of *Sud Ouest*. A story on the front page was headlined BRITISH SPYMASTER BURGLED.

"You're the only one who could have leaked that, Bruno. The brigadier's furious and I don't want him taking it out on me."

"Not guilty. Check with Sergeant Jules. He told me that the reporter had simply looked up Crimson on Google." He swallowed his irritation and scanned the story. It looked as if Delaron had transcribed the details of Crimson's career from some official biography. On an inside page was Delaron's photo of Crimson's house and a file photo of Crimson receiving his knighthood at Buckingham Palace.

"Well, it's building up. The BBC ran something on it, so now we're getting inquiries from the British press. You know how my boss hates working while reporters start running all over the place."

Why is this such a problem, Bruno thought, if she and her colleagues are simply making an effort to find Crimson's burglar as a matter of professional courtesy?

"What are you up to, Isabelle?" he asked.

"The brigadier is on the warpath and coming down here with Crimson when he flies in tomorrow. I'm not exactly sure why he's coming, but I need his backing to get that new job, so I'm doing all I can." Her voice softened. "Have you made any progress?"

"Maybe," he said, leaving the café to speak in private. "At least I've got a suspect. His name is Paul Murcoing. He has a low-grade criminal record, and his last-known address is in Bergerac. J-J has a team looking for him. Where are you?"

"I'm at Crimson's house, babysitting the place till he gets back. We've had forensics crawling all over it. If Murcoing's been arrested, we'll have his prints and DNA on file. Meanwhile I'll see if we can round up some gendarmes. The brigadier wants to keep the press away from the house. The question is whether this is a just a straightforward burglary or whether there's something more to it. Does this Murcoing have any British or American connections?"

"He's a suspect in the murder of the British antiques dealer," he said.

"Jesus, this gets worse." She hung up, leaving Bruno unexpectedly holding a dead phone. She, like him, suspected this might not be a straightforward burglary, but why had she asked about American connections? Apart from a retired New York lawyer, a widower, and two old ladies who had taught French in California high schools, he didn't know any Americans in the area. Jacqueline Morgan had an American parent, but she was a French citizen. Suddenly he remembered why she had looked familiar when he'd visited her. He had seen her at Crimson's garden party the previous summer. He remembered she wore a black cocktail dress. They hadn't spoken; there must have been forty or fifty people present.

Jacqueline knew Crimson, and she was writing a book that could make a big splash in the media about American money influencing French politics. But that was sixty years ago, the dawn of the Cold War. It wasn't the kind of issue that would have much political impact now. Most of the old parties had disappeared or merged into new ones; only the Socialist and Communist Parties remained from those days. He shook his head; that couldn't be it. However, there had been that cryptic remark Jacqueline had made about the French nuclear deterrent not being really independent.

Now *that* could have an impact. Nuclear weapons were the crown jewels of France's defense system, and since de Gaulle's day it had been a cornerstone of national pride that, unlike the British, France had developed its own warheads and missiles. The prospect of a scandal about dependence on the Americans was likely to worry the brigadier and his minister, particularly if a retired British intelligence chief was involved. Isabelle had said earlier that Crimson had just been in Washington for some high-level meetings. And the French elections were coming up. This was all way above his pay grade, Bruno thought. He'd better talk to the mayor.

His phone rang again. It was Monique, asking if he was still looking for Yvonne Murcoing. Indeed he was, he replied. Monique had just checked Yvonne's room to see if she might have returned, and on the notepad by the bed she'd found a phone number with the words "camper van."

Bruno scribbled down the number in his notebook, thanked her and dialed the number. The woman who answered said Yvonne had rented their camper van the previous year, and she'd recently asked to do so again. But she and her husband were about to take a week off themselves, so the camper wasn't available. When had Yvonne called? Bruno asked. In the evening, three days earlier, he was told. That would have been the day of Fullerton's murder. Bruno rang J-J and left a message asking if his team could start checking rental agencies. As he put his phone away, it gave the little ding that meant a call had come in while he'd been talking. The number showed it had come from Paris. He checked the voice mail and listened.

"*Salut,* Bruno. Gilles here from *Paris Match.* I'm interested in this burglary of your British spy chief. I thought I might come down to your part of the world, interview Crimson and see what I can turn up on other important Brits in Périgord. Please call me back, ciao."

Bruno knew Gilles from his time in Sarajevo, during the siege, and they'd renewed their friendship recently when Gilles had been more than helpful in the case of the Red Countess. Gilles was no fool. Once he learned that Isabelle, whom he also knew, was on the case, he'd know that there was more to this burglary than met the eye. Bruno would have to handle this with care.

The mayor looked cheerful when Bruno knocked and entered his office. The delay with the new sewers, Bruno now learned, had apparently been resolved, and the mayor asked Claire to make two fresh coffees. Bruno described his talk with Isabelle. Could her sudden interest in the Americans be somehow connected to the revelations in Jacqueline's book?

"I doubt it," the mayor said. "Her book won't be published until well after the elections."

"Bits could leak," said Bruno. "Has anybody seen it but you?"

"I don't know, and I haven't read all of it. I imagine she has sent most of it to her editor. And I know she's given talks to a couple of historical societies. This is history, Bruno, old stuff; most of the old passions have died."

"Not when it comes to nuclear weapons cooperation. And I got the impression this was much more recent."

The mayor nodded thoughtfully. "I know Jacqueline has been working with some newly declassified documents. Our officials involved have kept it quiet so far, so if the American archives are being unsealed there's probably a reason for that."

"Presumably Crimson would know about this," Bruno said. "The Americans and the British usually work closely on intelligence and on nuclear matters." He put down his cup and sat forward. "Maybe I'm adding two and two and coming up with five, but you know politics. This looks like a pretty close election we have coming up. Could something like this make a difference if it blew up?"

"Any little thing can make a difference in a tight race. The economy is in bad shape and there's this whiff of scandal around the interior ministry. A new row about the government mishandling nuclear matters could be just what the opposition needs," the mayor replied. "Let me think about this. After all, I'm involved." He leaned back in his chair, closed his eyes for a long moment and then opened them to look out of the window. "I signed the paper that secured Jacqueline special access to our Senate archives. My name will be on the paper trail."

Both men sat staring ahead for a moment. Then Bruno said, "How's Cécile? I hope she's not in too much pain."

"They give her morphine. I'll see her again this afternoon."

"And dinner?"

"Jacqueline is doing something with last night's leftovers. She's a good woman." Bruno took the cups and left the mayor staring out of the window.

After an hour searching on toutypasse.com for ads offering campers for rent in the region, Bruno had made more than twenty calls but with little to show for it. His labors were interrupted by a call from the curator he knew at the Centre Jean Moulin in Bordeaux, to report that nothing embarrassing had been found in Murcoing's war records. He had joined the Maquis in late 1943, after the Germans had occupied southern France and begun the STO, Service du Travail Obligatoire, the compulsory roundup of men and young women to work in labor camps in Germany. He'd joined the Groupe Valmy in early 1944, fought at Terrasson in June and took part in the battle to liberate Périgueux in August.

"Some of this we have confirmed by Marcelle Murat, a real Resistance heroine known as Le Caporal. She used her pharmacy as a mailbox and informal hospital and acted as a courier between the various groups. I'll draft something you can use in a press release or have read at the funeral," said the curator. "I'll miss Murcoing. He used to come and see us once a year, always to ask if there was anything new about the money he'd helped take from the Neuvic train. Do you know about that?"

"Yes, I even found a couple of banknotes he must have taken from the train. He had one clutched in his hands as he died."

"We'd love to have one for the museum, if you could ask his heir. That would be young Paul, I suppose."

"You know him?" Bruno sat up with a jerk.

"Yes. He'd normally come along with his grandfather. I remember he sat in when we interviewed the old man for the oral archive. He was just as bad as his grandfather, railing against the thieves and crooks who stole the Neuvic money.

It was all a capitalist plot, he said. Of course, Murcoing was in the FTP, the Francs-Tireurs et Partisans, the Communist wing. I don't know if Paul is in the party, but he certainly sounds just like the old man. He's a regular on the bulletin board we set up on the Internet, and he's always cropping up on the various history websites. The Neuvic train seems to be an obsession with him."

"That's interesting because we're trying to find Paul to talk with him about another important case. It's one so serious I'm beginning to doubt that he'll show up at the funeral. Can you give me details of these websites?"

"I'll send you a list. There are a lot. And I'll look up some of Paul's postings, ravings more like. I've got your e-mail address at the *mairie,* and anyway I'll see you at the funeral. There aren't many of the old veterans left, and I'd like to attend."

"What's Paul's e-mail address?" Bruno asked quickly. He wrote it down, hung up and checked his watch. School had started, so rather than calling Florence he sent her an e-mail, asking if she could track any activity on Paul's account at orange.fr.

He felt he was making progress, slowly. An image of Paul was beginning to build in his head. There was the photograph, that cheeky smile with its flash of intelligence. There was his relationship with his grandfather and their shared obsession about the Neuvic train, his fondness for serious films and his relationship with his sister. How often did siblings in their twenties go on vacation together? But there was so much yet to learn, so much of the image that was fuzzy or blank. What of the connection to Fullerton? Was it business or pleasure or both? And what would Paul have done with a van stuffed with Fullerton's antiques? If he and his sister were looking for a camper, they'd need somewhere to store Paul's van with the furniture. The old family farm had been sold. But perhaps

Paul knew of an abandoned barn up in the hills, which would only be a temporary solution.

There was a knock on his office door, and a tall, thin man with sloping shoulders and a mournful expression entered the room carrying a black briefcase. He shook hands as he introduced himself.

"Bernard Ardouin, *juge d'instruction*. We have a mutual friend in Annette, who says I have to be sure to listen to you."

An interesting start, thought Bruno, and unusual. Under French law since Napoléon's day, a magistrate appointed to be *juge d'instruction* in a case had almost unlimited control of the investigation. He could interview witnesses and review evidence, define the lines of inquiry the police should pursue, authorize arrests and prosecutions. Finally, he or she would present the case to a court. The job of a French *juge d'instruction* was to discover the full truth—unlike the adversarial system in Anglo-Saxon countries, where a prosecuting lawyer and a defense lawyer fought a case to win a verdict of guilty or not guilty—and he had broad powers to do so. That was why the French novelist Balzac had described such a figure as "the most powerful man in the world."

"I don't know about that, but I'll do what I can to help," said Bruno. "Do you want to chat here in the office or go down to the café?"

"Let's start here. Cafés tend to be full of people, listening for gossip. All I have so far is the certificate of death and a preliminary pathologist's report that says death was inflicted by a succession of heavy blows causing multiple fractures to the skull and facial bones. It also says that the victim was HIV positive and taking the usual drugs to keep the disease at bay."

Ardouin removed a thin file from his briefcase and reviewed the facts. The victim was a foreigner, Francis Fullerton, age thirty-six, a British citizen and antiques dealer. The body was discovered by Yves Valentoux, thirty-five, of Paris, a French citizen with whom the deceased was in a homosexual relationship. He looked up.

"I interviewed Valentoux yesterday and was satisfied that he could be released. I understand it was you who worked out his movements through the garage and *péage* receipts. The Police Nationale tell me they are looking for a possible suspect, Paul Murcoing. Can you take me through that from the beginning?"

Bruno described the steps he had taken, the visit to Dougal, the postman's identification of the van, the sign maker and the warehouse at Belvès.

"So the only evidence of his involvement is that this white van was seen by the postman approaching the *gîte* not long before Fullerton's death," Ardouin said. "Plus this Murcoing had been arrested on suspicion of dealing in stolen antiques and may also be homosexual."

"He's disappeared, and so has his sister. She tried to rent a camper on the evening of Fullerton's murder."

Ardouin looked up from scribbling notes on a pad and gave Bruno a look of amiable skepticism. "And he's the only lead you've got," he said. It wasn't a question.

"True," said Bruno. "But if somebody goes to the effort of buying a fake sign for his van with a fake address, and he pays in cash, then it's reasonable to assume he's up to no good."

Ardouin nodded. "But not necessarily murder. He could have met Fullerton by agreement, loaded his van with Fullerton's antiques and then left him alive and well. Then someone else could have come along and killed him."

"I agree," said Bruno. "Even so, he's someone we very much need to interview. He was close to his grandfather who died three days ago and is due to have a full Resistance funeral. If he misses that, he's on the run. Did the police send you the photographs of the furniture stolen from the other English-man's house and the list of wine that was taken?"

"No, what other Englishman?"

Bruno pushed across the desk a copy of *Sud Ouest*. "He's a very influential Englishman who has a team from the minister of the interior's office babysitting his property with their own forensics people looking for any trace that Murcoing had been there."

"Could be coincidence."

Ardouin's tone was matter-of-fact, rather than negative. Bruno got the impression of a solid, painstaking magistrate who would steadily let the evidence build while remaining wary of hunches and theories. There were not many magis-trates of this type. Many of them justified the usual police grumble that they were left wing, feminist and Green. On balance Bruno had concluded that this was reasonable. The law leaned to the side of property and authority; and it was no bad thing for some magistrates to tend a little in the other direction. In any event, he'd much rather deal with a *juge d'instruction* like the lugubrious but dependable Ardouin than with someone more flamboyant.

"Yes, but when we have so few other leads, coincidences are worth exploring," Bruno said. "I've also contacted people in the local gay community to see what's known of Murcoing, his usual associates, friends with whom he might be able to stay, that sort of thing. And we've circulated photos of the stolen furniture, in case some of it surfaces."

"What do you plan to do next?"

"I'm going to start looking into the *brocantes,* try to find people who might have known Fullerton and Murcoing. You probably heard from J-J that the Police Nationale have asked the British for any information they may have about the victim. His brother is arriving later today to make funeral arrangements, and he may be able to tell me more about Fullerton that might help us. Apart from keeping up the search for Murcoing, I'm not sure what else I can do."

"The Police Nationale tell me you've been seconded to the ministry to focus on the burglary of this Englishman. Will that leave you any time to help me?"

"If I'm right in suspecting the cases are connected, I'll be working for you while working for them."

"Very well, but please keep me informed. An e-mail each evening or a phone call will do." Ardouin gave Bruno an unexpected smile, a warm and genuine expression that lit up his usually mournful face. "And since it's a warm morning, let me buy you a beer in that café you mentioned."

12

Brian Fullerton had the look of a boxer going to seed and carried himself like a military man. He had big hands with a gold wedding ring, an amiable face with a broken nose and big ears. His gray hair needed cutting. He wore a blazer with an unidentifiable club badge on the breast pocket, the bowl of a pipe poking from it, and well-polished brogue shoes. Judging from Francis Fullerton's passport photograph, he would never have guessed the two men were brothers. Bruno estimated Brian to be in his mid-forties, about ten years older.

"My condolences on your loss," Bruno began, glancing at his watch. "You made very good time from Bordeaux." He hadn't expected the man until much later in the afternoon.

"I canceled the booking the consulate had made for me and took the Ryanair flight to Bergerac instead," said Brian, in excellent French. "It seemed a lot closer. Here's my passport, just to confirm I'm the brother you're expecting. I haven't checked in to the hotel yet, it seemed a bit early. They'd booked me into Les Glycines in Les Eyzies, but that's too pricey for me so I looked on the Internet and found a place in town, the Hôtel St. Denis. It looked cheap but reasonably comfortable."

"I think you'll be fine there. I'm surprised how good your French is."

"My mother is French, met my father when she came to work for some neighbors in England as an au pair in the early sixties. Where's my brother's body?"

"At the morgue in Bergerac. The autopsy should be finished by this evening. It will then be up to the magistrate whether the body can be released for burial. He was a bit worried about identification. Now that you're here, we can probably confirm that through your DNA. I'm afraid the head was too badly damaged to be recognizable."

Fullerton frowned. "That sounds bad."

"It was an extremely brutal killing, and we're determined to find the murderer. Were you and your brother close?" Bruno pulled out his notebook and began writing.

"Not really. Francis was eleven years younger and we led very different lives. But we tried to spend the usual family times like Christmas and the occasional vacation together so he could get to know my children. I'm a civil servant, married with a family, kind of conventional. Francis was the complete opposite."

"You mean that he was homosexual?"

"Ah, you know. It took our parents some time to adjust. We're an old-fashioned family." He went on to explain that Francis had never really settled down, perhaps had never really grown up. He'd been intelligent and managed to get a degree even though he dropped out of university for a while, but he kept getting into trouble with drugs and debts. "When Francis went to prison it broke my mother's heart. He was her favorite, the last baby, born long after my sister and me, and he always had this angelic look as a child." Fullerton frowned again. "I suppose I have to get used to referring to him in the past tense."

"We didn't know he'd been in prison," said Bruno, not altogether surprised. "We asked the British police if anything was known about him, but these inquiries take time. Why was he sent to prison?"

"Receiving stolen goods," said Brian. After some wild years in London and then in America, Francis had settled down with a steady partner, Sam Berenson, an older man, in the antiques business in a part of Brighton called The Lanes, full of antiques shops. Francis claimed he'd been the fall guy when the police found a haul of stolen silver at their shop, according to Brian. One of the burglars had turned queen's evidence, and since Francis refused to testify against his partner, he was sentenced to three years and was out in two.

"But he stayed in the business?"

"Berenson died of AIDS while Francis was in prison, and he left Francis everything: a house in Brighton, the shop and all the stock." Fullerton shook his head ruefully. "Almost worth it for two years inside, that's what my wife says."

"Did he specialize in silver?"

"No. The shop specialized in antique furniture, rugs and paintings. Anyway, Francis sold everything at the top of the market, just before the recession. He made a lot of money and then started his new business. He began going back and forth to France, selling British stuff over here and then buying French furniture to sell in Britain. He seemed to be doing very well out of it. He drove a Porsche, bought a house in Chelsea when the prices dropped. He always had a good eye for a bargain."

"How often did he come to France?"

"At least once a month. He had a big warehouse outside Brighton where he kept his stock. And he went back to the States a few times, using his old contacts in Los Angeles. Then he started exporting English antiques over there."

"Do you know if Francis made a will?"

"Yes, I checked with his lawyer before coming over here. Everything goes to me and my sister to be kept in trust for our children. I've got a letter from the lawyer saying I'm the executor. I made some copies. Here's one for you." He pulled a file from his briefcase and handed Bruno the letter.

"I suspect his dying in France may complicate the inheritance. You may want to consult a lawyer."

"I already have. He told me Francis's British property will be covered by the will, but the French property has to be different."

"What French property?"

"He had an old farm in the Corrèze, very picturesque but too remote for me and the children. We visited a couple of times as a family, and then I came down again last year with him, just the two of us. He bought the place when he sold the shop. That's why I was surprised to hear that he died here at a *gîte* he was renting. That seems strange when he had a place of his own."

"Does it have barns?" Bruno asked. "Could he have used it as a warehouse?"

"Yes, that's why he got it. It was cheap, of course, but with the new autoroute he could easily visit the various *brocantes* and estate sales from Bordeaux to Lyon."

"I think we'd better take a look at the place. Where is it exactly?"

"Just south of Ussel, about twenty minutes off the autoroute. I need to go there myself to see his *notaire* and work out the details of the inheritance. Is there anything more you need me to do?"

"If you know what you want to do with your brother's remains, I can introduce you to the local undertaker. But first I have to talk to the *juge d'instruction*. I think he'll want you to give a DNA sample, just to confirm the identification, and I'm sure he'll need to interview you. Let me see if he's still in St. Denis."

Bruno called Ardouin, who was still at the St. Denis gendarmerie, gave him a quick summary of what he'd learned from Brian Fullerton and arranged to escort him there. On the way back to his office, he stopped at Father Sentout's house to check on the details for Murcoing's funeral and called in at Delightful Dordogne to see if Dougal had heard from Yvonne Murcoing. Not a word, he said, and he was about to clear out her room at the staff house to make way for a replacement. As Bruno was leaving, he met Philippe Delaron coming in to pick up a list of new rental addresses to be photographed for Dougal's website.

"When's the English spy coming back to his house?" Philippe asked. He was wearing a new leather jacket that looked expensive. His sideline in news photos was evidently paying better than the family camera shop. "I'll need to take a photo. Gaëlle says she thinks he gets back tomorrow."

"In that case, she's heard more than I have."

"Why have they got gendarmes guarding the house?"

"Ask the gendarmes."

"Come on, Bruno, be a sport. You can tell me."

"The *procureur* has appointed a *juge d'instruction* for the murder inquiry, and the victim's brother just arrived from England," Bruno said, trotting down the steps. At the last step, he stopped and looked back. "Have you had a request from the Police Nationale to publish a photo of anyone they want to find urgently?"

"You mean a suspect? Not that I've heard. Give me a minute." Philippe thumbed an autodial number on his phone, fired off a quick question and then shook his head. "Not so far."

"I'll see what I can do," said Bruno. As he walked back down the rue Gambetta, he called J-J, who told him the press office was soon going to release Murcoing's mug shot from his earlier arrest.

"What if I let *Sud Ouest* have the more recent photo from the surveillance camera? They'll give it more prominence if they think it's their story rather than a routine police request."

"Go ahead. But don't get quoted saying this guy's a suspect. Let them take the responsibility for that and we'll give a 'No comment.'"

Bruno passed on what he'd learned from Brian Fullerton and said he planned to drive out with Fullerton to the Corrèze farm as soon as he'd finished with the *juge d'instruction.* Back in his office, he texted Delaron to come see him, prepared another copy of Murcoing's surveillance photo for the paper and began printing out the pictures of Crimson's rugs, paintings and furniture that had been given to Crimson's insurance agent. He was looking up the phone number of the *police municipale* in Ussel when Delaron appeared. Bruno handed him a copy of Murcoing's photo.

"This didn't come from me, understood? And I'm not saying he's a murder suspect, just that the police urgently want to interview him. I think the Police Nationale will be issuing his mug shot later today. He's Paul Murcoing, lives in Bergerac, makes a living as a driver—and his grandfather is getting a full-scale Resistance funeral here in St. Denis next week. That's it."

"Thanks, Bruno. Where was this taken? Looks like a print from a surveillance tape."

"I'm not saying, Philippe. *Bon courage.* By the way, there's something you can do for me in return." Bruno pulled out the photos of Loïc Murcoing as a young man in his Resistance unit and handed them to Delaron. "I'd like these blown up as large as you can make them. It's for his funeral. I'd like to put them by the coffin in the church."

Once Delaron had left, Bruno called Gilles at *Paris Match* to say he'd always be welcome in St. Denis, but he wasn't sure how much of a story there would be in a burglary.

"I see you've got a murder on your hands as well, the victim being another Brit. Any connection?"

"The victim is half French, and it's not clear yet if there's any connection. Look, Gilles, this is not an affair where I can give you much help. A *juge d'instruction* has been brought in, and I'll be in real trouble if I start feeding you stuff. Crimson isn't even back here yet."

"I was talking to one of the British reporters here in Paris. He said Crimson will get there tomorrow, and he and some others are heading down to St. Denis. I'll be arriving earlier. I'm booked into the Vieux Logis from tonight. I'll be in that café of yours by eight tomorrow morning."

"The Vieux Logis? I didn't know *Paris Match* was making that much money these days."

"Let's just say I have a hunch about this story. See you tomorrow."

When Bernard Ardouin called to say he was finished with Fullerton's brother, Bruno went to the gendarmerie to pick up Brian for the drive to Francis's farm in the Corrèze.

"There's nothing else for me to do," Fullerton replied. "They can't release the body until the identification is confirmed, and then I'll have him cremated and take the ashes back to England. If you take the autoroute to Ussel, I think I'll remember the way."

Brian said he should make a call first, pulled a mobile phone from his briefcase and began dialing. Bruno called J-J to tell him of his plans and then called Isabelle to keep her in the picture. Finally he made a courtesy call to the police in Ussel to say he was coming onto their turf. When he finished, Brian Fullerton was looking at him, a perplexed expression on his face.

"That's odd. I just called the number of the farm in Corrèze, wondering if my brother had left one of his messages about where to find the key. He had several different hiding places, each with its own letter. It was a sort of code he worked out with my kids when they spent a summer here, a family joke. But a woman answered, and when I gave my name and asked who she was, she slammed the phone down."

"Merde," said Bruno. Could it have been Yvonne? Was that where she and her brother were hiding out?

He called the Ussel police again and explained the situation. They knew where the house was and promised to send a car there.

13

A single policeman was waiting by his van in front of the farmhouse. It was similar to those around St. Denis except the stone was gray, not brown, and the shutters were painted bright red. One long, low barn was attached to a wing of the house, and a second, taller barn stood to one side. The garden was unkempt. Stalks of last year's dead geraniums lay forlornly in pots, and there was jungle where the vegetable garden would have been. The trees planted to the north and west looked stunted, as though hunched against the wind. It would be cold here in winter, Bruno thought.

"By the time we got here, the birds had flown," said the *flic*. He introduced himself as the town policeman from Neuvic, a name that startled Bruno. "I know, you keep thinking it's the one in Dordogne. This is another Neuvic, best known for the lake. You can't see it from here, but it's just over that ridge to the south."

Bruno introduced Fullerton as the new owner. "Have you been inside?" he asked.

"The main house was open, so I took a quick look around. The beds have been slept in, there are dirty dishes in the sink, and there's a cashier's ticket from Leclerc on the kitchen counter dated two days ago. I don't know if anything's been touched or stolen."

Bruno took two sets of gloves from his van, donned one and gave the other to Fullerton, who'd been peering in through the windows. Nothing seemed different, he said. Bruno led the way into the house. It was an odd mixture. Some beautiful pieces of old furniture, an Empire clock atop an Empire table, two Louis XVI chairs, a large tapestry on the stone wall that Bruno thought might be an Aubusson were scattered like islands of good taste among cheap modern stuff that looked as if it came from IKEA. There were layers of grime on the red tile floor in the kitchen, and the stove was worse. Bruno noted empty bottles in a box and dirty glasses in the sink.

He knelt down to look at the bottles. In two of them, the dregs were still moist. One was a Château Kirwan 2005, and the other was Haut-Brion 2001. He checked his notebook. They could have come from Crimson's cellar. In the dining room, some strips of wallpaper hung down forlornly, and a large brown damp patch covered part of the ceiling. His eye was drawn by an exquisite small oil painting of a young woman in eighteenth-century dress on a swing.

"School of Watteau, I believe," said Brian. "Were it a real Watteau, it would be worth more than the whole place."

Upstairs, the towels in the bathroom were damp, and the floor of the shower was still wet. In one bedroom they found female underclothes and a pair of tights; in the other, a pair of men's dirty socks was balled beneath the bed. Both beds had been left unmade.

"Looks like they left in a hurry," said Brian. "Maybe they were in a panic after I called."

"Have you looked in the barns?" Bruno asked the *flic*. He said no, adding that they were locked. Bruno asked Brian if he remembered the codes for the keys.

"*G* for the geranium pot, *L* for the ladder, *Ò* for the orangerie, which is what we called the little glass lean-to at the back, *R* for the rake in the toolshed, *I* for the iron seat that came from an old tractor and *A* for that artichoke pot hanging on the wall."

He lifted the terra-cotta artichoke from its hook to reveal a big iron key and a smaller one that looked like it fitted a Yale lock. Bruno and the *flic* followed him to the single-story barn. He used the big key to open a large, partly broken wooden door. Behind it lay a much more solid metal door, which he opened with the Yale. He flicked on an inside light, a fluorescent strip that flickered and buzzed before suddenly blazing into stark life.

Cases of wine were stacked against the far wall. In front of them were heaped rugs, rolled up and tied with lengths of orange plastic string. Alongside stood paintings wrapped loosely in canvas. Bruno went back to his van for the file of photos of Crimson's possessions. The first painting he uncovered was a thickly painted scene from a window, dominated by a flapping curtain and overlooking a dismal garden with dirty brick houses in the background. It was marked in Crimson's file as a Bratby, valued at eight thousand euros, and Bruno saw the artist's signature in the bottom right corner. To make sure, he unwrapped the next canvas and unveiled two gloomy watercolors of beach scenes, beautifully framed. Each was recorded in Crimson's photos and listed as a work by John Sell Cotman. They were valued at five thousand euros for the pair.

"No doubt about it, these are stolen goods," he said, rising and showing the photos to the *flic*. "They were stolen from a house in my commune at the beginning of this week."

"You mean my brother was up to his old tricks?" Brian asked.

"Not as far as these paintings were concerned. He was still

in England when these were stolen," Bruno said. "Let's look in the other barn."

It was locked, so in search of the keys Fullerton led them to the toolshed and the orangerie in vain before going to the back of the house, where an aluminum ladder lay propped lengthwise against a wall. He bent down at one end, slid a key from the hollow of one of the legs, and the three of them trooped to the large barn. This had two wide wooden doors, each about seven feet high. They were locked with a chain and a padlock. The key turned easily, and Bruno and Fullerton hauled the two doors open to reveal a tall white van. On its side were painted blue letters reading CHAUFFAGE-FRANCE with an address in the industrial zone of Belvès. Its rear doors were open, and the interior was stacked high with furniture, mainly tall wooden dressers, each protected from its neighbors by blankets.

"Bingo," Bruno breathed to himself. On the floor of the van by the open doors were four heavy iron tubes, each about three feet long, held together by elasticized bands with hooks at each end.

"Any idea what these might be?" he asked Brian, pointing at the tubes. He wondered whether he might have found the murder weapon.

"Rollers," said Fullerton, lighting the pipe he'd been filling. "It's how they move heavy furniture, sliding them along on those rollers."

More furniture was stored in the barn: large and small tables, more dressers, tall, glass-fronted bookshelves with ornate carved headings and sets of handsome dining chairs.

Bruno called Isabelle to tell her that he'd found at least some of Crimson's belongings and that his suspicions had been confirmed of the link between the burglaries and the murder. He allowed himself a few moments to enjoy her praise, feeling like a schoolboy rushing home with a prize, and then called J-J to get the arts squad and forensics team to the Corrèze farmhouse.

"We've found the white van, and we may even have the murder weapon," he went on. "It ties Murcoing with Fullerton, and we may be able to clear up a whole host of burglaries into the bargain."

"On my way," snapped J-J, and Bruno turned to see Brian delving into one of the dressers in the back of the white van. He was wearing gloves, so he'd do no harm.

"Is it okay with you if I head off now?" asked the local *flic,* looking at his watch. "I was due off at two."

"Sure," said Bruno, shaking hands and thanking him. He promised to send a copy of his report to the Ussel station and to make sure Ussel got some of the credit once Murcoing was caught. He watched the police van disappear down the bumpy track.

"Can you give me a hand to move this furniture a bit? I think I recognize it," Brian said from inside the van. "Just lean that dresser over to the left so I can get this drawer open."

Bruno complied. Brian eased a white Apple laptop computer from the drawer.

"That's where my brother always hid it when he was traveling," said Brian. "Do you think I might get it back when you're done with investigating what's on it? I always lusted after one of these."

"I thought you said you and your brother weren't close," Bruno said. "You seem to know a lot about his habits."

"We made the effort to keep up. Like I told you, I even came out here with him once, just the two of us."

"What about his mobile phone?" Bruno said. "We never found it. Just maybe that's here too." He sighed as he glanced at the mass of furniture to be looked through.

"No problem," said Brian. He took out his own phone, thumbed through the address book and dialed a number. "If it's here, we'll hear the 'money, money, money' song from the musical *Cabaret*. That's the ringtone he put on his phone."

No sound came. Brian shrugged and took the laptop into the house. Bruno followed him into a room that was used as a study, with a desk and crammed bookshelves and an old-fashioned phone. As Bruno glanced around, Brian ducked under the desk and pulled at a power cord still attached to a converter plug.

"Francis always left a power cord here, in case he forgot one," Brian explained. He plugged in the laptop and began muttering to himself as the screen opened and demanded a password. Suddenly he looked up and struck himself on the forehead. "Idiot!"

He turned to Bruno. "I forgot to look at the shrine. It's that big cupboard. Is it open?"

He pointed to a giant, built-in corner cupboard. It had two double doors that stretched from floor to ceiling, nearly ten feet tall, in heavy age-darkened oak. Bruno tugged at the handles, but the doors were locked. Brian pulled the drawer completely out from the desk and from the back of it took a key that had been attached with heavy-duty metallic tape.

"This may come as a bit of a surprise," said Brian, sounding apologetic as he inserted the key. "I should have mentioned it before."

"Mon Dieu," breathed Bruno as the doors opened and a rack of guns met his eye. There were two rifles, two old submachine guns, a revolver, a small mortar and an antique radio set, all grouped around a large framed photograph of a young man in a World War II British army uniform. He wore three white stripes on his sleeve. A smaller photo of a pretty young woman of the same era hung beside it. Draped

above the portrait was a flag from the FFI, the French Forces of the Interior. Below it was a row of medals, two Nazi daggers and an old Wehrmacht helmet. Between them, very expensively framed, was a Banque de France banknote that Bruno recognized—the same design and denomination as the one he had seen gripped in the hands of Loïc Murcoing.

"Meet Grandpa," said Brian. "That's the shrine. And that photo of Grandpa is a much better likeness of Francis than that passport photo of him you asked me to identify. It was uncanny how closely they resembled each other."

But what caught Bruno's eye were the two empty slots in the display of guns, one shaped like a handgun and the other like a small machine pistol, with the velvet backdrop unfaded where they had been.

"I wonder where they've gone," said Brian. "That was where the Sten gun used to be. And the other one was a Browning nine-millimeter. I'll be sorry if we can't find those."

"Are these in working order?" Bruno asked.

"They still work, and he cleaned them regularly. We used to do some hunting with the rifles. I used the Lee Enfield, but Francis always used the French Lebel. We also tried some target shooting with the Browning that's missing."

"What can you tell me about this shrine and your grandpa?"

Their French grandmother was from this part of the Corrèze, Fullerton began. Their British grandfather had met and made her pregnant during the war and returned after the war to marry her. Sergeant Freddy, as he was known, had been a wireless operator with the Special Operations Executive, SOE, the British agency established to build and train resistance movements across Nazi-occupied Europe.

That was Sergeant Freddy in the large photo, and Grandmère Marie beside him. The medals included his Distinguished Conduct Medal, the oak leaf for his mention in dispatches and a series of the usual campaign awards. He had been dropped into France in March 1944 to operate the wireless communications that brought in the *parachutages,* the airdrops of arms and equipment from Britain that went to the Resistance. The radio in the shrine was a genuine British model B Mark II, a device as crude as it was weak, with a signal at best of only twenty watts and requiring at least sixty feet of aerial. Constantly on the move to evade the German radio-direction-finder trucks, the wireless operators suffered a terrifying attrition rate. If they tried to transmit from towns, the Germans turned off the electricity in substation after substation until they found the one that caused the radio to die. Then they surrounded the area and closed in. If an operator tried to transmit from the countryside, they needed a big battery, heavy, cumbersome and not easy to charge.

Sergeant Freddy was smart. He developed a system to charge a battery with parts from an old bicycle and never transmitted from the same place twice. He managed to evade the Germans until the complete liberation of the region in August 1944. But in June of that year many Resistance groups came out of hiding prematurely, believing that the D-day landings heralded imminent victory. They were slaughtered by German regular units. In Tulle, the nearest large town to the farmhouse, one hundred twenty of them were hanged in a single day, and one hundred fifty more were sent to Dachau, where most of them died. Sergeant Freddy was also lucky; the FFI flag was from the Maquis du Limousin unit that had helped him get away from Tulle.

The guns were all genuine from the period, and some of the individual weapons had been used by the Resistance. Francis had bought them over the years, from collectors, estate sales and auctions of family heirlooms. The Sten gun and the German Schmeisser had been obtained from what Brian described as "very unsavory sources," which Bruno assumed to mean criminals.

"That banknote's a new one on me. I never saw that before," Brian said, leaning forward to study it more closely. "Would it be from the Neuvic train robbery?"

"I think almost certainly, yes. Any idea how your brother might have gotten hold of it?"

"No, but I'm not surprised. Francis was fascinated by that incident and read everything about it he could get his hands on. He even went around interviewing people. The nearest town to here is also called Neuvic, which kind of set him off. He spent a lot of time on it, often going to the Public Records Office in London. I know he was trying to find out if Freddy had been involved. He'd gotten hold of some account that confirmed Freddy had arranged some of the parachute drops that went to Groupe Valmy."

Brian stood up, looked around the room and shook his head. "All those bookshelves, full of stuff Francis gathered, but he never managed to find one of the original banknotes before. I wonder where he got it?"

"Did your brother ever mention anyone called Murcoing?" Bruno asked. "Paul Murcoing, a young man, or an old *résistant* called Loïc, his grandfather and one of the original Groupe Valmy members?"

"No, but I'll bet you'll find stuff about him in those files. Take a look in the bottom drawer of the filing cabinet; that's where he kept his photos. They'll all be in alphabetic order."

Bruno looked under *M* and found a file labeled MURCOING (VALMY). Inside it were three decent portraits of Loïc standing by a modern Neuvic road sign. There were also copies of the 1944 photos of the Groupe Valmy that Bruno had seen in the dead man's box of treasures. But there was no file for Paul Murcoing.

Brian went back to the laptop, trying to guess passwords, while Bruno searched the rest of the house. He examined the contents of the freezer section of the fridge and the cisterns for the WCs, looked under tables and on the tops of bathroom cupboards. Finally, taking a last look around the bedroom where he'd found the dirty socks, his eye fell on a framed photo on one of the bedside tables. There were Paul and Francis, arms around each other's shoulders, grinning for the camera while sitting at some café table in the sun. They were drinking what looked like Ricard, and between them two cigarettes smoldered on an ashtray marked DUBONNET.

"I found the password," came Brian's triumphant shout from below. "It was taped to the back of another drawer. He used *Neuvic1944*. He was obsessed with that damn train robbery."

Bruno turned to go downstairs to see what the laptop might reveal, but his eye was caught by a second framed photo on the other bedside table. A moody portrait of Paul Murcoing half smiling, something deliberately seductive in his eyes, was inscribed: POUR MON TRÈS CHER FRANCIS, JE T'EMBRASSE, PAUL.

14

The village of Paunat was one of Bruno's favorite places, a classic ensemble of old Périgord houses tumbling down a hillside to the stream and dominated by an imposing Benedictine abbey. Seated at a table for two on the terrace of the restaurant, Isabelle and Bruno kept glancing up to admire its floodlit wall as the twilight deepened. Once J-J and Bernard Ardouin had arrived at Francis's farmhouse with the forensics team, Bruno had been able to leave and drive Brian back to his hotel. Isabelle had called to invite him to what she called a working dinner, saying she needed to get all the details before the brigadier arrived with Crimson next day.

"You can pick somewhere discreet, if you're worried about word getting back to your Englishwoman that I'm in town," she had said, in a half-mocking, half-teasing tone.

Given the speed at which local gossip moved around St. Denis, Pamela probably already knew. He'd called her earlier from the Corrèze to explain that he wouldn't be able to exercise the horses that evening but that he'd join her at seven the next day for the morning ride.

For once, Isabelle had ditched her usual black and was wearing a starched white shirt that showed off her cruise-ship tan, over a pleated skirt that flared enticingly as she turned to wave at him after climbing out of her rented car. He told her he admired the way it looked on her. Smiling happily, she told him it had been made by Fortuny, and she'd found it at a vintage clothing shop in Paris.

"I'll take the *coquilles St. Jacques* and then the *blanquette de veau*," she said to Bruno, after looking appreciatively at the large blackboard with the day's menu that had been placed by their table. "I'd like a bottle of Perrier, and I'll leave the wine selection to you. And then tell me all about what happened today and explain why you didn't bring our puppy along."

"Balzac still has some manners to learn before I'd dare let him loose on a restaurant," he replied while trying to choose between the veal and the chicken. Finally he ordered the same dishes that Isabelle had chosen, along with a glass each of the restaurant's Bergerac Sec to go with the scallops and a half bottle of la Jaubertie's Cuvée Mirabelle to go with the veal. Then he told her how the day had unfolded from the moment Brian Fullerton had mentioned his brother's farmhouse.

"I'm worried about the missing guns," he said over the cheese course. "From the brother, it's clear that Francis was in the habit of using them, so it's a reasonable guess that Paul had learned to fire them. He's on the run with his sister, fleeing in a hurry from the place they thought was a refuge, and he's armed and dangerous. I don't envy the traffic cops who flag him down or whoever has to go in once he's cornered."

"They'll use the Jaunes," Isabelle said, referring to the Gendarmes Mobiles, their elite unit. "Nobody would shed many tears if Murcoing gets killed, but there'll be trouble if his sister gets shot as well. But that's somebody else's problem. Today, you did well. It's obvious that Murcoing is the murderer, and Crimson gets his stuff back, and so will some other victims as well. I imagine the local insurance agents will be giving you a very special dinner."

Bruno was about to say that it could not be nearly as special as this evening when he remembered the sharp way she had said, "Those days are over," when he'd made some quip about her wearing his shirt as a dressing gown. And now she was off to some European job in Holland. There would be no more special missions for the brigadier that sometimes brought her down to St. Denis. Perhaps this was to be their last supper together. A part of him would always be in love with her vivacity and her fire.

"Bruno, I wanted to warn you there's a buzz around the ministry that there's to be some kind of preelection surprise. People are nervous. And St. Denis seems to be caught up in it," she said, startling him. "Maybe you are too. I'm not sure exactly what this political intrigue might be, but the brigadier told me to ask you about Americans, and when he did I noticed your army file was open on his desk. I think that was why he was so quick to seize on Crimson's burglary."

"I don't understand. Crimson's an Englishman." One part of his brain was thinking that this had to be about Jacqueline's book and therefore implicated the mayor, while another was thinking that for once this was something he could not discuss with Isabelle. Her interest would be to protect the state; his would be to protect the mayor.

"English, Americans, two sides of the same coin," she said, waving his comment aside. "You know these old Gaullists; it's always been an article of faith that there's no difference between *les Anglo-Saxons*. And in intelligence, at least, they're probably right; the English tell the Americans everything. Just remember that as far as the brigadier is concerned, you have no secrets. He'll even know we're together this evening."

"Did you tell him we were having dinner?"

"No, but you remember in Bordeaux, after your phone was tapped and he gave you one of our secure ones? He can call up a screen that shows him where all of those phones are at any given time. And before you ask, yes, that means he knows when we've spent the night together."

Bruno felt himself blushing. "Is this rumor about an election surprise just in your ministry?"

She gave a wry smile. "You know Paris." She said it as if she'd been born and bred in the capital, when in fact she'd been based there less than a year and had spent much of that time in hospitals.

"Remember Gilles from *Paris Match,* the reporter I knew in Bosnia?" Bruno asked. "He's coming down here along with some British journalists. He said it was because of Crimson, but I wonder."

"Crimson is a good news story. Burglary solved, goods recovered, brilliant police work."

"I don't think that's it. This is election time, political season."

She nodded thoughtfully and took a sip of wine. "It's strange that we never talked politics, you and I, nor was there much of it when I was based in Périgueux. In Paris, after other people's love lives it's the main topic of conversation. I presume you lean to the right like most *flics.*"

Bruno raised his eyebrows. "I don't think I lean in any direction, and I suspect the old tradition of lifelong loyalty to a single party is fading pretty fast. Take you, for example; I'd say you were progressive on social matters like abortion and gay rights, but conservative on law and order and maybe on defense."

"That sounds like you too," she said, smiling.

"I don't pay that much attention to national politics. Locally, I vote for the man or woman I like." Bruno recalled his last trip to the voting booth for the municipal election. He'd voted for the mayor, who was center-right, and for the kindly retired schoolteacher who'd chaired the local Socialist Party for two decades. He'd also cast his ballot for Alphonse, an old hippie who was a passionate Green, and for Montsouris, the only Communist on the council. In the last national election, he'd voted one way for the presidency, and in the elections for the Assemblée Nationale he'd voted for the other side.

"But you're anti-European," she said. "You're a French nationalist, a real *cocorico*. And I've heard you moan about those bureaucrats in Brussels often enough."

"Absolutely not. I love France, but I'm a passionate pro-European. It's just some stuff that comes out of Brussels that irritates the hell out of me."

Bruno relished the way that other Europeans like Pamela, from Scotland, and his German friend Horst, the archaeologist, could live and work in France or anywhere in Europe they chose. He liked the principle of a single currency and travel without passports. But he was angry that rules made in Brussels were squeezing to death the small farmers around St. Denis.

"So who are you going to vote for?" she asked. "The devil we know or the devil we don't?"

"I don't know yet. None of them really impresses me, but maybe it's time for a change. That's the best thing about democracy, the feeling that you can throw the rascals out."

He signaled for the check, but the waiter pointed to Isabelle and shrugged. She'd paid when he went to wash his hands.

"Don't worry, you're going on my expense account," she said. "You got Crimson's stuff back."

"Thank you," he said, studying her and wondering whether to say what was on his mind. He decided to go ahead. "For a while, I thought you'd invited me to dinner to say a formal adieu."

She looked at him in silence, almost sternly, took a deep breath as if about to say something important and then stopped herself. She picked up her bag from the floor beside her, rose and turned to take his arm. She flashed him a brilliant smile, gave the skin of his forearm a gentle nip and said, "I thought I already did."

"Several times," he replied. "That's the problem. I never know if you mean it."

The kitchen and living room lights were still on, and Valentoux's car was parked in the driveway when Bruno got home. He must have heard the Land Rover, because as Bruno emerged he was standing in the doorway, a bottle in his hand, to welcome Bruno's return.

"This is for you, to say thanks," he said, handing Bruno a bottle of Lagavulin and leading the way into the living room, where two glasses were waiting alongside a jug of water. "Annette tells me it's your favorite scotch, and I'm celebrating. I'll be moving into her place in Sarlat tomorrow, if that suits you."

Bruno thanked him, put the bottle into his cupboard and brought out the bottle of Lagavulin he already had opened. He poured out two glasses and splashed a little water into each one. He noted with approval that there were no ice cubes.

"Annette told me how you drink it, no ice, just a touch of water."

"Dougal, a Scottish friend, showed me how the Scots drink it," Bruno replied. "I'm glad you're settled, and I've also got some reassuring news. It looks like you're in the clear and that it was Murcoing who killed your friend."

"I'm not surprised. I found out more about him from someone I've known for years, someone who's based in Bordeaux. He seems to be a mercenary youth who makes a habit of living off older men. Apparently he speaks good English."

Bruno was about to say that Francis Fullerton would fit that pattern, but thought better of it and instead sipped his drink. He liked Valentoux and did not want to offend him, but he wanted to know more about Fullerton's other affair. How far should he allow for some jealousy on Yves's part?

Valentoux noticed Bruno's hesitation and smiled. "You're very polite. I knew Francis was never faithful to me, and I accepted that. I fell in love with him, and I was very attracted to him. He was a wonderfully handsome man, full of energy and joie de vivre. There were times I thought I'd found the love of my life; times when we both thought that. But I think I always knew or perhaps feared that he was a bit of a rogue, not someone to rely on."

A parallel with Isabelle came into Bruno's mind. He'd trust her with his life, but he wasn't sure that he could rely on her, not if it came to a choice between her career and her heart. He dragged himself back to the conversation with Yves.

"When you say Murcoing was mercenary, you mean he went with older men for money?"

Valentoux shrugged. "Perhaps, I don't know. But I'd imagine it was mainly for presents, expensive clothes and trips, always at the best hotels, perhaps the occasional painting. I can't see Francis being involved with someone quite so crude as to demand cash."

Valentoux took a notebook from an inside pocket and handed Bruno a small color photograph. It showed a dark-haired little girl in a light blue dress sitting on the lap of a strikingly pretty woman. The picture had been taken in a garden, in front of an ivy-covered wall; an older woman stood beside them.

"You may be surprised but that's Odile, my daughter, and those are her parents, Francine and Hélène, an actress and a set designer whom I've known for years. They initially wanted to adopt, but when that proved difficult, they asked me to help and I fathered the child with Francine. Odile calls me Tonton, Uncle Yves."

"Congratulations," said Bruno, his eyes lingering on the little girl, looking for a resemblance. "I think she has your eyes."

"I have a whole photo album: her birth, her birthdays, going on vacation together at the beach in Normandy. Here's one of Francis with Odile, in my apartment in Paris. He thought she was marvelous, and I think he fell in love a little with Francine and Hélène, just as I had."

"She's lovely. How old is she?"

"She was four when that was taken, last summer, in my garden. Francine and Hélène are very kind; they make a lot of room for me to share in their joy. Perhaps they may have had some room for Francis as well. I know Francis hoped that might happen. That was something he wanted to talk about on this vacation we had planned. He was beguiled by his fantasy of giving Odile a little sibling."

"She's a lovely child. You're a lucky man," said Bruno, and meant it. He pushed the photo back across the table, poured two more drinks and asked, "Did you know that Francis had another house not far away, in the Corrèze? That's where I was this afternoon."

"I knew he had a place somewhere in the south, but he made it sound more like Languedoc or Provence. I had no idea it was so close."

Bruno described his meeting with Francis's brother, the trip to the farmhouse and the loot he had found there. He didn't mention the guns or the shrine, but he spoke of Francis's interest in his grandfather's wartime exploits and his obsession with the Neuvic train.

"On the evening we met he talked to me about his grandfather—Sergeant Freddy, he called him—and his work with the Resistance. I thought he might have been inventing it, a convenient line to attract a Frenchman. He sometimes talked about this mythical train with its billions of francs. I'd never heard of it, and I'd thought it might be another of his fanciful stories. He had quite a few, about his wild times in Los Angeles and New York in those halcyon days before the plague came, before AIDS."

"Did you know he was HIV positive?"

"Yes, he was honest about that from the beginning, and absolutely assiduous about safe sex. That's why I was reluctant . . ." Yves checked himself. "Francis was interested in the American moves to legalize gay marriage. I think it was as much the hope of sharing a child with Francine and Hélène or fathering another one as any great urge to settle down with me. For my part, I was worried about the HIV being passed on."

Yves drew his hand over his eyes. "How silly that all seems now that I'll never see him again."

Seeing his wistful expression, Bruno chided himself for being too intrusive. He finished his drink and rose to his feet.

"I'll be up early again tomorrow to exercise the horses, so I may not see you before your move to Sarlat. We've got each other's numbers, and I'm sure our paths will cross. Just toss the sheets and towels in the washing machine before you leave."

"One last thing before you go," said Yves. "I don't know if it could help, but when I first mentioned to Francis that I'd be directing in Sarlat this summer, he said he knew the area.

Apparently he'd been renting a place somewhere around here, near Les Eyzies, ten years or more ago. He'd taken the place with some friends and met a young French boy. There had been some trouble with local people—I'm not sure whether it was a fight or just the usual gay bashing—and they'd all left in a hurry."

Bruno felt a little shock of recognition and a renewed sense of his failure in an unresolved case whose memory could still occasionally trouble his nights. "Did he tell you the name of the French boy?"

"No, never. But when we were at his place in London one evening he showed me some poems he had written. They were very intense, not to my taste. But there was one about listening to a lover speaking French."

15

On his early morning drive to Pamela's house, Bruno was considering how to refer to his evening with Isabelle. As they saddled the horses, he said casually that he'd been summoned to "a working dinner with your favorite policewoman from Paris." To his relief, Pamela did not react. She was much more interested in his news that Crimson was expected to return to St. Denis that day, that his belongings had been found and that the local burglaries would now cease.

"That poor man, coming home to a ransacked house," she said. "Tell him to join us for dinner, Bruno."

After an invigorating ride and a refreshing shower, Bruno led Balzac on a leash through the temptations of the Saturday morning market. The young basset hound sniffed and then gulped down the scraps of pâté and crusts of brioche, the offcuts of great hams and rinds of cheese that kindly stall-holders tossed in his path. Finally Bruno thought, Enough. He scooped up his puppy to carry him past these well-meant offerings and fastened his leash to the leg of the chair opposite the one where Gilles was sitting on the terrace of the café. His laptop was open before him, and all the day's newspapers were piled alongside it. They shook hands. As Bruno turned to wave for Mirabelle, a schoolgirl who earned pocket money as a waitress on Saturday mornings, Gilles began feeding Balzac chunks of his own croissant.

"You'll make him fat," Bruno said as he shook hands. "I'm going to have to stop bringing this dog to market. What's the news from Paris?"

"Not much, which is why I'm down here hoping for some more," said Gilles. "Is this guy Crimson arriving today?"

"So I'm told, and we've found his stuff. The Police Nationale will be putting out a press release later today saying that all of Crimson's belongings have been recovered. If you're still running news on your website, you can have the scoop. You'll even beat *Sud Ouest*. We found the stolen goods in a Corrèze barn belonging to the murdered English antiques dealer."

"When you say 'We,' does that mean you were present?"

"Yes, but don't say that. Let J-J take the credit." A coffee and croissant appeared in front of Bruno and he nodded his thanks to Mirabelle, one of Florence's favorite pupils.

"Let me tweet this first, and then you can give me some more detail for the website."

Twenty minutes and another coffee later, Bruno had made his rounds of the market. He climbed the steps to the upper square and gazed down on St. Denis and its people. Farmers' wives with shopping bags were coming out of the bank, and teenage girls in market-day finery were giggling together by the bridge and deliberately not looking at the boys. Everything was normal, and all was calm, except that there was an armed killer on the loose.

His cheerful mood evaporated as he considered what he might do if Paul Murcoing suddenly appeared on the bridge carrying his stolen guns. He was paid to protect St. Denis. Reluctantly, because he preferred to do his job unarmed, Bruno descended the steps, walked across to the *mairie,* went up to his office and opened the safe. He took out his MAB nine-millimeter, stripped, cleaned and lightly oiled. He then carefully wiped the bullets before loading the magazine. It could take fifteen rounds, but like most former soldiers he left out one to loosen the spring and reduce the chances of jamming. He reassembled his weapon, checked the safety catch and strapped his holster around his waist. Feeling self-conscious at its unaccustomed weight, Bruno went back to complete his patrol and watch over the market. To his surprise, none of his friends and neighbors seemed to notice he was armed.

An hour later, however, it was the first thing Isabelle spotted when he responded to her phone call and arrived in his van at Crimson's house. As he climbed out to greet her, he could hear the distant sound of a helicopter. "Perfect timing, they're on their way in," she called from the doorway, then came down the path to greet him. "It's good to see you with a gun again. That usually means matters are about to get interesting."

She opened the front of her leather jacket so he could see her shoulder holster but then went down on one knee after Bruno opened the rear of the van and little Balzac leaped out and sprinted toward her. Ears almost as long as Balzac himself flapped like giant wings as he jumped into her arms, his tongue raking her neck and cheek. She laughed and hugged him and then seemed to lose her balance and toppled onto her back, Balzac standing foursquare on her chest to nuzzle at her face. Bruno felt himself grinning even as he thought how much he would miss her.

"Don't just stand there, help me up," she called from the ground, and laughing he stretched out a hand. The helicopter was much closer. She dusted herself off and watched Balzac follow his sniffing nose around the garden. Whether or not she would miss him, Bruno thought, she'd certainly miss Balzac.

One of the men in overalls who had been with her on her first day at Crimson's house was standing on the edge of the covered swimming pool, holding a red flare, its rising smoke giving the pilot the wind direction. The military helicopter flew past the house, turned and came back into the wind as it dropped. Bruno clamped his képi firmly to his head, noticing that the helicopter was a Fennec, one of the unarmed models used to transport senior officers. Balzac, who had darted into the shelter of Bruno's legs when he saw the helicopter descend, now barked in defiance as its rotors stilled. The door opened, and the brigadier, dressed in a suit and tie, groped with his foot for the little step attached to the skids and jumped down. He turned to help Crimson, a rather older man in gray slacks, blazer and open-neck shirt.

Crimson was the only man Bruno knew who seemed to have his hair cut once a week. It was always at a perfect length and never seemed to become disheveled, however strenuous the tennis or capricious the wind. At first, Bruno had thought it signified a touch of vanity, but now that he knew the man it seemed all of a piece with his self-possession and self-control.

"Bruno," said the brigadier, much more coldly than usual, reaching out for a curt handshake as Bruno's arm came down from the salute. "I believe you know Monsieur Crimson."

"Bruno and I have been on first-name terms for years," said Crimson, in his grammatical but strongly accented French. With careful courtesy he shook Isabelle's hand before surprising Bruno with a kiss on both cheeks. They had been amicable acquaintances but hardly good friends. Perhaps he was trying to send a signal to the brigadier. "I gather you've pulled off a remarkable bit of police work."

"You'll need to check the hoard, but I brought this as a token of the eventual return of your goods," said Bruno, and handed to Crimson the wrapped parcel he had brought with him from the back of his van. He was conscious of the brigadier glowering impatiently at him. Whatever credit he'd gained from solving the burglary did not seem to have impressed the brigadier.

"Let's do this inside the house," Crimson said, and looked down to where Balzac was sniffing at his perfectly tailored twill trousers. "And who's this little fellow? You finally managed to replace dear Gigi?"

Inside his kitchen, he unwrapped the two Cotman watercolors, which Bruno had selected as the most portable and identifiable of the loot from the barn. Crimson examined them both with deep satisfaction.

"These were the wedding presents my wife and I gave each other over forty years ago. I can't believe you pulled this off, Bruno. I'd been resigned to a long battle with the insurers, and then when I landed at Paris, there was Vincent waiting for me with the good news and his helicopter. I can't believe that you got my wine back too."

Bruno had never known the brigadier's first name, and from the way her eyes widened, nor had Isabelle.

"I'll want to see you at the gendarmerie at five this afternoon, Bruno," the brigadier said briskly. "I don't think we need detain you or your dog further. As soon as Monsieur Crimson has unpacked his things, we'll take the helicopter on to the Corrèze so that he can check on the rest of his property, and then we'll arrange to have them shipped back here."

Bruno replied with a crisp salute. His attempt at a dignified departure was undermined by Balzac, who was alternating his attentions between Isabelle's black sneakers and Crimson's

English brogues. Bruno finally had to bend and scoop Balzac into his arms to take his leave, aware of Isabelle's averted eyes and the half-baffled, half-concerned look on Crimson's face.

"Call me tomorrow because I owe you the best dinner in the Périgord," Crimson called after him.

16

His holster still around his waist, Bruno was in his office at the *mairie,* dealing with accumulated paperwork, when his phone rang. He put down the leasing contract for a big screen on which the council would project open-air cinema on summer evenings and answered.

"It's Jacqueline Morgan, and I'm not sure whether I'm in your jurisdiction, but I thought I'd better tell you first. I've been burgled."

She was in another commune, so technically the break-in at her house was none of his business, he told himself as he drove through Les Eyzies on the way to her house. But her tale was intriguing, she had been helpful in sharing her expertise, and any friend of the mayor deserved his best efforts. He parked behind her white BMW, pulled from the glove compartment a pair of latex gloves and a couple of evidence bags and knocked at the door.

The first thing he noticed was that Jacqueline had been to the hairdresser. The iron-gray curls he remembered had been tamed into soft waves and given subtle streaks of gold. She was wearing a well-cut dress that flattered her trim figure. On her feet were sneakers, but a pair of formal shoes with heels stood by the door, as if she'd kicked them off on entering. At their first meeting, she had looked like he imagined an American female academic would appear. Now, despite the shoes, she looked French and ten years younger. When she presented him her cheek to be kissed, he detected an attractive scent.

Jacqueline said she had spent the morning at the market in Sarlat and had then met the mayor for lunch before he went to the hospital. Bruno didn't think she was the kind of woman who'd dress up to go shopping in the market, so she must have wanted to look her best for lunch with the mayor. He smiled to himself at the thought.

She'd then driven home to find no sign of forced entry. But the books and papers on her table were not quite where she had left them, and when she'd looked into the kitchen she found the back door open and one of its panes neatly removed. She had checked the rest of the house, and a few small items of jewelry were missing from her bedroom, along with some silver, her TV set and the laptop.

She led him to the back and showed him the pane of broken glass on the kitchen floor, still mainly attached to a sheaf of greased newspaper. That was the technique that had been used at Crimson's house. Could this be Murcoing's work again? Or perhaps somebody who wanted to make it look like Murcoing?

He told Jacqueline to stay inside and went out to check the garden and outbuildings. They were all clear, but an army could have been hiding in the wooded slopes of the ridge that rose behind the house. Dirt roads led up through the woods, although he could see no other houses up there. About a kilometer from Jacqueline's home he had passed a duck and goose farm, which seemed to be her nearest neighbor. A burglar would have had no fear of being seen. The ground was too dry for prints, but there were tire tracks in the grass behind the house, out of sight of the road.

Inside, the house was strangely tidy for a burglary. Usually he'd have expected drawers pulled out and upended, mattresses shoved aside and ripped and cupboards dragged away from walls. In the bedroom a rather fine wooden box, obviously for her jewelry, had been tipped onto the bed. A charming nude sketch of a woman sitting on a bed, her shapely back to the painter, hung between the two windows. Even the least artistic thief would have thought that was worth money.

"I haven't touched anything since I found the house like this, except for some of the books and notes downstairs to see if anything was missing," she said. "The most important thing is the manuscript of my father's memoirs. I have copies, of course, but not here in France, they're . . ."

Bruno put a finger to his lips to signal for silence. He was not one to leap to conclusions, but there was a possibility that Jacqueline's burglars had been the kind of people who would also leave the house bugged. It was going to be a very interesting conversation with the brigadier.

"Are you insured against theft, madame?" he asked. She nodded, her eyes widening, understanding the signal of his formality. "And the value of your stolen silver and jewelry would be what in your estimate?" Bruno waved his hand upward two or three times to encourage her to set the figure high.

"Well over ten thousand euros," she said, "probably more. Some of them were antiques, irreplaceable family heirlooms. The silver coffeepot is eighteenth-century American, and since my father was descended from Mary Robbins, there's a family legend that it was made by Paul Revere."

Bruno looked at her blankly.

"He was a silversmith in Boston, a famous revolutionary who carried the news of the British raid that started the War of Independence. There are poems about him that children learn in school, at least we did in my day. Mary Robbins married his son."

Bruno nodded, thinking that would be useful for the plan that was forming in his mind. "Do you have a photo of this coffeepot?"

Jacqueline went to a two-drawer filing cabinet disguised as a wooden chest of drawers. He told her to wait and brought another set of gloves from his car. She put them on, muttering that the files seemed to have been searched, and gave him a postcard-sized print of a handsome coffeepot with a curved spout.

"I had to have a photo taken for the insurance once I'd listed it as a special item," she said. "I put the value at ten thousand."

"And your laptop? How much would that be worth?"

"Over a thousand. Both it and the TV were quite new."

"So altogether the value of what has been stolen could be as much as twenty thousand euros? Perhaps we'd better see if anything from the outbuildings is missing before I call the gendarmes." He steered her outside and into the garden at the rear.

"You think I'm being bugged?" she asked in a whisper.

He shrugged. "It's possible. What about the material on your laptop? Do you have it all backed up?"

"Yes, on the university mainframes, both in Paris and in the States. It's tiresome, but I won't have lost anything. Is this some government operation, spying on me?"

"I don't know but we'll do this by the book."

After a fruitless search of the barn and shed Bruno led the way back into the house and called the gendarmerie at St. Denis, where Sergeant Jules was on the desk. Jacqueline's house was roughly halfway between the gendarmeries in Montignac and St. Denis, so he couldn't be accused of deliberately calling in the gendarmes he knew. Bruno explained the burglary and the value of the items stolen and stressed the news value of Paul Revere's coffeepot. Most important, he added, was that the same method of entry had been used in the Crimson burglary, so that pointed to Paul Murcoing. That would get Yveline excited, Bruno thought.

He then went to his van and pulled out the cheap pay-as-you-go phone he'd bought in a previous case when Isabelle had wanted to contact him in a way that could not be traced. He used it to call Annette in Sarlat and explained not only the burglary but also his suspicion that the real target of the thieves might have been Jacqueline's papers. Could she make sure that the report of the burglary got special attention when the *procureur* came back to the office on Monday? Once the *procureur* listed the case as a *délit,* a serious crime, there would be a paper trail that would make any attempt at a cover-up very difficult.

"This sounds intriguing, so let's talk about it over dinner tonight," she said. "I'm with Yves at the house, and he's been shopping in the market to make that dinner he promised you. I already called Pamela and Fabiola."

"Is there enough for a couple of extra guests? My friend Gilles from *Paris Match* is in town, and I think you'd like to meet Jacqueline."

"The more the merrier," Annette replied. "My place in Sarlat, about eight? And by the way, Bernard Ardouin has brought me in to help on the Fullerton murder, so I need to call Sergeant Jules. I'll just ask him if anything has come up, and that way the *procureur*'s office will be informed."

Bruno hung up, called Gilles to tell him about dinner and smiled to himself at the difference between the way the French judicial bureaucracy was supposed to work with its separate jurisdictions and checks and balances and the way that in practice friendships and personal connections could cut through the red tape. He took a mischievous pleasure in the way that he, a village policeman, could play the system. But this time he would have to be particularly careful. Usually he could count on discreet support from the brigadier and Isabelle. This time the politics made that problematic, and he'd hate to have either one of them as an enemy. The brigadier could squash him like a bug.

Suddenly he looked at the cheap phone in his hand and cursed himself for being so foolish. Isabelle had the number. If she decided to track the phone records, his careful maneuvering could be uncovered. So much for his moment of self-satisfaction. He'd have to buy another disposable phone as soon as he got back to town.

He was taking this risk not for Jacqueline, whom he barely knew, but for the mayor, to whom he owed just about everything that made his life rewarding: his home, his work, his place in St. Denis. More than that, he had a visceral dislike of the way that agents of the French state often rode roughshod over the law. If the brigadier, say, had staged Jacqueline's burglary to protect the government from embarrassment, that would stick in Bruno's throat. He remembered the angry words he'd exchanged with Isabelle over the growing number of scandals piling up at the door of her ministry. At least she was making arrangements to move to another job.

"I thought you might like some coffee," said Jacqueline, coming out of the house with a tray. "I'm just sorry that I can't serve it in Paul Revere's jug."

She took the tray to a small garden table with two spindly metal chairs, tucked into a sunny corner among the rosebushes.

"I think you ought to know what's going on, or at least what

I think may be happening," he said. "Somebody in the French government is worried that a scandal could be unleashed just ahead of the election. There is some suspicion that Jack Crimson is involved. I presume you know his background?"

Jacqueline nodded. "And they think my research is somehow involved, is that what you mean? But it all happened so long ago. Anybody involved in that business with the slush funds and the Resistance money is almost certainly dead."

"You mentioned that you were working on something else, about the French nuclear deterrent not being truly independent. If the opposition could make an issue out of that in the next week or so, it could have an impact on the election."

"The Americans say it's not the crime, it's the cover-up that causes the trouble, and the cover-up has been going on for years," she said. It had started with Nixon's summit with President Pompidou in 1970, she explained. By 1973 the French were being given assistance in developing their missiles, their multiple warheads, and even being shown how to set up underground testing sites for nuclear weapons. They also received help on missile guidance systems. She had a Pentagon document that recorded the French saying they didn't need their missiles to be accurate enough to hit Soviet missile silos; they just wanted to be able to take out cities.

She had a whole file of documents, she said, memos of talks between Nixon and Pompidou, and between Kissinger and the French defense minister Robert Galley. The cooperation had gone a lot further under Presidents Carter and Giscard d'Estaing. Most of the material was marked TOP SECRET, but she had managed to get some of it declassified. There was a whole lot more in the archives of the Nixon Library, she said.

"So this material is now publicly available?"

"Only if you know where to look. Some of it's quite funny. There's a memo of a discussion between Kissinger and Defense

Secretary Schlesinger when they say the French have, and I quote, 'the worst nuclear program in the world.' Because of U.S. laws against the transfer of nuclear secrets, they set up a system called negative guidance, under which the French nuclear technicians would say they were thinking of doing it this way, and the Americans would shake their heads. They'd go through the various options until the Americans didn't shake their heads, and that's how they built the triggers for the French nuclear explosions. I had fun writing the chapter with all that stuff."

"Why would the Americans do this?"

"Kissinger made it quite clear that the purpose was to ensure that the French were dependent on American technology and stressed that 'the real quid pro quo is the basic orientation of French policy.' That's another quote. Once de Gaulle was out of power, Kissinger thought he could use the nuclear bait to turn the French into reliable allies again, on the American leash just like the British. And if the Americans withdrew their cooperation, the French would fall far behind in nuclear matters. And you know how important that is to Paris."

Bruno nodded and took a deep breath. Nuclear weapons were France's last claim on great power status. "Are these documents still in your files here? Or have they gone?"

"It doesn't matter. I photocopied them, scanned them into pdf files and have them all stored in the cloud. Get me a computer and a printer, and I'll print them out for you."

"Have you told the mayor all this?"

"Not in such detail, no. I told him the funny stuff. He was the one who said my book would make quite a stir. But I've given seminars on this material at the National Defense University and at the Woodrow Wilson Center in Washington. I have a couple of graduate students who'll get their doctorates out of this."

"Is your book finished?"

"The text is finished, and I'm just about done with the footnotes. I expect to send it to Yale University Press by the end of the month. My editor there has already seen most of it."

"This is the English version you're talking about. What about the French edition, when will that be ready?"

"I'll translate it myself, and I'm aiming to have it done by the end of the summer, which would mean publishing it sometime next year."

Bruno was thinking how this would play in French public opinion if extracts from the book or even a summary of its highlights turned up on the front page of *Le Monde* a week or so before the election. Nuclear independence had been one of the cardinal principles of French governments for the last half century, and to learn that it was all a sham would come as a national shock. The opposition would have a field day. He could envisage a row in the Assemblée Nationale, public inquiries, denunciations and even fistfights on TV talk shows.

"Tell me about the politics of this," Bruno said. "Were both parties involved?"

"Pompidou and Giscard were conservatives, so the Socialists could claim it was their fault. I don't have any documents about Mitterrand's time, when Reagan was in the White House."

"I can see why a conservative government would want this kept quiet," he said, wondering if Jacqueline had her own political motives.

"But it's our history, Bruno, yours and mine and that of every other French voter and taxpayer. Why shouldn't they know about it?"

Why not indeed? he thought. But the timing would be important, the timing and the way the information was released. Was it unreasonable for the brigadier and his political masters to delay the information for a few weeks until the election was over? Would it not even be a huge distortion of the political process to have the final days of the election campaign dominated by an angry public debate over France's nuclear status?

Bruno shook his head, suddenly angry at himself. He was thinking like the brigadier or like a politician. These were not decisions to be taken by agents of the state, thinking of the French electorate as so many children to be protected from monsters in the dark. This was a free country, and such an issue was for the French voters to decide.

"You look like a man who's just made his mind up about something," said Jacqueline. "Are you going to tell me about it?"

"First, you're invited to dinner tonight with me and some friends in Sarlat, and if you agree I'd like to share this with them," he replied. In the distance, he could hear the familiar sound of a police siren. The gendarmes were on their way. "One's a magistrate and another is a journalist with *Paris Match.* I trust them, and I'm confident that you can, and giving them this information may be the only way that you can control how this story is released and presented."

"Rather than suppressed by the kinds of people who burgled my house and bugged my home," she said. "That's fine with me. I wonder, can the mayor come too? I was going to make dinner for him, but I think he'd want to be a part of this."

17

His shoes polished and his uniform jacket and cap brushed, Bruno presented himself at the gendarmerie at one minute before five, shook hands with Sergeant Jules and was shown into the commandant's office. The brigadier was standing beside the desk, studying a series of framed photographs on the wall of Yveline playing hockey. On top of her computer sat a small stuffed toy in red cloth. As Bruno came to attention before the desk he could see it was a monkey, and was surprised that the brigadier had not tossed it into a wastepaper basket. He braced himself for an encounter of the kind he had learned in the army was best handled by saying "Yes, sir," and as little else as possible.

"How are you, Bruno? Sit down, take your hat off and have a seat." The brigadier sat down at Yveline's desk, pulled a bottle of Balvenie scotch from his briefcase, poured generous slugs into two water glasses and added a couple of splashes of Evian. He pushed one glass across the desk to Bruno, who stared at it suspiciously.

"Well done on the burglary. Crimson is delighted and so am I."

"Thank you, sir," he replied, trying to keep the surprise from his face.

"You're no fool, so you'll have worked out why I was curt with you at Crimson's house."

"Yes, sir." It could only be because the brigadier wanted to mislead Crimson. He had no idea why.

"I won't enjoy my drink until you enjoy yours, so please take a sip and stop playing the old soldier."

Bruno obeyed but hardly tasted the whisky as he watched the brigadier pull a slim file from his briefcase.

"You won't be surprised to learn that Crimson is someone we keep a friendly eye on, but we're also interested in Jacqueline Morgan and how they know one another. Just over a year ago she was invited to give a faculty seminar at the Wilson Center in Washington on her research into European-American relations during the Cold War. Crimson was her guest, invited along to give a commentary from the British point of view. Since the seminar covered some very sensitive aspects of French nuclear policy, we were fortunate that a visiting French academic was in the seminar room and spoke to us afterward."

He fixed Bruno with a piercing look and asked: "Why did you not tell Isabelle that you'd been to a party at Crimson's house last year with the pair of them?"

"I told Isabelle I'd been to parties at his house, but I didn't know her. In fact I didn't meet Jacqueline Morgan until the day before I met Isabelle at Crimson's house, and I called on her as a historian who knew a lot about Resistance finance. She was in work clothes; no makeup, her hair a mess. Having previously only seen her dressed up for a cocktail party I wouldn't have recognized her."

"How well do you know Crimson? He seemed very fond of you this morning." The brigadier refilled their glasses.

Bruno recounted the tennis games, the drinks at the club bar, the garden party and the dinner. "Until Isabelle told me his background, I'd assumed he was just another retired civil servant."

"You understand that it's him we're really concerned with rather than her. He's always been very close to the Americans, and it was interesting that after meeting him she got those documents declassified. I doubt whether the Americans give a shit who is the next president of France. But the British certainly do."

"I'd have thought they'd be happier with the devil they know."

"You could be right; I wouldn't know. But even if the Brits don't want to interfere in our elections, they may think it useful for us to know that they could upset our applecart if they chose to. There are lots of items on the European agenda where London will need help from us—protecting their precious financiers in the City, concessions on European affairs. A little leverage is always good."

"This is all way above my head," Bruno said. The refilled glass was looking very attractive, but he restrained himself.

"In that case let's talk about Jacqueline."

"She strikes me as an interesting woman," said Bruno.

"You are known to have a soft spot for women, Bruno, a sentiment that in general I applaud. But it can lead to misapprehension."

He pulled out another file from his briefcase and began reading phrases at random. "Arrested in Paris, May 1968, at a barricade on the rue St. Jacques while a student at the Sorbonne . . . arrested August 1968 at the Democratic Party convention in Chicago, received a broken jaw from a police baton . . . September of that year she takes up an exchange scholarship at University of California, Berkeley . . . December

1969, a delegate to the final convention of Students for a Democratic Society in Flint, Michigan, voted to wind up the SDS and reform into the Worker-Student Alliance, a group closely associated with the violent extremists known as the Weathermen . . . arrested in May 1971 during a march on the Pentagon to protest the Vietnam War."

The brigadier paused in his reading, looked up and took a sip of his drink. "Quite the little activist, this Jacqueline Morgan. A member of Redstockings, a radical women's collective, and a contributor to a collective book titled *Our Bodies, Ourselves.* And she never gave up. Arrested again in 1985, this time in Britain, when she was staying at the women's camp protesting against American missiles at the Greenham Common airbase. She was arrested again that year during a demonstration over the miners' strike but was released without being charged. She was supposedly a visiting professor at the University of London at the time. I suspect that was the moment she came up on Crimson's radar screen. Most recently she attended our Green Party's summer university last year, where she spoke as a member of the advisory board of Greenpeace in the United States. I have to hand it to her, she never stops."

He tossed the file onto his desk. "And now the radical Professor Morgan is connected to a British spymaster. If this were the Cold War, I'd suspect a honey trap and start looking for a Moscow connection. These days, who the hell knows?"

"You know she was burgled today?" Bruno asked. "Her laptop and documents were taken, along with some silver and jewelry to make it look genuine."

"It wasn't us, but I hope you'll understand that I can't answer for all the less public arms of the French state, however much I may disapprove of what they do in the name of national security."

Bruno sipped at his drink, wondering what the brigadier's real agenda might be but mainly thinking of the epic of Jacqueline's life. She'd plunged into the history of her time and also made a distinguished career by writing some of that history. He did not feel surprise but rather admiration.

"Why not say what you want to do?" Bruno asked. "Are you trying to suppress her work, or do you just hope to delay it until after the election?"

"Why on earth would I want to do that? This is our history. The French public is entitled to know it."

Bruno sat back in his chair, completely baffled. He reached for his scotch, took a long sip and then looked thoughtfully at the photograph of the president of the Republic that hung on the wall by the door.

"You want him to lose the election," he said. The brigadier shrugged, poured himself another drink and waved the bottle toward Bruno, who put his hand over his glass.

"I couldn't care less who wins the election, they're all pretty much the same," the brigadier replied. "But there's something rotten in the entrails of the state, some of it in my own ministry. You know what I'm talking about because I'm told you said much the same thing to Isabelle. Tapping the phones of journalists and opposition leaders, burglaries, suitcases full of secret campaign funds, crooked deals, planted evidence, enemies lists and worse. That's what I'm sick of. To save France from that requires a change of government."

"No, it doesn't. It means we need a free press and a fair election." Bruno pushed the half-full glass of scotch back across the table, picked up his hat and walked out.

As Bruno approached the mayor's house, he saw that the mayor had returned from the hospital and was engaged in that most restful of chores, watering his garden. The mayor turned at the sound of Bruno's footsteps, offered him a friendly nod and then raised his eyebrows.

"You look cross," he said, over the patter of spray on leaves. "Jacqueline called to tell me about the burglary. She also told me about dinner with your friends in Sarlat. I could use a respite from going to the hospital. She'll be here shortly. We can have a drink before we head over there."

Bruno took a deep breath and asked, "How's Cécile?"

"Asleep in a morphine dream. Her hand twitched when I held it. We grew these plants from seedlings, and now she won't live to eat them. I've accepted that. What's the matter with you?"

Bruno recounted his conversation with the brigadier.

"I wish I could identify for you one election when nobody in the state apparatus tried to put his thumb on the scales," the mayor said. "It's what they do, part of the price we have to pay for the existence of an intelligence service. We expect them to keep us safe from terrorists, but we've never been very good at defining the lines they should not cross."

The mayor walked to the tap on the side of the house, turned it off and wound the hose into neat loops. "You know what I mean, Bruno. You cross a few lines yourself from time to time, and so do I," he said. "It's an imperfect world, so it comes down to personal judgment. I let you get away with a few things because on the whole I trust your instincts and your motives. It's for you to decide how far you trust the brigadier."

"I'm not sure there's anything I can do," Bruno said. "I thought I was doing the right thing in advising Jacqueline to release a summary of her work, so at least she keeps control of it, and it doesn't get suppressed. But now it turns out that's what the brigadier wanted all along."

"Not quite. The brigadier wants it released. So do you and

so does Jacqueline. But if you think that the brigadier wants a wave of heated headlines to emerge like a bombshell in the final days of the campaign, you don't have to let him get away with that. Ah, there she is now."

The white BMW pulled into the drive, and Jacqueline stepped out. She was wearing high heels again and a silk dress in pale green. Its sleeves came down just below her elbows, and somehow she made the plain black plastic watch on her wrist look like the height of fashion. She kissed the mayor on the lips and hugged him briefly before turning to Bruno and offering her cheek.

"I took your advice," she said to Bruno, and pulled two folded pages of typescript from her bag. "Here's a first draft of an article I'm thinking of sending to *Le Monde.*"

Bruno read out loud. " 'Recently declassified documents from American archives suggest that U.S.-European nuclear cooperation went further than has been hitherto believed and that, like Britain, France's development of missiles and nuclear weapons benefited from the discreet sharing of U.S. technology . . .'

"It reads like *Le Monde,*" he said, handing it to the mayor, who skimmed the whole draft quickly.

"Those who know will understand the significance of this, and those who don't will probably not get past the first paragraph," the mayor said. "Perfect—it's all there but not sensationalized." He gestured to the table on the terrace where a bowl of olives and another of nuts awaited and invited his guests to sit before he went into the kitchen and returned with a tray bearing three champagne flutes and a half bottle of champagne.

"Just enough to wet our lips before we head for Sarlat," he said, and turned to Bruno as he opened the bottle. "I hope you're not planning to go in uniform."

"I've got a jacket in the van. I'll look like a boringly dressed civilian."

"Talking of wetting our lips," said Jacqueline, "I was thinking about Bruno's friend at *Paris Match*. It might be a good idea to have him run a small item first, a teaser to whet *Le Monde*'s appetite. In my limited experience of the media, they seem all the more interested when they know a rival publication is sniffing after the same story. Would your friend be amenable to that?"

"I don't know, but it's worth asking," Bruno said. "You may have to succumb to the *Paris Match* treatment, a flattering photo and an interview with the glamorous historian who straddles two continents."

"That doesn't sound too bad."

"That's not all. You can expect quite a lot about your past to come out, May '68, Vietnam protests, SDS, radical feminist, Greenham Common."

The mayor raised his eyebrows, and Jacqueline gave Bruno a sharp look. "You've been doing your homework."

"Not at all," he replied. "It was just read out to me from an interior ministry file on you that's currently sitting in the gendarmerie."

18

They were climbing into Jacqueline's car for the journey to Sarlat when Bruno's phone rang, and J-J's gruff voice told him that new evidence had emerged. Yves Valentoux would be arrested that evening for questioning.

"It looks bad." J-J went on, "Yveline has evidence that he wasn't at home in Paris all evening, contrary to what he said. She went through all his credit card statements and then through the individual bills and found that he bought a disposable phone about six weeks ago which we've tracked moving down here from Paris on the day that Fullerton was killed."

"How do we know it was Valentoux's phone?"

"It's on his credit card. He bought it at a Leclerc. At the same time he put twenty euros onto it prepaid, so we were able to identify the SIM card."

"What does he say?"

"I haven't spoken to him yet. I'm on my way to Sarlat to arrest him. I cleared it with the magistrate. Ardouin will join me at the police station. I thought you might want to be there."

Bruno explained to Jacqueline and the mayor and then called Annette.

"I know about it," she said as soon as she answered. "Ardouin just called me. So much for our happy dinner party."

"Does Yves know?"

"Yes. He's sitting beside me, shattered. He's agreed to go to the station, and I'll go with him. All we know is there is supposed to be new evidence. Will I see you there?"

"Yes, J-J invited me to the station. They can't keep you on the case, not now that you're sharing a house, so obviously I can't talk about the new evidence. Find him a good lawyer. I'll stay in touch."

Bruno hung up and called first Pamela and then Gilles to explain and felt relieved when Gilles offered to take Pamela and Fabiola to dinner. Driving to Sarlat, he welcomed the time to himself so he could consider just how little he really knew of Yves. He knew that Yves was a skilled actor, able to perform and entertain at a dinner table within a day of finding his lover's dead body. He had abundant charm, and Bruno and his friends had all warmed to him. Bruno had been touched when Yves showed him the photograph of his daughter, but that could have been a theatrical ploy to secure his sympathy.

He would have to wait until he saw the details of the new evidence. And there would be questions to answer. If Yves had driven down with his disposable phone, he hadn't used his own car. What transport had he used? Could he have driven down earlier, parked at a station and then used the trains to get back and forth? He'd still have to provide himself with an alibi in the form of autoroute toll receipts. Bruno tried to remember exactly what Yves had said about the evening he spent at his apartment in Paris. And if he had followed Fullerton down to the Périgord and killed him, then he'd have needed to clean up and change. Where had he done that? The forensics team had been sure nobody had stayed at the *gîte* since Dougal's employees had cleaned it.

As he navigated the series of roundabouts that led into Sarlat, Bruno concluded that even if Yves had been lying, that didn't mean he had to have been the killer, though it made him into a top suspect along with Paul Murcoing. Could they somehow have been in it together?

Bruno usually enjoyed being in Sarlat, a town where he half expected to walk into a film crew making yet another version of *The Three Musketeers.* The set designers might need to tidy up a few shop fronts and remove the chairs from a few café terraces, but otherwise they wouldn't have to change a thing. The town had been preserved as if in aspic since the sixteenth century, a glorious jumble of medieval houses and narrow alleyways, dark tunnels and grand Renaissance town houses, all built around a monastery and an abbey that dated back to Charlemagne's time. Sarlat was the capital of the Périgord Noir and one of the most visited towns in France; Bruno never tired of wandering its cobbled streets when he went to the movies with Pamela and Fabiola. Like Annette, they were passionate about film, and Annette's decision to settle in Sarlat had made their own visits more frequent.

This was a more somber visit. When Bruno arrived at the town's subprefecture, which housed the commissariat of police, Ardouin was already questioning Yves. J-J and Yveline were side by side at the desk normally used by the duty officer and going through the file of her research.

"Valentoux lied about being in his apartment that evening," she said, flashing Bruno a triumphant smile. "I checked his landline records with France Télécom, and he got two calls that he didn't answer. I tried the number, and it was an actress he knew. She wanted him to engage her for the festival here. He didn't reply, so it looks as if he wasn't home."

Bruno nodded. "Maybe she was someone he was trying to avoid. What does he say about the disposable phone he bought?"

"He hasn't said anything to us. He said he'd wait until he spoke to the magistrate."

"What was the timing on those two phone calls?"

"The first was seven-twenty, the second at seven twenty-four," she replied.

"So he could have gone out to buy a paper or some cigarettes, something so routine it could have slipped his mind."

"It's possible," J-J said. "But when he was being questioned for murder, I would think he'd have remembered. And then there's the disposable phone. Anyway, it's up to Ardouin now. I've ordered some pizzas; I think it could be a long night."

J-J pushed the file across to Bruno, who reviewed the cell-phone-tracking report. The scan had started at noon at Villejuif, just south of Paris, on the day of the murder. Then the phone had followed the Aquitaine autoroute through Orléans and Limoges. The tracking had stopped at six in the evening when the location was St. Denis.

"Do we have any more data for before noon and after six?" Bruno asked.

"I just picked those as the relevant times," Yveline replied.

"Were any calls made or received on the phone?"

"There was a call to a St. Denis number and another to a disposable phone somewhere in Bergerac, but we don't know who owns it. I've asked France Télécom to let us have the records of the number, but they can't do that until Monday."

"Do we know whom he called in St. Denis?"

"Delightful Dordogne, a rental agency. That's all we've got."

Bruno asked himself why Yves would be calling Dougal's agency when Fullerton had been making the arrangements.

"Can we get some more tracking on the phone, before noon and after six?" he asked.

"What's the point?"

"If Valentoux was the killer, we need to know how he faked his alibi with the autoroute tolls. The phone tracking could tell us that."

"That makes sense," said J-J and asked Yveline to see to it. The pizzas arrived as she was on the line to France Télé-com, and Bruno took some slices in to Ardouin and Yves, who looked relieved to see him.

"Monsieur Valentoux says he bought the disposable phone when shopping for groceries with his friend Fullerton when they were together in Paris," Ardouin said. "It seems Fullerton had wanted one because he didn't want to pay the roaming charges on his English phone. Did you find any such phone among his possessions or in his van?"

"No. But we didn't know we should be looking for one. We didn't go through everything."

"Monsieur Valentoux also insists he was home on the evening in question but might have gone out briefly to buy ciga-rettes at a local *tabac* on the avenue Mathurin Moreau, where he says they know him," Ardouin continued. "They may be able to confirm this. Could you call them, please, and check?"

"It's called the Café Moreau," Yves added. "I always buy my cigarettes there."

Bruno left the room, found the number of the café and called it. A woman answered, and he introduced himself and explained his business.

"I remember Yves bought a lottery ticket early in the week because he said he was leaving Paris the next day. He bought a couple of extra packs of cigarettes for the journey," the woman said. "But I can't remember whether it was Monday or Tuesday or Wednesday. If he still has his ticket, it should give the date and time."

Bruno thanked her, put the phone down and knocked on the interview room door. Ardouin told him to enter, and Bruno asked Yves if he still had his lottery ticket. He opened his wallet and handed Bruno the ticket.

"Purchased at Café Moreau in Paris on the third, that's Tuesday evening, at seven twenty-four," Bruno read aloud. He scribbled down the number and handed the ticket to Ardouin. "The woman in the café remembers selling it to him along with some cigarettes. And that would explain why he didn't answer his phone."

Ardouin nodded and closed the file before him. "So your story holds up, Monsieur Valentoux. One of those rare occasions when cigarettes may actually have done you some good."

The whole St. Denis contingent had gathered at Pamela's place for an impromptu meal of Fabiola's risotto. The mayor had brought wine and two cans of his own pâté, and Pamela contributed salad from her garden and cheese. After calling to see where they had all gone, Bruno was able to join them in time for coffee and relate the dramas of the evening.

"So you're back looking for Paul Murcoing," said Pamela when his tale was complete and a toast drunk to Yves's release.

"Well, I am," said Bruno. "He was the last person we can place at the murder scene, so we have to talk to him even if the *procureur* says the evidence against Murcoing is only circumstantial and there's no obvious motive. Yveline still suspects Valentoux, and J-J wants to start looking at other antiques dealers who might have had a motive to kill Fullerton."

"Maybe there's an English connection, somebody living here who knew him," Pamela suggested.

She was looking well, the pallor of a Scottish winter beginning to give way to the beginnings of a tan, her bronze hair
piled loosely atop her head to display her long neck and the
emerald earrings that suited her. She was wearing a pale blue
blouse of heavy silk over perfectly cut jeans. Bruno smiled,
enjoying the look of her, the clear skin and bold eyes, the shape
of her neck and the delicate scent of her hair. She returned
his gaze, a fondness in her eyes, and placed her hand on his
where it rested on the table. That was unusual; Pamela seldom
showed her affection in public.

His attention was distracted by sounds of argument from
the other side of the table, where Gilles and Jacqueline had
been locked in discussion. Distracted by the events of the evening, Bruno had forgotten that Jacqueline wanted him to help
promote her story in *Paris Match*.

"Bruno, could you explain to Jacqueline that I'm not a
little clockwork toy that can be wound up and sent marching
away and then turned off?" Gilles said, filling his glass with
wine. "There's a big story here, but all I'm getting is hints
about nuclear strategy and warnings not to make a big sensa-
tion. You know I can't work like that."

"I'm just saying that I don't want my work to be overinter-
preted," said Jacqueline crisply. "This is a serious matter."

"I've known Gilles a long time, and I trust him," Bruno
replied. "Why not show him that draft you showed me earlier
and then explain how you would like the story to emerge? He
knows more about the way the media works than anybody
else here, and I'd like to hear his views."

Giving Bruno a dubious look, Jacqueline shrugged, took
the folded typescript from her bag and passed it to Gilles. He
pulled a candelabra closer, put on a pair of reading glasses and
began to study it closely.

"Lousy lede," he muttered, and Jacqueline's lips tightened.

This was not going well. Bruno helped himself to some cheese and bread. Gilles finished reading, took his glasses off and handed back the typescript.

"This is based on your book, which won't be published in the U.S. until later this year. Is that right?" Gilles waited for Jacqueline's nod of agreement. "But you want to get the facts out now because you're worried that the government wants the story suppressed, and you think the French people have a right to know how they've been lied to for forty years about our precious *force de frappe,* how that nuclear arsenal isn't really ours, it comes courtesy of the Americans, just like Britain's. The technology for our missiles, our guidance system, our warheads, our test sites, even the triggers for the bomb itself, all come from the U.S.A. although we have been proclaiming for decades that we are independent. In return for this, our president agreed to modify French foreign policy. And you want me to run a vague little teaser piece in *Paris Match* to build up interest before you run this as an op-ed piece in *Le Monde*. Am I right so far?"

"Yes," said Jacqueline in a clipped voice.

Gilles put his hands together, looked from Jacqueline to Bruno and back again. "And in return for running this teaser, rather than getting the credit for breaking what could be one of the stories of the year, all I get is the offer to write a nice soft feature with a full-color photo about this intriguing Franco-American historian who's blowing the whistle on one of the biggest strategic secrets of the Fifth Republic. It doesn't sound to me like a good deal."

"I could let you have some of the documents to publish, but I'd also insist on approving whatever you write," Jacqueline said stiffly, sitting back and folding her arms. The body language between her and Gilles was verging on hostile. "I have transcripts of Kissinger's meetings, including his jokes about France having the world's worst nuclear program. All of it is headed 'Top Secret.'"

"Let me explain my problem," Gilles said, leaning back and sipping at his drink. "I go to my editor who looks at me like I'm an idiot and wants to know why we don't keep the story to ourselves and screw *Le Monde.* That's what I'd be asking, in his shoes."

"You would get an exclusive on the documents," said Bruno, before Jacqueline could respond. From the way she was bristling, he was sure she was about to make some cutting remark about *Paris Match* not being taken as seriously as *Le Monde,* which would only make matters worse.

"The documents have been declassified," Gilles replied. "That means we could get our U.S. correspondent to hire a history graduate student tomorrow and tell him to go to the Nixon Library first thing Monday morning and find them."

"What might help you persuade your editor to do it our way?" Bruno asked.

"What else have you got?"

"Another story altogether. Have you ever heard of the great train robbery and the mystery of the Resistance billions?"

19

Bruno woke to the smell of coffee, a tongue licking briskly at his ears and the weight of a soft, squirming basset puppy on his chest. He opened his eyes, moved Balzac's rump out of the way and saw Pamela, already dressed in riding clothes, standing by the bed with a tray.

"Breakfast in bed, what a treat," he said, wriggling his way upright. She put the tray on his lap, plumped up the pillows on her side of the bed to sit beside him and took hold of Balzac before the puppy could attack the croissants. They were still hot from the bakery; she must have gone to town for them. There was also orange juice for him and a bowl of Stéphane's thick yogurt and a banana for her. Balzac turned to lie on his back, legs pedaling the air. The pads on his paws were already starting to darken from the pink of puppyhood but his tummy was a lovely soft rose color.

Bruno scratched Balzac's belly and looked out of Pamela's window at the sky, bright with a few high streaks of cirrus; it promised to be a fine day. He glanced at his watch, almost nine. It was Sunday, so there was no pressure. The others had left the night before around midnight, and he and Pamela had said good night to Fabiola and taken Balzac into Hector's stall so he could sleep beside his friend the gelding. Then they had stood awhile, Pamela leaning her back against him as they looked at the vast reach of the stars against the clear night sky. When he began to kiss her neck, she'd unpinned her hair to let it float down around his head, turned to kiss him properly and then taken his hand to lead him to her bed.

"Thank you for this," he said, gesturing at the tray. "And thank you for last night. I feel wonderful."

"You know, there was a moment last night when I thought Gilles might be staying the night with Fabiola," she said. "They lingered together over coffee and exchanged what my mother would have called meaningful looks."

"You mean like the looks I was giving you?" He took her hand and raised it to his lips.

"No, you knew exactly what would be coming next. And so did I. But they didn't. The looks were exploratory, aware of possibilities in one another, looks full of uncertainty about how the evening might end. It was quite romantic, just watching them. Maybe she's finally ready to have an affair, but I don't think she's yet made up her mind about him."

"Gilles is a good guy, she could do a lot worse."

"He's a few years older than her, which might not be a bad thing," Pamela said. "And he's a bit plump. But she could always shape him up. I'm sure he lives on pizzas and sandwiches in Paris, and he probably drinks too much."

"You sound like you're planning the wedding and thinking about names for their first child," he said, surreptitiously giving Balzac the final bite of his croissant as Pamela stared up at the ceiling.

"I saw that, and you'd better be sure he leaves no crumbs in the bed," she said, turning onto her side to face him and putting a hand on his bare chest. Her face bore a serious look. "Do you think Fabiola's happy?"

"She seems to be. She's got an interesting job, earns more money than me, has lots of friends, horses to ride, and she's passionate about that women's shelter in Bergerac she volunteers at."

"Does it worry you that she earns more than you do?"

"No, because I don't spend the money I do earn. I get my food for free from the garden or hunting or cheaply from my farming friends. My uniforms are free, so I don't spend much on clothes. The *mairie* pays for my gas and my phone bills. I don't owe a penny on my house, I have a wonderful horse, and I have some good wine in my cellar. Other than raffle tickets at the tennis club, I don't gamble, and I just spent the night with a beautiful woman who brings me hot croissants in bed. All that makes me the richest man in St. Denis."

"I'm happy to hear that." She paused. "Do you think Fabiola's attractive? She's so sensitive about that scar."

"I think she's very attractive with a lovely figure, and that scar's not prominent, and it's the kind of feature that makes a man look twice, curious about how she got it. When she says it was a mountaineering accident, it's like she's handed him a rope. Once he starts talking to her about where she's climbed and why she likes it, then he'll realize what an interesting, intelligent woman she is, aside from being a doctor. Plus she makes a great risotto, and those fondues of hers are irresistible."

"But that's the thing. Intelligent women make men nervous. Maybe that's why she's started learning to cook."

"You don't make me nervous." He kissed her hand again.

She gave him a playful slap and said, "Time to get out of bed. The horses need riding. I'll go and see if Fabiola's awake while you get dressed. See you in the stable." She kissed him on the forehead and headed for the stairs. As his eyes followed her appreciatively, he was sure she was putting a deliberate extra wiggle in her hips.

An hour later Bruno arrived at the gendarmerie, summoned by a message on his phone from J-J.

"We know Murcoing's sister rented a camper, but we can't find it," said J-J, averting his eyes from the little red monkey that still sat atop Yveline's computer. "One of the Bergerac cops was trawling through every ad on the Internet and came up with a guy in Issigeac who rented it to her. We're checking every campsite, and the *motards* are checking every camper on the roads. We've even mounted checks at the Spanish border. Any ideas?"

"We're still watching his mother's house in Bergerac and checking every day with his aunts," said Yveline. She looked exhausted, nothing like the fighting-fit athlete in the photos on her wall. "We'll get him eventually when he runs out of cash. They've got to turn up somewhere."

"I've had a detective taking Paul's photo around to all the gay bars in the region," said J-J. "A lot of people know him. He's not popular. We followed a few leads and called on some old boyfriends, but no luck so far."

"What about the *brocantes*?" Bruno asked. Some of the antiques fairs had already begun, early in the season though it was. Bruno supposed that Murcoing could be raising cash by selling off some of the more portable items from his loot, jewelry and silver, either at the fairs or directly to antiques dealers.

"We've visited the ones we've had suspicions about, and we've had a cop looking at every antiques fair that's going on in the whole of southern France," J-J said. "We can't afford to keep up this level of manpower much longer, so we need some new ideas."

"If he's not on the road in the camper, then either he's found a place to hole up or he's already out of the country," said Yveline. "It would have taken him just four hours to get to Spain. I know we've got Interpol on this, but can't we get the Spanish police to make more of an effort?"

J-J looked at her, glanced at the stuffed toy on her computer and rolled his eyes at Bruno.

"There's no shortage of vacation homes all over southern France. He could have found one that's empty and holed up there, just as he did at Fullerton's place," said Bruno.

"There are thousands of such places, and we can't send a cop to check out each one. Plus we think this guy's armed."

"Was there nothing on Fullerton's laptop that might give us a lead?" Bruno asked.

J-J looked up sharply. "Fullerton's laptop, where's that?"

"The Apple laptop that belonged to the murdered man, the one we found in the van in the Corrèze barn."

"*Putain,* now you tell me. I didn't see any laptop." He leafed through his file and pulled out some papers stapled together. It was a long list. He ran his finger down each page. "There's nothing on the inventory about a computer. Where the hell is it?"

Bruno remembered Brian Fullerton's cry of triumph when he found his brother's password for the laptop.

"Fullerton's brother must still have it," he said.

"Where is he now?"

Bruno was pulling out his phone and looking up the number in its address book even as he answered. "Hôtel St. Denis? I'm calling now."

Fullerton was still checked in but had gone to church, he was told by Mauricette at reception.

"It's my fault," Bruno said. "I should have made sure you knew about the laptop, but I was just distracted by finding the stolen goods. *Merde,* J-J, I'm sorry."

Yveline made a sound of disgust and shook her head.

"It's our fault as much as yours," said J-J. "I remember seeing a power cord on the desk in the study where the guns were. I should have made the connection."

"I'll go to church and get Fullerton out. I'll come back with the computer," said Bruno, heading for the door.

"These village coppers are all the same," he heard Yveline say as he left. "Amateurs, all of them. God knows how we'll explain this to the *juge d'instruction.*"

Bruno almost ran down the steps of the gendarmerie, heading for the rue de Paris and the church, when he heard the cheerful toot of a horn and managed to stop just before he had dashed into the path of Dougal's daughter Kirsten on her Mobylette.

"You better look where you're going, Bruno," she said. "You'd have done more damage to my bike than I'd have done to you."

"Sorry, something's come up," he said, and she drove off. Suddenly a thought came to him. If Murcoing wanted to be sure of finding an empty holiday home, his sister would have known of one from Dougal's list. He ran down the street to the offices of Delightful Dordogne, hoping to find Kirsten. Sure enough, she was there.

"Could you print me out your work list for this week?" he asked her. "I need to see which houses will be vacant; it's about the burglaries."

"No problem, just give me a minute to turn on the computer," she replied, taking off her helmet and shaking out her white-blond hair.

"I'll be back in five minutes." This time he looked both ways before he crossed the road and headed for the twelfth-century church of St. Louis that dominated this part of the town. Built in an age of faith to hold hundreds, today it could count only a handful of worshippers, who seemed to be outnumbered by the choir. Father Sentout's sonorous voice was stressing the importance of these weeks after Easter in the lives of the faithful and rolled on undeterred by Bruno's entry. From habit rather than devotion, Bruno dipped a knee and crossed himself, then moved discreetly to the shadow of a pillar and looked for Fullerton. He spotted him in the center of an empty row of chairs, kneeling and apparently in prayer, and waited until Fullerton resumed his seat.

"Sorry to disturb you, but the chief of detectives for the region wants to see you, and we also need to check your brother's computer," he whispered.

"Can't it wait?"

"Sorry, no. My colleagues are making a fuss about your taking it."

Fullerton sighed at Bruno's words but nodded agreement, and the two men crept as quietly as they could along the row and out of the church. Father Sentout ignored their movement, and the rest of the congregation seemed too intent on his sermon to notice, or perhaps they were simply asleep.

"Sorry to have caused a problem. Once I had the password and got in, I couldn't wait to find out what was on the hard drive," Fullerton said. "I didn't think you'd need it right away; you all seemed so caught up in the stolen goods. Anyway, I hope you'll be pleased with my progress."

As they walked to the hotel, Brian explained that he'd found a long trail of e-mails between his brother and Paul, some about *brocante* sales, some personal and a lot about their shared interest in the history of the local Resistance and the Neuvic robbery. There were also exchanges of e-mails with other men, including Yves. Francis Fullerton had kept a separate file for his travel reservations and expenses, and each of his many trips to France had been carefully itemized with dates and hotel costs. It was pretty clear from the exchanges with Paul about which houses would be empty, Fullerton explained, that his brother had been up to his old tricks with stolen goods again. And there were hundreds of photos of furniture on the hard drive, each one labeled with a reference number for the house it came from.

"Will you give me a receipt for it, since I want to be sure to get it back?"

"Yes, of course. I'll wait here, and you can bring it down."

He returned within two minutes, and Bruno handed him a receipt torn from his notebook. Fullerton said the magistrates were hoping to release the body on Tuesday, and he had tentatively booked a cremation for Wednesday. They parted, and Fullerton ducked back into the church.

Armed with Dougal's list and the laptop, Bruno reentered the room where J-J and Yveline were comparing photos of items of furniture against the inventory of the barn. He put the laptop on the desk, scribbled down the password and explained how Dougal's list showed the vacation homes that Paul Murcoing and his sister would know to be empty.

"It's a total of twenty-two houses, but I know some of these addresses, and they're close to a town or to neighbors who would spot people coming and going. There are maybe fifteen that are remote enough to give Murcoing the security he'd need. One of them is Crimson's house, so that cuts it down to fourteen."

J-J looked at Yveline, who pursed her lips and said, "We

can't do fourteen simultaneous raids, not without bringing in *mobiles* from all over France. Three at a time is the best we could do, and that would mean getting an extra squad from Bordeaux."

She picked up the little red monkey from the top of her computer and began to pace the room. As if talking to herself she went on: "Then we'd have to get approval from the *juge d'instruction,* and that would mean helicopters, thorough reconnaissance, warnings through a bullhorn. Each squad could do a maximum of two hits a day, and you can't keep that kind of activity quiet, so it would be all over the local radio. And what if they're moving around from place to place?"

Yveline replaced the monkey on top of the computer and glared from one man to the other. "It's not going to work, is it?"

J-J cleared his throat and said, "She's got a point, Bruno. We'd have to bring in the *juge.*"

"What about sending out police in plain clothes, with a pair of binoculars to see if there's any movement at the house or maybe spot the camper?"

"I'm not sending anybody poking around in range of the houses," said J-J. "This guy is armed and dangerous. What we need is to set some kind of trap, something that would tempt him out. Still, I like the idea of taking a careful look at these places. You're the local man, Bruno; get me some big maps and mark down each house, see if you can locate a likely place nearby where you could stay in cover and watch. Meanwhile, Yveline and I will have a look at the laptop."

An idea was forming in Bruno's head, a way to take a discreet look at each of the houses without needing the elite *mobiles* squads from the gendarmes. Armed to the teeth and encased in body armor, they were trained for terrorist and hostage situations; they'd blunder all over an unfamiliar countryside. But he had friends who knew the area. Moreover, it was hunting season. He began making a mental list of the friends he could trust enough to call out on a job like this.

"I've got to do a report for the *procureur* on that burglary yesterday, the one with the American coffeepot," Yveline said, giving Bruno a suspicious look. "I don't suppose you'd know why his office seems to be taking a special interest in it."

He was about to respond with a sharp comment that it was because whoever broke in used the same method as in the Crimson burglary but restrained himself. She was a young woman, nervous at this first job in command, and she was evidently under strain. Older and wiser people had helped him when he was making the inevitable mistakes that came with a lack of experience. He should do the same for her.

"I don't really know," he replied from the doorway. "I'm off to pick up a sheaf of maps from my office. If you want some advice from a village policeman, I'd get ready for a few calls from the local papers about the value of this coffeepot. And I'd look up the name of Paul Revere, who's supposed to have made it."

20

Hector picked his way down the steep bridle trail through the woods until Bruno reined in his horse at a place where there was a break in the trees and he had a clear view of the isolated house below. Pamela was on her mount beside him. For once the binoculars case was being used for its proper purpose rather than as a way to carry Balzac while on horseback. He took out the heavy Second World War binoculars that had belonged to Pamela's father and brought the house into focus. The shutters were all closed, the cover was still on the swimming pool, and there was no sign of heat from the chimney. A tarpaulin was snugly tied down on the woodpile, covered in last autumn's leaves and bird droppings. There was a barn, but its door wasn't high enough to accommodate a camper. He scratched it off his list.

"It's empty," he said to Pamela, settling his shotgun back more comfortably on its strap around his shoulder. He was dressed as a hunter: camouflage jacket, brown trousers and a brown woolen cap instead of the usual riding helmet. If he had to dismount and search on foot, he had to look the part. "Give me a moment to check with the others."

He pulled out his phone to scroll through the text messages.

There was one from the baron to say that the first house he'd been assigned was certainly empty, and similar texts from Sté- phane, Maurice and Raoul. Bruno had been confident that his friends, experienced hunters who had tramped over these val- leys for years and knew each fold of ground, represented the most natural and least obtrusive means of checking the rental homes on Dougal's list. He acknowledged each message and sent a query to his other hunter friends as to their progress.

He knew this was a long shot. There were many rentals not on Dougal's list, and Paul Murcoing might be smart enough to have worked out that the police would make the connec- tion between his sister and Dougal's spreadsheet. But at least Bruno felt he was doing something positive in this increas- ingly frustrating hunt for Fullerton's murderer. He put his phone away, checked that his handgun was still on safety and spoke to Pamela in a low voice.

"If we head across the field below and up the next ridge, we should be able to see the third house."

"Good, I could do with a canter and so could Bess. These woodland trails can get tiresome."

Bruno decided not to point out to Pamela that she had insisted on joining him, suggesting that two people out riding would look much less suspicious than one, and nobody would ever mistake her for a policewoman. She was probably right, but her presence made him nervous. There was an outside chance that this mission could be dangerous, and a small voice in the back of Bruno's head murmured that he was putting her at risk because of his own pride, his desire to show Yveline that with his friends and local knowledge he could achieve results that her gendarmes couldn't.

He flicked the reins, and Hector walked on until the woods gave way to moorland. At the prospect of an open field Bruno's horse tossed his head and moved smoothly into his stride.

Bruno looked at the house before he dismounted, but the place remained still, no flicker of sunlight reflecting from some lens in one of the upstairs rooms, no empty bottles or garbage bags outside the kitchen door. They rode on, making their way up the ridge and then skirting some woods and hedges before getting to the long arm of woodland that slanted down toward the next house on the list, promising good cover. There was no trail, and the undergrowth was thick, so he went forward on foot, then pulled himself up on a couple of low-lying branches until he had a clear view of the isolated house. He checked carefully with the binoculars but saw no sign of habitation. The barn was big enough to take a camper, but he couldn't see its doors from this side. The dirt lane up to the house was thick with weeds that looked unbroken by any passing wheels. He walked back to Pamela and the horses.

"You go on ahead along this ridge. There's a firebreak through the forest that leads toward that hunters' shack where we had a picnic, remember? I'll meet you there. We can look at one more house, and that's it for today."

"I remember the hunters' shack, but what are you going to do?"

"I need to take a look at the barn doors on the other side, see if they're big enough for the van. Don't worry, I won't get close."

"If it's safe enough for you, it's safe enough for me. Besides, I'm getting bored. Let's go."

Pamela put her heels into Bess's side and cantered down the hill, gathering speed as she headed directly for the house. Quickly he mounted and chased after her until he was alongside and she could see him gesture to his left. He was indicating he wanted to stay on the high ground, but she thought he was inviting her to race. She bent forward in the saddle to urge Bess to go faster.

"No, no," he shouted, feeling a sense of alarm as he tried to catch up with her to head her off. "Go left, up the slope."

Hector stretched out his neck and stepped up his pace, soon outpacing Pamela's much older mare, but the gelding ignored Bruno's efforts to stay in front so he could start nudging Pamela to the left. Hector raced on ahead and only then would consent to heed the rein, veer to the left and go back up the hill. Bruno reined him in and risked a look behind to see Pamela, thrilled by her speed, continuing her gallop down the hill on a course that would take her close to the house.

Bruno's heart was in his mouth. If Murcoing was hiding inside, a burst from his Sten gun could be lethal at that range. Cursing, Bruno took Hector on a tight rein down the hill after her, conscious of the gun bouncing on his hip. He hoped it was covered by the hunting jacket he wore. Suddenly his horse jerked to one side, surprising him. Bruno looked down and saw Hector had sidestepped to avoid a fold in the ground, the grass scratched away at one side. Then he saw the holes and realized they were riding into a rabbit warren.

Before he could shout a warning he heard a scream. He looked up to see Pamela tumbling through the air and her horse sprawling, one foreleg still trapped in one of the dozens of holes made by the rabbits.

Skirting the holes, he rode as fast as he dared to where Pamela lay, dreading what he might find as he jumped down from the saddle and bent over her still form, trying to block out the hideous screeching from her stricken mare. He felt the pulse at her neck, and it was still beating. He didn't dare to move her, fearing a broken neck. Her limbs were lying straight, and when he pinched the tendon above her knee her lower leg twitched. The spinal column was still functioning.

He fumbled for his phone and called Fabiola, who was supposed to be waiting for them with the horse van near the next house they were to check. Bruno told her what had happened and where he was.

"I'm in the next valley, but I'll get there as soon as I can," she said. "Listen, Bruno, calm down. Call an ambulance right away. Above all, don't move Pamela."

Feeling as if his mind was working slowly, he dialed 15, the number for medical emergencies, and found himself connected to Ahmed at the St. Denis fire station. They would be there within fifteen minutes.

"What's that screaming?" Ahmed asked, and when Bruno said it was her horse, he replied, "Shoot the poor animal."

As he trudged back toward Bess, he realized that no sign of life had come from the house. Nobody could have ignored the dreadful noise that Bess was making. His eyes filled with tears when he saw that Hector was standing over Pamela's mare and tenderly nuzzling her, as if giving what comfort he could. Bess didn't seem to notice. Her foreleg was still trapped inside the hole, and the rest of her leg lay at a brutal angle. Her entire weight must have pivoted on the trapped hoof and snapped all the delicate bones. There was no way Bess's leg could be saved, and she was an old horse.

Even if Murcoing and his sister were inside the house and would flee as soon as they heard gunfire, Bruno didn't give a damn. He pulled his automatic from the holster on his belt and flicked off the safety catch. He slapped Hector's rump to push him away, knelt beside Bess and tried in vain to still her tossing head. He could barely think with the noise as he looked at this faithful horse on whom he had learned to ride. He drew an imaginary *X* from right ear to left eye, and right eye to left ear.

Bess suddenly seemed to be looking at him, and the thrashing of her head stopped for a moment. Aiming for the center of the *X* he put the muzzle close to her forehead to avoid any chance of a ricochet and fired twice into the skull. That was the rule; if the first shot failed to penetrate, the second one would. Bess's great head jerked and then sank to the ground.

The echo of the shots, so different from the sound of a shotgun, seemed to rock the air around him as he closed the safety catch, reholstered the weapon and went back to Pamela. He slipped the shotgun from his shoulder and took off his jacket to cover her. There was no movement on her face, no flickering of eyelids, but her hands were warm, her pulse still firm.

He tried to remember how she had fallen. She had tumbled over Bess's head, exactly as if turning a somersault. Thanks to the way she'd been galloping, her waist and knees had been bent and her head tucked low. That was the shape he remembered seeing as she turned through the air, rising almost slowly before she came down fast, her body still curved. Had she landed on her head or her back? He tried to remember. She had rolled once and again, then her limbs had gone loose and she'd sprawled. He closed his eyes and squeezed them tight, trying to conjure up the visual memory of her landing, but it had been too fast. The exact way she had hit the ground was not clear in his mind.

A sound came from behind him. Hector, stepping slowly, was looking from Bess's body to Bruno. He came another step, lowered his head and moved again, close to Bruno, shaking his head nervously. Bruno remained still until Hector brought his nostrils down to breathe on Bruno's neck. Slowly, his hand stroking Hector's neck, Bruno rose to his feet and mounted his horse.

He turned Hector's head away and trotted around the side of the isolated house to check the far side of the barn. It was open to the elements, with no wall and no door. Half a dozen campers could have parked inside, but there wasn't a single one, just some scattered hay. As he completed the circuit, he heard the sound of the ambulance siren in the distance and checked his phone. All the hunters had now reported in. Each of the houses on Dougal's list had been checked and pronounced empty. It had all been for nothing. He dismounted and led Hector back to Pamela's still form.

Fabiola arrived first, the horse van that was attached to Bruno's Land Rover bouncing and jolting on the dirt track. She left the engine running, glanced at Bruno without speaking and went to Pamela, the medical bag she always kept close jerking as she ran. Kneeling, she checked for a pulse and then gently pulled back an eyelid. She opened her bag, took out an instrument and used it to peer into Pamela eyes, into her ears and then up her nose. Finally she ran her hands carefully over Pamela's limbs and then stood as the ambulance came into view.

"She's concussed, unconscious, no sign of bleeding from the ears," she said. "How did she land?"

"I'm trying to remember, but all I can be sure of is that she was tucked in like a ball, as if somersaulting. She rolled once when she hit the ground and then again before she sprawled."

Fabiola glanced at the dead horse. "You took care of Bess? I thought I heard two shots."

"That was me."

Ahmed and Fabrice ran from the ambulance with a stretcher. Dr. Gelletreau heaved his bulk along behind, carrying a neck brace. He slowed to a walk as he recognized Fabiola.

"I was nearby with the horse van," she explained, and repeated what she had told Bruno. "We'll need an X-ray and a scan, so that means we take her straight to Sarlat. I'll go with her."

"I'll come too," said Bruno.

"No, you won't," she said, in a tone so harsh that Bruno felt she was accusing him of doing more than enough damage already. He felt a savage sense of guilt. He should never have allowed Pamela to come with him. And it had all been pointless, his little glow of pride at thinking of Murcoing's access to Dougal's list now destroyed. If he'd been a better rider, perhaps he could have headed Pamela off before she reached the rabbit warren. He should have found the words to dissuade her from joining him on the search. At the least he should have realized that his slow, cautious searching of the deserted houses was leaving her bored and eager for a gallop. He'd been so focused on his task that he'd barely thought of her.

Now as he watched Fabiola help Ahmed and Fabrice put the brace on Pamela's back and head before gingerly edging her onto the stretcher, he felt a surge of something much deeper than concern flood through him as he pondered what Pamela meant to him. She had created a private world for herself with her pool and horses and tennis court and her own little community with Fabiola. And she had generously and without any demands shared it with him. There was always good food and a welcome, horses to ride, companionship and easy conversation, and above all that sensuous warmth and pleasure that she offered him in the privacy of her bed. There were many forms of love, Bruno reflected, but he had no doubt that many of the deepest and sweetest kinds were embodied for him in this woman who was now being placed in the back of the ambulance.

Fabiola stared at him impassively from inside until Fabrice closed the rear doors. After the ambulance pulled away, Bruno took the saddle and bridle from Bess's body and then called the vet to arrange for Bess's removal. He unsaddled Hector, led him into the horse van and drove gingerly down over the rough field and onto the path that led to the road. As he reached it, his phone rang.

"I'm at the hospital," said the mayor, his voice hollow. "Cécile passed away peacefully this afternoon." He hung up before Bruno could say a word.

21

There was no sign of the mayor's Peugeot when Bruno pulled into the parking lot of the hospital just east of Sarlat. He asked for Pamela in the emergency wing and was told she'd been taken to the main hospital for X-rays. He found his way to the right department, and a tired-looking nurse told him to wait. He showed her his police ID, and she said she would try to find the doctor who had treated Pamela. A young man in a white coat soon arrived to say she was concussed and the X-rays had shown a broken collarbone. She had now been admitted at least for the night and was scheduled for a scan sometime the next day. If complications developed, she might have to be moved to Bordeaux.

"Has she come around?"

The young doctor told him no, adding that Fabiola was still with her. He gave Bruno the room number.

Fabiola was sitting beside the bed where Pamela lay with an intravenous drip in her arm and a small tube feeding oxygen into her nostrils. Electrodes were attached to her temples, and more wires snaked under the hospital nightgown and onto her chest. Displays on the machines behind the bed showed bright lines dancing rhythmically. Her face was white, her lips pale, her neck and throat encased in a foam brace.

"How serious is it?" he asked.

"It's always serious when someone's unconscious, and the longer it lasts the more serious it is. It looks like there's no cervical spine injury, but we're watching for any buildup of intercranial pressure or any lesions. From the marks on the back of her helmet and riding jacket it looks like she landed partly on her head but mainly on her shoulders and back. You said she was rolling when she landed, which may have saved her from a broken neck. Were the two of you racing?"

"No, she was galloping, but I wasn't. I was some way behind her. It took twenty or thirty seconds to reach her, and she was completely still by the time I did. I'd been trying to get her to turn away from that house. It was Hector who spotted the rabbit warren, and I tried to shout a warning, but too late. I should never have allowed her to come with me."

"Probably not." Fabiola turned her face away to look at the machines.

He couldn't tell if there was some medical duty she had to perform or if she couldn't bear the sight of him. He knew from the look she had given him as the ambulance doors closed that Fabiola was furious with him and probably blamed him for Pamela's fall. That was fair enough; he blamed himself. Was this the end of his friendship with Fabiola or an anger that would pass as Pamela recovered? He hadn't really considered the prospect that Pamela might not recover fully. He'd assumed that since her neck was not broken and her limbs seemed to work she would wake up and be back to normal in a day or so. But what if it wasn't so simple, or if she had suffered lasting brain damage or would eventually awaken with some change in her personality?

He quelled the thought and looked around. There were

three more beds in the room, two of them empty and someone lying still in the third, bandages wrapped so thickly around the head that Bruno could not tell if it was a man or a woman. There were no paintings, no TV set or radio in the room.

"Are you planning to stay here?" he asked.

"No, I'll come back with you. I'm just giving the staff a bit of a break by being here, otherwise that nurse would have to be in and out. I'll come back tomorrow to have a look at the scan results. They'll tell us more. If she's not awake by then . . ." She broke off and glanced at her watch.

"Can I touch her?"

Fabiola nodded. "Could be a good thing."

Bruno went to the far side of the bed, took Pamela's hand and stroked it, thinking how odd it was to feel no returning pressure. Trying to avoid the wires and tubes, he bent forward to kiss her cheek, smelling the antiseptic wipes they had used on her.

"What worries me is that she told me once that she'd fallen before and had been concussed," Fabiola said. "Over dinner one evening she was explaining why she'd given up show jumping. She was thrown off when her horse shied at a fence, and she blacked out for a few minutes. A second time can make it much more serious."

"Can I come back with you tomorrow?" Bruno felt that dismaying sense of helplessness that a nonmedical person feels in a hospital, dependent on the staff for information, for reason to hope.

"I'll call you after we look at the scan, but I expect she should have surfaced by then, at least I'm hoping for that. We can go when you're ready. I'll tell the nurse and have a word with the doctor. They're pretty good here." She left the door open when she left the room.

Bruno didn't know if he was imagining things, but he

thought he felt some movement of Pamela's hand where it lay in his. He looked at her eyelids but there was no sign of any quivering. He told Fabiola when she returned, and she checked the screens on the machines.

"Her pulse rate is up a little." She lifted Pamela's eyelids again, looked for a long moment. "No change."

"What are you looking for?"

"If the pupils are of different size, that's a clue to look for brain damage. It doesn't mean there is any; it's just an indicator. And you want to see how the pupils react to light."

"You think there might be brain damage?" The words were out before Bruno could stop himself.

Fabiola paused before she answered and turned to look him in the eye. "We're at one of those unpleasant moments when doctors are as much in the dark as laymen. Until we see the scan, or until she recovers consciousness and we can start to assess her state, we don't know what the outlook is going to be, and there's not much point in speculating.

"I know it was an accident, and I know how Pamela sometimes rides like a madwoman. But I'm not just a doctor; I'm her friend, and I'm human. Right now I'm furious with you and looking for someone to blame. So please just drive me home with the radio on and let's not talk. There's nothing more I can tell you."

Back in St. Denis after dropping off the still silent Fabiola and collecting Balzac from the stable, Bruno called at the mayor's house. No one was at home. He debated whether to drive to Jacqueline's to see if the mayor was there and decided against it. But he felt the urge to do something, anything, rather than sit and worry about Pamela and feed his sense of guilt. He checked his phone for the text messages from the hunters, none of whom had found any sign of Murcoing or a camper. He rang the incident room at the Bergerac station where the hunt for Murcoing was being coordinated and reported the empty houses to Inspector Jofflin. There was no news from the search of the campsites or from the road patrols.

He called Crimson to tell him of Pamela's fall and to postpone the dinner he'd been planning. When he explained how he and Pamela had been looking for Paul Murcoing, Crimson interrupted: "Was that the chap who burgled me?"

"Yes, but he's now a murder suspect, either on the run or in hiding somewhere. That's why we were searching the *gîtes* that were listed as empty."

"Do you have some way to smoke him out?"

"Maybe." Bruno remembered that J-J had wondered whether Murcoing could be lured out of hiding into some kind of trap. They had thought perhaps his obsession with the Neuvic money could be used as bait. He explained this to Crimson and said, "Nothing's been decided yet, but if we try it, what kind of bait could be used?"

"What if some new documents were being released from the archives in London that cast new light on it all, maybe giving the names of which Resistance leaders were authorized to control the money?" Crimson said. "They'd have to come from SOE, Special Operations Executive, but you wouldn't even need real documents. Just forge a couple of file references and a page of contents from an archive catalog and a sample page, scan it all and send an e-mail message to Murcoing. I presume he's got Internet access of some kind, if only through a phone."

"We'd have to send it to Murcoing in a way he'd believe it," Bruno said. "I'm not sure how we could do that. We know that

Francis Fullerton was equally fascinated by the Neuvic business. Maybe we could concoct a message to Fullerton about new documents with a copy to Murcoing. That might work."

"Let me think about this," Crimson replied. "I have one or two old friends who're familiar with those archives, including the ones still sealed. We have our quarry, we need a trap, and I think I may be able to provide the bait. I'll need someone here who's good with computers. Who's that woman teacher, the one who set up the computer system for the schoolkids?"

Bruno gave him Florence's phone number and then set off in search of the person who had best known the murdered man. He found Brian Fullerton at the Hôtel St. Denis, sitting in the courtyard under the plane trees with his pipe and a glass of kir. A bowl of olives and an open laptop lay on the table. This was his own computer, he explained, and he was looking forward to replacing it with his brother's once the police had finished with it. He fussed over Balzac, who was always delighted to make a new friend, and offered Bruno a drink. Bruno joined him in a kir, and when Brian asked how the search for Murcoing was progressing, Bruno simply shrugged.

"I'm getting quite a sense of the guy from the e-mails," Brian said, gesturing with his pipe at the laptop.

"But they're on your brother's machine," Bruno said, and then saw the small thumb drive fixed into a socket on the side of the device. "Ah, I see, you copied your brother's stuff onto that."

"Not all of it, but the e-mails," Brian replied. "It's going to be a hell of a job working out which parts of his stock are really his and which were stolen. Sorting out his will and his financial affairs will be difficult enough, so I thought I'd try to do some work on that while waiting for the body to be released. But instead, I've been going through the e-mails with Murcoing."

There was material in here for half a dozen police investigations, he explained, including Murcoing's role in helping buy some of Francis's guns from some shady types running a bar in Toulouse. There were several long e-mails from Murcoing, recounting all his grandfather's theories and suspicions about who got the money from the Neuvic train. The old man had seen suspects everywhere, starting with Malraux and some Russian who was in the Maquis in the Limousin; he even claimed that some big insurance firm had been started with part of the loot. There was a long account of some impoverished mechanic from Cadouin who was suddenly able to buy three trucks as the war ended and set up a successful carting business.

"It's hard to tell what's true, what contains a grain of truth and how much of it is pure invention," Brian said.

"Did your brother have anything to contribute?"

"Yes, indeed. He took it all very seriously." Brian relit his pipe and sat back as he began to explain that Francis had made several visits to the Public Records Office in Kew, just outside London, looking up the SOE archives. Many of them had been declassified, and Francis had scanned photocopies into his computer and sent them off to Murcoing with a rough translation. There were desperate missives to London from Resistance chiefs about how broke they were and how they needed money to feed their men and help support their families.

"But nothing more about the Neuvic train?"

"That's what Murcoing was really interested in, but my brother only found snippets in the SOE archives. But he told Murcoing that more files were scheduled to be declassified, and he'd hired a researcher to keep an eye out for them. One of the last e-mails said he'd gathered lots of new photocopies that he was bringing with him."

"We didn't find those at your brother's house," Bruno said, thinking that this could gel with Crimson's idea for new documents to lure Murcoing out of hiding.

"Murcoing must have taken them," Brian replied. "He's obsessed with this Neuvic business. He compiled a list of names of Maquis types from the Groupe Valmy and other networks, people he claimed were suspects, or ones that he or his grandfather believed had gotten away with some of the loot. Lord knows there was enough money at stake. He gives their addresses, the names and addresses of their heirs, the family businesses and farms that suddenly had money to expand with after the war. Two or three of his e-mails end up with the phrase 'They will pay for this!' But he doesn't say whether he wants to denounce them or blackmail them or what."

"Could you collect those names for me and e-mail them to me at my office?" Bruno asked. "I'd like to check them against our list of burglaries. What was your brother's reaction to this kind of thing?"

"It didn't seem to surprise him. But that was Francis, he was always an enthusiast. Even as a little boy he'd take up some hobby like stamps or aircraft recognition and hurl himself into it for weeks at a time, just like he did with Grandpa Freddy's wartime career and this venture with Murcoing. I went with my mother to see his specialist when he was in one of those expensive treatment centers where they try to wean people off drugs, and he told us that Francis had an addictive personality."

"What about their personal relationship? Did Murcoing know about Francis's affair with Yves or his liaisons with other men?"

"Francis was e-mailing all sorts of different men in ways that made their sexual relationship pretty clear, but he was at pains to keep them all separate," Brian replied. "With Murcoing,

I think there was much more passion on Murcoing's side. It reminded me a bit of that line from La Rochefoucauld, that in love there is always one who kisses and one who offers the cheek. Murcoing was very much the one doing the kissing."

"I'm wondering if that could have been a motive for the murder," Bruno said. "Murcoing could have felt betrayed if or when he found that Francis was about to have a romantic liaison with another man."

"I've asked myself the same question. The relationship with Murcoing had lasted for a long time, according to the e-mails. That was unusual for Francis. I used to wonder if Francis ever really loved anybody, except maybe his nephews and nieces, my children. It's hard to tell, and even harder to match the charming little brother I knew with what he became later. He could be a monster when he was on drugs."

Brian called up the final exchange of e-mails and turned the laptop so Bruno could read them.

The last e-mail from Francis had been sent on Monday, and he'd arranged to meet Murcoing at his Corrèze farm "after the weekend," presumably meaning this weekend. Francis said that he was bringing a full load of furniture from England to be unloaded and would then return across the Channel with French furniture from the barn. Bruno worked out the timing. Today was Sunday. The e-mail had been sent the previous Monday, and on Tuesday Francis had taken the Chunnel train and called at Dougal's to pay for the extra days' lease and to pick up the keys.

"So my brother would not have been expecting Murcoing when he suddenly showed up at the *gîte*. There could have been an angry scene," Brian said. "But I don't understand how Murcoing knew that Francis planned to arrive early for a romantic interlude with this other man."

"His sister works for the rental agency," Bruno said. "She

knew which *gîtes* were going to be occupied and when. And the name of the tenant is also listed for the relevant week, so the cleaners and gardeners know who'll be there. She'd certainly have recognized your brother's name, since this affair with Murcoing had been going on for over a year, you say."

"Maybe even longer. Look at this." He scrolled back to the beginning of the chain of e-mails between the two men, the first one dated in September, more than eighteen months earlier, and sent by Murcoing when Francis had returned to England after their affair had begun, or perhaps resumed. He pointed to a line in the rambling and passionate message.

"I have often thought of you even before that magical reunion when I saw you at the fair in Monpazier," Bruno read, and wondered just how long it had been between the reunion and their previous meeting.

That triggered a memory, something he had noted at the time and planned to follow up on but that had slipped his mind. It was to do with Valentoux and the night he had told Bruno about his daughter. Valentoux had been asking around the gay community in the region for information about Paul Murcoing and had been told he was known as a mercenary.

The conversation began to play back in Bruno's head. They had been standing on the steps of his home because Yves had wanted a cigarette. Yves recalled that Francis Fullerton had recounted some story of being in this region and meeting a boy a decade or so ago. And then an image suddenly appeared in Bruno's mind of the studio portrait of a sultry-looking Murcoing that had been on Francis Fullerton's bedside table in Corrèze and of Yves mentioning a poem that Francis had written about a boy named Paul.

Mon Dieu, he thought to himself, it's the missing boy from Bergerac who gave the medical clinic a false name on that case

I could never resolve, the one that kept me awake at night. It will be in one of my first notebooks.

He began to rise clumsily, jolting the table and startling Brian, who reached out to steady his drink. Bruno was thinking of the pile of cardboard boxes in his barn where he stored his old papers.

"Sorry, I just remembered something," he said.

"Is it to do with the case?"

"Maybe, but it's probably not that important, it's just that there may be a connection with something that happened a long time ago."

"Can you tell me about it? Does it involve Francis?"

"I think it might, it happened about ten years ago. A group of English gays rented a *gîte* and invited some French boys back to their pool. But the fathers turned up as well and beat the hell out of the Englishmen. I tried to sort it out, but the English guys left the area. The French boys were sent away on sudden vacations, and everybody clammed up. There was one boy I could never track down, who may have been young Murcoing."

"Ten years ago, that's just before Francis went to prison. And I recall that he did go on holiday not long before he was arrested. I don't remember him being beaten up."

"Did your brother drive a Range Rover?"

"No," Brian answered. "But his partner did, Sam Berenson, the one who died and left him the antiques business."

The names of the Englishmen had been on the rental agreement and on the car registration forms. Bruno was sure he'd have copied them down in his notebook.

"Did you find any poems on your brother's laptop?" he asked.

"Yes, he wrote a lot, poems, short stories. He even wrote a

few songs when he was in New York, made a couple of CDs, which I still have. I don't know for sure, but all his writings are probably in his computer. Why?"

"Yves Valentoux told me the other day that he remembered Francis reciting a poem he'd written about a French boy. That may have been where all this started. I'm going to have to look in my old notebooks."

"That's a shame, because I was just about to invite you to dinner, if you're free, that is," said Brian. "I've had enough of going through these e-mails and the mess of my brother's life."

"You're very kind, but I have some horses to take care of and a friend who's in the hospital. I may have to leave at any moment."

22

It was Bruno's day off, and after he'd phoned the hospital and Fabiola hoping in vain for some news of Pamela, he decided to plunge into activity rather than sit around worrying. He'd started by hunting through the cardboard boxes containing his old notebooks. Each box was sealed with Scotch tape and identified by the years the notebook had been filled. Inside, wrapped in the plastic bags the dry cleaner used to protect Bruno's uniforms, the notebooks were in rough chronological order. He found the relevant one, resisted the temptation to read it through and relive old events and cases and checked on the names of the Englishmen he'd written down from their car insurance forms. One of them was Francis Fullerton and another was Samuel Berenson.

The only French name he found was Édouard Marty, the boy who'd disappeared to England before enrolling at the university. While his notebook didn't say so, Bruno was sure he remembered that it had been the University of Bordeaux. And Marty had planned to study architecture. His parents had been old when he was born, and Bruno knew the father had died and the mother had moved away to be near her sisters. He called the faculty of architecture at the university, asked to speak to the director's office, identified himself and explained that he was trying to trace a former student, Édouard Marty.

"He's still here," she said. "What are you after him for, speeding again in that new Jaguar of his?"

Nothing like that, he replied with a laugh, just a routine inquiry about a possible witness. But how could Édouard still be at the university?

"He's not teaching today, he's only part-time," he was told. Bruno was given the name and number of a company named Arch-Inter where Marty could be found when he was not teaching a course on the history of interior design as an associate professor. Bruno searched for the company on his computer and found an elegant website, with the words "Arch-Inter" forking out to say "Inter-national" and "Inter-iors." To his great surprise, it boasted offices in Bordeaux, Cannes, London and Los Angeles.

The company offered services in architecture, interior design and furnishings in different traditions, from English country house and minimalist modern to French ancien régime or Empire. There were photographs of very grand-looking rooms furnished in various styles, each of them captioned in Russian and in English. It seemed to be a one-stop service for wealthy Russians, who would buy a house or apartment and have it filled by Arch-Inter in whichever style the client chose. How long, Bruno wondered, before they added Shanghai to their list of offices?

Bruno clicked on the section titled "About Us" and saw that Francis Fullerton was listed as the London representative. Bruno sat back, reflecting on the chain of circumstance that connected the beating up of some foreign gays a decade ago with this international company today. And what better outlet could there be for Fullerton's haul of French and English antiques? This was clearly a much bigger and more lucrative operation than Bruno had assumed, and perhaps one that could present some alternative explanations for Fullerton's murder.

He phoned Bernard Ardouin, who called up the website on his own computer as they spoke. Ardouin asked whether Bruno recognized any of the items in the photographs as stolen. No, he replied, but the art squad of the Police Nationale might be able to, and the place to start would be to compare the website pictures with the photographs on Fullerton's computer. Bruno explained the original connection between Fullerton and Édouard and asked whether Ardouin had any objections to Bruno's driving to Bordeaux to interview the architect.

"I'd rather you didn't do that yet," said Ardouin. "We don't want to alert him before we're sure stolen goods are involved. And as you say, this looks like a matter for the art squad rather than you, but all credit to you for opening up this lead. I'd better brief J-J and get him to print out those photographs on Fullerton's laptop."

"Still no sign of Murcoing?" Bruno asked.

"Nothing from J-J or the Bergerac police, and he hasn't used his bank card. He'll have to show his face at some point; it's just a matter of time. I've asked J-J to have some plainclothes types mixing discreetly with the crowd at the funeral tomorrow."

As he ended the call, Bruno wasn't so sure that finding Murcoing would be quite that simple. He shrugged. It was time to resume his training session with Balzac, who was by now so accustomed to being hugged and caressed by every human he met that Bruno had some difficulty in getting him to associate achievement with reward.

The special dog biscuits he prepared each month helped. Bruno mixed together a liter of milk, a bag of brown flour, an egg and a handful of brown sugar. He cut a slice of fat from the ham that hung from the beam in his kitchen, fried it and then poured the rendering into the mix along with a shredded clove of garlic. He then added tiny morsels of the ham. If he had any gravy left from one of his own meals, or any other useful leftovers, they went into the mix. If it was still too moist, he added bread crumbs. Baked for thirty minutes in a hot oven, the biscuits had proved irresistible to his previous dog, Gigi, and now to Balzac. Lured by the scent, Balzac would come when called and had learned to approach Bruno from the left with one whistle tone and from the right with another.

It was when he'd ended the training session with a grooming session and was cleaning Balzac's ears that he'd been reminded by the identifying tattoo inside the ear of one avenue he had not tried.

Bruno went into his study, pulled out the phone book, turned to "Tatouages" in the *pages jaunes* and found two tattooing parlors in Bergerac. He checked his watch, donned his uniform and headed into town, where he'd be in time to catch Pascal at the post office taking his midmorning break. He dropped off Balzac in Hector's stable, and armed with Paul Murcoing's photograph and the sketch Pascal drew from memory of the tattoo on the arm of the driver of the white van, he drove to Bergerac. Stopping to buy diesel fuel, he made the obligatory courtesy call to Inspector Jofflin to say he'd be coming onto Jofflin's turf and might have a lead on Murcoing. To Bruno's relief, he was passed to voice mail and left a message without having to explain his hunch.

At the first parlor, a place in a run-down part of town that seemed to specialize in gothic images, he drew a blank. The second place was just outside the old town, not far from the river, in a street where flower shops alternated with organic food stores, hairdressers and vegetarian restaurants. Ahead of him two women, one with a severe crew cut, were strolling hand in hand. The shopwindow of the tattoo parlor was dominated by a dramatic collage composed of posters advertising local concerts. Inside, a shaved-headed man in black leather pants and a matching vest, his arms and chest covered in ornate and colorful designs, glanced at Pascal's sketch and said proudly, "That's my Maori warrior."

"Your what?" Bruno asked.

"Maori warrior, from New Zealand. I saw it on one of their players in a rugby match on TV. Different designs say different things about how many fights you've been in, how many of the enemy you killed. I adapted it and made my own design."

"Did you do one for this guy?" Bruno showed him Paul's photo.

"Paul, yes, I did that one, and another that only his best friends would see. But I haven't seen him for a few days. He's usually in Marcel's at night."

"Is that a bar?"

"Bar, bistro, little theater in the back, its real name is Proust, but we all call it Marcel's. It won't be open now, though. Weekend nights run late, so they don't open Mondays until the evening. Is he in trouble again?"

"No, he's a witness in a case. What was he in trouble for?"

"I don't know, it's just something you say. But I make sure he pays me cash in advance," the man said. "You know what I mean?"

"Do you know where he lives?"

"You might find him at Marcel's. He's got one of the rooms

upstairs, but I don't know if he lives there or just uses it for pickups. Like I said, I haven't seen him for a bit. And if you find him, don't tell him it was me who told you."

Bruno found the place easily enough, between a dog-grooming salon and an antiques shop with a single Buddha head in gray stone dominating its window. Proust was painted black, and the windows were filled with movie posters of Jane Russell and Lana Turner flanking a blown-up photo of a beautiful woman's eyes. Bruno thought they might have belonged to Elizabeth Taylor. Below the eyes was a photo of Marcel Proust in profile. The door to the bar was closed, but it opened when he tried the handle. Inside, chairs were piled atop tables, the floor was wet, and a black woman who was mopping it looked up guardedly at his police uniform.

"I'm looking for Paul Murcoing," he said, showing the photo.

She shrugged and slopped water on the floor. "Boss not here," she said, not looking at him.

He walked across and put the photo in front of her face. "Do you know this man?"

She closed her eyes. "You talk to boss."

Bruno sighed. She was almost certainly an illegal immigrant. He disliked doing what he was about to do, but he didn't want to waste time.

"Your papers, please, madame."

"Papers at home." Now she had stopped mopping and was standing still, head down.

"You have a choice, madame. You either show me Murcoing's room right now, or we go to the police station and check your papers."

She shrugged again, this time with an air of defeat, pulled a large ring of keys from the pocket of her apron and led the way up two flights of narrow stairs to an unpainted wooden door. She unlocked it and let Bruno step into a room that was clearly unoccupied. There was a plain double bed, with a mattress and a pillow but no bedding, a small table with a water jug and basin, a hard-backed chair and a handsome armoire that had seen better days. It was empty.

"Paul gone," she said, a phrase she repeated when he asked when he had gone, how long he had been there and who else had stayed.

"His things, his possessions?" he asked. "Where are they?" He knew that when a policeman wanted to intimidate, he took out a notebook. Bruno fished in his jacket pocket for something to write with, remembering with a sinking feeling that he had left his pen in his car when checking the tattoo-parlor addresses on the map. The notebook was sufficient. Sullenly, she led the way downstairs to the cellar and pointed to two cardboard boxes.

"Boss packed these when Paul gone. He leave Tuesday."

That was the day of Fullerton's murder. He put the notebook away and opened the first box, full of unwashed clothes and a pair of dirty sheets. The second box contained shoes, toiletries, a small TV set, some books and what Bruno assumed were sex toys. They included leather manacles with straps, a battery-driven vibrator and what looked like clothespins in brass. He guessed they were nipple clamps. There was a small brown bottle with a label describing it as leather cleaner, which Bruno suspected was amyl nitrate, a drug that was sniffed and supposedly enhanced sexual pleasure. At the bottom was some mail. The biggest envelope had an English stamp and postmark, and inside was a printout of two crude photos that appeared to have been taken with a cell phone. One was of Yves Valentoux and Francis Fullerton standing together, eyes only for each other, at a bar. On a counter behind them was the kind of dimpled beer mug that you only found in English pubs. The second photo was in the same place and showed the two men kissing. Was this the trigger for Paul's jealous rage? Who might have sent it, and with what motive?

Most of the mail was junk, but he found an insurance form for the white van, a pharmacist's receipt for eighty-three euros that had not yet been claimed back from the health insurance fund of the transport employees section of the Force Ouvrière trade union. Finally he found a bank statement that showed Paul with just over two thousand euros in his account. The address for the account was the bar.

"No more," said the woman, and made no objection when Bruno took the papers. She followed him upstairs, and by the time he opened the door to leave she was mopping the floor again. He suspected her boss would never learn of his visit. He left messages for both J-J and Jofflin to pass on Murcoing's old address and to suggest that a visit to Marcel's bar might produce some leads. Since he was in Bergerac, he looked up the address he had for Joséphine, Murcoing's aunt. She worked with old people, Father Sentout had said. She lived not far from the first tattoo place he had visited, a crumbling neighborhood where the butchers advertised halal meat and several of the woman were veiled.

Joséphine answered the door in a housecoat with a towel wrapped turban style around her head and flapping her hands in a way that suggested she was drying her nail polish.

"I've come to give you fifty euros," he said, showing the banknote.

"I thought you'd pay me at the funeral tomorrow."

"I was nearby so I thought I'd deal with it now. You might be busy tomorrow. If you'll just sign this receipt for two of your father's old banknotes, one for the *mairie* and the other for the Resistance museum, I'll be on my way."

She invited him in, offered a cup of coffee, and as her kettle boiled she glanced casually at the receipt he'd brought and pocketed the fifty euros. Bruno had drafted the receipt with care, saying that the sum was received "in return for two invalid banknotes of a thousand francs, dated 1940, said notes to be used for historical display only." The space to be signed and dated by Joséphine identified her as representing the lawful heirs of Loïc Murcoing.

She sat at the kitchen table to sign it and made no objection when he pulled out a chair and joined her, resting his arms on the slightly sticky waxed tablecloth. The kitchen looked as though it hadn't been changed for decades. There were none of the usual fitted cupboards but racks of shelves for the plates and a small refrigerator that growled and wheezed. Joséphine wrote clumsily, as one not much accustomed to writing, and made the coffee, grinding the beans and then using a *cafetière.* The coffee was good, and he said so.

"I'm never one to scrimp on a good cup of coffee," she said, adding three lumps of sugar to her cup. "One of my only treats these days."

"Everybody in the family coming to the funeral?" he asked.

She eyed him narrowly, her hand sliding down to the pocket of her housecoat as if to make sure the banknote was still there. "I'll say this for you, you're the first *flic* who didn't push his way in and start asking where I was hiding Paul. And before you ask, I don't know where he is, and my sisters don't either. And nobody will be more surprised than me if he shows his face at the funeral and gets arrested."

"I heard he was living over a bar, a place called Proust, known to the customers as Marcel's."

"You know more than the police around here then. He was supposed to have part ownership of that place, but I don't know what came of it. Probably nothing, like most of Paul's big ideas." The words were harsh, but her tone was fond, Bruno noted.

"He seems like a bright kid, from what I hear, someone who should be going places rather than just driving a van."

"His grandfather was so proud of him, always at the top of the class," she said. "We all were when he passed his *bac* and went off to the university, first time anyone in our family ever did that. He was always too clever, but he was a sweet kid. Everybody liked him, even animals. He always had one in tow, a dog or a cat. He had a way with them. Stray dogs used to follow him home. He always wanted to keep them, but his father walked out soon after he was born, so there was no money."

"He did well to get to the university," said Bruno.

"Yeah, but that's when it all went wrong. He was easily led astray, fell in with the wrong crowd, and that's why he dropped out. I blame those damn drugs. He could really have made something of himself."

"What did he study?" Bruno was happy that she was talking; he still didn't feel he knew much about Murcoing.

"He was specializing in architecture. He could always draw beautifully, even as a little boy. Portraits, landscapes, he had a real gift. He drew one of me, and I didn't even know he was watching me. It was so good I framed it, look." She heaved herself to her feet, went into the sitting room and brought back a cheap plastic frame. The pencil sketch it contained was not simply recognizable as her, it conveyed something of the determination with which she had endured a hard and ill-paid life.

"That's very good."

"He was only fourteen when he did that. You ought to see his landscapes, ones he did when he was a bit older." She gestured to the kitchen wall behind Bruno, and he turned to look at something that had not registered when he first glanced around the kitchen. Now he looked more carefully and saw a framed watercolor of a Bergerac street scene in autumn, leaves turning brown and the stone of the buildings merging with the gray sky. It felt sympathetic rather than gloomy, an attempt to find some beauty in a drab scene.

"He could make a living at this."

"He made a few francs in the summer, doing sketches of tourists down by the statue of Cyrano, but they wanted quick caricatures, not the little portraits he liked to make. Come and look at this."

She led him back into the sitting room, dominated by an elderly three-piece suite of furniture around a TV set, and from the cupboard beneath the TV she drew a thick sheaf of paintings, sketches in pencil or chalk and some more watercolors. Bruno leafed through, thinking of the waste of talent that Paul's life represented. There were a couple of scenes of Périgord villages and churches that he'd have been proud to own and some more fine portraits. He stopped at one that looked familiar, and he realized it was Édouard Marty as a grown man, perhaps in his late twenties. That meant it must have been done recently. There were three exquisite portraits of Francis Fullerton, one of him dozing in a summer hammock, another in a formal pose in a chair and a third on a beachfront, hair ruffled by the wind. There was an intimacy about them, a depth of affectionate knowledge that suggested love.

"He's really gifted. I wouldn't mind buying some of these from him, or from you maybe." He pulled out a watercolor of a river scene and another of a Périgord village. "If I gave you the money, I know you'd see he got it eventually, right?"

"In prison, you mean, once you round him up?" The

moment of shared appreciation had gone, and Joséphine was back in her defensive stance.

"I just like the paintings," he said genuinely. Her glance softened.

"He used to charge twenty, thirty euros down at the statue. Give me fifty, and you can have both."

23

This time Bruno's police uniform ensured that he was shown directly to Pamela's room in the hospital. Fabiola's phone call with the good news had reached him as he was leaving Bergerac. Pamela was awake and lucid. The scan had shown no lasting damage beyond a broken collarbone and two cracked ribs. All tubes and wires had been removed. She was sitting up with one arm in a sling, looking at an English newspaper with a pen in her good hand, when he poked his head around the open door. He gave her the overpriced flowers he'd bought at the hospital shop.

"They're lovely, Bruno, thank you," she said, after returning his kiss. She tasted of toothpaste, and there was a scent of lavender he'd not known her to wear before. She filled in one of the clues in her crossword puzzle before continuing. "Fabiola was here earlier and told me about Bess. It's very sad. I'll miss her very much. But I know you had no choice."

"She was in great pain. It had to be done," he said. He paused before speaking again. "When will they let you go home?" There was a rather battered metal vase on the cupboard. He filled it with water from the tap.

"Maybe tomorrow, the doctor said, since Fabiola will be

there to keep an eye on me. But why the uniform? Isn't today your day off?"

"Something came up on this murder case, so I had to go to Bergerac and look official." He placed the flowers in the vase and turned back to her.

"Bruno, really, you can't just dump them in like that," she said in mock reproof. "Bring the vase to me and hold it while I arrange them. Honestly, you men have no idea." She began to arrange the mixed red and white roses with her good hand, making him strip some leaves and bend some of the stems to change their height.

He was pleased to hear her sounding so normal and looking so much better than he'd expected. Fabiola must have brought in some makeup and the pretty white nightgown that he recognized. The newspaper was probably her idea too.

"I hope these are tough enough for you." Bruno laid a booklet of Sudoku puzzles on the bed beside her. Normally she raced through them almost as quickly as she could fill in the numbers.

"Lovely, such a treat, but now I want to hear all about the murder case. Have you traced Murcoing yet?"

No, but he now knew a lot more about the young man, and he explained his findings in Bergerac and the Arch-Inter connection.

"So who would have sent Murcoing the photo of his lover kissing Yves?" Pamela asked. "Who might have had an interest in trying to drive him into a fit of jealous rage? And who would benefit from Fullerton's death? It's obvious, it must be the brother. He stands to inherit, after all."

Bruno shook his head. "Brian says his brother's will leaves everything to his nieces and nephews, to be held in trust. He may be lying, but we can check that through the British police. Now that they have a death certificate, there's no reason for the will to be secret. If Brian is lying about the will, then obviously he becomes the main suspect. But how would Brian or anybody else have known that Paul would be driven to kill just by that photograph? And we might never have known about the Corrèze farm if Brian hadn't told us. It doesn't hang together."

She nodded. "How certain are you that Murcoing is the killer?"

He shrugged. "We can place him at the murder scene at about the relevant time, but mainly his running off is what feeds our suspicion. He had a romantic motive and maybe also a financial one, if he thought Fullerton was cheating him. Certainly Fullerton had a lot of money, and Paul seems to have been getting very little."

He'd switched both his phones to vibrate that morning before going to see Joséphine, and now the second, private one vibrated. He glanced at the screen, recognized from the number who was calling and said, "I have to take this." He excused himself, heading into the corridor and out of earshot as he answered Isabelle.

"Have you seen the *Paris Match* website?" she began, her voice neutral rather than angry. "Your friend Gilles is making news again."

"I haven't seen it, but I think I know what it's about."

"The brigadier knows you're behind it. And there's a rumor that there's something coming in *Le Monde*."

"I don't understand why he thinks I'm involved. Gilles talked directly to Jacqueline Morgan. Her book is finished, and she's looking for publicity. I know she's written something for *Le Monde*, but it's up to them to decide what to do with it."

"Don't be coy, Bruno, not with me. And I don't care

whether her story runs or not, but there are aspects of this that you don't know. Can we meet?"

"Did the brigadier tell you about the difference of opinion between him and me at our last meeting?"

"Yes, and that's partly why I need to talk with you."

"Where are you?"

"I'm in Périgueux. I need to be discreet, so can I come to your place?"

Bruno checked his watch. "All right, let's say five this afternoon."

They hung up, and he went back to Pamela, who greeted him with a question. "Are you absolutely certain that your corpse is the man you think it is? The head was destroyed. How did the brother identify him?"

"They're doing a DNA test and the usual fingerprints. The dead man had served a prison term, so they're on file. We'd have used dental records, but as you said, the head was smashed."

"But right now you're assuming that your dead man is who you think he is and not the brother. Am I right? What if your corpse is the brother, and the man you think is the brother is in fact the crooked antiques dealer and also the murderer?"

Pamela had been doing too many crossword puzzles, he thought. "If it's the crooked antiques dealer who's alive, why would he have led me to his hoard of stolen goods? And he had to assume that we'd check the fingerprints. That's routine."

"Who called you?"

"It was about Gilles. His piece on Jacqueline's nuclear secrets is on the *Paris Match* website."

"Are you trying to avoid telling me that your caller was the person you refer to as my 'favorite French policewoman'?"

He nodded, feeling guilty and reminding himself that he should never underestimate Pamela's powers of perception.

"Will this *Paris Match* story mean trouble for you?" she asked.

"Maybe, I don't know. As long as the mayor stays in office, there's not much anyone can do, beyond taking my special phone away, which I wouldn't mind. Life was a lot simpler before the brigadier had me on speed dial."

"Presumably Isabelle wants to see you about it."

He nodded again and warily scanned Pamela's face. She looked neither cross nor suspicious, simply thoughtful.

"Have you looked into this Arch-Inter group you mentioned? If it has offices in California, it must be a big operation. Wouldn't it have to fill in some type of customs form if it ships goods overseas?"

"Yes, but not within Europe. Fullerton could bring in and take back truckloads of antiques to Italy or England with no problem. For Russia, he'd need a customs declaration, and for America they'd have to go by container, so there'd be records. The art squad can handle all that, they do it all the time."

"Pass me my laptop. Fabiola brought it." She asked him to plug it into the wall socket and inserted the little plug that connected to the Internet through the cell-phone system. While she booted up, he took the opportunity to visit the men's room, his uniform provoking the usual range of curious and worried glances.

"This Arch-Inter firm is pretty big in the States," she said when he returned, gesturing for him to look over her shoulder. "That's quite a showroom they have in Santa Monica, and they're promising regular new deliveries of English and European antiques. Hmm, I wonder . . ."

She did a Google search for Companies House, London, accessed the website for the register of British companies and typed in "Arch-Inter." Up came the name and a number. She tapped twice on the number and up came a list of documents filed by the company, each of which could be downloaded for one pound.

"Here are the names of the directors of Arch-Inter. Surprise, surprise, look who we find."

Over her shoulder he read the names: Paul Murcoing, Brian Fullerton and Édouard Marty, all added to the board on the same date three years earlier. Francis Fullerton had been a director since the company was formed in 1986. There was another English-sounding name, Alan McAllister, which Bruno recognized from the California branch of Arch-Inter.

"The plot thickens," she said, sitting back and looking extraordinarily pleased with herself.

"You should be doing my job."

"Too easy," she replied with a grin. "And you might want to check whether Murcoing had a company credit card. If it's attached to a British bank, he could have access to money that your systems aren't tracking."

"*Mon Dieu,* we never thought of that." He wondered how Pamela knew about such matters and then remembered her account of spending hours with lawyers and accountants, while sorting out her mother's estate.

"Now you need to get your *juge d'instruction* to check the annual reports to see just how much money the company is making," she went on. "Above all he needs to find out how many shares each director owns. That's how you can tell who's really in charge."

"With Francis Fullerton dead, the question now is what happens to his shares. Presumably that'll be in his will," Bruno said, reaching for his hat. "I have to go and see Ardouin, the *juge,* and then relate all this to J-J." He bent down and kissed her. "Did anybody ever tell you that you're as brainy as you are beautiful?"

"Never in quite this context, with me lying in bed and a man who ought to be much more grateful just about to don his hat and leave me to languish."

He kissed her again. "Close your eyes and think of justice."

When Bruno returned to his home with Balzac he saw no sign of Isabelle or a rental car. Balzac scooted from the back of the Land Rover and around the side of the house to the chicken coop, where Isabelle was sitting on a tree stump in the late afternoon sun, watching the birds and smoking. She stomped out her cigarette just before Balzac leaped onto her lap and used his back legs to pedal his way up to lick her neck. Holding the puppy in both hands, she rose and offered Bruno the cheek Balzac was not monopolizing to be kissed.

"You walked here?" She was dressed like a hiker in walking boots and jacket and somehow still managed to look chic. A light rucksack was on the ground beside her.

"I parked at the hunters' blind on the far side of the ridge and walked the trail. You should be impressed that I remembered the way."

"Why the discretion?"

She gave a slow smile. "I could say I was thinking about your reputation or maybe I just wanted to take a gentle walk through the woods to see how my leg had recovered." She took a paper-wrapped bottle from the rucksack and passed it to him. "But I'm also bringing a message from the brigadier along with this peace offering. He says you passed the test."

Did the brigadier never stop playing games? He opened the tissue paper and found a bottle of Balvenie. "It didn't seem like a test to me."

"I know, he put me through a similar interview. The mood in Paris is poisonous right now with the election so close, people worried for their jobs, lots of documents being shredded, files being sanitized. It's hard to know who to trust."

"That's the life you chose, Isabelle."

She nodded. "It's what I thought I wanted, what I still want, if only it weren't so damn political all the time. It's like living in Machiavelli's kitchen. Anyway, it looks like I could be getting that European job. I'm on a short list of three, and I'm the only candidate who speaks English and has experience of international liaison. I go up to The Hague for the formal interview on Friday morning. You ever been to Holland?"

Bruno shook his head.

She gestured to his house. "I see you finally put the windows in the roof. Will you show me?" She picked up Balzac to carry him with her.

Bruno led the way inside, remembering how he had talked of his plan as they had lain in bed, sharing that special territory of new lovers as they spoke of plans and dreams and explored possible futures together. Always practical, Isabelle had said he'd have to knock down walls to install stairs. So Bruno was proud of the solution he'd found, to put the staircase into the small room he'd used as a study, fitting his desk and books beneath the stairs and not taking space from his sitting room. When she climbed the stairs ahead of him, her limp was still noticeable.

"It's great, Bruno," she said, putting Balzac down to explore as she looked into the smaller room to the left and the much larger room to the right and then poked her head into the small shower room he'd inserted between them. The rooms were still empty of furniture. She looked again into the smaller room.

"The children's room you always planned," she said. Her voice was flat.

"That depends if there's more than one, then they get the big room, or maybe both of them."

"Aren't you planning to move up here yourself?"

"Not yet," he said. "There's the painting to finish, blinds and curtains to choose. And I like that bedroom downstairs." He did not have to add that it was the bedroom that they had shared.

"How will you get the beds up that staircase?"

"I just have to get the mattresses up. The beds I can build myself."

She walked to the window, opened it and looked out at the view across the steadily rising ridges, fields and woodlands with not another house or road in sight. Then she turned, leaned with her back against the windowsill and looked carefully around the big room as if furnishing it in her mind. He wondered if she was thinking of what might have been, but she pushed herself off from the windowsill, flashed him a determined smile and headed down the stairs, speaking over her shoulder.

"I've got something for you as well."

Balzac was too small to get down the stairs without tripping over his ears, so Bruno scooped him up and followed her. Outside, she went back to her rucksack and pulled out a stiff cardboard envelope and handed it to him.

"We were interested in her too, not just Crimson," she explained as Bruno pulled out a grainy surveillance photo of Jacqueline taken at a hotel entrance. She was with a tall and slender man with a thick head of flowing white hair, a man instantly recognizable to anyone who read French newspapers. The next photo showed the two of them embracing in the shadows of an entrance courtyard to what looked like a very plush apartment building.

"That's your boss," Bruno said, finally realizing why anything to do with Jacqueline could set off alarm bells in Paris.

"That was before he became a minister, five or six years ago, when he was still mayor of Orléans and she was teaching at the Sorbonne. The building is where he kept a discreet pied-à-terre on a fancy street behind the Parc Monceau."

"Did the RG get photos like this of everybody?" he asked. The Renseignements Généraux had been famous for their voluminous files on left-wing parties, but he wasn't very surprised that they had been keeping an eye on fast-rising politicians of all stripes.

Isabelle shrugged. "Who knows if they were watching her or him? Does it matter? They both turn out to be people of interest, particularly now."

Bruno was trying to work out the political implications. "So now the minister is worried that Jacqueline's book might rebound on him, and he would be blamed if his party loses the election?"

"That's why he needs to find someone else to take the rap. That's one of the first laws of politics," Isabelle said. "And if the blame somehow falls onto the Americans or the British and their shadowy secret services trying to manipulate our elections, not to mention our foreign policies . . ."

She took the cardboard folder and the photos back from Bruno. "I'd better go. Will you walk back to the car with me, you and Balzac?"

He printed some names on a page of his notebook and gave it to her, explaining the results of the Web search at Companies House. "We need to see a copy of the will Francis Fullerton made in England. J-J is trying to get it through the usual channels. If you can find out faster it would help. And

I'd like to hear if anything is known about these people, directors of this Arch-Inter Company."

"I thought you already had your suspect, Paul Murcoing. Or are you following one of your hunches?"

"Never leave potentially useful information unchecked—isn't that what you used to tell me?" Bruno asked.

Isabelle shouldered her rucksack and began to walk around the chicken coop to pick up the track into the woods. Bruno saw her grimace, her limp apparent. He took her arm and turned her around and steered her toward his Land Rover.

"I'm getting a bit pressed for time," he lied. "I'd better drive you back to your car."

She gave him a sharp look but agreed, saying, "I've got something to tell you, and it might be easier to tell you in the car when I don't have to look you in the eye."

"If you want to tell me that it's all over between you and me, I've been expecting it," he said, carefully keeping his voice neutral. "We've both known long enough that there's no future for us. You're not coming back to Périgord, even if you are giving up your career in Paris."

To get to her car by road would mean driving two long sides of a triangle, so he was taking the shortcut along the bridle path. It meant driving slowly but they would still be there in a fraction of the time, and this was not a conversation that he wanted to prolong.

"We've lived with that," she said. "This is something else." She paused, and they drove on in silence, Balzac resting quietly on her lap, content just to lie there and feel her hand stroking his back.

"I don't really know how to begin, because I know that as soon as I say this it really is over between us." Her voice didn't sound like Isabelle's at all, none of that energy and eagerness he knew so well. "There'll be no more surprise reunions, no more fantasies of having you for a weekend in Paris. It's final. You'll never want to speak to me again."

He rounded a bend and saw her car parked by the hunters' shack, perhaps a hundred yards ahead. He had a sudden presentiment of what she might be about to say and felt a great hollowness begin to gather somewhere deep in his gut.

"I have done something unforgivable," she said as he drew up beside her car. Her head was bowed, and she seemed to be speaking to Balzac more than to him, or perhaps making her farewell to the puppy she had always called "ours."

"It was that night before the summit, the night before Gigi was shot, when we were together."

Bruno was sure of it now. Her voice seemed to be coming from a long distance away. He wasn't sure that he could speak.

"I got pregnant and I didn't tell you." He heard her open the car door and felt her place Balzac gently on his lap, but he couldn't turn his head to look at her. "I had the abortion and never told you. I think I knew that you'd talk me out of it, or you'd try, and that was a conversation I couldn't face."

Her hand touched his cheek, and he felt the vehicle shift as her weight left it. "I know what this means to you. I'm sorry, Bruno."

He sat immobile, stunned, barely registering the way she limped to her car without looking back, unlocked it, climbed stiffly in and drove away. It was Balzac who brought him back to reality, clambering up the steering wheel to get close enough to lick Bruno's chin before tumbling back onto his lap.

24

"Why did you race off like that? I said I was sorry, that I knew it wasn't your fault. Pamela told me all about it, and she's as good as new." Fabiola was breathing hard as she brought her mare to a halt beside Bruno.

"It's nothing to do with you. It's me," he replied. "Something happened today, so I thought a fast gallop might clear my head. I'm the one who should apologize."

Even during the ride, Hector racing beneath him faster than they had ever gone together, the finality of Isabelle's revelation still stunned him. There had been a new life, and now there was not. It would have been kinder of Isabelle never to have told him, but that was not her way.

Fabiola eyed him curiously. "So if it's not me you're angry with, let's not take it out on the horses. Can we go back more slowly? Victoria's too old for a ride like that, and I don't think Balzac enjoyed it."

Bruno looked down to where the puppy was huddled as deep inside the binoculars case as he could go, staring up at Bruno with wide eyes. He was being selfish, Bruno chided himself, and foolish to think that he could escape dealing with this by pushing his horse and his own horsemanship to their limit. He turned Hector and began to walk him back along the ridge, Fabiola falling in alongside but wise enough not to speak. He knew that some unpleasant nights lay ahead of him, but that was for the future. He had a job to do, a murderer to hunt down, a suspicion to pursue and friends like Fabiola to whom he owed more than this surly silence. At that moment, duty itself vibrated for his attention from the phone at his belt. He answered and heard J-J's voice.

"We found the plates for the stolen camper. Some Dutch tourist realized his own vehicle had suddenly grown French plates, the ones we were looking for. It looks like Paul put the Dutch plates on his own camper."

"Where was this?"

"A campsite just outside Hendaye, down by the border. Maybe he got into Spain. Or that's what he wants us to think. Still, we've alerted the Spanish police."

"Have you gotten anywhere on Francis Fullerton's will yet?"

"We have the one with the *notaire* in Ussel. It's boilerplate. All his French property goes to his nearest family, which means his brother and sister. He cites the Corrèze farm and a bank account. We're still waiting for the British will. And we're having trouble with Fullerton's computer. A lot of stuff had been deleted, and the files written over, so it's not so straightforward to dig stuff out from the hard drive. We'll have to send it to the specialists in Paris, and that costs a fortune. This job's breaking my budget as it is. And we heard back from the phone trackers. Valentoux's story about that disposable phone he bought holds up. It was switched on in Calais on the morning Fullerton was killed, and the cell-phone towers tracked it all the way down to St. Denis. It looks like it was with him all the time, and it hasn't been switched on since."

"Murcoing could have taken it when he killed Fullerton and switched SIM cards," said Bruno. "What about this guy in Bordeaux, Édouard? I asked the *juge* if I could go and interview him, but he said he wanted the art squad brought in. Have they been in touch with you?"

"Yes, two of their guys are going through Fullerton's photos and the Arch-Inter customs forms; that also goes on my budget. There won't be anything left for my salary at this rate."

Bruno hung up and turned to Fabiola. "Do you have plans for dinner, or shall I make us an omelette?"

"I've got plans, I'm afraid, but thanks." She colored a little and changed the subject. "Whatever it is that's on your mind, you know I'll help if I can."

"I know. If you're in a rush, I can rub the horses down." He carefully didn't ask where she was going.

She looked at her watch. "Thanks, that would help." As soon as they reached the stable, she darted into Pamela's house, taking off her riding jacket as she ran.

That gave Bruno time to do something that had been on his mind. Once the horses were settled and fed, he climbed into his Land Rover and took the road to the end of the commune, to the vacation rental cottage he remembered from his first year as the policeman of St. Denis. He knew his district so well by now that he could have found it blindfolded. Rather than dwell on Isabelle's decision, he turned on Radio Périgord for the news, none of which concerned him, except for the final item.

"Police are still searching for Paul Murcoing, said to be the chief suspect in the St. Denis murder case of Englishman Francis Fullerton. Juge d'Instruction Bernard Ardouin refused to comment on reports that Murcoing was believed to have fled to Spain. And finally, who was Paul Revere, and why is his coffeepot said to be worth as much as a hundred thousand euros? Coming up next, on Radio . . ."

Bruno switched off the radio as the *gîte* came into view, looking a great deal more weathered than when he had last seen it. The roof tiles had turned to the soft red color that was so characteristic of the region, and the gravel of the drive had turned gray. One gable end was now green with ivy and some badly pruned roses straggled around the door. A Volvo with Dutch license plates was parked at the side of the place and a child's bike lay on its side on the bumpy lawn. In the ten years—no, eleven—since he had been here, hundreds of vacationers must have lived and eaten and swum and sunbathed on the property, overlaying that day when he had walked to the rear and seen blood on the tiles and those wisps of blood hanging like red smoke in the water.

Balzac had clambered forward from the back of the Land Rover and over the hand brake to sit in the passenger footwell. Bruno scooped him up and put him in his lap. Maybe at last he was on the way to finding some resolution of that case that had haunted him. But as he sat there, thoughts of what Isabelle had done flooded over him. He tried to understand it from Isabelle's point of view as well as his own. He argued to himself that it was Isabelle's life, her body, her future, and that she alone was entitled to make the decision. The baby that had been aborted was the promise of new life, but for Isabelle it must have seemed like an almost mortal threat to the life she had planned for herself.

But couldn't she have had the child and given it to him to raise? He'd have found nurses, babysitters, taken it to the crèche and the infants' school, taught it to fish and to cook, to know the woods and the ways of dogs and horses. Why had she never even given him the chance to make that suggestion? Did not a father have some rights over the future, over the life and death of his child? Isabelle knew he did; it was why she had admitted that what she had done was unforgivable.

He understood that Isabelle must have thought it through. She was aware of the physical changes that would come as the pregnancy progressed. She understood what the impact on her psyche would be as the hormonal shifts brought forth the maternal instincts that would wrench at her whole being when it came time to part with her child. Even if she gave the child to Bruno and returned to Paris or to Holland to resume her career, there would have been the guilt as her child grew up without her. She must have looked ahead to desperate Christmases and birthdays, brief reunions and heartrending farewells, and decided against that course. Unlike him, she was trapped by the iron laws of biology.

He was aware that tears were running down his face and onto Balzac, and now he saw that a man had come out of the *gîte* ahead and was staring curiously at him. He put on his cap and climbed out of the vehicle so that the tourist could see his uniform.

"Tout va bien?" Bruno called. "All okay? Just making a routine check. Sorry if I bothered you."

The Dutchman nodded and waved back. Bruno returned to his seat, noticed that the engine was still running, turned his car and drove away, heading automatically to St. Denis but not sure if he was in any mood to go home and spend the evening alone.

He was saved by a phone call. He glanced at the screen and saw it was Florence, so he pulled to the side of the road to answer.

"Bruno, I'm with Monsieur Crimson, and he wants to invite us both to dinner if you are free. I have a babysitter. Here, he wants to talk to you."

"Bruno," came the familiar cheery voice. "I just got a call

from the Vieux Logis. They have a cancellation and can give me a table for three in an hour. Can you join us? I want the three of us to put our heads together over an idea I've had."

"That's very kind of you, and I'll see you there in an hour," Bruno said. "I just need to go home and change and look after the dog, then I'll head straight for Trémolat."

"Bring your puppy. The waiters will love spoiling him. See you there."

They sat in the garden, beneath the plane trees whose leaves seemed almost to be growing as Bruno watched, surging with the energy of a Périgord springtime that was about to burst into summer. Whether indoors in winter or outside as the warmth came, it was the restaurant that Bruno would choose if it were to be the last meal of his life. He could afford to dine here only rarely but always ordered the same *menu du marché:* whatever the chef had managed to acquire that day and assemble into a wonderfully balanced meal.

There were always little amuse-bouches to begin, baby pizzas the size of eggcups or a morsel of *boudin noir* stuffed into a fig or something equally inventive. Then the meal took its usual course, a crème brûlée of foie gras or a chilled soup, and then some confection of fish, sometimes a seviche of raw fish cooked in the acid of some exotic fruit rather than the usual lime juice. The meat could be rabbit or lamb, veal or venison, but always with perfectly cooked vegetables. That was the difference between his own efforts and the meal of a professional chef, Bruno thought, the blending and balance of dishes and the arrival of each component at just the right moment.

The evening's pleasure was enhanced by the sight of Florence, seated between himself and Crimson, in a simply cut linen dress of pale blue that brought out the color in her gray eyes. Her hair, which had been lifeless and dry when he had first met her at the truffle market in Ste. Alvère, now shone with life and had been shaped to highlight her fine bones and slim neck. She looked around the garden and eyed the ordered shapes of the topiary, the obelisks and spheres, with cool interest rather than open curiosity, as if she were accustomed to dining at a place such as this.

"This dinner seems small thanks for your efforts in recovering my rugs and paintings, Bruno, and for your remarkable skills with a computer, Florence," said Crimson. "I wish you'd been on the team in my old job. Take a look at this document she cooked up, Bruno. That should smoke our quarry out."

He pushed an iPad across the table, and on its screen was what looked like a photocopy of an aged document from some official archive. It looked genuine down to the ancient typescript, the utilitarian gray of the official paper and the marks of little holes where papers had been pinned together. It appeared to be the contents page of a file, and Bruno recognized some of the words and acronyms: Neuvic, Valmy, FFI, FTP. Other names were new to him, and some words, DIGGER and ARCHER and WHEELWRIGHT, were in capital letters. He asked Crimson to explain.

"The names are simple enough," Crimson replied. "Maurice Buckmaster was the head of SOE's section F, which ran operations in France, and Gubbins was the major general in overall charge. The document refers to Buckmaster's report to his boss on the Neuvic train, which makes it look as though London was much more involved in the whole business. The words in capital letters are the names of operational networks. Digger was one of the SOE networks active around here in 1944, run by a Frenchman called Jacques Poirier who joined the British army, where he was known as Captain Jack. He became friendly with Malraux, and that document is supposed to be Poirier's account of what happened to the money. You know the other acronyms, Francs-Tireurs et Partisans and so on?"

"They look very convincing. Well done, Florence," Bruno said, nodding that he understood the terms. "But do these documents exist?"

Crimson pursed his lips. "Some of them do, like the reports from Buckmaster and Poirier, but they haven't been declassified yet. I know roughly what's in them, and there's no smoking gun, as our American friends say. It's fairly routine stuff, reporting rumors about the Neuvic money and saying there's no confirmation. The fact is, we didn't really want to know. What we've concocted here is just the contents page, but that should be enough to smoke Murcoing out. And Florence also cooked up a new e-mail to Francis Fullerton, with a copy to Murcoing, claiming to come from the Public Records Office as a notice that new files which Fullerton had requested have now been declassified. She copied their official format, and it all looks very persuasive."

"So it does, but now that we have the bait how do you propose to draw Murcoing out into the open if he bites?"

Crimson ran his fingers over his iPad, and another document appeared that looked like an e-mail. It was in serviceable French, but obviously written by a foreigner.

"I set up a new e-mail account with a fake name and e-mailed Murcoing," Florence said, evidently proud of her work. There was a slight flush to her cheeks, as if she were excited by her unexpected role in the venture.

Bruno quickly read the e-mail, which purported to come from a professional researcher in London who claimed to have done regular archive work for Fullerton at the Public Records

Office. It said he'd been sorry to see news of Fullerton's death in the British press, but Fullerton had earlier given him Murcoing's address and the researcher wanted to know if Murcoing was still interested in the documents. Murcoing should know that much of the contents of the supposedly declassified files had been blacked out, but the researcher had personal contacts who had given him the uncensored version. He was coming to France and would be happy to arrange a meeting, if Murcoing was able to pay the sum Fullerton had offered.

"We attached the faked contents page to the e-mail," Crimson explained. "I'm rather proud of that last document, the one dated 1946 that claims to come from the British Embassy in Paris, reporting a meeting with American and French government officials on the Neuvic affair."

As two black-clad waiters approached the table bearing plates, Crimson ran his fingers over his device, and the documents disappeared. He slipped the iPad into a briefcase that rested against his chair. The sommelier arrived and refilled their glasses with the champagne Crimson had ordered, a Celebris from Gosset, one of the oldest of the champagne houses. Bruno had heard of it but never tasted it before. With just a faint hint of sweetness, it went perfectly with the scallops in beurre blanc.

"So now we wait for Murcoing to log on to his e-mails and then to contact you at your fake e-mail address," Bruno said. "And then you arrange a meeting. What do you suggest should happen then?"

"I assume we can arrange the meeting at a place where you can organize a police ambush," Crimson replied.

"We know he's armed and dangerous, and he's already killed once. I don't think you should be anywhere near the meeting place," Bruno said firmly.

"I hope you're not planning to be involved yourself, Bruno," Florence said. "This is a job for a specialist police unit."

"Of course, you're right," Bruno said. "What worries me is that we may be underestimating Murcoing. He's no fool, and he must be suspicious of something like this falling so conveniently into his lap. I'm not sure he'll just come waltzing to some prearranged meeting spot. If he takes the bait, he'll try to set up a meeting at a place he can control, and he'll certainly check it out beforehand for any sign of an ambush. That's what I'd do. Still, we may be lucky. Filial piety may bring him to his grandfather's funeral tomorrow, which would save us all a great deal of trouble."

The sommelier brought the decanter with the red wine Crimson had ordered, laying the cork beside it so Bruno could make out the stamped capital letters that spelled CHÂTEAU HAUT-BRION.

"Le quatre-vingt-quatorze, monsieur," murmured the sommelier, a man who had learned his art in the old school. Instead of pouring some wine for the customer to taste, he poured a tiny sip for himself and then sniffed and tasted it to pronounce it good before half filling the three glasses.

The '94, thought Bruno, a wine made when he'd been dodging mortar bombs in Sarajevo, when Paul Murcoing had been a young teenager and Francis Fullerton had been attending funerals in New York of friends who had died of AIDS. Crimson had been doing whatever the interests of the British crown required, and Florence had been at school amid the dying coalfields of northern France.

Bruno's eye was caught by a movement at the far side of the garden, where two diners had been hidden by the trees. He saw Gilles offering his arm to help Fabiola rise from her seat. The couple then strolled hand in hand from the garden and out into the night. Well, well, he thought. If Fabiola had been at school when the wine was bottled, Gilles had been darting across Sniper's Alley in the same wretched Bosnian siege that he had known. Curious, the strength of the bond that such a shared experience could forge, and it left him confident that his dear friend Fabiola was in good hands.

25

Bruno was almost always proud of his town, but he felt an extra glow as he stood at the big wooden doors of St. Denis's church greeting the steady flow of mourners arriving for Murcoing's funeral. Some he had expected, like his friend the baron, wearing his medals from the Algerian War, and Joe, Bruno's predecessor as the town policeman. Joe wore in his lapel the small red rosette of the Légion d'Honneur, awarded for his boyhood exploits as a Resistance courier. Then came those inhabitants of the retirement home who could still walk; they always enjoyed a good funeral, if only to remind themselves their turn had not yet come. What Bruno had not expected was the turnout of youngsters. He assumed at first it was because of the presence of Florence, their favorite teacher, in the choir. Then he saw Rollo, the headmaster, bringing up the rear.

"I thought it made a good teaching moment," Rollo said, shaking hands. He spoke over the slow, sad tolling of the church bell. "We held a special lesson this morning on the history of the local Resistance for the senior classes and then asked if any of them wanted to join me at the funeral. I'm proud of them: not one stayed behind."

Crimson murmured, "No reply from Murcoing yet," as he arrived with Brian Fullerton, followed by Monsieur Simpson, the retired English schoolteacher who had been called up in the closing weeks of the Second World War and thus counted as a comrade-in-arms of the dead man. He was flanked by the only two other citizens of St. Denis who could claim the honor, Bachelot and Jean-Pierre, one a veteran of the Gaullist Resistance and the other a fighter for the Communist FTP. After a lifetime of enmity that had made their families the Montagues and Capulets of St. Denis, they had finally in old age and retirement become friends.

Jacqueline came alone, rather than arrive with the mayor, who stood beside Bruno at the door to greet the mourners. Since he was to give the eulogy, the mayor was wearing his sash of office and accepted with quiet dignity the murmured condolences on the death of Cécile. "Friday," he kept saying, again and again, as the old folk asked when her funeral would be.

Joséphine and her sisters were already installed in the front row, Gilles sitting behind them, his notebook open to scribble details. Plainclothes police were scattered throughout the congregation. More police were in the nearby cafés, and J-J himself stood just inside the door of the Maison de la Presse, pretending to study the magazines. There was no sign of Paul and his sister.

Out of respect, Bruno was wearing the medal of the Croix de Guerre he had won in Bosnia, which he normally kept in a drawer at his home. He was in full-dress uniform, freshly pressed, and he had polished his boots and leather belt that morning. Philippe Delaron was taking photographs of the honor guard: eight soldiers and a junior officer from the garrison at Agen who stood at ease in the churchyard. The officer looked at his watch. The mayor looked at Bruno, who glanced across to J-J in the shadows of the shop and shrugged. It was time.

"Escadron, garde à vous," the officer called. The troops came to attention and marched in pairs into the church, down the nave and, as Bruno and the mayor followed them, took their places at each side of the coffin. The futuristic shape of their FAMAS rifles looked oddly out of place amid the ancient stones. Loïc Murcoing lay in state before the altar, on which stood giant photographs of the young fighter he had been. The coffin was closed, and on its lid rested his Resistance medal.

The tolling bell had fallen silent, and from his place before the choir, a schoolboy began to beat on his drum the slow, steady rhythm of a march. The choir began quietly to hum the familiar chords of the Resistance anthem, "Le Chant des Partisans." Slowly their voices grew louder, and then Florence's pure soprano rang out high and clear throughout the church.

"Ami, entends-tu le vol noir des corbeaux sur nos plaines?" Friend, do you hear the dark flight of the crows across our land?

The handful of words and the tune were made heavy by the weight of history. As Bruno shifted his eyes from Florence to the coffin and the photographs of the young fighter behind it, he felt tears begin to gather. He was not alone.

He saw the eyes of the young officer glisten and Father Sentout weeping openly as Florence reached the line: *"Ce soir l'ennemi connaîtra le prix du sang et des larmes."* Tonight the enemy will learn the price of blood and tears.

"Bring the guns from the haystacks, careful with the dynamite." Behind him he heard the quavering voices of the old people take up the words, and then the full choir joined in with *"Si tu tombes, un ami sort de l'ombre à ta place."* If you fall, a friend will come from the shadows to take your place.

It had all happened a lifetime ago, a generation before he

had been born. Bruno wondered why it moved him so. He suspected it was less the words and the music than the images they summoned in his head: jackboots marching through the Arc de Triomphe, de Gaulle speaking from London to pledge that France would fight on, General Leclerc's Free French Forces racing into Paris as young men like Loïc Murcoing fought against tanks with a handful of weapons in their own streets and villages. He thought of his predecessor Joe recounting how as a boy he'd watched as the collaborators of St. Denis had been lined up on the bridge Bruno knew so well and shot so that their bodies crumpled into the timeless flow of the river below.

But as Father Sentout began the Mass, there was something else that stirred Bruno deeply, beyond these wartime pictures flickering in his mind. It was the presence around him of the folk of St. Denis, young and old, conservatives and Communists, men who had worn a uniform and women who had kissed them farewell and waited for their return. It was this gathering to commemorate and to remember, to pay tribute to one of the last of the old men who had gone to the hills to take up arms against the invader knowing that death would be the price of defeat. It was fitting, Bruno believed, that the young people were here, to understand what it had meant to France to be vanquished and occupied by foreign troops who did not bother to hide their contempt for the conquered. And it was right for those youngsters to know that in a nation like France, no defeat was ever final, no fate was ever foreordained, that even amid the ruins and corpses of defeat, rebirth and recovery and renewal could always come.

The Mass ended and the mayor came forward to stand by the coffin, his head bowed in homage before he turned to address the crowded church.

"*Françaises et français,*" the mayor began. "Dear friends and citizens of St. Denis, we are here to pay honor to a brave son of France and to the cause of freedom for which he fought. Nothing I could say here would match the courage and sacrifice of thousands of our young men and women who stood for France in our bleakest hour, when that dark flight of the crows haunted our sweet land and the panzers rolled through our villages. We thank them for what they have taught us about this France that we love. We stand in awe of their courage and we extend our sympathies to their families for their loss. And we give thanks to the Lord, in this church where our ancestors have prayed for a thousand years, that Loïc Murcoing was able to live the rest of his life in pride and dignity in this valley that he had helped to free. And we pray that our sons and daughters will never again have to bear such burdens. *Vive la France, vive la République.*"

While the soldiers presented arms and the choir burst into the "Marseillaise," Bruno joined in the words as he reflected that the mayor had a rare gift among politicians: he never spoke too long. Along with the mayor, Jacquot the builder, Joe, the baron and Montsouris, Bruno took his place beside the coffin, and as the anthem came to its end he gave a quiet word of command, and they lifted it onto their shoulders. The officer ordered his men to port arms and, stooping a little under the burden, the coffin-bearers followed Father Sentout and the file of troops down the nave and out through the churchyard to the cemetery.

"Now," said Bruno, and the six men began to lower the coffin slowly as the first shots of the salute rang out. As the echo of the third and final volley died away, Loïc Murcoing rested in the soil for which he had fought. One by one, his relatives and neighbors came up to pick more of that soil from the heap by the grave and toss it onto the coffin lid. By the time each of those present had dropped a handful of earth, the coffin was no more to be seen.

Bruno scanned the wooded hill behind the cemetery and then across beyond the church to the hedges that lined the winding road to the hamlet of St. Félix. He felt certain that somewhere in that shadowy terrain Paul Murcoing was watching the interment of his grandfather. A cruel irony, thought Bruno, that Loïc Murcoing was being honored for taking to the hills to fight the enemy, while his grandson was now hiding in those same hills to evade the justice of France.

In Paris, *Le Monde* was published as an evening newspaper, but it did not reach the provinces until the following morning. The Internet, however, had made it universally available as soon as the print edition was published, so Jacqueline was reading the text of her article on her smartphone, the mayor peering over her shoulder to make out the words on the tiny screen. Around them in the council chamber of the *mairie* the crowd lined up for glasses of wine and tiny sandwiches and canapés. The *vin d'honneur* the mayor had arranged to follow Murcoing's funeral was in full swing.

"It's weird," said Gilles, squeezing his way through to Bruno with two glasses of red wine and handing one to him. "My teaser piece on the nuclear stuff ran on the website yesterday and got almost zero reaction. But this morning's article on the great train robbery has really started something. There was so much traffic that it nearly crashed the website. My editor's ecstatic."

"That's another dinner you owe me," said Bruno.

"I know, but I've been working nonstop."

"That's not what I hear. The word is that you were dining

with a beautiful brunette at my favorite restaurant last night. Hand in hand, is what I heard."

"Do you know everything that goes on around here?"

Bruno grinned at him and clinked their glasses together. "She's a fine woman, and you're a lucky man. But watch yourself; if you trifle with her, you'll have me to deal with, and you'll wish you were back in Sarajevo."

"Trifling is not what I had in mind, Bruno. I think I'm smitten."

"She's a serious woman, and she's also the best doctor we've ever had in this town, so don't even think about trying to lure her away. Meanwhile, tell me about the reaction to your Neuvic article."

"A couple of deputies have called for a parliamentary inquiry, the Banque de France is under pressure to hold a press conference, and the Socialists have issued a statement denying that they got any of the money."

"Never believe anything until it's been officially denied," Bruno said with a chuckle.

"But something else has come up you ought to know about. I've had an e-mail from Paul Murcoing. It came through on my phone just now as I was coming into the *mairie,* and there's a big document attached. Can we get out of this crowd and find a quiet place to read it?"

Bruno led the way back to his office, noting with approval that Gilles managed to pick up two full glasses as he ducked and darted through the thickening crowd. He turned on his own computer and gestured for Gilles to take the chair and use the big screen to read whatever Paul had sent.

It began with an e-mail, sent to the electronic address listed for Gilles on the *Paris Match* website, congratulating him for "bringing this scandal from the shadows of our history into the light of day." But he'd only scratched the surface of the story, Paul went on, and the real truth had yet to emerge. Gilles clicked on the attachment to open the document.

"J'accuse," read the title page, a cliché in French political journalism since Émile Zola had used it on the front page of *L'Aurore* to condemn the miscarriage of justice in the Dreyfus case. "I accuse André Malraux of theft from the people of France . . . I accuse the British government of using their influence over the Resistance to manipulate French politics in their own interests . . . I accuse the government of the United States . . . I accuse de Gaulle . . . I accuse François Mitterrand . . ." And on and on it went, some of it taken wholesale from the rants Paul had posted on the Resistance websites. The attack on British intelligence contained a scan of the concocted document Bruno had seen on Crimson's iPad the previous evening.

"In the old days before the Internet," said Gilles, "this sort of stuff used to be written in green ink with lots of underlinings and capital letters and usually finished up with claims they were being bugged through the fillings in their teeth. Except this British document looks new. Is this for real?"

Bruno made a quick decision. You either trusted a man or you didn't. "No, it's a fake," he said. "It was cooked up and sent to Paul to smoke him out. It looks like he's taking the bait."

"*Putain,* this story gets better and better, and *Paris Match* is at the heart of it. A dead Resistance hero, his grandson on the run for murder, British spymaster faking documents to help the French capture him; all this and a conspiracy theory around the great train robbery. And he's got his sister with him. You couldn't make it up."

"Are you planning to use some of this?" Bruno asked, a little nervous at the prospect of a media circus.

"You bet I am. This is a manhunt story made for the Internet age; and I'm in touch with the target. I'll send out a tweet that he's reached me and then do something for the website, but first I have to call Paris and brief them."

"Just don't say anything about the document being faked. And make me a couple of printouts of that rant of his for me."

Bruno pulled J-J out of the party and took him onto the balcony outside the mayor's office to brief him and give him one of the printouts.

"It was all your idea, J-J," Bruno said. "You were the one who asked if we could set a trap for Murcoing. He didn't show for the funeral, but he's biting at this. We need to find out where the computer is that he used to e-mail Gilles. I'm betting he's still in France and that camper with the Dutch plates was just a ruse."

"You haven't thought this through," J-J replied, looking cross. "So he gets in touch with Crimson. What then?"

"Then I go to whatever rendezvous he nominates and bring him in. I wear a tracker in my shoes so you know where I am. You can have cars and a helicopter on standby somewhere close in case we need reinforcements."

"This is a job for the Jaunes, not for you. They're trained for this."

"It has to be one man, someone who knows him."

"You don't know him."

"I know enough about him and his family to have a chance of talking him into giving himself up. With the Jaunes a shoot-out is just about guaranteed. Let's find Crimson and see if he's heard from Murcoing. He should be inside."

They found the Englishman squeezed into a corner by the window that overlooked the River Vézère, trying to rescue Florence from the admiring attentions of the young officer who had led the guard of honor. J-J used his bulk to clear some space around them, introduced himself to the officer and asked him to give them some privacy. With the sensitive antennae of a lifetime in politics, the mayor realized that something important was happening and suddenly appeared alongside Bruno just as he was explaining that Murcoing had swallowed the bait.

"We won't know if he's contacted us until we can get to a computer and check that e-mail address I set up," Florence said. "I've got my laptop in my bag."

The mayor led the way to his own spacious office, which to Bruno's knowledge had never yet been polluted by the presence of a computer. Florence sat down at his desk and fired up her machine.

"Don't you need a plug or something?" the mayor asked.

Florence gave him a maternal look and shook her head before turning back to open the e-mails. "He's sent something. He wants a phone number to reach you," she told Crimson.

"We'd better buy you a disposable," Bruno said. "He's going to be expecting to hear an Englishman and someone who knows what he's talking about."

"Can you find out where he sent the e-mail from?" J-J asked.

"Not discreetly and we don't want him to know we're looking. But you should have experts with the equipment to track it."

"The first thing I have to do now is call the *juge d'instruction* and tell him what's happening," said J-J. "He's in charge of this inquiry."

"But it isn't just an inquiry anymore. It's a manhunt," said Bruno. "And we have some time. When Crimson answers that e-mail and gives Murcoing the phone number, we have to say that he's just arrived in France, let's say in Paris, coming in from London on the Eurostar train. It will take him some time to get down here so there'll be no meeting until tomorrow. And Murcoing will need time to arrange the right place for a rendezvous."

Crimson let out a short, excited laugh. "I'm almost beginning to enjoy this."

26

"The English are mad," said J-J as they drove to Bordeaux. "Did you hear Crimson say he was enjoying himself?"

Bruno had persuaded J-J to make a last appeal to the *juge d'instruction* on the need to interview Édouard Marty, even though the art squad had reported they could find nothing questionable in his accounts. J-J had been successful. Bruno was convinced that Édouard must know something more than the bland statement he'd given to the art squad. Yes, he had readily admitted, he was a director of the company that Francis Fullerton had founded, but he claimed to be a very minor shareholder and was concerned solely with the interior design side of the company, specializing in modern and minimalist design. He had nothing to do with the antiques, he said. And his work for Arch-Inter was simply a sideline to his own architecture practice and his teaching at the university.

But that left out the connection from a decade ago, when Paul Murcoing and Édouard Marty had been the boys at the swimming pool and Paul's more recent portrait of Édouard as an adult. The link between Fullerton, Paul and Édouard might be important. An old friend from Paul's youth, with whom he remained connected in Fullerton's crooked business, was someone to whom a man on the run could turn for help or money or transport. And Bruno was dubious about Édouard's protestations of innocence about the antiques trade. The website of the showroom in California had shown a lot of antiques, and Édouard's office seemed to organize the shipping.

"How do you want to handle the questioning?" Bruno asked. He knew from experience that J-J was a relentless interrogator, and while his sheer bulk could intimidate most suspects he also had a subtle sense of the psychology and timing of the art of questioning. "Shall we do it the usual way, you play the tough guy, and I'm the understanding one, or what?"

"Probably," grunted J-J from the passenger seat, flicking through a file of spreadsheets as his new aide, Josette, drove the big Peugeot along the autoroute to Bordeaux. "If this goes on much longer, it's going to eat up ten percent of my investigation budget for the year. And with the new cuts there's no reserve fund. Christ, look at the overtime for the plainclothes guys at the funeral, a complete waste of money."

Bruno reminded J-J how many burglaries had been cleared up from the haul at the Corrèze farm.

"How are things between you and Isabelle?" J-J asked, closing his file and thrusting it into the overstuffed briefcase at his feet.

"Over," said Bruno.

"That's what you always say, but she keeps coming back."

"Not anymore. She's moving to Holland to join Eurojust; she has her interview Friday, but it sounds like a formality."

"*Putain,* and I've just about persuaded the prefect to let her take my job when I retire. She'd come down to Périgueux as my deputy and then only have to wait a couple more years. I was hoping to get her down here before the election and all the backstabbing starts at her ministry. You've heard the rumors about that?"

"No, but I know what I've read in the papers. And who knows how the election will turn out? If this current bunch get reelected, there'll be no change."

"That's where you're wrong. Even this minister of the interior's own party is just looking for an excuse to get rid of him. He's a liability. And this new superagency for intelligence that he's set up is a menace. That's why I want Isabelle out of it before the shit hits the fan."

Bruno seldom talked national politics, partly because his interest was limited and partly because he reckoned there wasn't that much difference between the parties. He remembered some graffiti he'd seen: IT DOESN'T MATTER WHO YOU VOTE FOR, THE GOVERNMENT ALWAYS GETS IN. But he'd rather talk politics than talk about Isabelle. The wound was still fresh.

"The problem is that Isabelle says she doesn't want to come back here," J-J went on.

"I think she means it," Bruno said, when it was plain that J-J was waiting for him to respond.

"She's under a lot of strain," said Josette from the driver's seat. It was the first time she had spoken. "She was crying in the ladies' room the other day. It's not like her at all."

Bruno felt her cast an accusing glance at him in the rear-view mirror. He turned his eyes away to look at the country-side flashing by the car. Josette had put the magnetized blue light on the roof, and they were doing a hundred and eighty kilometers an hour. At this speed, they'd be in Bordeaux in less than an hour.

When they reached the Pont d'Aquitaine, the great bridge over the River Garonne, J-J made a courtesy call to his Police Nationale counterpart in the Gironde *département* to explain his presence in the city. The *juge d'instruction* had already telephoned, J-J was told, and if any assistance was required

Bordeaux would be happy to help. Josette's GPS directed them to the plush suburb of Caudéran, and then to the most exclusive area of all where gardens backed onto the Parc Bordelais. Bruno and J-J exchanged glances, and J-J rubbed a finger and thumb together to signify the price of such a property as the car pulled up in the driveway of the distinctly grand *maison de maître* where Édouard lived and kept his showroom.

"Very tax efficient, home and showroom in one," grumbled J-J. "I dislike this guy already."

J-J hauled himself out of the car and up the wide steps to the double doors. A discreet brass plaque on one of the columns that flanked the doors read ARCH-INTER.

"Commissaire Jalipeau and Chief of Police Courrèges to see Monsieur Marty," he announced to the elegant young woman in black silk who answered the doorbell. Behind her, the hallway was uniformly white—the stairs, the tiles, the walls and woodwork and the single tall-backed wooden chair that was the only furniture.

"Do you have an appointment?" she asked coldly.

"Do you want an appointment with the inside of a jail cell, mademoiselle?"

"It's all right, Clarisse," came a voice from the upper landing, and Édouard appeared. "May I help you, gentlemen?"

"Where do you want to start being questioned, here or in police headquarters? Since I suspect you'll end up in custody, it might save time if we went straight there."

"Let me see if I can help you here," Édouard replied calmly, descending the staircase as if making an entrance. He was wearing a black suit over a T-shirt so white that it gleamed. "I thought this had all been settled with your colleagues from the art squad."

"They're not colleagues. They're specialists who sip tea and make polite small talk about Monet and Manet and money. I deal in murder and violence, and that's what I want to question you about."

Édouard led them into a large room, opposite the one to which Clarisse returned. It too was all in white except for a strikingly red chaise longue with chrome legs at one side of the fireplace and two very modern chrome-and-black-leather chairs facing it. A block of polished steel sat between them to serve as a table, and inside the large fireplace stood an African carving of a woman with row upon row of breasts descending the length of her torso. Above it hung a bizarre and multicolored modern tapestry of jazzy abstract shapes from which hung festoons of blue and yellow fabric.

"Where is your old boyfriend Paul Murcoing?" J-J began.

"I have no idea. I haven't seen him for several weeks."

"Where were you last Tuesday afternoon and evening?" J-J was referring to the time around Fullerton's murder.

"I think I was out of town with clients. It will be in my diary."

"Have you communicated with Paul in the last week in any way?"

Édouard paused and examined his fingernails. "A couple of phone calls, perhaps, and some e-mails, all to do with business."

"You'll have no objection to our going through your phone bills and e-mails?" J-J's aggressive delivery made clear that he was not asking a question.

"Perhaps I'd better discuss that with my lawyer."

"Discuss it all you want, I've got an order from the *juge.*" J-J waved the document he'd obtained from Bernard Ardouin and turned to Bruno. "Call Josette in and tell her to get that computer from the secretary and have a look around for any more. Tell her to bring me any mobile phones she finds."

"Don't I know you?" asked Édouard, studying Bruno.

"The last time we met you were naked and your friends' fathers had beaten the hell out of you. That was at the vacation home where you and Paul Murcoing and Francis Fullerton were first together."

Édouard nodded. "I remember. You pestered my parents and my school friends until you got bored and gave up."

"You're wrong," J-J said. "He never gives up. That's why he's here. But compared with me, he's a pussycat. Now, about your little playmate Paul . . ."

Bruno went outside to call in Josette from the car. She was scanning a list of numbers on the screen of her own phone when Bruno passed on J-J's instructions. She handed him the phone.

"I just downloaded his phone records from France Télécom. He had a lot of calls in the last week from a number that looks like a disposable phone and some more from public phones, paid for with one of those cards you can buy."

She slipped on a pair of evidence gloves and went into the house and into Clarisse's room. Bruno heard angry female voices as he handed Josette's phone to J-J, who began scanning through the France Télécom records.

"You get a lot of calls from public phones, do you?" J-J inquired. "Only in the last few days. I wonder who that could have been. Wouldn't have been the man we're hunting for murder, would it?"

"I don't know where Paul was calling from, but yes, he has called several times in recent days."

"What about?"

"Business, the legal position of the company after the death of Monsieur Fullerton, that sort of thing."

"Did you discuss anything else?"

"No."

"Did you know that we had put out public statements in

the press and on TV saying we wanted urgently to interview him?"

Édouard paused and then nodded his head.

"And you want to tell me that that important little detail never came up in your business chats?"

"I told him that he should go to a police station and offer to help you all he could. I cannot believe he's a murderer, least of all that he killed Francis. They were very close."

"So you knew how to get in touch with him but decided against doing your duty as a law-abiding citizen and informing the police. You're in big trouble, Édouard."

"I didn't know where he was. He said he was moving around."

"I'm getting bored with this," J-J said, turning to Bruno. "Let's take him back to the station, charge him with obstruction of justice and conspiracy. We'll get around to the murder later. Get the handcuffs from the car and let the press office know we can offer everybody a nice picture of Édouard here being led out of his fancy house in chains."

"No need to rush things," Bruno said, and turned to Édouard, who was now looking alarmed. Bruno let the silence build as J-J thumbed through the phone records.

"What did Paul use for money?" Bruno finally asked. "Did you give him any?"

"No, I didn't see him. I don't know what Paul did for money." Édouard was sweating and his immaculate T-shirt was starting to look rumpled at the neck.

Bruno knew the signs. Soon there would be a little act of resistance, a token defiance to retain some shred of self-respect. Then Édouard would break and start to treat J-J as some father confessor whose approval he could win by telling him everything he knew.

"What company records do you keep here?" Bruno asked.

"Your art squad colleagues went through all the records." There it was, the moment of defiance. Now J-J would move in for the kill.

"No, they didn't," said J-J. "They didn't put a freeze on your bank accounts and company credit cards, which is what I'm about to do. I want all checkbooks, statements and credit cards."

Josette came thumping downstairs carrying an expensive-looking weekend bag. She put it on the steel cube and began to pull out phones, an iPad and laptop. Édouard put a hand to his mouth and stared in disbelief at this lawful rifling of his life, as if finally understanding the sweeping investigative powers of the police backed with a signed order from a *juge d'instruction*.

"This one's a disposable," Josette said, holding up a cheap handset. "It was by the bed. Its memory goes back as far as the day after the murder, and all the calls in and out are with the same number, that other disposable on the list. I bet it's Murcoing's."

"*Putain,* you really are in trouble," said J-J. He pulled a notepad from his briefcase and began copying down the times and dates of the various phone calls. "You've been in touch with him never less than twice a day. So where is Murcoing now?"

"I don't know, he never tells me. I really tried to persuade him to give himself up. He gets this way sometimes, single-minded, determined . . ." Édouard's shoulders heaved as if he were about to be sick, but instead he gave a sound that was half cough and half sob.

"Has he been here, to this house?"

"Not lately, not since all this began." Édouard was wiping a handkerchief at his mouth, his brow, his neck.

"Do you know how much money he's withdrawn on the

company's English credit card?" Bruno asked. "We know about that."

Édouard swallowed and nodded. "I checked online this morning; it's just over three thousand euros."

"Maybe we won't freeze it just yet," said J-J. "If he tries to get more out and finds it's frozen, he'll suspect we've got Édouard. We'll keep the phone line going as well, so long as Édouard can only answer in our presence and we tell him what to say."

He told Josette to set up a tracing system on the phone, then asked Édouard for the code required to open his iPad. Édouard shook his head and remained silent.

J-J sighed and pulled out the *attestation* from the *juge d'instruction* and handed it to him. "See that, where it says electronic records? You've got no choice, Édouard. The law says so."

When Édouard stayed silent, J-J shrugged and said, "Give me your ID card."

Édouard took out his wallet and handed the ID card to him. J-J put it beside the iPad and said conversationally: "Over seventy percent of people use four-digit codes for their PIN numbers that are taken from their birth date. Let's try that."

He tapped four numbers, but nothing happened. He tried another combination, and the screen opened. Édouard stared at him as if witnessing some magical trick and then shook his head. He looked at J-J scrolling through various icons on the screen and seemed to reach a decision. Another little act of defiance, thought Bruno, another confession now due to come.

"He said he keeps his phone turned off except when he calls me every day at eight in the morning and eight in the evening," Édouard burst out. "You can see that from the dialing logs."

"And do you have any little code between friends to say that all is well and the stupid police haven't yet caught on?" J-J asked.

Édouard began to babble, as if he could not wait to tell them everything that he knew or suspected. But Bruno noted that everything he said was about Paul, not a word about himself, about Arch-Inter or even about Francis Fullerton. Maybe Édouard was made of sterner stuff, after all, giving up whatever he thought the police wanted to know. But perhaps there were other secrets still unspoken and still protected behind this flood of confession. Maybe it was time to push Édouard a bit harder.

Bruno waited until Édouard stopped talking and then spoke thoughtfully, as though thinking aloud. "Why don't we get the art squad back in here to have another crack at him? They'll be really angry that they missed all this so they'll drop the kid gloves this time. We've got enough to hold him so we might as well let them have some credit."

"I think we can bring in more than just the art squad," said J-J, swiveling the iPad so Bruno could see the images of naked boys on the screen. "This looks like a different kind of art to me. I'm disappointed in you, Édouard, I didn't expect this. Tell me, Bruno, how old do you think these kids are? These two are underage, I'll bet. Josette, who runs the pedophile squad in Bordeaux these days? Is it still that old brute Pontin?"

"It's still him, *chef,* the last I heard." She rose and turned to look at the images. "Definitely underage, I'd say."

"Inspector Pontin's a legend in this business," J-J said conversationally, scrolling through more photos. "You're going to have a very interesting time with him, Édouard. This kid can't be more than thirteen. Pontin won't like these pictures at all. And you a professor at the university. Well, I think we can say your teaching career's over. And do you have any idea what happens to pedophiles in prison?"

Édouard had drawn up his legs and shrunk into a crouch on the chaise longue, his hands over his face.

"Last chance, Édouard," said Bruno. "Maybe there's some more help you can give us on finding Paul."

27

Bruno was outside the Moulin bakery when it opened at seven. In his Land Rover was a thermos with fresh coffee, in the cooler a half-bottle of champagne, some fresh-squeezed orange juice, butter and his own homemade black-currant jam. He bought three croissants, three *pains au chocolat* and a baguette, all still hot from the oven, handed them to Fabiola in the passenger seat and drove to the Sarlat hospital to give Pamela a special breakfast before taking her home.

It had been the mayor's idea. When Bruno had called him late the previous afternoon from Bordeaux to say he was driving back to Périgueux with J-J and Édouard, their prisoner, the mayor insisted on driving to Périgueux to bring him home. When Fabiola had called Bruno's mobile to say they could bring Pamela home the next day, the mayor had insisted that Bruno leave the town to police itself until Pamela was safely installed back in St. Denis.

The mayor took him to Jacqueline's for supper and they found her on the phone, being interviewed by France Inter on her article in *Le Monde*.

"Just before the two of you arrived, I had a difficult call

from Paris," Jacqueline said when she put down the phone. "It came from the minister of the interior, a deeply unpleasant man with whom I was foolish enough to have a fling some years ago. He asked if I was seeking to destroy his career."

"I don't see the connection," the mayor said, looking confused.

"Our affair was not exactly secret, although he was married at the time. I'd met some of his political colleagues at dinner parties and receptions, you know how it is in Paris. And of course when they saw my name on the piece in *Le Monde* they assumed that he was somehow behind it and began wondering about his motives. He must have had some angry phone calls as a result, and that's why he called me."

"You must have seen that coming," said the mayor.

"Of course I did, which was an excellent reason for publishing the article. He was a charmer, of course, and very good-looking, but I found that I couldn't stand his utter pomposity, which is why I ended the liaison. His subsequent political career has plunged him even further down in my estimation. He was a bully in private, and he's been a bully as minister. The man's a disgrace. I won't be at all embarrassed if this becomes public so long as it ends his political career."

Bruno exchanged looks with the mayor and felt himself grinning. "You have been warned," he said.

The mayor looked fondly at Jacqueline and said, "I'll take my chances."

After the meal, the mayor drove Bruno back to St. Denis, where Bruno's car was parked.

"I don't sleep there, you know," the mayor said as they set out. "It wouldn't feel right, certainly until Cécile's funeral is over."

"And perhaps the election," Bruno replied, thinking of the

impact on the voters of the mayor starting an affair when his wife had just died.

"Perhaps. But when you get to my age, Bruno, and you find yourself fascinated by a woman and feeling like a youngster again, that's not something you can afford to ignore. I'd rather be with Jacqueline than get reelected. To be in love again is like a gift."

"It always is, at any age." Bruno felt the mayor take his eyes briefly from the road to glance at him as if about to speak and was relieved when he didn't. He didn't want any conversation about Isabelle.

"I spoke to Monsieur Crimson today about this trap you are setting for Murcoing," the mayor said after a silence. "Are you planning on going yourself?"

"Yes, to try and talk him into giving himself up."

"You'll be armed?"

"No, I don't think so."

"Are you mad? He's killed already, and now he has these guns."

"If he sees I'm armed, he'll be tempted to shoot. If he knows I'm unarmed, we have a chance to settle this peacefully. We are all assuming that Paul killed Fullerton in a *crime passionnel,* but from what I've learned about him, I'm not sure it's as simple as that."

"But it's an insane risk to take, Bruno. I can't allow it."

"You'd rather Crimson went instead?"

"No, of course not. Some hostage expert from the special gendarme unit, that's who we need to send."

"Yes, but to send him where? And with what instructions? To shoot Murcoing like a dangerous dog? That would be illegal. Paul's in charge of arranging a meeting place. He'll set this up carefully, probably insist that he can inspect the documents he's been promised before he shows himself. I've thought this through, and it's the only way."

"What does J-J say?"

"He began by objecting, but he came to see that it makes sense to do it this way. I'm not convinced that Paul did it, or that he acted alone, or that he's so crazy that he's staying on the run with no plan to get out of France and make a new life somewhere."

"You sound as though you know him."

"I don't, but I know about his grandfather and his obsession with Neuvic. I've met his aunt Joséphine, and I was the one who organized the funeral for the old man. He was close to his grandfather, and he'll have heard about that. I wouldn't be at all surprised if he has given his aunt or his mother a disposable phone so they can stay in touch. A lot of planning has gone into this, which is why I think he must have an escape route planned. And then there's his painting."

"What do you mean?" the mayor asked, as he pulled into the parking lot behind the St. Denis *mairie* alongside Bruno's police van.

"I bought a couple of his paintings from his aunt. They're very good, landscapes. His portraits may be even better. There's a sensibility . . . I don't know how to put it, but I find it hard to equate Paul the artist with the brutal way Fullerton was killed."

"So how do you explain it?"

"I don't, I can't."

The two men sat together in companionable silence, the engine still running. Finally the mayor spoke.

"Give my regards to Pamela when you take her home from the hospital. And take my tip, make an occasion of it. Take her some flowers. Maybe you should take her some croissants."

"Thanks for the tip, and for the dinner and the ride," said Bruno, climbing out of the car. "I'll let you know how things develop. Sleep well."

"What a wonderful breakfast," Pamela said as Bruno placed the tray on her lap, poured her a glass of champagne mixed with orange juice and kissed her on the forehead. Somehow she'd managed to fix her hair and face and look beautiful for their arrival. Fabiola had smuggled Balzac into the hospital in her bag and now held him back from leaping onto the bed. She allowed him to give Pamela a single token lick on the neck before putting him on the floor with his own chunk of baguette.

"It's a special occasion," said Pamela. "I think he deserves a corner of my croissant."

"I'll fit you with a bandage we call a figure eight. It will keep your collarbone in place," Fabiola said, passing the treat down to Balzac. "You should still wear the sling most of the time because otherwise you'll try to do too much with that arm. I'll be there to help you dress until you get used to it."

"The doctor here said it would take at least six weeks for the bone to heal," Pamela said. "And longer before I can ride again."

"He's right," said Fabiola. "I'd like you to wait three months."

"But that's my peak season. If I can't look after the guests I'll lose my regular visitors."

"We've taken care of that," said Bruno. "Florence has recruited two girls from her oldest class who'll come and clean the *gîtes* and your house and change the bedding. They'll also take care of the washing and ironing every Saturday morning for twenty euros a week each. And Yannick, who lives at the end of your road, will look after the garden for ten euros an hour."

"Thank you both, you've been marvelous. And thank you for arranging Bess. I'll miss her, of course, but I've been looking on the Internet and there's a *jument* for sale up near Limoges," Pamela said. "She's a *selle français,* Bruno, like your Hector, and I'm thinking about breeding her. It would be lovely to have some foals around the place."

"You can't buy a horse till you've ridden it, and that's a good three months away," said Fabiola. "Now let's get you packed up and dressed, and we'll take you home. Bruno, you take the food and the suitcase and the dog down to the car, and I'll help Pamela dress. I want to fit this new figure-eight strap. Then come back and get us."

He was delayed by a phone call from Yves, who apologized for calling so early, but he'd been having breakfast with Annette. He'd mentioned something about Paul Murcoing, and she had insisted he call Bruno at once. Bruno told him to go ahead.

"When I last spoke to you about him, it was after I'd talked to someone who evidently disliked him. Last night at one of the rehearsal dinners I spoke to somebody who liked him, or at least thought well of him. Apparently he'd met Paul when they were both volunteering at a hospice in Bergerac. He said he thought Paul was a kindly young man and found it hard to believe he'd killed anybody. That's it, Bruno. If I hear any more, good or bad, I'll let you know."

Bruno had just passed through Meyrals on the way back to Pamela's when his phone rang again. Fabiola, who had dealt with too many car-crash victims to let a driver use a cell phone, took it from the pouch at his waist, accepted the call and held it to his ear.

"It's Crimson. It's all gone wrong. I've just heard from

Murcoing. He doesn't want to meet me and says that instead I should get in touch with Gilles from *Paris Match* and let him have the new documents. He's even sent Gilles's e-mail address. What do we do now?"

"*Putain,* let me think. I'll call you back as soon as I can."

Fabiola put the phone away. "Bad news?"

"Our plan to smoke out Paul Murcoing just collapsed, and I don't have another."

He explained the ploy that he, Crimson and Florence had developed and his intention to go to the rendezvous instead of Crimson to talk Paul into giving himself up.

"Thank heavens that's not going to happen," said Pamela from the rear seat. "It's a ridiculous risk for you to take. Why not just leave it to J-J and the rest of the police? They're bound to pick him up eventually."

"I don't think it's that simple," said Bruno.

"Didn't I hear Gilles's name being mentioned on the phone?" asked Fabiola, a note of concern in her voice. "How does he come into this?"

"Gilles has been in touch with Paul, or rather Paul e-mailed Gilles after his piece appeared on the *Paris Match* website. Now Paul wants Crimson to give the documents to Gilles."

"These are the documents you faked?"

"No, we only faked the title page of a file. The documents don't actually exist, but Paul doesn't know that."

"Why should Crimson do what Paul wants and hand the documents over to the press?" Pamela asked. "I thought you said this researcher you invented wanted money for them."

"You're right," Bruno replied. "And he was supposed to be expecting them to go to a private person, not to the press."

Might the plan be saved, Bruno asked himself, if Crimson just said no and insisted on the original arrangement? He'd have to think this through and keep his thoughts to himself.

He didn't need the distraction of Pamela trying to talk him out of it.

"How much money did this researcher want?" she asked.

"I'm not sure any deal was reached. The story is that this was a professional researcher who used to do occasional work in the archives for Fullerton, paid by the day. Crimson thought that would be at least two hundred euros a day, but these documents are supposed to be special, classified papers that have not been publicly released. I imagine the price would be two or three thousand, maybe more."

"Where would Paul get that sort of money?"

"He got three thousand on the company credit card." Bruno turned onto the long lane that led to Pamela's house. "Maybe that was why he wanted the cash. Look, we're almost home."

He always enjoyed this approach, the long ridge climbing to the left and then the fringe of poplars that shielded the house and grounds from the north and east, the ivy-covered pigeon tower and the welcoming sight of the house itself, the courtyard formed by the flanking barns that Pamela rented as *gîtes*.

"The sooner that gardener gets here the better," said Pamela. "I've got three families arriving Saturday."

"And I have to get to work," said Bruno, helping her from the car.

"Dinner tonight after you ride Hector?"

"Let me call you." He kissed them both and headed back toward town, punching Crimson's number into the phone as he drove.

28

Crimson's house was not quite in order. The rugs had been laid, the pictures hung, and most of the furniture was back in place. But the dining room table was still to be reassembled, and cases of wine were stacked beside it. Crimson took Bruno to his study, where a desk phone and a cheap disposable were lined up on the desk. A large-scale map of the area and a laptop stood open on a small table beside the desk.

"You dyed your hair," said Bruno. As arranged, both men were wearing khaki slacks and blue shirts.

"It was the nearest I could get to looking like you. Even with binoculars, if we have the same clothes and hair color he won't be able to tell us apart. We'd better synchronize watches and be sure we have each other's phones on speed dial."

"Quite a little operations room," said Bruno.

"I've got other maps as well, notepads and tape recorders, and there's coffee in the thermos. Why did you bring the dog? I mean I'm delighted to see the little fellow, but you can't intend to take him along."

"He's my secret weapon. Murcoing likes dogs." Bruno looked around the study. "It looks like you've done this sort of thing before."

As soon as he was out of sight of Pamela's house, Bruno had called Crimson and suggested that he reply to Paul by saying he had no intention of giving the documents to the press. He wanted to deal only with someone who was personally known to and trusted by Fullerton. Otherwise he'd return to England and forget the whole thing. Crimson had agreed and sent the e-mail.

"Florence is teaching, but she wants to drop by after school. She's arranged babysitters," Crimson said. "Now we just wait."

"Not quite," said Bruno. "If you can find a screwdriver we could put that dining table of yours back together."

It took them twenty minutes and would have taken longer but for J-J's arrival with Josette, who explained that she and her husband had just furnished their new house from IKEA so she knew about putting furniture together. She added that she loved dogs, and Balzac was the friendliest little charmer she'd seen in years, which sent her soaring in Bruno's estimation. She took off her jacket, rolled up her sleeves and took charge. Crimson excused himself to make more coffee. When he returned with a tray, the table was assembled.

"Well done, we can spread out the other maps now," he said, gingerly resting the tray on it as if unsure of Josette's skills.

"Don't worry, monsieur. I sat on it to be sure I'd done it right."

"Before we start on today's operation, I have some interesting news," said J-J. "When Josette looked at Édouard's mail, she found a letter from the traffic police. His Jaguar was caught by a speed camera on the autoroute from Périgueux to Bordeaux just after eight on the evening of Fullerton's murder."

"That means he was there," said Bruno.

"He was certainly in the general vicinity. And the *juge*

d'instruction shares your suspicions, but Édouard now has a lawyer, and he's not saying a word."

"*Putain,* I was sure you'd broken him yesterday."

"Me too, but it seems we were wrong. I'll get back to him when this is over. Now listen carefully because I have something I'm required to say," said J-J. "This is not an officially sanctioned operation. You are doing this at your own risk, and I know nothing about it, understood?"

"Yes, I understand."

"Here's a slim-line flak vest, not the latest model, but it will stop a handgun. We've changed the license plates on your car so it looks like it was hired in Paris," J-J went on. "And here are the shoes." He handed over a pair of black hiking boots. "The tracker's in the heel, and Josette has the monitor. We'll need to be no more than a mile away for it to work, so keep me informed by phone of where you are. Inspector Jofflin has a second car waiting outside Bergerac with another monitor."

"Any support?" Crimson asked.

"Somebody owes me a favor, so a team of Gendarmes Mobiles will be doing an antiterrorist training exercise with live weapons and a helicopter at the Golfech nuclear power plant near Agen. They're about fifty miles away, say thirty minutes, but give me some notice, and I'll have them moved closer. They've been informally briefed and we're on the same communications network."

Bruno nodded, and inquired innocently: "The favor would be from the brigadier?"

"Don't ask. And here's a wire for each of you so we know what you're saying if you can't use the phones. It goes under your clothes, and we have to attach the transmitter to your backs with tape, so get your shirts off. It's very short-distance, maybe three hundred yards if we're lucky."

Bruno and Crimson began to strip. J-J waited until they

were taped, the system tested and Bruno had the flak vest under his shirt.

"And here's the gun I want you to use." He put his foot up on a chair and drew up his trouser leg to reveal an ankle holster in black webbing and Velcro and drew out the gun.

"It's a Smith and Wesson Centennial Airweight, designed for this holster. It's an American thirty-eight, which is pretty much the same as our nine-millimeter. A revolver, because it's less likely to get jammed by sock lint or any kind of debris you pick up walking through rough ground. And I want it back."

"I don't want to carry a gun."

"Take it, and don't be a fool."

"At least this way you have the option," said Crimson. "And it really is concealed."

Reluctantly Bruno strapped it on, privately suspecting with a soldier's superstition that this would probably ensure that Paul never made contact again. Crimson's disposable phone rang.

"Hello," he said, his English accent more evident than usual. Bruno saw the little cogs on the cassette recorder moving. Josette turned away to make a call, presumably to start the trace.

"Yes, I have a car, a rental, a white Peugeot, a 207." Crimson continued speaking in English.

"I'm at a hotel on the autoroute outside Périgueux," he said, after a pause. "Francis told me he had a place nearby."

Another pause.

"Yes, I have a map. Yes, I've found Les Eyzies. Okay, the public telephone outside the post office on the main street. How long will it take me to get there?"

Bruno felt frustrated hearing only one side of this conversation. Couldn't they have rigged up some extra earphones?

"You'll call me there at one precisely. I understand."

Another pause.

"Francis promised me two thousand pounds. Let's say twenty-five hundred euros."

He waited for a response.

"Very well, at one." Crimson closed the phone.

"Fifty seconds," said J-J looking at his watch. "That should be long enough to trace it. Josette?"

She held up a hand to silence him as she listened and scribbled on a notepad.

"It came from a public phone booth outside the *mairie* in Coux," she said, and turned back to speak into her phone. "We expect the next call will be at eleven to the public phone outside *la poste* in Les Eyzies. Can you set the trace up now? Thanks."

"Call Jofflin, tell him to get to Coux and then call in," said J-J. "Murcoing won't still be there, but this looks like the area."

"He might be watching the phone booth, or Yvonne might be watching," said Bruno. "He's not alone."

"We'll be careful." J-J turned to Crimson. "We'll follow you to Les Eyzies, and we'll park down the road but in the line of sight. There's a gas station on the corner we should be able to use. I want Bruno hiding on the floor of your car in the rear. I suspect Murcoing will have a second public phone arranged after Les Eyzies, one he can watch for any funny business. When you've fixed the final rendezvous, you hand the car over to Bruno. You'll have to find a spot which is undercover. When Bruno drives off, stay undercover until you see my car, and we'll pick you up. Make sure you can recognize my car and keep talking so we can pick you up on the mike."

"You've done this before," Crimson said to J-J.

"There was a kidnapping case a few years ago. We set up

a similar tracking system for the plainclothes guy who carried the ransom."

"And how did that turn out?"

"The plainclothes guy took one bullet, but he lived to arrest the pickup team. One of them led us to their safe house, and the hostage team did the rest. We saved the kidnap victim."

"Don't be so modest, *chef*," said Josette. "You were the one that took the bullet."

"And if I hadn't been given the ankle holster, I'd be dead. Remember that." J-J looked at his watch. "Right, let's run through the checklist. Radios, phones, tracker shoes, ankle gun, pen and notepad. Anything else?"

Josette checked her list. "A folder for the documents he's supposed to be carrying. Phone cards in case they need them." She looked at Bruno. "Don't you need a leash for the dog?"

"You're not taking the dog along?" J-J said.

"I've got the leash in my back pocket. Paul Murcoing loves animals but was never allowed to have one as a kid. His aunt told me. This gives me an edge."

J-J shook his head and rolled his eyes at Josette. "Let's go."

Bruno lay hunched and sweating under a blanket on the floor in the back of the Peugeot. Even with the passenger seat as far forward as it would go, it was a squeeze, particularly with Balzac squirming on his chest. He had an open phone line with J-J as Crimson came back from the phone booth.

"The next call will be to a phone booth in Campagne in fifteen minutes," he said, and drove back to the small roundabout by the Hôtel Centenaire and turned off toward Campagne.

"Okay, we heard that," said J-J over the phone that Bruno held to his ear. "We'll take the lower road past St. Cirq so he won't see you're being followed. We can park at the place where they sell foie gras, and we should still be in range."

Another uncomfortable ride and then a further hot and stuffy wait until Crimson returned from the Campagne phone booth and reported: "He says I have to drive to another phone booth, in Audrix, by the *mairie*. I take a left on the road to Coux and then a right at the top of the hill. He must have scouted this all out carefully."

"*Putain,* he'll see us coming up that long hill if we follow," said J-J. "Josette, get Jofflin to drive up from Coux, go past Audrix and then wait at that cheese shop just below the village. We'll go the long way around through St. Denis and use the parking lot at the big cave. And see if they can get a trace on the Audrix phone booth."

Crimson drove up a long hill with endless bends. Bruno felt his right leg start to cramp. He braced it against the door and tried to bend himself double at the waist so he could straighten the leg. Realizing something was wrong, Balzac wriggled up Bruno's trunk to lick his face and then found his way out from under the blanket. Audrix was one of the highest villages in the region, a good place for someone with binoculars to follow the progress of approaching cars.

"Are you all right?" Crimson asked.

"Just a cramp, I'll be fine."

"Sorry, we're almost there. If I'd thought, I'd have rented a bigger car. By the way, I told Paul I have my dog with me. He asked what it was and I said a basset hound puppy. He laughed."

At Audrix, the wait for Crimson to return was considerably longer, and J-J told Bruno over the phone that he could not hear the mike. J-J's voice was nervous. He kept asking what the delay was and why Crimson was not returning. Bruno replied that he didn't know. He could see nothing, and it would be too risky for a head to suddenly appear from the rear seat of the Peugeot.

"It's probably taking time for Crimson to write down the directions," Bruno said into his phone. "That would mean we're on the last lap. Wait, I hear footsteps. That's probably Crimson coming back to the car."

The driver's door opened, and Crimson spoke as he settled himself and attached the safety belt.

"I'm to drive on down the hill, cross the railway line and then take the first road on the left, at a sign marked Tennis," he reported. "Are you hearing this all right, J-J?"

"You're faint, but we can hear you. Speak the directions slowly, and, Bruno, could you hold the phone out from under the blanket? We should be able to hear it better."

Crimson repeated the directions. The terrain was all familiar, and Bruno followed the route in his head.

"We'll do the switch immediately after you turn left at the sign for the tennis club," Bruno said. "There's good cover there from hedges. Leave the engine running and wait for J-J."

"I heard all that," said J-J. "But be sure Crimson stays in hiding when he's out of the car. I'm coming, but I don't want to arrive there immediately; it would look too suspicious.

"Bruno, the chopper's on its way. I'll hold it at Le Buisson until I hear from you."

"I'm turning now at the sign to the tennis club and stopping," said Crimson, and Bruno felt the weight shift as he left the car. "Good luck."

29

Bruno climbed over the seats and took his place behind the wheel, closed the door and drove into the parking area. He turned off the engine, left the key in the ignition, picked up the file on the passenger seat and caught sight of himself in the mirror. His hair was a mess from being beneath the blanket, so he ran his fingers through to straighten it. He climbed out of the Peugeot and freed Balzac to scurry around the car. The dog lifted his leg against a wheel, darted to the tennis club building and sniffed around the door. When Bruno began to walk, certain that binoculars would be watching, Balzac followed.

The shoes he'd been given felt odd, as if one heel was higher than the other, presumably for the tracker. It was a warm day, and the flak vest was already damp under his jacket from his being beneath the blanket. Bruno checked his watch as he passed the small vineyard. He'd been walking five minutes. Another eight minutes took him to a railway crossing, where a pair of Alsatians barked at Balzac when he went up to their fence to make friends.

Bruno smiled wryly to himself as Balzac, looking puzzled at his harsh welcome, scuttled back to his master's side. They continued to follow the route he'd been given. As he turned up the gravel path that led to the woods where the rendezvous would take place, Bruno wondered whether that might be an omen for his own reception. What might he expect from this encounter? He went through the traditional soldier's catechism. He either secured his objective of persuading Paul to give himself up, in which case there was nothing to worry about, or he didn't. If he failed, either he'd walk away free, in which case there was no problem, or he wouldn't. If he did not walk away free, either he would not take a bullet, in which case, no problem. If he was shot, he'd either recover, which meant no problem, or he wouldn't, in which case he wouldn't be able to worry.

The crude fatalism cheered him a little, but that was not the calculus that had sent him trudging up this winding slope in the hot sun. Bruno's knowledge of Paul Murcoing had gone beyond the crude caricature of a violent psychopath who had butchered his lover. Bruno saw him as a human being, close to his sister and his grandfather, and as an accomplished artist who refused to do cheap sketches for cash and preferred more serious works. Paul possessed an easy charm that worked on women as well as men, and on dogs too, Bruno recalled. He had volunteered at a hospice for the dying. Bruno could not make all this fit with the simplistic category of killer. Paul had to know the game could not go on much longer, and he had his sister to think of.

Up to Bruno's left was a hill topped by a water tower and a cell-phone transmission tower. Was that a flash of sunlight on binoculars he saw? It would be a perfect location to track Bruno as he walked to the rendezvous and keep watch for any suspicious cars. Ten more minutes took him along a dirt track, and Bruno started the climb through the woods to the enormous clearing that had been turned into a motocross circuit.

As he looked at the plunges and humps and muddied

curves of the circuit, he felt certain that Paul would be using one of the motorbikes designed for such tracks. It would take him cross-country and through woods in a way that would evade any pursuit. Why hadn't he thought of that and advised J-J to have some *motards* on standby? He checked his watch; he had been walking for twenty-five minutes, and he'd gone at least a mile and a half. That could be beyond the maximum range for the tracker, particularly since trees would cut down reception.

Jofflin's car would be the closer of the two. There was no discreet place nearby for J-J to park and no proper roads, only dirt tracks that would challenge even his own Land Rover. Bruno had hunted around here, ridden over the land on horseback with Fabiola and Pamela and even come through this forest looking for mushrooms with the baron. The nearest road in the other direction was two or three miles away, and J-J's car could not handle the rough forest tracks. Bruno would have to assume he was on his own.

He got to the concrete stand and waited, Crimson's disposable phone in his hand. Paul would be expecting the English accent that he already recognized and that Bruno could not possibly hope to impersonate. That would make for a difficult moment.

The phone rang. He put it to his ear and began working his mouth as though saying "Hello" again and again but keeping silent. He heard a male voice speaking English and carried on miming his response. He took the phone from his ear, looked at it, shook it, returned it to his ear and began once more miming his "Hello." Faking a bad connection was his only chance.

Across the clearing perhaps two hundred yards away he saw a flash of movement through the woods. Then he saw it again, farther along through the trees, and realized it was someone on a mountain bike, wearing a cycling helmet and shorts. Very clever, he thought. Nobody could catch a mountain bike in these woods, and someone riding one could avoid all the roads. Cyclists were so common that Paul could probably risk the gendarme patrols and go cross-country again if he had to.

There was a sound behind him, and he turned to see another mountain bike coming slowly down the slope from the woods toward him. The cyclist in helmet, shorts and a long-sleeved cycling vest in green stopped, perhaps thirty yards away, feet on the ground but poised to pedal away swiftly. From a waist pouch, the cyclist took an automatic pistol and pointed it at Bruno. It was big and flat, an automatic, probably the Browning.

No matter how good his training or how thoroughly he had tried to think through this moment, Bruno learned anew that there was nothing quite like the adrenaline shock of a gun being aimed at him. He told himself that the vest was designed to stop a nine-millimeter round and tried to repress the thought that an untrained shooter usually fired high and there was no vest to protect his head.

The file in one hand, the phone in the other, Bruno ignored the tremor in his legs and raised his hands above his head as Balzac wagged his tail and trotted up to the bike to sniff at the cyclist's feet.

The second cyclist came out of the woods to Bruno's right and paused, perhaps twenty yards away. He took off a small backpack and removed a slim black weapon, its magazine sticking out sideways from the barrel. Bruno recognized it was a Sten gun. After he'd learned that it was missing from Fullerton's collection, Bruno had looked it up. It has thirty-two rounds, nine-millimeter bullets, a tendency to rise when fired and very prone to jam. The cyclist held the butt in his right hand, finger on the trigger, and his left hand on the magazine. That meant he didn't know the gun well. Holding it there meant pressure on the magazine, which could alter the angle at which the bullets were fed into the chamber and cause a jam.

"It's not him," shouted the first cyclist, the one holding the automatic. It was a female voice. "I know this guy, he's a cop from St. Denis. It's a trap."

"Bonjour, Yvonne—bonjour, Paul," Bruno said, his arms still high and his eyes fixed on the gun that threatened him. He was conscious that his voice was a notch or two higher than usual, and there was a chill lump of fear in his belly. "I've come to ask you to give yourselves up before anybody gets hurt."

"Did you see any cars, anybody else following him?" Paul asked his sister. His face was covered in fashionable stubble. The sleeve of his cycling vest had ridden up enough for Bruno to see the beginning of the Maori warrior tattoo.

"No, but it's got to be a trap."

"The bikes are a good idea," said Bruno, straining to keep his voice calm. He settled back on his heels to stop the quivering in his legs. "Even if there were any cars, you can get away again. I'm hoping you won't do that. There are no charges against Yvonne. Think of her future."

"Go back up the hill and keep watch," Paul told his sister. He pulled back the bolt to cock the Sten, holding it steady and aiming low. Bruno's heart thumped as he realized that he was now one pull of the trigger away from all thirty-two rounds of the magazine hitting him in less than three seconds. "You expect me to believe that you came just to tell me to give up? Have you got the documents?"

As Yvonne stood on her pedals to cycle back up the hill,

Balzac trotted across to Paul and made a friendly bark of greeting. Paul ignored him, not taking his eyes away from Bruno for a moment.

"There are no documents, Paul. We cooked up that page as bait to get a chance to talk to you. I knew about your grandfather's war record, about the Neuvic train, about his suspicions." The words came out in a rush, and he knew that he was not sounding persuasive, even to himself.

"They aren't suspicions. He spent half his life trying to find out what happened to that money. What about the contents page you sent me from the archive? Was that faked too?"

"Not entirely," he said, straining his ears for the sound of a helicopter or even a car engine, for some indication that he was not alone facing a submachine gun. He had seen how the bullets could stitch their way up a human body. "Most of the documents exist, they're just not declassified yet. But I'm told they don't provide much evidence for your theories. The British really didn't know what happened to the Neuvic money."

"Crimson probably told you that, the guy the papers call the spymaster. So he's in on this as well."

Paul's voice was even, not carrying any tone of anger or frustration. Bruno hoped he would stay this calm.

"Crimson got involved when you burgled his house. But we got all the stuff back from Fullerton's place in the Corrèze. We very nearly caught up with you both there."

Paul nodded. "So what brings the St. Denis policeman into this?"

"Apart from the burglaries being on my turf, I was at your grandfather's deathbed. He had one of the Neuvic banknotes in his hands as he died. I'm keeping his Resistance medal for you and the photos he had of himself in the Groupe Valmy."

Bruno's legs had stopped trembling, and he felt the first glimmer of relief that this encounter was turning into a dialogue, just as the book on hostage negotiations said it should.

"One of the photos was of the Neuvic operation. And after he died I found some photos of you and him together. I've got one in my shirt pocket. I thought you'd like to have it. Can I get it out and show you?"

"Just keep your hands in the air. Does that mean you were the one who organized the funeral?"

Bruno nodded. "Your grandfather got a good send-off. Half the town was there with a military honor guard and we sang the 'Chant des Partisans.' Did you get close enough to see anything of it?"

"Not as close as I'd have liked. But I heard the music."

"I went to see your aunt Joséphine."

"So I heard. You bought a couple of my pictures, got them cheap, just as you did with the Neuvic banknotes."

"I paid what I was asked."

Paul considered that and nodded. He glanced down at Balzac, who was sniffing around his ankles. "That's a nice basset, what's his name?"

"Balzac."

Paul smiled, that same smile Bruno had seen in the surveillance photo at the printing shop. Bruno understood why the shopgirl had been charmed.

"Tell me, why did you bring Balzac?"

"Because I know you like animals."

Paul laughed. He looked calm and self-possessed, with none of the nervous stress Bruno had expected. Bruno found that at last he was able to swallow as his own tension began to ease.

"You're a strange kind of cop. What's your name?"

"Bruno, Bruno Courrèges. I'm the town policeman at St. Denis, as your sister said."

"Bruno, I've heard that name before. I seem to remember seeing something in the papers about your pulling a Chinese kid out of a fire, and that thing in the big cave, was that you?"

Bruno nodded. Paul eyed him curiously.

"How did you get onto me?"

"A postman remembered the van and the France-Chauffage sign you faked, so I went to the sign shop, where they had a security camera. Then I took your picture to the *zone industrielle* in Belvès and met one of your admirers, a woman called Nicole. She recognized you from the security photo. So then I had a name, and we began to check known addresses and went to see Joséphine and began looking for Yvonne."

Paul laughed. "I haven't thought of Nicole in a while. So it was all because a postman saw the van. Would that have been somewhere near the place where Francis was killed?"

"On the road up to the house. He was leaving after delivering some mail; you were heading toward it. I presume Francis was still alive then."

"Assume all you like." He paused and then cocked his head as if remembering something. "How long have you had this job?"

"Eleven years, and yes, I was the cop who came to investigate the attack on that vacation place eleven years ago when you and Édouard Marty were beaten up with the older English guys. You were the one with the broken nose who was taken to the clinic where you gave a false name and address. Either Francis Fullerton drove, or he was the one with the broken arm."

Paul nodded slowly and studied Bruno without speaking. The Sten did not waver. "Are you armed?" he asked.

"I have a small gun in an ankle holster. A snub-nose revolver. It couldn't reach you at this range. I wouldn't have worn it, but senior colleagues insisted. They think you're a murderer. I'm not so sure."

"Why do you say that?" Paul sounded genuinely curious. "The papers and the radio are all saying I'm guilty."

"Partly it's the hospice where you volunteered, partly it's your paintings, but it's mainly because I can't bring myself to believe you killed Francis in a *crime passionnel*. I think you loved him, but I can't see you being jealous in that way. And I can't see you beating him to death like that, so brutally."

"Well, you're right about that." He gave a short laugh. "All of it."

"Tell me what happened, Paul. If you didn't do it, who did? Give yourself up and come with me and we can find out what really happened. You haven't got much time. We know about the British credit card and we're blocking it. You'll have no more money. There's a helicopter nearby with a team of Gendarmes Mobiles aboard. You know how they're trained. They'll take one look at that Sten and they'll shoot first and ask questions later. Think about Yvonne; do you want them gunning her down alongside you?"

"It needn't be like that," Paul replied. "Thanks for the warning, but this isn't over."

"So what now?"

Paul looked at Bruno thoughtfully. "It's a pity there are no documents. That story needs to come out."

"Gilles from *Paris Match* is a good reporter. Once he gets his teeth into something, he keeps on chewing."

"You know him?"

"We've been friends for a long time. We met in Sarajevo during the siege. He was a reporter. I was in the army."

"Interesting, Grandpa would have approved. Now since I

don't want to make more trouble by shooting you, I'd like you to put that phone down and take your shirt off. Leave the photo in the pocket."

"I'm wearing a flak vest and a wire."

"That's what I expected, so take them off. I imagine you've got a cordon forming around this area while you engage me in friendly chitchat."

Bruno complied, wincing as he ripped off the tape that held the transmitter to his back, and laid them on the ground in front of him. He opened the button on the shirt pocket and slightly withdrew the photo so Paul could see it.

"Now, sit down on the ground. Keeping your hands well away from that ankle holster, take your shoes off. Use your feet to get them off, that's right. Now take off that ankle holster. If you try to open it I'll shoot you. Don't get up. Just raise your arms and put your hands on your head and keep them there. Now start shuffling back on your bum and call your dog to join you. Keep on backing away."

Bruno called Balzac from sniffing at his abandoned shoes and wriggled back down the slope. Paul kept the Sten gun aimed at him as he stepped off the bike and put Bruno's shoes, phone and the transmitter into his rucksack. He left the gun in its holster on the ground. Finally he took the photo from Bruno's shirt pocket and then remounted his bike.

"Good luck, Bruno. Sorry your feet are going to get a bit torn up, but stay in touch with Gilles. I may have something to communicate, and I'll do it through him."

"Can you at least tell me who killed Francis?" From far in the distance, Bruno could hear the first, faint chattering of a helicopter.

"It wasn't me. I was there, but I didn't kill him. I couldn't have, despite what he was doing to us." Paul cocked his head, hearing the rotor blades.

"That's the Gendarmes Mobiles." Bruno said. "For God's sake, think of your sister. This doesn't have to end with you both dead."

Paul shook his head, looked up the hill and whistled. After a moment his sister appeared. He stuffed his gun into his rucksack, shouldered it and rode off along the side of the hill, disappearing into the woods, his sister following close behind.

Bruno lowered his arms at last. They felt so light they seemed to want to rise again of their own accord. His body was sending waves of relief through his frame that the danger was over while his mind felt disappointment that he had failed to bring Paul in. He took a deep breath and stretched. The gendarme chopper was still too far away to be seen.

He retrieved his shirt, flak vest and the ankle holster, wincing as the sharp pebbles bit into his stockinged feet. Feeling a curious mixture of elation and humiliation, he hobbled very carefully down the motocross circuit to the track that led back to where Jofflin's car was waiting. When he saw it, he waved and then heard the engine start up. He'd held the suspect in place for more than twenty minutes, which should have been long enough for whatever plans J-J had prepared for an ambush.

30

J-J had not been happy. His car had gotten stuck on a trail in the woods far behind the motocross circuit and required a tow truck to come and drag it out. His phone couldn't get a signal, and the helicopter with the Gendarmes Mobiles had beaten its way back and forth along the ragged edges of the woods, and they had never seen a soul, let alone two cyclists. He grudgingly accepted the return of his revolver and flak jacket, listened to Bruno's account of the conversation with Paul and only smiled when he saw Bruno's bare feet. The ruined socks had been thrown away, but Balzac had gleefully rescued one and carried it dangling from his mouth.

Jofflin drove Bruno and Crimson back to Crimson's house, where Bruno borrowed a pair of socks and put his own shoes back on. Thanking Crimson for his trouble, he drove to his office to report to the mayor, who warned him that Delaron was asking questions about unusual police activity.

"You met this young man, Paul?" the mayor asked.

"Yes, and we had an interesting conversation given that he was holding me at gunpoint. He wouldn't explain what had really happened, just that he was at the scene but hadn't killed Fullerton, despite 'what he was doing to us.' That's the bit I don't understand. I've no idea what Fullerton was doing, or who Murcoing was referring to when he talked of 'us.' But he was very self-confident, as though he knew it would all work out for him. I never saw anyone who looked less like a hunted man on the run."

"What happens now?"

"I tried to tempt him out of hiding and bring him in and it didn't work. I suppose now it's up to J-J and the *mobiles,* which means there's a strong chance that Paul gets killed and we never learn the truth."

"It's out of your hands now. And I imagine you haven't heard the news. The minister of the interior has resigned, pleading reasons of health, a very unusual development this close to the election. Jacqueline is delighted and called to say she's putting some champagne on ice to celebrate. Gilles will be joining us, since she now sees him as a worthy fellow conspirator. She made a point of saying that you were also invited along with Balzac and what she called your various womenfolk. I think that was meant to be a joke."

"I suppose you can never be sure with a woman like Jacqueline."

"*Bien entendu.* It makes life much more interesting."

Back in his office, where a full in-box and a pile of unopened mail awaited him, Bruno opened his computer and groaned as he saw screen after screen of unanswered e-mails. It would take him days to clear the backlog. He looked out of his window. The cars at the roundabout had stopped for a line of cyclists to pedal through. They were all on racing bikes, rather than the sturdy mountain bikes Paul and his sister had been riding, and none of them was wearing a green vest. He studied them anyway, wondering how far away Paul and Yvonne could have gone by now.

J-J had made it clear that Bruno was off the case, now that

his ploy to smoke out Paul with the forged papers had run its course. Murcoing was henceforth the concern of the gendarmes and the Police Nationale. Bruno was back in his usual routine, taking care of the affairs of St. Denis. It was a job he much enjoyed, but he was aware of a sense of letdown, of unfinished business.

His desk phone rang, and he looked at it glumly. What would it be this time? A lost cat, or a denunciation of some unemployed guy working for cash, perhaps a complaint about the new parking restrictions.

"Bruno, it's Jack Crimson. I'm at home, and Florence is here along with Brian Fullerton. But so are Paul Murcoing and his sister, and they're pointing guns at us." He was trying to make his voice sound calm, but Bruno could almost feel the tension through the phone line. "They're holding us all hostage . . ." Crimson's voice cracked, but he went on: "And Murcoing wants to speak to you."

"Bruno, I told you this wasn't over," came the now-familiar voice. "This is why."

"*Putain,* I didn't think you could possibly get into worse trouble, but now you have." Bruno's mind was racing as he tried to recall the checklist of procedures for a hostage situation. "What do you want, Paul?"

"A presidential pardon, safe passage out of the country for Yvonne and me and the promise of a public inquiry into the Neuvic money. I'll release Crimson when those conditions are met."

"What about the others, Fullerton and Florence? You don't need them; you could let them go."

"After what you told me about the *mobiles*? I don't think so. Call me back on Crimson's landline one hour from now, or things will start to get unpleasant. I have three hostages, don't forget, and I only need the one."

He hung up. Bruno immediately dialed J-J and walked briskly back to the mayor's office as the call connected. He saw the mayor's startled face when for the first time in his career Bruno entered without knocking. His eyes on the mayor, Bruno said into the phone: "J-J, I've just had a call from Paul Murcoing at Crimson's house. He's taken Crimson hostage at gunpoint along with two other people."

The mayor rose, looking stunned, and then sank back into his chair as Bruno recounted Paul's conditions.

"J-J, I'll meet you at Crimson's house, and I'll arrange for a doctor and an ambulance to be on standby. I have my mobile phone, and for anything else the mayor will be in his office. I'll patch my phone through to his and rig up a tape recorder."

"Mother of God," said the mayor as Bruno hung up and called Fabiola's cell phone.

"I'll be right back with the recorder," said Bruno, and left for his office. When Fabiola answered, he briefed her and asked her to arrange for an ambulance and someone to check on Florence's children. One of her pupils was probably baby-sitting but could not be expected to stay all night. He opened his safe and took out his gun and a spare magazine and put on his holster and uniform jacket. He forwarded all his calls to the mayor's extension and took the recorder back with him along with two spare cassettes and rigged it to the mayor's phone.

"I'm going to Crimson's house, where I'll meet J-J," he said. "You're the communications backstop. Get Roberte in to answer your phone rather than Claire; she's more levelheaded. Fend off all calls that aren't related to this hostage situation and make sure you keep your mobile charged and ready, since I'll use that to stay in touch with you. Is that clear, sir?"

"Yes, Bruno."

"Please make a note to call me in exactly fifty minutes to remind me that's when Paul is expecting me to call him again."

The mayor looked at his watch, took the top from his fountain pen and scribbled a note to himself on a clean pad.

"And nobody, nobody, is to talk to the press. If Delaron gets hold of this, we'll have a circus."

Bruno was already dialing again, the special number that he was only to use in emergencies.

The phone was answered, but there was no reply, just a silence. "This is Bruno Courrèges in St. Denis, and I need to speak to the brigadier urgently."

"Bruno?"

Oh, God, it was Isabelle's voice. Of all the people in the ministry she had to be the duty officer of the day. Firmly squashing all the emotions and recriminations that flooded through him, he kept his voice crisp and neutral.

"Crimson has just been taken hostage at his home," he began, and explained the details.

"*Putain,* the brigadier's not here. He's gone to the Élysée, and there's complete chaos here. You heard our minister just resigned? I'll try to patch you through, but if he's with the president he can't take the call."

"Stay on the line to see if he answers and, if not, keep calling him until you can brief him. I'm on my way to Crimson's house where J-J will join me. We have some Jaunes in the vicinity with a chopper, but they're trained in antiterrorist response, not hostage rescue. So do your best to keep them out of the way."

"You got it. If the brigadier doesn't answer in ten seconds leave it to me. And Bruno, please take care."

He waited the ten seconds, but the brigadier did not pick up. He hung up and then began to dial the gendarmerie when the mayor coughed and said: "Er, Bruno?"

He stopped at the door, about to trot down the *mairie* stairs, phone to his ear.

"I'll look after Balzac, don't worry."

The pup was sitting on the rug beside the mayor, looking up at Bruno in perplexity. Was his master going for a walk without him?

"Thank you, I know he's in good hands."

He ran down the stairs as the call went through, hoping that Sergeant Jules would answer rather than Yveline.

"Gendarmerie, St. Denis," came a female voice, but it was Françoise.

"It's Bruno. Is Jules there? It's an emergency."

"He's right here. I'll put him on."

As he got to his Land Rover, Bruno explained to the unflappable Sergeant Jules that he wanted all available gendarmes deployed to form a distant cordon around Crimson's house. They were to stay out of sight and keep all traffic away unless it was official.

"It's a hostage situation, so you know the procedure. I've informed J-J. Perhaps you could inform the prefect's office and the *proc*. We'll probably need more gendarmes from St. Cyprien on standby if this goes through the night. Tell Ivan to start making sandwiches and pots of coffee. If you call the mayor, he'll arrange for someone to bring them out. Where's Yveline?"

"It's her day off. She said she was going shopping in Périgueux."

"Call her and brief her and suggest that when she gets back she holds the fort at the gendarmerie, but I need you and the rest of the squadron out there as soon as you can."

"Understood. I'll see you there. I'll get Ivan to make ham and cheese; they're always the most popular."

Bruno grinned. He could always count on Sergeant Jules

for the essentials. He put his phone in his breast pocket and tried to concentrate on his driving while, despite himself, his brain kept building mental maps of Crimson's house and grounds, access points and vulnerabilities. He knew the rough technique of the hostage-rescue squad; plastic explosives on front and rear doors simultaneously, as flashbang grenades, meant to startle and stun, not to kill, went through each of the windows, followed by the first assault team. A second team would use ladders to break into the upper floor.

But he remembered wooden shutters on Crimson's ground-floor windows. If they were closed, they would have to be broken before the flashbangs could be launched through the windows, so they'd lose the benefit of surprise. Drenching the place in tear gas and smoke was the usual alternative, but it was risky. The other options were even worse: snipers, starvation and stealthy entry.

When he arrived at the entrance to Crimson's driveway, Bruno was alone. He parked out of sight, leaving the side-lights on so Sergeant Jules would see his Land Rover. Avoiding the driveway Bruno slipped through the woods at the side of Crimson's property to scout the sides and rear of the house. The shutters had all been closed, and he could see no open windows on the upper floors. Inside the garage was a rented car, presumably Crimson's. Brian's car was parked in front of the doors and Florence's bicycle leaned against the side wall. There was good cover by the garage for an assault team to form up, and only a single window, probably for a staircase landing, on the nearest wall. The *mobiles* could cover that window with a silenced gun, put up two ladders and break in that way. That's how he would do it.

Bruno crept close to the shuttered windows, each of which showed chinks of light from inside, but there was no sound from the rooms at the rear. One of the mountain bikes was leaning against the kitchen door, something that might give them a warning if it was moved. Gently he felt along the frame, and his fingers touched a taut piece of string that led through the keyhole into the house. There would probably be a bell or something on the other end that would make a noise if the bike was moved.

At the front of the house, in the room he recalled as Crimson's study and which had earlier that day been his makeshift operations room, he heard the murmur of voices. The sound was not clear enough for him to tell with certainty who was talking, but he thought it sounded like Florence. At least he knew where some of them were. The other bike lay against the front door. Paul had probably rigged a warning system on that one too.

As Bruno withdrew to the fringe of trees and back to his Land Rover he was sure he was forgetting something. Had there been another door into the house? Perhaps he could find a way to break silently through the French windows. He cast his mind back to his previous visits and remembered the descent to the wine cellar and the hatch for the fuel-oil delivery. He crept back to the rear of the house and felt for the metal plates and the padlock that sealed them. Bolt cutters could take care of it. Damn, he should have made a sketch of what he could recall of the interior for J-J. There would be five in the house, Paul and Yvonne, Crimson, Florence and Brian.

Crimson had explained that Florence would be coming to his house after school to hear what had happened with the trap they had set. But why was Brian Fullerton inside? Wasn't he supposed to be flying back to England today with his brother's ashes? Bruno had heard nothing about a delay in the release of the body, but that had to be the explanation, and Brian had become friendly with Crimson. Maybe he'd simply dropped by to say good-bye and walked into the kidnapping. Bruno knew from Pamela's trips that the Ryanair flight left at around five, so Brian would have missed his flight back to England from Bergerac by now.

Bruno stopped, struck by something he had not considered before. That flight usually landed around four, so how had Brian arrived in Bruno's office on Friday morning? Brian said he had canceled the flight to Bordeaux the consulate had booked for him and flown into Bergerac instead. And he'd added that he'd come straight to Bruno's office from the airport and had not even checked in to his hotel.

The thought nagged at him, so he called the security office at the airport where Marco, one of the shift chiefs, had been in Bruno's class at the police academy. Bruno asked about the inbound flights from Britain on Friday morning. There had been none. He asked Marco to check if there were any records last week of a Brian Fullerton arriving. He heard the sound of a keyboard being tapped.

"Nothing on the computer," said Marco. "Let me check other airports? It's all on the same database now. Here he is, flew into Bordeaux Monday last week on British Airways from London Gatwick. Open return."

"Thanks, Marco. You're sure it was Monday? Could there be any mistake?"

"No, this comes from the airline boarding lists. If they're not on the flight they're not listed."

Monday last week was the day before his brother was murdered. Why was Brian flying in then? And why had he misled him? Brian had flown into Bordeaux. Édouard was in Bordeaux, and his Jaguar had been caught by a speed camera returning from Périgueux to Bordeaux on the evening Brian's brother was killed. And Brian, Édouard and Paul were all directors of Francis's company. But this couldn't be about inheritance; Francis's will put everything in trust for his nieces and nephews.

Was he sure about that? Hadn't he asked Isabelle and J-J and even Crimson if there was some way to check Francis's will? Suddenly he remembered Pamela telling him that, unlike in France, under English law you could leave your property to anyone you chose. If Francis was planning to leave his property elsewhere, that could be a motive for murder.

As he reached for the phone at his belt, he felt it vibrate.

"Bruno, it's J-J. I'm on my way, I'll be with you in ten minutes or so. The brigadier just called me. They can't get a hostage-rescue team here before tomorrow morning, and he suggests we use the *mobiles*. He doesn't seem to care too much about taking Murcoing alive, and we can have them here in ninety minutes. What do you say?"

"If they go in guns blazing, there's always a risk to the hostages. Is the brigadier ready for that?"

"He says he is. But that kind of operation has to be authorized by a minister, and we don't have one. That's the problem."

"We'll talk it through when you get here."

Bruno saw headlights coming around the bend from St. Denis and stepped into the middle of the road to flag down the vehicle. It was the gendarmerie van, Françoise at the wheel and Sergeant Jules beside her, with the ambulance following close behind. He was advising Jules where to position his men when his phone vibrated again. It was the mayor.

"Bruno, it's time to call Paul Murcoing."

"Thanks. Any developments?"

"Everything's fine. Roberte is handling the phones, and Jacqueline is looking after Florence's children. I'll call if anything happens. Isabelle called, asking for news."

"Could you call her back and ask if she had any reply from England about Francis Fullerton's will?"

"Okay, but you'd better phone Paul."

Bruno found Crimson's home number in his phone and dialed it. Paul responded instantly, as if he had been standing by the phone.

"It's Bruno. There's a problem. If you turn on the TV or radio you'll realize this is no trick. The interior minister has just resigned for personal reasons. Normally that's the man who would have to make a decision about your conditions, but right now the post is vacant."

There was a silence as if a hand had been placed over the mouthpiece at the other end. Bruno could faintly hear the sound of Yvonne's voice, high and angry. Then Paul spoke, trying to sound calm but not succeeding. "There must be a deputy or an acting minister."

"Yes, but without lawful authority. We're trying to get this clarified, and I've asked the mayor of my town whether this can go to the Élysée for the president to make a decision. Can I call you back as soon as I hear anything?"

"Where are you now?"

"Near the house, and there's just me, so far. A couple of gendarmes are setting up a roadblock to keep other traffic away. We're waiting for the Police Nationale from Périgueux."

"Call me back in an hour, and tell those people in Paris that if they don't have a decision by then, I will start putting bullets into hostages. I'll start with feet and knees, unless I think you're dicking me around, and then I'll get serious. One hour, Bruno.

"Don't make this worse," Paul said, and hung up. Bruno called the mayor to pass on the message.

"I spoke to Isabelle," the mayor said when Bruno had

finished. "Apparently Francis Fullerton changed his will very recently. His estate goes to any natural child of his own and, failing that, to Yves Valentoux to be held in trust for a girl called Odile. Who on earth is she?"

"I think she might be the key to all this, and that's exactly what I needed to know. Thank you, and thank Isabelle for me when you speak again. What do you think the chances are of the Élysée intervening?"

"Very slim. It would mean potentially taking responsibility for the death of Crimson and the others. The fact that there's a vacuum at the top of the interior ministry is just the kind of escape clause politicians like."

Bruno hung up and immediately called Yves Valentoux. From the background sound, he was in a bar or restaurant.

"Yves, this is really important. Lives may hang on it. How serious was Francis about asking you to marry him?"

"I know he was planning a trip to the States for us to get married there. I hadn't agreed, but he was always so confident about everything . . ."

"Would it be legal for a non-American?"

"He'd obtained U.S. citizenship when he lived there in the nineties. Apparently it was quite easy before 9/11. He also kept his British passport."

"And you told me he wanted to give Odile a little brother or sister. What about his HIV?"

"He said he'd researched it, and there were ways to sanitize his sperm. I never took it that seriously, but he certainly did."

"I think this plan to marry you and have a child was what got Francis killed. It would have changed the inheritance."

31

J-J closed his phone with a snap. "They won't make any decision in Paris, and they won't authorize using the Jaunes. I guess it's down to you now." He looked with sympathy at Bernard Ardouin, the *juge d'instruction,* who was standing beside Sergeant Jules's gendarmerie van. It was the nearest they had to a mobile operations room until the real one arrived from Périgueux with reinforcements.

"You could order the gendarme general for the *département* to send in the Jaunes," J-J went on. "But he'd probably want to consult the defense ministry, and we'd be back where we started. The only people you can be sure will carry out your orders are my team and Bruno."

Ardouin's own boss, the chief *procureur* for the *département,* was at a gala dinner and opera in Bordeaux along with the prefect. Their phones were turned off.

"I have to call Paul again in ten minutes," said Bruno. "Damn it, does nobody have the balls to make a decision?"

"There must be an intermission coming up," Ardouin said, trying to sound decisive. "I'm sure we'll be able to reach someone soon."

Bruno had expected better from Ardouin. He turned away to hide the disgust on his face and called the mayor.

"Nobody wants to make a decision. Will you authorize me to go in? I think Paul will speak to me."

"Bruno, whatever you decide to do will have my full support, and Roberte who's sitting here heard me say that."

Bruno was dialing Crimson's number when a shot came from inside the house followed by the piercing note of a woman shrieking.

"I'm sorry I had to do that," Paul said as he answered Crimson's phone. "I warned you this would happen."

"I have no news and no official response from Paris on your conditions, but a superior officer is now here, Commissaire Jalipeau, head of detectives for the *département.* The *juge d'instruction* is with him, and he wants to talk to you."

Bruno handed the phone to J-J and went back to Sergeant Jules.

"Since nobody else will do anything, I'm going to try," he said. "I'll need your people to break a window on the upper floor and pull down the bike that's leaning against the front door, both at the same time. Ten seconds after that, I want the bike leaning against the back door to be pulled away. There's an alarm rigged to each one, and it will distract them. And I'll need those bolt cutters you have for traffic accidents."

"All right, do you want me to come with you?"

"I'm not sure you'd squeeze through the gap I'm planning to use, but thanks for offering. Who are the best people on your team?"

"Françoise, no question. She's also the best shot. By the way, Yveline's back and calling every few minutes to ask if anything's happened. She told me somebody left a cardboard box on the steps of the gendarmerie with an old silver coffeepot inside. It must have happened just after I left. She says it looks like the American one that was stolen. What do you want her to do?"

"Tell her to call the owner and see if she can identify it," Bruno replied. "But first, let's talk to Françoise."

Jules beckoned Françoise to join them. He asked her if she was ready to volunteer to go in with Bruno.

"About time somebody did something," she said. "If he's shot Florence . . ."

Bruno explained his plan. He went to his Land Rover, pulled out his spare roll of fishing line and measured out two lengths of twenty yards each. He gave one to Françoise. She crept to the front door and tied the line to the bike while he did the same at the rear.

They rejoined Jules, who had collected a handful of fist-sized stones and positioned himself below the window that looked onto the garage. Each of them gave the sergeant an end of the fishing line.

"Pull on that, and the bike topples, and the alarm goes off," said Bruno. "When you hear the click of the bolt cutters, count to twenty and then pull the back-door bike."

Jules repeated the instructions.

"Then count to ten and break that window and start shouting. Stay tucked up against the wall so they can't see you or shoot you, but keep on throwing stones until that glass breaks."

"Count to ten, window," Jules said.

"I'll go in first and try to get up the stairs to the landing to get the high ground, and Françoise will stay at the top of the cellar stairs."

"What's this?" J-J demanded, joining them. "What are you up to, Bruno?"

"Since you people won't do anything, the mayor has told me to do something."

"You're not doing anything."

"You're not my boss."

"No, you fool, I'm your friend. What have you got in mind?"

Bruno explained his plan. J-J nodded. "It might help if I were to call him when I hear your bolt cutters and say we just heard from Paris."

"It would help a lot. If I can open the front door on the way up, I'll try it."

Bolt cutters in hand, with Françoise carrying an aerosol can of lubricant, they crept around to the rear of the house, to the edge of the terrace and the access for the fuel oil. Françoise sprayed the lubricant onto the hinges and then held the padlock so Bruno could get some purchase. With a powerful heave of his shoulders he closed the long handles of the cutters and heard a loud snap. Françoise dislodged the broken padlock, and then Bruno took a deep breath, seized the edges of the two metal plates and in a swift move pulled them up and open. The entry to the cellar, not much wider than his shoulders, loomed dark at his feet.

He let himself into the hole, counting under his breath, and lowered himself until his feet touched the floor, and the count was ten. He whispered to Françoise to follow, helped her down and then took out his gun. He released the safety catch. Fifteen.

He opened the door to find the cellar in darkness. He groped his way to the stairs and began climbing at the count of eighteen. He had just reached the top of the stairs when he heard glass break and then a noisy clatter as a bike fell. He opened the door, the light suddenly very bright, and heard a woman's voice shout, "Back door." Footsteps ran down the stairs from the upper floor. He had reached a new count of three, now four.

To get to the back door, Yvonne would have to come past him. He had never hit a woman, but it would be better than shooting her. As Yvonne jumped down the last stairs and turned to face the back door Bruno put his entire weight into a punch that started at his knees and ended in the center of her stomach, just below the rib cage. There was a great whoosh of air being expelled from her lungs, and then she bent over double and fell as if she'd been poleaxed. The automatic pistol fell from her hand.

The count was seven as he grabbed her gun and tucked it into the back of his waistband, so there was no time to open the front door. The count was ten as he began leaping up the stairs as the first rock came in through the landing window.

Bruno lay flat on the landing, pointing his gun down the stairs and planning to shoot Paul somewhere around his waist, to stop him but with luck not kill him. He would have one clean shot at a moving target before Paul's Sten began hosing the stairs with bullets.

Then he heard the sound of a blow, a grunt and something clattering as it fell. There were confused voices, shouting, protesting. Then came a burst of automatic fire from inside the study, shockingly loud.

Then silence.

"*C'est fini, c'est fini,*" came a shout. "It's over. I got him. Here's the gun."

The study door was opened and the Sten gun, minus its magazine, was pushed out into the hall.

"Can we come out now? This is Brian Fullerton. Murcoing is dead, and we are all safe."

At that point Sergeant Jules pulled the second length of fishing line, and a new clattering came as the bike toppled and the glass jug filled with teaspoons that had been resting on a chair was pulled down by the falling bike to tinkle against the door.

"Françoise, secure the prisoner on the floor," Bruno called. "Then go out and get J-J and the sergeant, the doctor and a stretcher."

"She's choking, it sounds very bad," Françoise said. "I've cuffed her." Her gun poised, she went to the front door, clambered over the bike and shouted for the others to come.

"Come out one at a time with your hands up," Bruno called.

Brian came first, looking defiantly around him, then Florence, her face drained and her hands and lips trembling, though she looked unhurt. There were no bullet wounds in her hands or feet. Paul had been bluffing with that shot. Crimson came last, looking back into the study, from which drifted whiffs of cordite.

"It's clear," said Crimson.

"What happened in there?" Bruno asked.

"I tripped him, grabbed the Sten and shot him," said Brian. "It was him or us."

"There was a shot earlier and a woman's scream," said Bruno. "We thought he might have shot Florence."

"He fired into the ceiling, and his sister did the screams," said Crimson. "It was a bit of theater."

J-J was the first in the door, Fabiola on his heels, and then Sergeant Jules and the *juge*. Bruno pointed Fabiola to Yvonne, still straining for breath, rocking back and forward from her waist, her eyes wide with terror. The three hostages dropped their hands, and Florence turned accusingly to Brian Fullerton.

"You didn't have to shoot him," she said. "He was helpless, spread-eagled on the floor. He'd dropped the gun."

"We'll sort this out later," Bruno said, and told them all to get back as he looked into the study.

Paul Murcoing lay in a spreading lake of blood. His handsome face was unmarked, but a trail of bullet holes rose from his left hip, across his stomach and up the right side of his chest. His eyes and mouth were open, with a look that might have been surprise.

"Good result," said J-J, coming into the room, the others following. "Hostages all saved, the bad guy dead, the girl lives to go on trial. We charge her with kidnapping, resisting arrest."

"I think there might be another trial," said Bruno. He turned to Crimson. "Tell us what happened in there."

"They panicked when the first bike fell. Paul had sent his sister upstairs; he was worried about the window up there. Then he took a phone call. As he was speaking we heard her shouting and running downstairs and then nothing until the windows started breaking. That's when Paul dropped the phone and ran out."

"I tripped him," Brian interrupted. "That's when I grabbed the Sten and shot him. I thought he might have another gun."

"How convenient for you that he's dead," Bruno said. "Paul can take the blame for all of it, the thefts and the murder of your brother."

"You didn't have to kill him," Florence repeated. "He'd fallen, lost the gun, and you had him covered. I couldn't believe it when you opened fire."

"He killed my brother, and he would have killed us too," Brian retorted angrily. "I was saving our lives."

"It didn't look like that to me," said Crimson. "Florence is right. I won't mourn for him, but there was no need to shoot the man."

Brian ignored him and lifted his head defiantly. Bruno stared at him a moment, remembering what he'd learned about Brian's flight times, and then addressed him.

"When we met last Friday you told me you had just flown into Bergerac, hired a car and come straight to St. Denis. Is that right?"

"That's right. I changed the flight the consulate had booked."

Now Bruno knew he was lying, and everything fell into place—Brian's attempt to sanitize his brother's laptop, his false arrival date, his shooting of Paul. He felt he even understood Paul Murcoing's phrase, "what he was doing to us."

"When did your brother tell you he was intending to marry Yves Valentoux?" Bruno asked.

"What, my brother marry?" Brian scoffed. "He was gay."

"But he wanted a family. He wanted a child, and he had found a partner he loved and wanted to live with. He told you that, didn't he?"

"My brother had all sorts of wild ideas: adoption, fatherhood. His enthusiasms never lasted more than a week or two."

"This one did. Francis told you he was going to father a child and have it brought up by two friends of Yves who were already raising Yves's daughter. And you realized that he would thereby disinherit you and your children and leave the control of his company to strangers."

Brian glared at him, his fingers curling into fists, but Bruno carried on.

"So with Paul and Édouard Marty, your fellow directors in Arch-Inter, you decided to take steps to ensure the company, not to mention the house in Chelsea and the Porsche, stayed in your hands."

"This is all bullshit, Bruno . . ."

"Édouard Marty was arrested yesterday and is telling us everything. How he picked you up at Bordeaux airport last Monday, drove you out to confront your brother."

Bruno was making it up as he went along but had never been more certain of anything.

"You hated him because he was your mother's favorite, because of all the money they spent on his debts and his rehabilitation, while you were the dutiful son, the hard worker. He was gay, and you were straight. You gave them the grandchildren, but he had all the love. He goes to prison, but his old sugar daddy dies and leaves him the house and the business. As your wife said, not bad for two years inside. Then his business took off, and he had all the money. And all you had was a token share and the hope that your children might inherit something, and then you learned that even that was going to be taken away from you."

Brian stared coldly at Bruno and said nothing.

"We have Édouard's testimony, we have your flight details, we have a speed camera that took your photo as you drove back in Édouard's Jaguar, and we'll have your clothes, where I think we will find microscopic specks of your brother's blood from when you beat him to death. And now you killed Paul so that he conveniently takes the blame for it all."

"Brian Fullerton," said J-J, and Bruno turned to listen. "You are under arrest for the murder of your brother, Francis . . ."

Bruno felt a punch on his back, stumbled forward, and the pistol that Yvonne had dropped and that he had stuffed into his waistband was wrenched from its place. For the second time that day the adrenaline flooded his body. Brian was pointing the weapon at him.

"You think you're so bloody clever, but you've no idea what it was like. He was a monster. My parents had to sell their house to pay for the little queer's treatment, and what do you think there was left for me? I'm glad I did it . . ."

There was a great clunk, and Brian's eyes went glassy, his knees buckled, and he fell as Florence completed her follow-through after the forehand drive had slammed her precious laptop into his temple. The sheer metallic case cracked open, and components and letters from the keyboard tinkled to the floor.

"Thank you," Bruno said, his legs still trembling and his mouth dry. Painfully, he swallowed and bent to grab the pistol that had fallen from Brian's hand. "We'll get you a new computer."

Florence let out a great sob, threw down the wrecked computer, put her hands to her face and crumpled into Bruno's arms.

"Can you please take me home to my children?" she asked him as J-J handcuffed the unconscious man.

Bruno led her out, leaving J-J and the rest of them to clear up, complete the paperwork and file the charges. He settled Florence in the passenger seat of his Land Rover and called the mayor.

"It's over. Paul is dead, shot by Brian Fullerton, who has now been charged with the murder of his brother. No hostages hurt. I'm taking Florence home to her children. If Paris calls, tell them it's all ended well. If Pamela calls, tell her I'm on my way. I'll see you tomorrow."

Bruno hung up, feeling a great wave of tiredness that slowed him as he climbed behind the wheel and set off back to St. Denis. He thought of Yves and the way he'd spoken of his daughter, Odile. He thought of the murdered Francis Fullerton and his yearning to be a father. He felt himself awed as he contemplated these deep and potent tides of parenthood and family, the waves of ancestry and succession that tied past and present together.

He looked at Florence, aching to be back with her children, and he thought of the risks he had taken that evening. And he wondered if he'd ever have stepped into such danger if Isabelle had still been carrying his child.

Acknowledgments

This is a work of fiction, and all characters, places and institutions are inventions, except for the historical facts cited below.

The Resistance train robbery at Neuvic in July 1944 took place exactly as described here, and the haul was 2,280 million francs. The final months of the war were a period of sharp inflation, so comparative values are difficult to establish, but the exchange rate calculated for the U.S. Federal Reserve by the U.S. Embassy in Paris in 1945 suggests that the sum taken was around 300 million euros in today's money, or $400 million. See http://www.federalreserve.gov/pubs/rfd/1946/47/rfd47.pdf.

In financial terms, it was by far the greatest train robbery of all time. In suggesting that this was five times the national budget for education, I used the best detailed analysis of the French state budget for 1946, which can be found online at http://www.persee.fr/web/revues/home/prescript/article/pop _0032-4663_1947_num_2_4_1873.

I am grateful to my friend Jean-Jacques Gillot, an eminent local historian and coauthor of the *Résistants du Périgord,* an authoritative encyclopedia of the Resistance in Périgord, for his invaluable research into the Neuvic affair. He generously shared his archives with me, including those of the Paix et Liberté movement, a shadowy anti-Communist group with access to police archives, which was set up after the war to monitor the French left, apparently with clandestine U.S. support. M. Gillot is also the author of the best account of the fate of the Neuvic money, *Le partage des milliards de la Résistance,* and of *Doublemètre,* an enthralling account of the Resistance leader Orlov, almost certainly a Soviet spy, who suddenly became exceedingly wealthy after the war. So did many others, including André Malraux. Despite repeated official inquiries, the fate of much of the Neuvic money remains unknown.

The use of the Marshall Plan slush funds to finance U.S. intelligence operations in Europe after the war is a matter of historical record. My own book, *The Cold War: A History,* covers much of the ground. Preventing a Communist takeover in France and Italy after 1945, when the Communists were the largest and best organized of all political parties, was a top priority for the United States and Britain. George F. Kennan, the career U.S. diplomat whose famous "Long Telegram" from Moscow in 1946 sketched out the grand strategy of containment that was to guide U.S. policy throughout the Cold War, argued for U.S. military intervention if the Communists looked like they would win power through elections.

My account of Jacqueline's research into secret U.S. assistance to the French nuclear program after 1970 is historically accurate, thanks to the work of my colleagues at the Woodrow Wilson International Center for Scholars in Washington, D.C. Their Cold War research center has assembled an extraordinary archive of documents and astute analysis that illuminates much of the secret history of modern times. Some of the documents I cite on French dependence on U.S. nuclear technology may be consulted at:

http://legacy.wilsoncenter.org/va2/docs/doc%2016a%203-10
-70%20k%20to%20Nixon%20%2092253.pdf

http://legacy.wilsoncenter.org/va2/docs/doc%2052%20%
206-23-75%20underground%20testing%20coop%20%20
111968.pdf

http://legacy.wilsoncenter.org/va2/docs/doc%2047%20
memcon%209-5-75%20Schlesinger%20Kissinger%20%
20112907.pdf.

In the last of these selected documents, the transcript of a Pentagon meeting on September 5, 1973, with Defense Secretary James Schlesinger and future national security advisor Brent Scowcroft, Dr. Henry Kissinger notes that "the real quid pro quo is the basic orientation of French policy."

The interpretation of the likely impact of such revelations on French politics is my own invention for fictional purposes.

The brunochiefofpolice.com website has had several queries about some of the foods mentioned in the Bruno novels. The splendid Tomme d'Audrix cheese and the *aillou* are indeed made by my friend Stéphane Bounichou, who can be found in the markets of Le Bugue on Tuesday and Saturday mornings, Le Buisson on Fridays and St. Cyprien on Sundays. Mail order is possible in some European countries. He can be reached via http://www.facebook.com/pages/Fromagerie-Le-Ptit-Jean-De -Mai/171737676196647?sk=info.

Like Bruno, I am torn between trumpeting the excellence of the wines of Bergerac, and particularly the Pécharmants, and worrying that greater renown might make them too expensive to afford. For the moment, they remain very reasonably priced, and details of some of my favorites may be found on Bruno's website. The magnificent wines of Château de Tiregand, particularly the Grands Millésimes of 2005 and 2009, can be found at www.chateau-de-tiregand.com/index1 .html.

I am grateful to the Dordogne tourist board for its enthusiastic support for Bruno's adventures. The board is offering to provide by mail a book of vouchers for reduced admission to the Lascaux Cave and many other caves, castles, gardens and tourist attractions in the region to any reader who sends his or her name and address to bruno.perigord.tourisme@orange.fr.

As always, the real heroes of the Bruno books are the astute and kindly people of the Périgord and the wonderful *paysage* and the way of life they have crafted over the centuries. It is a privilege to live among them and to share it. Once again, I must ask forgiveness from my friend and tennis partner Pierrot, our local policeman whose genial personality and wisdom first inspired the Bruno stories, for covering his placid and law-abiding countryside with fictional corpses.

Bruno would not be Bruno without Jane and Caroline Wood in Britain and Jonathan Segal in New York, and without Anna von Planta and Ruth Geiger in Zurich. My wife, Julia, and our daughters, Kate and Fanny, have always been the first to read each new Bruno and have been as perceptive as they are supportive. The food in the Bruno novels owes just about everything to Julia, Pierrot, Raymond the retired gendarme and my other friends and neighbors. Much of this book has been written with Benson, our basset hound, sitting or more often sleeping at my feet until I take him out for a walk and to enjoy a *p'tit apéro* with Raymond or the Baron or Joe my neighbor, and often with all three.

The Bruno, Chief of Police Series

BRUNO, CHIEF OF POLICE

Meet Benoît Courrèges, aka Bruno, a policeman in a small village in the South of France. He's a former soldier who has embraced the pleasures and slow rhythms of country life. He lives in a restored shepherd's cottage, shops at the local market, and distills his own *vin de noix*. He has a gun but never wears it; he has the power to arrest but never uses it. Most of his policework involves helping local farmers—his friends and neighbors—to avoid paying E.U. inspectors' fines. But then the murder of an elderly North African who fought in the French army changes all that. Now Bruno must balance his beloved routines with an investigation that opens wounds from the dark years of Nazi occupation, and he soon discovers that even his seemingly perfect corner of *la belle France* is not exempt from his country's past.

Fiction

BLACK DIAMOND

Something dangerous is afoot in St. Denis; in the space of a few weeks, the normally sleepy village sees attacks on Vietnamese vendors, arson at a local Asian restaurant, and subpar truffles from China smuggled into outgoing shipments at a nearby market. All of it threatens the Dordogne's truffle trade, worth millions of dollars each year, and all of it spells trouble for Benoît "Bruno" Courrèges, master chef, devoted oenophile, and beloved chief of police. When one of his hunting partners, a noted truffle expert, is murdered, Bruno's investigation into the murky events unfolding around St. Denis becomes infinitely more complicated. Because his friend wasn't just a connoisseur of French delicacies, he was a former high-profile intelligence agent—and someone wanted him dead.

Fiction

THE CROWDED GRAVE

It's spring in the idyllic village of St. Denis, and for Chief of Police Bruno Courrèges that means lamb stews, bottles of his beloved Pomerol, morning walks with his hound, Gigi, and a new string of regional crimes and international capers. When a local archaeological team searching for Neanderthal remains turns up a corpse with a watch on its wrist and a bullet in its head, it's up to Bruno to solve the case. But the task will not be easy, not with a meddlesome new magistrate, a series of attacks by animal rights activists on local foie gras producers, and a summit between France and Spain approaching—not to mention two beautiful, brilliant women vying for Bruno's affections.

Fiction

THE DEVIL'S CAVE

It's spring in St. Denis. The village choir is preparing for its Easter concert, the wildflowers are blooming, and among the lazy whorls of the river a dead woman is found floating in a boat. This means another case for Bruno, the town's cherished chief of police. With the discovery of sinister markings and black candles near the body, it seems to Bruno that the occult might be involved. And as questions mount—most notably about a troubling real estate proposal in the region and the sudden reappearance of an elderly countess—Bruno and his colleagues are drawn ever closer to a climactic showdown in the Gouffre de Colombac: the place locals call the Devil's Cave.

Fiction

ALSO AVAILABLE
America Reborn

VINTAGE BOOKS
Available wherever books are sold.
www.vintagebooks.com